RECKONING AT LITTLE BEAR

To Jim,
Hope you Enjoy!
Rick

ICEFEST 2024
(June 13, 2024)

RECKONING AT LITTLE BEAR

A GHOST CREEK NOVEL

RICK LEY

LUMINARE PRESS

WWW.LUMINAREPRESS.COM

Cover Design by Melissa K. Thomas

Luminare Press
442 Charnelton St.
Eugene, OR 97401
www.luminarepress.com

LCCN: 2020921008
ISBN: 978-1-64388-501-8

For:
My faithful readers who have read my works
and thus far said, "Not too bad!"

With special thanks to:
Bob Carnein, my friend, mentor, and voice of reason.
Doc, without your help Reckoning at Little Bear
would be little more than, "Not a bad try."
And to Patricia Marshall and the good people at
Luminare Press who made RLB a reality.

Interior artwork by Laura Ley
Photography courtesy of the Ley family

ALSO BY RICK LEY

Jolie Rouge

Ghost Creek

CHARACTERS

(in order of relevance/hierarchy)

Primary Players

Michelle Snow (Kozlowski)—Author, and Nick's wife and business partner. Michelle returns to Breckenridge, Colorado to research her current literary project—a sequel to *Ghost Creek*—about the 1988 Sacred Lands disaster that occurred in the Little Bear mine.

Nick Kozlowski—Michelle's husband and fellow Sacred Lands disaster survivor. Nick is an environmental consultant and is the technical advisor for Palmetto State Transformer and Relay's (PSTRE) environmental litigation case against Athens Petrolatum (Athens).

Melanie Sutton—Travels with Michelle to Breckenridge in a mutual search for closure. Her late brother Garret was responsible for the atrocities that left several dead and nearly killed Michelle and Nick that fate-filled July day, in what became the latest Sacred Lands disaster.

Chris Orrey—Nick's friend and long-time business associate. Leader of the technical team subcontracted by MacDonald & Carlyle Law Firm, LLP (M&C), PSTRE's legal representation in its suit against Athens.

Dylan Streeter—Missing person of interest from the past.

William Laney—Missing person of interest from the present.

MacDonald & Carlyle Law Firm, LLP (M&C)

Bill Carlyle—Senior partner and lead counsel for PSTRE in its litigation case against Athens.

Smithson ("Smitty") Griffin—Partner and second chair.

Brant Sutherland II—Associate attorney. Liaison between Smitty Griffin and Chris Orrey.

Ainsley MacDonald—Managing partner (referenced character).

Wendy—Scone-making administrative assistant (referenced character).

Charlene—Human-resources contact for concierge needs at Ashley House (referenced character).

Palmetto State Transformer and Relay (PSTRE)

Stan Merrill—Irascible president with a long-standing family feud with Athens.

Hal Cole—Senior officer and financier for PSTRE's overseas-business venture.

Gerry Dawson—Moody facility-operations manager.

Tarryall Mountain Foundation

"Jodi"—Mysterious cyber pen pal, who bodes Michelle warning not to return to Colorado.

Beth Stockwell—Directorate member and Michelle's principal point of contact at Tarryall.

Joe Hayden—Directorate member in charge of day-to-day affairs.

Bill Clay—Directorate member.

Hollis ("Bud") Walker—Directorate member and emeritus.

Teddy Monroe—Directorate member and president.

Judith Barrie—Staff employee.

Derrick ("Storm") Schmidt—Summer intern.

Vikki Atkinson—Summer intern.

Carol Jones—Summer intern (referenced character).

River City Environmental (RCE)

Sam Piersall—Project manager for the environmental consulting firm tasked with collecting field data for the PSTRE/Athens case. Reports to Nick in the technical team hierarchy.

Jay Watkins—Geologist and field-team leader. Reports to Sam Piersall.

Tricia Bell—Field geologist.

Mindy Porter—Field geologist.

Brandon Butler—Geographic information systems (GIS) specialist (referenced character).

Athens Petrolatum (Athens)

Mike Dodd—President and Stan Merrill's counterpart in the PSTRE/Athens feud.

O'Reilly, Kreider, Ftorek & Gare, Attorneys at Law

Ted Carlson—Lead counsel for Athens in its litigation case against PSTRE.

Jim Cresson—Geologist and technical advisor. Nick and Chris's counterpart on the PSTRE/Athens case.

Clair Underwood—Paralegal.

Henry—Inattentive intern.

Operation Timberline Task Force

Colorado Task Force

Ron Sanderson—FBI special agent and Colorado task force team leader (introduced in *Jolie Rouge*).

Ryan Wells—FBI special agent and lead field agent assigned to Sanderson's Colorado task force.

Amy Morgan—FBI special agent and Wells's partner.

Agent Hernandez—FBI special agent and Morgan's backup partner (referenced character).

Agent Perry—FBI special agent assigned to Sanderson's Colorado task force (referenced character).

Agent Cullen—FBI special agent assigned to Sanderson's Colorado task force (referenced character).

Agent Donaldson—FBI special agent assigned to Sanderson's Colorado task force (referenced character).

Susan—Administrative Assistant at the FBI Denver office.

Brian—Technical support group employee at the FBI Denver office (referenced character).

Charleston Task Force

James Granby—FBI special agent, Operation Timberline team leader, and head of the Charleston task force (introduced in *Jolie Rouge*).

Steve Bonino—FBI special agent assigned to Granby's Charleston task force.

ICF Partners, Inc. Task Force

Catherine ("Cat") Solomon—Senior Project Analyst at ICF Partners, Inc. (ICF) and subcontracted Operation Timberline team member (introduced in *Jolie Rouge*).

Janelle Stone—Associate Project Analyst at ICF and Solomon's Colorado task force colleague (introduced in *Jolie Rouge*).

Kim Parsons—ICF president (referenced character from *Jolie Rouge*).

Missy Sparling—Assistant Project Analyst and Cat Solomon's protégé (referenced character from *Jolie Rouge*).

Other Players

(in order of appearance)

Garret Sutton—Michelle's former boyfriend and Melanie's late twin brother, who found the lost Little Bear mine while attending geology field camp in 1985. Garret's failed efforts to control the demons that haunted him since childhood resulted in the 1988 Sacred Lands disaster, and in the process fueled the belief by some that the area was still plagued by the centuries-old Curse of Coronado (referenced character from *Ghost Creek*).

Tracy Sheridan—Michelle's lifetime friend (referenced character from *Ghost Creek*).

Christa Longo—Michelle's deceased friend and mentor at Roberts Ecosystems (referenced character from Michelle's past).

Connor Lewis—Michelle's literary agent (referenced character).

Jordy—Poorly dressed young man talking with a friend on Ashley Avenue.

Mark Boone—Photographer for Michelle's book project.

John Parker—Prospector from Breckenridge's gold rush past. Parker was Garret's soulmate, whom the psychologically-impaired Garret believed he could communicate through time with in his thoughts and dreams. Parker's 1892 discovery of gold at Ghost Creek would lead to the development of the Big Bear and Little Bear mines (referenced character from *Ghost Creek*).

Miguel ("Mike")—Emotional artist for one of Michelle's children's books (referenced character).

Sylvia—Resident director for Michelle's dormitory at Huron College (referenced character from *Ghost Creek*).

Kerry (Sutton)—Melanie's younger sister and voice of reason (referenced character from *Ghost Creek*).

Brad (Sutton)—Melanie's older brother (referenced character from *Ghost Creek*).

Jamie Mason—Student who accompanied Michelle, Nick, Garret, and Tracy to field camp in 1985 (referenced character from *Ghost Creek*).

Aunt Joan and Uncle Terry—Relatives who took in Melanie and Kerry after Garret's childhood transgressions that disrupted the Sutton nuclear family (referenced characters from *Ghost Creek*).

Aunt Carol—Relative who took in Garret (referenced character from *Ghost Creek*).

Kyle—Melanie's ex husband (referenced character from *Ghost Creek*).

Erin Marten—Melanie's former roommate (referenced character from *Ghost Creek*).

Danny Schaize—Melanie's would-be boyfriend (referenced character from *Ghost Creek*).

Dave Hoffman—Anthropology major who figured out Garret's secret use of the Little Bear mine (referenced character from *Ghost Creek*).

Aunt Beth and Uncle John—Relatives who took in Melanie's brother Brad (referenced characters from *Ghost Creek*).

Ranger Rick—Charismatic park ranger at Dinosaur Ridge.

Billy—Boy with an imagination filled with wonder at Dinosaur Ridge.

Kristian Fletcher—Pollen scientist whom Michelle and Melanie meet at the Garden of the Gods.

Amy—Fletcher's geologist partner (referenced character).

Calvin Pearcy—PSTRE president in 1928 (referenced character).

Olivia—Help-desk attendant at Cordilleran Media Resources.

Dave Kerrigan—Wealthy citizen seeking to place land in trust with Tarryall.

Ian Prescott—Timberline syndicate thug.

Adeline—Help-desk attendant at the Charleston Register Mesne Conveyances.

Brett Carr—Cat Solomon's former friend and pirate-museum heist nemesis (referenced character from *Jolie Rouge*).

Damon Elliott—A college chum of Cat's who, along with her husband **Pete** (Hampton) and mutual friend (**Rey** Cruz), survived their high seas kidnapping at the hands of Haitian Timberline syndicate thugs (referenced characters from *Jolie Rouge*).

Marchand—Brett Carr's nemesis from the botched pirate-museum heist (referenced character from *Jolie Rouge*).

Patrick—Assistant Engineer at the Charleston City Special Projects Office.

Karen Lanier—Project Engineer at the City Special Projects Office.

Evan Barrow—Smitty's friend in need of legal assistance (referenced character).

Dan Thompson—Scheming businessman associated with the Ghost Creek legend. Thompson developed John Parker's claim into the Big Bear and Little Bear mines; in doing so, he allegedly resurrects the Curse of Coronado that some claim was responsible for the 1898 mine disaster at Little Bear (referenced character from *Ghost Creek*).

Marguerite—Head of airport concierge.

Shannon—Flight attendant.

Benjamin ("Bennie") Barrie—Beth Stockwell's high school sweetheart who, Beth believes, deserted her and his familial responsibilities after a bungled Tarryall heist (referenced character).

Rillieux—Unexpected person from Cat's past with ties to the Timberline syndicate (referenced character from *Jolie Rouge*).

CHAPTER 1

FRIDAY

MacDonald & Carlyle Law Firm, LLP
Broad Street, Charleston, S.C.
3:38 P.M.

Michelle stumbled in her flight to escape the beast. She collided with one of the stony walls lining the subterranean corridors of the living hell in which she was trapped, her feet failing to move as fast as her legs tried to carry them. Only good fortune kept her from falling completely, thereby preventing further damage to the scar tissue that had opened below her knee during her frightful passage through the bowels of the Earth at the hands of the creature. Hunched over, chest heaving, Michelle struggled to contain her sobs. Gathering her will, she pushed off hard against a thigh, propelling her body back to a standing position. With her free hand she probed at the spot where her head glanced off the rough surface of the corridor wall. The crown of her forehead was ragged, numb to the touch. Michelle drew her fingers to her nose and sniffed at the sticky wetness between the tips. She recoiled at the nauseating odor of iron, confirming what she feared: that she was now bleeding in two places. Without a means to stem the flow of new blood, there was nothing she could do to prevent that dreadful man-beast out there in the dark from homing in on her scent.

Michelle looked for a place to hide. Which way should she go? What a ridiculous question. Where else could she go except straight ahead until the next corridor, room, or ladder access materialized from the gloom. Compounding her woes, Michelle didn't know how far she would have to go. Worse, she couldn't run—or limp along with any semblance of haste because the visibility was poor, and she had to tread carefully to avoid falling into yet another one of those blasted areas where the ground, mysteriously, was missing. Yes, there was only one logical choice to make. All the same, Michelle still found herself perplexed by indecision. That was until her mind came back around to reality and forced her to take…the next step she couldn't make. To her horror, Michelle discovered that she could no longer move her legs because her feet had inexplicably become one with the rocky floor, her shoes having merged with the very granite within which she was entombed. Powerless, her situation dire, Michelle risked betraying her location by screaming out in desperation for the help that could never find her, lost as she was so far within the Earth.

Her morning started off well enough, the day clear, sky sunny, the gentle warm breeze kissed by a piney fragrance that tantalized the senses. Michelle was following Fred and Wilma, two of her mountain bluebird subjects, across the college field-station grounds. Up one hill and down the other, across this stream and that, she followed them—even across the ramshackle fence that defined the forbidden Sacred Lands—into the dreaded Ghost Creek valley, all the while jotting down salient observations in her field logbook. It was an exciting time for Michelle because recently, the birds had begun to deviate from their otherwise predictable behavior, for reasons she was determined to unravel. True to their new habits, her feathered friends did not disappoint this day either, offering their secret admirer one exciting insight after another. Why, Michelle could see the beaming smiles on her advisors' faces now when they read what would go down in the annals of Huron College as the most remarkable master's thesis ever written.

"There you two are!" she labored between breaths. Michelle was deep within the Sacred Lands, struggling to keep pace with the birds up the tricky slope toward Little Bear Mountain. She had lost, found, and at last tracked her subjects down again. This time they alighted on a pine bough just ahead and slightly beyond a spindly stand of aspens that struggled to fill a void in the otherwise expansive blanket of evergreens. *What's he doing?* Michelle wondered. She was spying on Fred from her hiding spot behind a fallen log, wondering why the strikingly handsome bird kept looking over his shoulder and bobbing his tail. *He's agitated. Fascinating.* Several feet away and closer to the trunk of the same tree, a disconcerted Wilma was doing the same.

The bluebirds suddenly took flight. Their path led straight away, obliging Michelle to meet their challenge. "Wanna play games, do you?" she yelled after them, pushing herself up from the ground. Dusting pine needles and spider webs from her clothing as she shimmied past and sometimes bull rushed her way through both bough and branch, Michelle forged her way ahead, somehow maintaining eye contact with her quarry the whole time. At one point, Michelle even thought she saw Wilma peer back at her as if making sure that their pursuer was still giving chase. *That's odd. Why would—*

The birds then did the unexpected for a second time in as many moments; they picked up the pace of their flight and started weaving through the foliage instead of flying around it. Michelle tried to keep up but soon found herself lagging farther and farther behind, her lungs burning to strain every stray oxygen molecule from the rarefied air. *Oh, no!* Michelle pleaded in silence. *Don't let me lose you! Where are you going?* And she did lose them, at least she thought she did, until she burst through a dense tangle only to spy them again flitting between the branches of two opposing trees. Grateful to have found them again, Michelle came to an awkward stop at the near end of a small clearing offering a good view of her subjects, where she collapsed, exhausted. The pine-needle bed beneath her knees was comforting. Michelle took advantage of the situation to catch her breath. She wiped the sweat from her eyes. Fred and Wilma were no longer flitting between branches, but hovering like butterflies before a great pile of rocks that appeared from out of nowhere. "What the hell?" There was no time to contemplate the fantastical appearance of the rocks, or why the birds were acting so strangely, because Fred and Wilma abruptly disappeared into one of the rock pile's many recesses.

Michelle was dumbstruck. She had never seen such a thing. In fact, she was certain nobody had. Excited by her discovery, she scribbled down her observations as fast as she could, and even doodled a sketch of the rock pile and surrounding area before chasing after the birds. Michelle closed the distance as fast as the terrain allowed. She really hoped to observe what the birds were doing in there. Mountain bluebirds nest inside the cavities of trees not *rocks*.

The first sign of trouble came when Michelle realized that she wasn't running so much as being pulled toward the rock pile, as if on some invisible conveyor moving at a speed much faster than she could run on her own. Distracted, she looked from her magically propelled feet to the obstacles in her path, wondering how this could be happening. Trepidation replaced curiosity about the out-of-body experience, when the skies suddenly darkened and the rocks ahead began to *move*. Michelle tried to turn away but her legs wouldn't obey her command. There was nothing she could do to keep from running haplessly on the invisible conveyor toward the jumbled pile of possessed granite. As far as the rocks were concerned, they weren't just moving, they were *growing*. Before her very eyes, the rocks transformed into massive boulders that had the magical ability to alter their position, forming the entrance to a great cave.

"*HELP ME! SOMEONE! PLEASE, HELP ME!*" she shrieked. The cave was fast approaching. Michelle remained powerless to avoid being sucked into the gaping hole. If this was not enough, she was working alone in the Sacred Lands, a place with purported supernatural properties that was out of bounds to professors and students alike. The sanctuary of the field station lay at least half a mile and a world away. It was an apocalyptic moment. The heavens darkened, the winds whipped to a fury, and lightning tore great white fissures across the sky. Claps of thunder echoed savagely off the mountainsides. The last thing Michelle remembered before being thrown violently into the cave was the dull red glow of two burning embers coming from deep within the inky blackness.

Michelle jerked awake with an eye-fluttering groan. Wherever she was, it was very dark and much cooler than the sunbathed slope she'd left behind. Her body shook from the uncompromising bite of cold that wicked up from the stone floor she found herself sprawled upon. Michelle tried to pick herself up, failed, then tried again. This time she was more successful, managing to struggle to her knees. She saw little more than faint shapes in the darkness, when the gloom suddenly vanished and refreshing warmth spread across her back. Michelle pivoted about to discover, much to her relief, that the tempest had passed as quickly as it had come and that the world outside was again bathed in sunlight. *Where am I? What am I doing here?* Michelle was confused. She had the feeling of having lost time, her mind clouded by the uncertainty that any of this was actually real. She stood with some difficulty and tried to take in her surroundings. Oddly, she found herself standing in the middle of a gently inclined antechamber hewn right into the bedrock. Ahead, wooden timbers lined the entrance to a corridor leading off into blackness. The barn-wood-like odor emanating from the timbers pleased her. It was also strangely familiar. *Wait! Fred, Wilma—*

The second harbinger of the terror to come appeared in the form of a faint grating sound from somewhere down the desolate corridor. Michelle froze. She cocked her head and listened. Several seconds passed, and then a few more. Nothing. She dismissed the sound as a figment of an over-active imagination. Perhaps it was her missing bluebird friends. No, she told herself. That was silly.

Little birds can't make sounds like that. They must've escaped while she was passed out on the floor. She wouldn't blame them if they had, because this place was beyond creepy. Michelle took one last, uneasy look around and decided to follow their lead and make her own escape—or better yet, flee the confounded Sacred Lands altogether—before taking one more step down this macabre rabbit hole. The exploits of Fred and Wilma could wait until another day.

The simple act of making a decision calmed her. Michelle was in the midst of completing her turn when she heard the grating sound again, and along with it what sounded like a long, low moan. *Or was it a growl?* This sound was even more chilling than the first. Michelle again stopped in her tracks. She would hear nothing more for a spell, save for the beating of her heart reacting to anxiety's tug. Then she heard it again: the grating sound, a definite growl, and this time the fluttering of wings. "Fred! Wilma! You are in here!" Michelle yelped with relief. She wasn't alone after all, nor was she imagining things. Her elation, however, was short lived, lasting only long enough to realize that the sinister sounds meant that she and her feathered friends were in peril from whatever was stalking them out there in the dark.

She reacted in a flash—remarkably, out of curiosity and not fear—when a profound thought emerged from all of the irrational ones swirling around inside her head. Her mind wasn't playing tricks on her and she wasn't in some magically transfigured cavern. No, she was in a mine, and by all accounts it was occupied. Michelle scampered across the remaining expanse of antechamber to the timber support framing the corridor entrance and listened once more. The corridor was dark, too dark to see very far without the flashlight she did not have. Michelle huffed in irritation. She ventured forward anyway, feeling her way along the nearest corridor wall. There was definitely something out there; of this, she was sure. She hadn't travelled far when she saw a faint orange glow in the distance. "Someone is in here," she muttered. "He's working on something...and that growl, it must be his dog!" she rejoined, trying to come up with a satisfactory explanation of her observations. Michelle raised a hand to her chest, grateful for having finally figured out what was going on, more so to revel in the feeling of relief. Burden lifted, she resumed her pursuit with haste toward the light and whoever else inhabited this suddenly not so strange place.

Her progress was arrested by a haunting wail that assaulted her from every direction. It was a melancholy, resonant moan—as if the interring granite was groaning in perverse agony. Michelle looked wildly about for an explanation. Her predicament became clear when, from out of the shadows strode a vision from her worst nightmare: the silhouette of a hulking monster—a menacing, bipedal creature with glowing red eyes. Transfixed, she watched the monster make its advance. That was until the wailing suddenly stopped, as did the monster's grip on her ability to take flight, which she did with haste. Michelle raced back in the direction of the mine entrance, screaming in terror. The walls ahead soon brightened, and a moment later she could see the entrance itself, which became larger with every step. She tripped at the junction of the corridor and antechamber, but was able to maintain her balance with a well-placed push off a timber post. If she could just make it outside, Michelle was certain that she could find a place to hide.

The monster closed the distance faster than Michelle anticipated. It was so close now that she could hear its breathing and smell its putrid breath, the spittle spray from its yawning mouth brushing the nape of her neck. But it was not until she was blanketed by its towering shadow that she dared look up at her would-be killer— the most dreadful creature imaginable, a man-beast covered with thinning, coarse red hair, a heart-shaped head, and a weasel's snout filled with dagger teeth that matched neatly with the claws on its remarkably short, gangly arms.

Michelle cowered before the beast. She watched with fright as it circled her, sizing her up, attempting to figure out just what kind of prey had entered its domain. When it flinched, Michelle collapsed completely. She raised a hand to shield her face when the man-beast leaned forward, opening its mouth. But instead of devouring her, the creature roared down at her, a bellow so loud that it made the ground shake. Somehow, Michelle found the wherewithal to spring to her feet and run. The beast took great delight in her plight and started to laugh, a heckling baritone of a laugh that chased after her like some imaginary attack dog. Michelle was so thrown off-stride by the hooting that she started to run crazily in an attempt to shake its advances. She was a mere body's length away from reaching the light of day when the man-beast snatched away all remaining hope. It grasped her with one of its reptilian hands and, with a jerk, dragged her back into the mine with long, pounding strides.

The beast toted Michelle down one corridor and relict ladder after another until she was hopelessly disoriented. She was bounced against so many rocky, metallic, and timbered surfaces that her body was battered numb. The beast stopped in the middle of a great room somewhere deep underground where it brusquely released its grasp and, after offering one last haunting chuckle, vanished before her eyes. It was from here that Michelle was left to find her way out of what proved to be a sadistic game of hide and seek that, owing to the beast's supernatural powers, would end only when *it* decided the game was over.

Michelle had eluded the beast through an endless warren of passageways only to find herself now trapped in her enchantment-bound shoes. She pulled and tugged until her hips and ankles felt as if they were going to be yanked from their sockets. She was scrunched into a seated position, weeping, rubbing at her sore ankles, when the revelation occurred to simply untie her shoes. Michelle managed a feeble laugh at her own expense between sobs as she fumbled with the laces in what proved to be a new race to extract her feet before the enchantment turned her shoes completely into stone. With not too much effort, Michelle extracted first one foot and then the other. The beast, though, wouldn't afford her the luxury of joy, for no sooner had she regained her freedom than she again heard the grating sound, along with what sounded like the whumps of heavy footfalls closing in the distance.

Michelle made her barefoot escape and reached the end of the passageway without incident. There, she was confronted with the option of turning left or right or taking the ladder before her to the next highest level. She favored changing floors, but wouldn't that be what the beast expected? *Screw it!* she cursed under her breath. She had had enough of the monster's game and didn't want to waste one more second in this hellish place, so she struggled her way up the rickety ladder for the fifty-odd feet it took to reach the next level, where she continued her flight.

She hadn't gone far when her senses detected a change in the shadow pattern ahead, the gray dim yielding to an expansive blackness. Michelle skidded to a halt mere feet away from yet another mysterious hole in the floor. She reached down to grab several pebbles from underfoot. She threw the first. It fell a considerable distance before hitting ground. She heard it bounce, then bounce again at regular intervals farther and farther down and away until, eventually, she heard nothing at all. *It did hit bottom, right?* She tossed the next stone farther out and didn't hear it hit anything at all. Dizziness washed over her at the thought of skidding into the abyss.

An angry wail punctuated the stillness. Michelle's heart did somersaults in her chest—the beast! It was homing in on her trail. Desperate, she reached down and grabbed another pebble. This time she threw it at an angle hard left. She shouted out with joy when she heard it skitter to a stop against what must be a wall. Buoyed with hope, Michelle hurried off in that direction and in short order found another corridor. Her spirits were lifted further when she again spied the orange glow down this new passageway. Michelle was determined that this time she would make it to her would-be savior and, together, they would get out of this godforsaken place.

The glow actually made it more difficult to see her immediate surroundings. Michelle had to use a hand to guide herself along the rock wall in the direction of the light, stopping only when her shoulder collided with something metal hanging from a timber-framed support. She reached with haste to steady a time-forgotten lantern that rocked noisily on its hook. Michelle cursed, hoping she hadn't betrayed her location. She held her breath for several long seconds, letting it out only when she heard nothing—nothing from the beast that is. But she did hear something: faint voices drifting toward her from the same direction as the glow.

Michelle hurried to reach the safety of the light, which she determined was coming from a side room cut into the rock off to her right. It was the comfort of the welcoming light that had occupied her focus to this point, but now that she was near her safe haven, she suddenly found her senses confounded by the reality that the glow wasn't a steady ray at all, but a menacing flicker that snaked its way through smoke-filled air emanating from the room beyond. As for the voices, they were neither neutral nor happy, but a frightful chorus of shrieks—*FIRE!*

Michelle was devastated. There was no safe place to turn. What she thought was her salvation was a room filled with dying souls who needed her more than she needed them—*WAIT!* That's not quite true. What was she to do? What could she do but stay and try to help. Michelle crept toward the side room, stopping just outside the entranceway. There, she pressed her back to the rock wall to steady her nerves, her mind torn between fight and flight. Michelle was vexed. Her would-be rescuers were trapped in the room in a state of extremis, and yet she hesitated because the last thing she wanted to do—could afford to do—was to go looking for more trouble. But considering that she had no idea where she was and that a fantastical monster was chasing her, there was really only one path she could take, and that was to forge ahead and meet danger head on. Perhaps if she could help at least one of them, then together they could make their escape and return with a rescue party to save the others. Her mind made up, Michelle gathered what remained of her will and, after a settling breath, wheeled about and barged into the unknown.

Rick Ley

The depth of human suffering in the chamber was unfathomable. At least half a dozen silvery-gray human forms staggered about the smoke-filled chamber, hands clutched to their throats. On the ground, she counted a similar number of men writhing in the throes of death. Still others wandered zombie-like, wailing in despair. Michelle clutched at her own throat in wonderment at why she was not affected by the smoke or lashing flames. It was as if she'd been immersed in someone else's terrible dream. She had to constantly sidestep like a sandpiper scurrying to pace itself with the ebb and flow of the waves along the strand to keep from bumping into one of the damned. She had wandered deep into the room when she realized that there was no one left to save.

Michelle hopped over one of the fallen and successfully eluded the hapless advances of a soon-to-be-departed soul when a sudden movement in her peripheral vision made her jump, regrettably a moment too late to avoid being fallen upon by a third. Michelle crossed her arms to brace for the impact...that did not happen. The man collided into her, this much was certain, but he didn't just stumble into her, he tumbled *through* her. That's when Michelle recognized the men for what they were—*GHOSTS*—spirits of the tortured souls who'd perished in this dreadful place some time before.

Everything then went terribly wrong. The chamber started to vibrate and then contort. The walls buckled. Fissures opened and started to bleed, casting great pools of blood across the floor. An inferno of fiery daggers erupted from everywhere at once, from the walls, from out of the smoke, and in some instances out of thin air. Overcome by the supernatural reality of her situation, Michelle crumpled to the ground and cried. She grasped her head between her hands and squeezed tight to rid herself of the debilitating feeling that she was about to die.

But not just yet…

A dreadful, reverberating chant that overrode the zombie spirits' desperate wails and the roar of the flames sounded from across the room. The beast. It had found her. Michelle was too traumatized to attempt an escape. It wouldn't have mattered anyhow because in the time it took for her to gain a fix on the origin of the sound, a shape emerged from the murk—

"GARRET!" Michelle screeched. "What? How? Please Help Me!" she choked between sobs. Michelle reached out for Garret to help her, but he didn't take her hand. And that precocious smile of his, it drained away to nothingness. For several long seconds, Garret stared down at her in silence through black, emotionless eyes. "Garret? What's the matter?"

Without warning, Garret went into convulsions and before Michelle's horrorstruck eyes transformed into the monster. His skin split along the spine, and out from the dermis emerged the beast, this time in near human form—a gigantic Indian, its head covered by a gruesome mask with menacing eyes that shone like red hot coals through holes burnt through the surface of the knotty shield. The creature looked down at her and started to laugh, and like before it circled her. Michelle pleaded for the beast to take her, only it wouldn't oblige. It just kept laughing and circling and circling and laughing until at long last, it lashed out with one of its devilishly clawed hands.

———

The thump from a car door closing rescued Michelle from her latest nightmare. A woman was preparing to back her car out of an adjoining parking space. Michelle stole a glance to her left, thankful to find the driver's seat unoccupied. They must have—yes—they were stopped at a rest area. *Good.* She needed time to regain her composure before Nick returned from the facilities. Wherever they were, it was a good ten degrees warmer than it was before she'd fallen asleep. The topography was much flatter as well. Michelle closed her eyes and smiled. *Finally!* They must be in South Carolina. Michelle found extended bliss in the interstate roar, which her over active imagination transformed into the sound of crashing waves.

Nick said that Chris Orrey, the friend whom they would meet later that afternoon, had guaranteed them free and unlimited use of the legal firm's beach house for the duration of their stay. This was a promise Michelle intended to take full advantage of. A girl needs to work on her tan, especially one pasty white farm girl from Ohio.

Sweat trickled down her temples; her eyes stung. Michelle raised an arm to wipe the sweat away. With her free hand she groped between the seat and center console and then the floor beneath her legs for the missing sunglasses she habitually parked on the top of her head when not in use. "Where'd I lose them this time?" She murmured. Michelle was surprised to find the same car that had just backed away again pulling forward into the adjoining spot. "Excuse me. Miss? Are those your glasses, down there—under your car?" the woman asked with a suggestive nod. Michelle cracked open the door, looked down, and lo and behold, there they were, her favorite pair of sunglasses peeking out from beneath the floorboard. *How in the hell?* Michelle picked them up and thanked the woman, who again backed away with a departing smile.

Michelle wrenched a crook from her neck. She sputtered a woeful sigh. There was only one way her sunglasses could have ended up on the pavement like that. She ruffled her fingers through her sweat-dampened hair to discover that her forehead hurt at precisely the same spot where she'd struck one of the stone corridors of the ill-fated Little Bear mine in her dream. On the dash she saw a greasy smudge where she struck her head in real life; the blow having jostled her sunglasses off her head, whereby they tumbled out of the open window. Overcome by a nervous chill, Michelle flipped down the visor to look into the cosmetic mirror. She saw nothing, but when she pressed on the spot, it hurt all the same. Michelle sighed, again, thankful that there wasn't a mark she would have to explain. As for the reddening around the scar tissue below her aching knee, this she could pass off to the cramped space. She must have cracked it into the dash in her throes of panic. There was no mistaking the intensity or vividness of her nightmares, which were escalating with each event—just like they had done to poor Garret decades before.

Michelle was comforted by the sound of Nick's approaching voice. He was speaking on his cell phone with Chris. When Nick paused outside the driver-side door to fumble through his pockets for his keys, Michelle took advantage of the time to again check on her appearance. She looked like hell. This she could chalk up to the sweltering heat.

"Shit. Can you hold a minute?" Nick said opening the door. He looked inside to find his wife's haggard face peering back at him. "You, *ah*, okay in there?" he asked, his eyes fixated on the fresh bead of sweat rolling down her cheek.

"You left her in the car?" Chris's distant laugh resonated through Nick's phone.

"No! I didn't just leave her in the car. I parked in the shade and put the window down before I went inside." A pause. Nick peered again inside the car. "It's Chris. He says hi."

Michelle waved her fingers lazily back at him and blew a sweaty curl from her face. She tilted her head in the direction of the travel-center building and waited for Nick to announce, "Michelle says hi, back," before she stepped out of the car.

Nick was still on the phone when she returned, refreshed after wiping the sweat from her arms and splashing cold water on her face. A fortuitous breeze helped to dry what would have to suffice for a *wild* look of loose, tawny curls. Michelle slid back into the passenger seat. Beside her, Nick was struggling to talk while managing a road map spread out across the steering wheel. "We're still planning to meet, right?" he asked Chris. "Uh-huh. Come again? Carlyle, Griffin, and Sutherland but no MacDonald…and you and me and Michelle. Got it. Huh? Oh. No, getting a head count is all. You know, to see what we're up against." They shared a laugh. "That? Oh, that was Michelle. She just got back in the car. We're at a rest stop, remember? Wait a sec. Here, let me put you on speaker." Nick did and Chris Orrey's voice erupted from the phone. "Change in plans," Nick said to Michelle. "Chris says the big guy, Bill Carlyle, is going out of town. He wants to meet with everyone involved with the case before he hits the road." Taking in Michelle's unkempt appearance, Nick gave her a devilish smirk and asked Chris if they should stop by the house first and freshen up. Michelle smacked him with the back of her hand. Nick dropped the phone. They heard Chris's raucous cackle calling out to them the entire time it took for the device to bounce off the steering column and land in a center console cup holder.

"You shit!" Michelle yelled. "If you didn't lock me in a hot car on a ninety-degree day!"

"There's no need to worry about what you look like," Chris said. "It's a business casual Friday. And, hey, you never did tell me where you are."

"Right," Nick said, yelling at his phone. "The tourist center on I-26 near Landrum, a little north of Spartanburg. We're still on track for a three-thirty arrival."

The *South Carolina Junket* was an exciting twist to the environmental litigation work that Nick and Michelle had become accustomed to. Nick was an environmental consultant, and over the eleven years since going into business for himself, his workload had slowly but surely shifted from the collection, interpretation, and reporting of field data to providing expert-witness testimony on the same information generated by others. He performed most of this work with Chris, with whom Nick had worked before at Wyatt Geosciences, first in Minneapolis and then in Grants Pass, Oregon, where he and Michelle lived for a brief stint in the early 1990s.

Michelle's initial dabbling into Nick's private practice consisted mostly of critiquing his arguments, which Nick then passed along to Chris. The problem was, in her opinion, she often knew too little in the way of the case details or that her experience on the geological side of the environmental profession was lacking, too limited to provide much in the way of useful insight. To this end, she asked for a larger role and worked Nick's needs in around her own publishing requirements. Nick recognized her contribution by changing the name of his company to Kozlowski & Associates, the aft end of the moniker made plural because of Michelle's ability to quickly and thoroughly make higher-level reviews of widely dissimilar information: in other words, she could do the work of a slew of staff-level employees.

Expert-witness work lent a certain panache at social functions, where friends gathered 'round for juicy anecdotes about legal conquests of disreputable corporations. Nick couldn't help but admit, though, that tort work, for all its potential, invariably fell short of expectations. This was not because the work wasn't interesting. Rather, it was the tedium of poring over paid-by-the-pound consultant reports followed by the preparation of carefully crafted summaries of cause and culpability that ultimately went nowhere beyond chamber doors—if that far. The high drama of a John Grisham legal thriller had thus far eluded him. False hopes notwithstanding, Nick still approached each new case with the wide-eyed expectation that *this one* might be his very own Pelican Brief.

The *Junket*, to which the new case's name was shortened for simplicity's sake, promised to be different from any of their other legal cases for any number of reasons, not the least of which was location—Charleston, in the heart of the Deep South. As if the image it conjured were not enough, an Internet search revealed Charleston to have a vibrant nightlife, proximity to upscale shopping and beaches, trees draped with Spanish moss, and restaurants serving low-country cuisine alongside those hifalutin fusion meals so popular today. What was not to like?

Their last two cases found Nick ensconced in Detroit, followed by a shithole gem of a place for much of March in a downtrodden part of Boston, places that Michelle refused to go and Nick said would be better served plowed under. But this one promised to be different. This was why they reconfigured their summer plans to work alongside MacDonald & Carlyle's coveted client, Palmetto State Transformer and Relay—PSTRE for short—with their little problem. Besides the location, what made the case worth considering was the Southern hospitality Chris said M&C promised to provide as compensation for an indefinite stay. In addition to handsome pay and unlimited use of the corporate beach house, Nick and Michelle would be guests at Ashley House, an auxiliary workspace and the private temporary living quarters reserved only for M&C's VIP clients.

They were primed for what promised to be a fantastic experience if it weren't for one—well, two—exceptions: Michelle's latest book project, a return to Ghost Creek; and, more to the point, a visit to the Little Bear mine. The mine was not only the location of Michelle's nightmares; it was the place where she and Nick were almost killed so many years ago by their former friend Garret Sutton. Her side trip was a pleasure-dampening diversion scheduled for the following week, just as work on the PSTRE case would be ramping up. "Nothing good can come from opening old wounds," Nick warned her. He never could come to terms with the atrocities Garret had inflicted upon them and the others on that dreadful July day in 1988. He remained adamant that Michelle risked further emotional pain, all to appease an overly zealous agent pressing for increased book sales. "But I need to do this," she implored. "And so does Melanie. We'll be fine. Besides, we'll be with an escort the entire time, and should be back the following weekend."

Michelle and Nick met at Huron College in the fall of 1985 on a geology-club field trip. Michelle and her childhood friend Tracy Sheridan were zoology majors who decided it might be fun to do something different for fall break and tag along with some geology majors on their rock and mineral collecting trip to Sudbury, Ontario. Michelle remembered vividly the moment she and Tracy laid eyes on Nick and Garret. Tracy acted first and captured Nick's attention. Michelle followed suit by accepting Garret's advances. Her three-year relationship with Garret proved trying, leaving

Michelle to wonder who, or what, was hiding behind his hauntingly dark, alluring eyes. What none of them knew until it was too late was the depth of the psychological burden Garret had shouldered since childhood. As time wore on, he became increasingly withdrawn and prone to sudden fits of rage. Swimming against a heavy emotional tide, Michelle found herself leaning more and more on Nick for support, as Nick did her, when he and Tracy started having troubles of their own. It was no small wonder that Nick and Michelle would find themselves desperately entangled in the wonders of situational love. The fallout from the changes in their relationship dynamics—all on account of Garret—placed them in the mine that day, the consequences of which would leave five dead and Nick, Michelle, and Tracy irrevocably scarred, both physically and emotionally.

It took Michelle several years to recover from her injuries, during which time she wrote a harrowing account of their tumultuous college days as part of her mental therapy. For a brief period in the early 1990s, she rode a groundswell of fame when *Ghost Creek* climbed the bestseller charts. The book captivated her audience with the chilling details of Garret's emotional destruction and a seemingly impossible link to a centuries-old Indian curse. In April 1993, Nick and Michelle were married and started life anew in Grants Pass, Oregon. The move was a simple intra-company transfer for Nick. There he reconnected with Chris, and, together, they conducted land acquisition surveys for Wyatt Geosciences' client, MinTech. For Michelle, it was an exciting new beginning. She would finally be starting her professional career working as a field biologist for Roberts Ecosystems.

Fate landed them on opposite sides of a political powder keg within months of their moving to the Pacific Northwest. It was the logging industry against an obscure adversary, the spotted owl, an endangered bird with endearing, human-like eyes. These were heady days when the triumphs and failures of owl and logging industry alike were played out daily on television and in the newspapers. Michelle found tramping the verdant forests, assessing habitat quality with Christa Longo, her mentor and new friend, exhilarating. It was a near vertical take-off for her career: a polarizing issue of international magnitude, and she was a part of it.

And then everything came crashing down...

Unbeknownst to everyone, they—Michelle, Nick, and Chris—not to mention the loggers, the loggers' families, even the hapless owl, were pawns in a much larger game being played out by bitter foes with ulterior motives far removed from mere timber sales or the fate of a reclusive bird few even knew existed. First, their relationship was strained from the pinch of opposing forces. Then Christa was murdered and Michelle discovered that she was the next target of a faction of Roberts's employees belonging to an ultra-radical environmental terrorist group called EcoGenesis. Alone and against great odds, she pieced together the fragments of her fractured will to stand before her attackers and reveal them to the world for what they were—misguided, remorseless *killers*.

Shortly after the EcoGenesis affair, Nick and Michelle retreated to the safety of Michelle's suburban Cincinnati home. Michelle had had enough trauma in her life and wanted to return to Darrtown to be close to her mother, who took this latest tragedy even worse than she had Ghost Creek. Nick needed to recover as well. He was laid low by a case of Hanta virus, the cause of which was hotly debated by tree huggers and tree fellers alike, who respectively attributed the outbreak to the lack of owls or insufficient predation by lazy birds.

In a curious turn of events, shortly after their return, an Oregon reporter leaked the first snippets about the same environmental cover-up Nick and Chris unraveled regarding MinTech's parent company, Carson Chemical. "Had the devastation ultimately caused by Carson Chemical been left unchecked," the reporter wrote, "unrepentant greed would have altered the ecology of a wide swath of southwest Oregon for decades to come." No sooner had the news started to attract attention than Michelle's agent, Connor Lewis, called her. He pressed her to strike while the proverbial iron was hot. "Michelle, you've got to do this. *Do it now!* Get your account of the story to market before someone steals your thunder. It'll be a smash success!"

Lewis knew what he was talking about. *EcoGenesis* peaked at number three late in 1995 and remained on the charts for much of the following year. Michelle had once again become America's favorite heroine, and in the process acquired the nickname "Calamity Girl" from a Cleveland newspaper literary critic. Michelle accepted the nickname as a badge of honor. Fame, though, wasn't something she coveted. In fact, it embarrassed her, and at times she found it downright frightening, so much so that Michelle more often than not declined public signings and only answered her agent's calls when she felt that she had to. By this time, writing had become more than therapy, it was her passion, and, through the tapping of keys, she found a whole new mental outlet writing children's books. As a result, she elected not to reenter the standard workforce and instead use her education and interests to teach children how organisms interacted with the world around them. It was a therapeutic process that filled her audience with wonder. Moreover, Michelle felt safe, and it was only recently that she dared even to think about branching out to help Nick with his private practice.

Michelle was on the phone with Lewis one day last November to discuss concerns she had about a draft of the artwork for her latest children's book. After assuring Michelle that the proposed artwork was not offensive—that, if anything, the ethnic appearance of the character in question would only help to promote book sales—the agent broached the subject of a *Ghost Creek* sequel. "The book companies, they all want to compete with reality television. You know, offer real-life personal interest stories, especially those where the story takes the writer back to their roots, to the scene of the crime, if you catch my drift," he told her. "They want to publish real stories and not that scripted tripe pawned off as reality." Lewis was a brilliant pitchman who knew how to play on her emotions. "I bet there's still so much you want to know, that you need to know, if you truly want to put this to rest. Don't you think that your loyal followers deserve the same?"

So now you're my therapist…thanks for the guilt trip, Connor.

If nothing else, Connor Lewis could be exasperating. "What are you proposing I write about?" Michelle asked, uncertain about the idea. Lewis's unexpected proposal resurrected long repressed feelings that made her uncomfortable. This angered her, yet she couldn't help but feel excited all the same. Connor was also right. She did still have unanswered questions.

"That's up to you, but I was thinking that you might start with a walk and talk through the area. You know, meet and interview people. Find out how much or how little the community has changed since then. How did they cope with the tragedy? Are they still being affected?" Michelle recalled liking this obvious angle. She had long felt that she didn't give the local community a fair shake in her cursory wrap-up at the end of *Ghost Creek*. "It would also be interesting to know what happened to the mines. Did they plug them up, or whatever you do to them?" Reading her mind, Lewis then coaxed in a low voice, "If they aren't plugged, wouldn't it behoove you to revisit them? You know, to go inside? Imagine the tension *that* would bring to the story!" And sensing Michelle's interest still wavering, he added, "All of us want to know how you're doing now. And what about that fascinating new avenue you're pursuing with Nick?" Michelle remembered Connor closing his sales pitch with, "We can still play up the twenty-five-years-later angle. Think about that! Rest assured, Michelle, there's no question that your audience will love reading about the past…your past. They'll eat up reconnecting!"

Now I'm vintage, too.

Nick was opposed to her returning to the Little Bear mine for obvious reasons. Michelle didn't blame him. But when his opinion changed little after she insisted she would not be alone, so did her patience for what she thought was self-centered patronizing. She had a professional commitment every bit as important as his. "Do I try and stop you whenever you go into the inner city to inspect supposedly deserted buildings for your clients?"

Arguments flared with increasing frequency as the months leading up to the inconvenient scheduling of her Colorado trip melted away. The Tarryall Mountain Foundation, the 'Conservancy' as she and Nick called the land-conservation organization that had purchased the Sacred Lands parcel from Huron College, took several months to finally grant her access to the mines, and then a much longer time for the lawyers to agree on the language for a remarkably complicated set of waivers, disclaimers, and non-disclosure mumbo jumbo that she could have cared less about. It was no wonder people simply trespassed on other people's property and asked forgiveness later.

Nick even tried to use the several Bankers Boxes crammed full of documents that Chris had sent them as leverage. He told Michelle in no uncertain terms that she needed to complete her inventory of the files and provide him with a chronological listing and highlight summary of each before she left for Colorado, so that he could focus on closing out his other client obligations. It was a reasonable request. Nonetheless, Michelle was certain Nick thought that she could never finish the assignment in time and that she would forego the Colorado trip altogether once she'd become immersed in the PSTRE case. Alas, she surprised him by working diligently to finish a week ahead of schedule, well before he had completed his own tasks. Impressed as well as defeated, Nick apologized and agreed to support her commitments from there on out, with the caveat that he would not stop worrying about her or Melanie until they both returned safely. And therein lay the problem. Nick may have been right all along. She hadn't even left and trouble was already brewing in the form of a series of cryptic emails she'd received over the past eleven days from someone at the Conservancy named *Jodi*, warning her that a certain element didn't want her meddling with the past.

"What's up with you?" Nick asked, interrupting Michelle's hum-along to a Hootie and the Blowfish tune on the radio.

"Huh? What are you talking about?"

"You keep fiddling with your phone. You seem preoccupied."

"Oh, it's nothing," Michelle lied. "I was just thinking about all of the little things I need to do before Melanie and I head out next week."

"Right."

Nick's attempt at conversation startled her. Michelle wasn't aware of just how long she'd sat in silence or absentmindedly played with her phone since they'd gotten back onto the highway. She had zoned out trying to comprehend the meaning of her dream and had become hopelessly lost in her thoughts, wondering if it meant anything that the nightmares began after she started receiving the emails, or whether Jodi, her *de facto* protector, was friend or foe. Michelle again looked to her phone, relieved to find nothing new from Jodi.

"By the way," Nick said, "I stopped again a little way back to get gas while you were napping. I got you a Coke and soft pretzel. They're back there." Nick jabbed a thumb over his shoulder in the direction of the floor in front of the back seat, where they kept travel snacks in easy reach.

"What did you say?" Michelle snapped, spinning around, looking to the floor then back at Nick with alarm. Michelle was overwhelmed with déjà vu. The Coke and pretzel sequence played out once before, back in 1985, on their maiden cross-country car ride to field camp, only then it was Garret who starred in Nick's current role.

First nightmares and now this...

"I got you a pretzel and a Diet Coke. Is that a problem?" Nick said. Probing for an explanation he teased, "I tossed a few bottles of that capuchin monkey piss stuff you like in the cooler before we left Cinci, if you'd rather."

Michelle burst into laughter. "That's kombucha! No thanks, but thank you. I thought—never mind," she said, stopping herself before continuing an explanation that could only lead to unnecessary complications. "A Diet Coke's fine."

The miles drifted by and so did her worries. They worked their way through the gray dinge hovering over the Appalachians, emerging on the far side of the mountains into rolling piedmont foothills bathed in glorious sunshine. They made small talk about the case for a while, but for the most part their attention was focused on all of the touristy things they planned to do and see during their stay in Charleston. The sudden appearance of the sun certainly had much to do with the vacation-like feel they shared, though it was the subtle change in vegetation that invigorated them most. An appealing mixture of evergreen and deciduous trees intermixed with tropical plants greeted them the closer they got to the coast. There was something about the vibrancy of the waxy foliage that told them they were approaching someplace special.

"Where do we get off the highway?" Michelle asked.

Nick tapped on the GPS to zoom out the field of view. "Like I thought. We stay on 26 until we hit 52. Somewhere in town, 52's name changes to Meeting Street and we take that the rest of the way down to Broad." Nick resumed his looking from the traffic to the street signs to the changing surroundings. Michelle commented on how the bedraggled vegetation even in the rag-tag commercial areas north of downtown proper looked so much better than its counterparts did in the cold climes back north. Nick concurred, pointing here and then there to an increasing number of palmetto (*or were they palm?*) fronds poking out from the scrub.

"You said Chris doesn't think the meeting will take too long?"

"That's what I understand. I think it's a meet and greet session. I'm guessing Carlyle wants to make sure the legal prep starts off on the right foot. I don't expect that you'll need to say anything. Hell, I mightn't either. Afterwards, Chris said that he'd take us to the place we're staying. It's supposed to be pretty posh."

"Works for me," Michelle said. She was tired and didn't feel like diving straight into a marathon work session on a Friday afternoon. "Wow! It's *really* nice down here, Nick," she commented, back to admiring their surroundings. "Look at all of the wrought iron fences. I love how the black color compliments the buildings. And all those neat lamp posts." Nick whistled through his teeth. "Impressive," he agreed. Then they encountered Spanish moss hanging from the trees shrouding the highway near Charlotte Street, and finally, the low, well-maintained flat-topped buildings south of Calhoun that captured the very essence of Victorian Charleston. "Really impressive!"

They turned onto Broad Street. "There! I think I see it," Michelle announced. "That pastel green-and-white-colored building there; the one with the bay windows." She pointed ahead and to their right. Nick acknowledged with a grunt and turned on his signal. "Do you see it?"

"Yeah, I see it, the one with the art gallery on the first floor." Nick called Chris the moment they parked. "Let's go," he said upon ringing off. "Chris is finishing with a meeting there, up on the third floor." Nick pointed skyward. Michelle cocked her head to see a rush of shadows pass by an upper floor window. "He'll meet us at the front desk where we sign in."

Like everything they'd seen thus far in Charleston, the law office of MacDonald & Carlyle was innately inviting. Michelle hadn't visited too many law firms before, but she'd been inside enough of them to recognize that this place did not suffer from the usual pompous intimidation. The floor and walls were covered with cypress planking. Massive yellow pine beams supported the ceiling and walls. Great circular rugs rested in all the right places, like the one covering the floor in front of the same bay window she saw from the street; it supported a parlor suite and side table, on top of which rested a water pitcher and a plate of scones. It was a welcome change from high gloss cherry wood and the spines of pretentious law books staring back in false welcome.

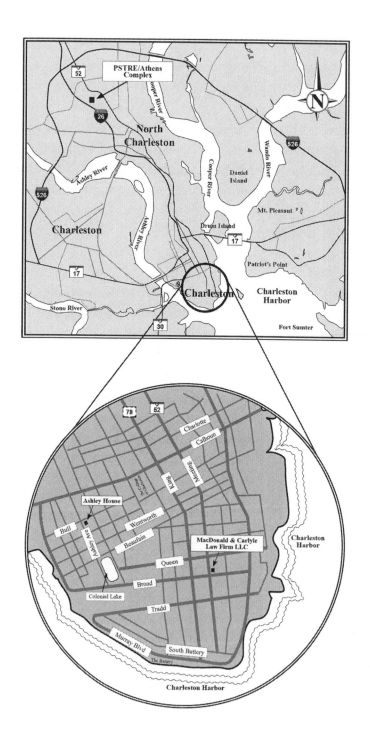

Rick Ley

This place was once an inn, Michelle thought. Taking in the airiness of the place with its charming post and beam structure, she reckoned that a major renovation had once taken place, all of the interior rooms having been removed and replaced by a series of offices and conference rooms that now surrounded an open-concept office space. Over-sized plate-glass windows mounted to rough-hewn pine posts accentuated the open feeling. An elegant glass chandelier hanging over the common area showcased a sweeping staircase leading to the third floor. Michelle dreamily imagined the place being used back in the day as a ballroom.

Nick nudged her shoulder. He handed her a badge with her name written neatly in fountain pen: "Ms. Michelle Kozlowski." Michelle affixed her name tag and followed Nick to the plate of scones. "Wendy told me she made them this morning."

"There you two are!" Chris announced, his voice booming as he strode down the staircase, arms wide in greeting. "Welcome!" Nick and Michelle were standing by the side table, struggling to choke down the dry pastry. "I take it you had a safe trip?"

It took a moment for them to respond. Nick was still chewing and Michelle feigned a swallow to conceal her bemusement at Chris's appearance. He always did have longish hair and a wild Scandinavian look about him, but this? Dressed in a tweed jacket and blue jeans, his hair pulled back in a graying, unkempt ponytail, he looked every bit the scary English lit professor she had back at Huron.

Pulling his gold wire-rims down to the end of his nose, Chris whispered, "I will shave and cut my hair before trial, if it goes that far." Leaning still closer, he whispered even lower, "I think the M&C folks are afraid of me." With a clap, he abruptly switched gears. "Do you two need to sit a few minutes, or are you ready to go upstairs? We have some time."

"We're good," Nick said. Michelle nodded. "We've sat long enough."

"Very well. Follow me."

Chris led them up the staircase to the third floor. They paused outside a conference room where Chris knocked lightly on the open door. Inside, an older man in a suit, Bill Carlyle, Nick surmised from Chris's description of him, was speaking to several younger men and a woman. The older man waved them in and said that he would be with them shortly. Nick passed the time admiring some old photos hanging on the wall. "Huh," Nick said. "Fort Sumter. That's around here, right?"

"Yeah, right here in Charleston Harbor," Chris said. "Maybe we'll go there Sunday if you're game, definitely before the two of you leave. Like the plaque says, the Civil War started right here, in April 1861, when the South bombarded the fort. The question of the day is, do you know who fired the first shot for the Union?" Nick and Michelle stared blankly back. "That would be Abner Doubleday, the guy wrongly credited with—"

"Inventing baseball. Incredible. Who won?" Nick asked, his eyes trolling the photos for an answer to the outcome of the battle.

"You skipped class that day," Chris wisecracked. "That would be Johnny Reb, though you didn't hear that from me. Some folks around these parts still take great pride in their secessionist past."

"Everyone sure is friendly," Michelle said, distracted by the attention she was attracting from several lawyers milling about in the hallway beyond the plate glass.

Chis panned the audience and chuckled. They were ogling Michelle as if she were a baby in a maternity ward. "Ah! Yes. Plenty of beautiful and famous people come through these doors, but rarely do they arrive in the same package. You do know that you and Nick are famous, right?" he said, "Particularly you, *Calamity Girl!*" The lookyloos dispersed when Chris placed his hand on her shoulder. "I wouldn't be surprised if a few figure out a proper way to ask you for your autograph." Michelle blushed. "But hey, if you're feeling denigrated, there's a real good sexual harassment firm across the street." Michelle chirped a little laugh and punched Chris lightly on the arm.

Rick Ley

"Chris?" the older man interrupted. They turned to find Bill Carlyle making his way in their direction. A large, pudgy man with pleasant blue eyes and soft features, Carlyle had the kind of face that made everyone around him feel instantly at ease. "You must be Nick Kozlowski," Carlyle said, shaking Nick's hand. "And you, my dear, must be his better half." Carlyle enveloped her hand between his.

"Yes. I'm Michelle. Pleased to meet you!"

"The pleasure's all mine. I'm Bill Carlyle. Please, take a seat." He gestured to several chairs parked around the nearest end of the conference table. With the departure of the woman and a male colleague, the two remaining members of the PSTRE legal team stepped forward to make their introductions. They were Smithson "Smitty" Griffin, a tall man with a refined grace who looked to be in his early thirties, and Brant Sutherland II, a thickly built twenty-something with flushed cheeks and muddy red hair. Sutherland gave the impression of being the rich kid bully sort out to make his mark on the world.

Carlyle waited for the commotion to settle before proceeding. He directed his preamble to his guests. "As each of you are aware, our good friends at Palmetto State Transformer and Relay—or PSTRE, which is pronounced 'pass-tree'—are suing their neighbor, Athens Petrolatum, citing damages from a wrongful action. PSTRE claims that an oil-like substance, possibly creosote, originating from Athens, has migrated onto PSTRE property, contaminating a production water-supply well PSTRE says is critical to their plans for business expansion. Athens at one time used creosote for the preservation treatment of utility poles for PSTRE, though the product found in the well might also be a conventional oil of indeterminate age. As I'm sure you're aware, Athens has a large aboveground storage-tank farm located along the property boundary that could easily be the source." Taking a cursory look at the information packet on the table before him, Carlyle made it a point to add, "As I can see from this summary, which I took the liberty to peruse before you arrived, both of you are also aware of the long history between the plaintiff and defendant. Lastly, the available environmental data are limited. This is a very nice summary, by the way. It gets to the crux of each of the reports that we had Chris provide to you. Very nice."

"Appreciated," Nick said. "It was Michelle who did the legwork, though I am reasonably familiar with the pros and cons of the information that I've had a chance to review thus far."

"The pros are?"

Nick rolled his eyes in sync with the rocking of his head. The crap quality of the reports Chris had given them to review was a problem. There was nothing in them that could honestly be used to support PSTRE's claim in a court of law. Nick did his best to dance his way around the question. "The long and continued use of both properties for industrial purposes has no doubt impacted soil and groundwater quality, the degree of which we still don't know. I'm certain that we can piece together what's going on underfoot with all of the new information PSTRE's consultant has and will be collecting over the near term. I look forward to seeing this information." Nick then ventured to press his concern for the lack of supporting data and logical recommendations that should have been made in the old reports. "These, I'm certain..." Nick hesitated to recall the name of the consultant, "yes, River City Environmental, has also identified."

"Such as?" Carlyle frowned.

Nick was uncomfortable for as long as it took to remind himself that he was neither casting stones nor implying that PSTRE's case was baseless. "We still need soil-lithology information from between the property line and the production well to demonstrate encroachment of an oil—or should I say creosote—plume. Chis and I plan to meet with RCE on Monday following a recon of the property and the surrounding area."

Carlyle weighed Nick's less than glowing endorsement carefully. What site data they did have had nothing to do with the core of the suit—the production well that PSTRE intended to put back into service. Carlyle searched skyward for the proper words to summarize his thoughts, his pronounced blinking failing to disguise his concern for the merits of the case.

"Bill," Chris interrupted, "I've scheduled a meeting with Sam Piersall for two-thirty at RCE's office in Columbia. We'll first take a look at what they're doing at the site, and from there we'll speak with Sam about focusing the ongoing investigation. Like Nick said, we'll know where we stand one way or the other before long."

For the life of him, Nick didn't foresee the discussion taking this path. None of this should have been a surprise…unless M&C was forging ahead with the suit regardless of not understanding the facts, or lack thereof. The latter apparently was the case.

"And the cons?" Carlyle asked, resigned to the certainty that the obstacles ahead were many.

Nick waited for the junior attorneys to shuffle the contents of several manila folders back and forth. The disruption ended when the surly-looking Brant Sutherland pulled out a copy of RCE's field schedule. Smitty and Brant tag teamed an explanation of the well drilling and test-pit work planned for the following week. Nick was not yet privy to the actual schedule and was encouraged by what he heard. Brant pointed to several drilling locations along the property line precisely where subsurface conditions were unknown on the PSTRE side of the Athens aboveground storage-tank farm. Encouraged by the program, Nick suggested what he would do with the data. "The first thing I'd do is confirm that there actually *is* oil—can we just call it 'oil' until we definitively figure out what it is?—encroaching onto PSTRE's property from Athens's operation to the north. From there it's imperative that we nail down the groundwater-flow direction. This might be tricky considering that PSTRE and Athens are pretty much centrally located between the Ashley and Cooper River drainages."

"RCE already has some piezometers in the ground and they are installing pressure transducers. That should answer the problem," Brant answered matter-of-factly while picking at his thumb.

"Oh." Piezometers are small diameter wells typically used only for the recording of the depth to groundwater below ground surface. Consultants convert the water depth measurements to elevations in feet above sea level that can then be plotted on a map. The data from at least three locations allow a flow direction to be determined. More than three data points and the map is that much more accurate. "And?" Nick begged when Brant left him hanging.

"Haven't heard one way or another. They were having equipment issues."

Nick was becoming irritated. He had no idea that RCE had already installed piezometers. He should have been informed of this. Nick made a mental note to speak to Chris later. The important take was that RCE was thinking like he was and understood that, shy of sabotage, the case hinged on demonstrating that local groundwater flow was primarily north to south, down the spine of the peninsula that terminated at Charleston a half dozen miles to the south. This being the case, the groundwater would carry oil from the Athens property onto PSTRE's and into the PSTRE production well.

"I'll give Sam a call when we're done here to find out if they've been able to make a determination," Chris said, acknowledging Nick's aggravation.

"Good," Nick said to Chris. "What I'm trying to say is that there's a lot of groundwater sloshing around, so to speak, beneath the Charleston peninsula, what with the tides and slugs of freshwater coming down the rivers with each rain event complicating things. It might take some doing to figure out the flow regime."

"I presume that you will *figure things out* if we focus our time and resources?" Carlyle said, probing for affirmation.

Nick peered into Bill Carlyle's pale eyes and flashed a confident smile. "Yes, we will," he said. "Do bear in mind that Athens could be positioned cross gradient rather than up gradient from PSTRE. In that case, groundwater could be flowing preferentially east *or* west toward either river drainage. We don't know where the divide is. Contamination from Athens, therefore, could miss PSTRE's property or the production well altogether." Nick raised a hand to stifle the lawyer's concern. "As we know, the Athens tank farm is situated rather close to the PSTRE production well. Assuming that any of those tanks or any other historical features standing there before them had leaked, simple dispersion could certainly account for off-site contamination reaching the PSTRE well, regardless of the prevailing flow direction. I was also thinking that if we dig further into the use history for Athens's property and perform a fingerprint analysis on the oil in PSTRE's well, then we might be able to unearth definitive evidence that finds Athens at least partially liable. Am I right?" Nick's question was received with sage nods from the legal team. "Good. We can use that information as leverage to perhaps pressure Athens to an out-of-court settlement that provides the monies necessary to clean up PSTRE's well."

Nick had hardly concluded his spiel when a satisfied Carlyle announced, "Very well. Make it happen!"

Nick puffed out his chest, relieved that he'd satisfied the boss. And so that Bill Carlyle was clear about the money he was investing in him, Nick insisted, "You can count on it. When we see RCE on Monday, Chris and I will ask if they can use the transducers to collect long-term water-level data if they're not already doing that. As part of the data scrubbing process, we'll ask that RCE account for tidal and river discharge effects and evaluate whether there are any area pumping wells or other draw sources we need to know about that could impact flow direction. It's logical that they're thinking about this, too. Either way, Chris and I will make sure that the bases are covered." Carlyle again expressed his endorsement. Out of the corner of his eye, Nick saw Michelle beaming with admiration.

"Okay," Carlyle said with a clap much like Chris's before. "I need to be leaving, and I do apologize for the limited time I had to speak with all of you. Before I go, let me explain the chain of command so that everyone is clear. Smitty, here, he will be lead counsel and will keep me appraised of progress." Smitty lifted his hand in acknowledgement. "Brant will support Smitty and act as principal liaison with Chris. Nick, Michelle," Carlyle said with a warm smile, "you will—"

"Report to me!"

"Indeed they will Mr. Orrey!" Carlyle said, sharing in Chris's good humor. "Now, this doesn't mean we cannot communicate freely with one another, but I do expect that all important information will be passed through the chain of command so that there's no confusion as to where we stand. Got that?" Everyone agreed. "Very good. Now, Smitty, don't be surprised if you hear from Athens's counsel next week. I told them to wait until I returned, but I'm not counting on them listening."

"About?" Smitty asked.

"After my meeting this morning between the principals with both firms, it's become clear that neither side is budging. Stan's—that's Stan Merrill, PSTRE's president, if you didn't know, Nick—really stirring the pot, itching for a fight with his counterparts at Athens."

Nick and Michelle looked to Smitty, who responded with an affirming *that sounds about right* arch of his brow.

"Afterwards, I received a call from Ted Carlson—he's chief counsel for Athens, Nick. Ted informed me that Athens intends to disclose something that will give Merrill pause to reconsider his lawsuit—no idea what that may be. I recommend that if they call before I get back, don't wait for me. Take Ainsley with you to act as a buffer. I will brief him before I leave."

"Not a problem," Smitty replied. Everyone started to rise. Smitty asked if he could speak with Chris in private.

Bill Carlyle made for the door before the others had picked up their things. He stopped at the jamb. "Ms. Snow?" he said, catching Michelle's attention, "I was wondering…when I return from my trip, would you be so kind as to tell me all about your latest book?"

Michelle was startled by the sudden attention, more so by Carlyle's use of her maiden name, which doubled as her surname pseudonym in the literary world. It was an offbeat question, given the nature of the meeting. Apparently the others thought so, too, by the way that they looked at their boss. "Of course!" Michelle said clumsily. "It would be my pleasure."

"*Excellent*! And autograph my copies of your other books?" Michelle again agreed, to which Carlyle tapped at the jamb and made his exit into the hall.

Ashley House
Ashley Avenue, Charleston, S.C.
7:35 P.M.

They followed Chris west on Broad Street for several blocks, then turned right onto Ashley Avenue. Michelle marveled at the immaculate architecture, the buildings all neatly constructed of stone, brick, or wood, and finished in hues of white, gray, or soft pastel. Many buildings also had balconies with wrought-iron or mill-turned wooden spindle railings from which to watch the hubbub on the streets below. Michelle thought the balconies added that perfect touch to a community clearly wanting to preserve its architectural past. All in all, it was a pleasant drive on a gorgeous afternoon. The sun still hung high in a cobalt blue sky accented with the wispy curls of cirrus clouds. A light breeze shimmered through the fronds of what Michelle finally determined to be sabal palmettos—South Carolina's state tree. Nick, the hopeless romantic, culminated their Mitch and Abbey moment when he cued up *The Firm* soundtrack on his iPhone upon turning onto Ashley, where they followed the west bank of Colonial Lake, the focal point of a block-sized town park. Michelle remarked that she looked forward to unwinding before dinner with a skate around the walking trail bordering the rectangular expanse of lake, on her roller blades.

Nick, like Michelle, was taking in the idyllic setting of the lake and Mayberryesque yards bordered by white picket fences when he failed to notice that Chris had pulled to the curb a few blocks past the lake. "We're staying here?" Michelle gasped, stepping out of the car that Nick managed to lurch to a stop mere inches behind Chris's bumper, "This place is gorgeous!"

"Yes, and I'm jealous for you! Welcome to Ashley House. Just wait until you see inside," Chris said, closing his door. "Go ahead through the fence, there, and take a look around. I'll meet you on the porch. I have a few boxes to bring in. Nick, do you mind?"

Michelle was giddy. It was the type of house that every little girl dreamed of one day living in, a monstrous place with an impeccably manicured yard surrounded, of course, by a white picket fence. Michelle walked the grounds while the boys retrieved the file boxes from the trunk of Chris's car. The house was constructed of wood and painted a pleasing light blue. Entrance to Ashley House was via a wrap-around porch with round wooden columns, painted white, that supported a second-floor balcony overlooking the yard. A lush hedge, highlighted with beautiful red flowers, bound the rear perimeter of the property. A very large flowering magnolia tree, complete with a dive-bombing mockingbird, shaded much of the central courtyard. High above, in the crook of a small branch shrouded by deep waxy green leaves and pinkish-white blooms, Michelle spied the nest mamma bird was protecting. At the south end of the property stood a garage, over which Michelle assumed was a caretaker's apartment.

"You can drop your things here for now," Chris said, once inside.

"Pretty impressive," Nick said, taking in the surroundings.

"It's not a bad place to stay," Chris deadpanned, watching Michelle run her hand along the length of the extraordinarily long table that dominated the great room. "I understand that the table you're admiring was milled from a pecan tree standing on the property when the lot was first cleared by some axe-wielding Scotsman a ways back in the early 1800s."

"I count five extra leaves, and it was hand-planed! Who owned this place?" Michelle asked, awestruck, sweeping her eyes across the expanse of the room. "Just imagine all the debutante balls for generations of Southern belles coming out into society. *Ohhh! I just love it!*"

"Wow. I never thought about that. I bet you're right," Chris encouraged. "As for the house, it's been in the MacDonald family since it was built. The MacDonalds were a well-to-do family, rich from the cotton trade. As I understand it, the family owned a sizeable spread back in the day. This is all that's left. Brant, the punkish one at the meeting, told me that the MacDonalds had butlers, a coachman, and slave maids who lived in an older cottage where the current garage and caretaker's apartment now stands." Chris then made it a point to say with a tantalizing whisper, "Supposedly General Beauregard, the dude commanding the Southern defenses of Charleston at the start of the Civil War, was a frequent visitor in the days leading up to the opening cannonade on Fort Sumter."

"Incredible!" Nick said. Michelle again gasped with excitement.

"It makes for a good story at least. The place fell into disrepair during the *War of Northern Aggression*, as they call it around these parts, and was nearly leveled during the quake of 1886. The house was rebuilt and then slowly deteriorated to a mere shell of its former glory until Ainsley MacDonald, the other principal partner of the firm, decided to restore Ashley House to its current use as an off-site work space and refuge for honored guests. After he and Carlyle started their law practice...come on," Chris said, putting words into action, "let me show you around instead of bullshitting. Then I gotta cut out and head back to the office to speak with Smitty before he leaves for the weekend. I'll give you a call when we're done and we can talk about meeting up later for dinner. Sound good?"

Food remained a topic of conversation as Chris took them on a tour of the first floor, which also included a bookcase-filled parlor, a spacious kitchen with an adjoining butler's pantry, and a half bath, along with various closets and other professional-use rooms and storage spaces. The upstairs was a utilitarian arrangement of bedrooms that included a communal full bath with a claw-foot tub that Michelle simply adored, and a newer half bath at the far end of the hall that adjoined a massive walk-in closet. "Stay in any room you like. And get this, Nick; on Monday I'll introduce you to Charlene who will schedule your *maid service*. Yeah, exactly!" Chris said in response to his friend's eager gapes. That was my reaction the first time they let me stay here. M&C pulls out all the stops for special guests. You can have your room cleaned daily if you like. And, oh yes, if you need groceries or shit like that and don't think you'll have the chance to go to the store—or if you just don't feel like it—you can tell Charlene and she'll see to it that someone brings over what you want."

"*Ah!* I can get used to a place like this," Nick said with satisfaction. "Remind me to thank Bill for the hospitality."

Outside, Chris led them across the grounds to the second floor caretaker's apartment. "Here's where we're keeping the files for the case," he said, stepping aside so that Nick and Michelle could enter.

"All these?" Nick said, shaking his head. The length of one entire wall of the main room was lined with file cabinets like so many soldiers standing at attention.

"Oh, my!" Michelle followed with no small measure of distress. There was no way that she could wade through them all before her Colorado trip. Michelle peeked inside the nearest drawer to find the neatly labeled tabs of dozens of file folders.

"Don't look so distraught," Chris snorted. "You already have most of what we know, though I'm sure there might be some intriguing nuggets still buried in here." Observing Nick's continued headshaking, Chris elaborated, "No, seriously. I sifted through each cabinet and pulled out what I believe is the most valuable stuff to get you going. As for these cabinets here," Chris added, pointing to the three closest to the door, "these just arrived and consist of what Brant and his minions found at the state file review for Athens Petrolatum. I haven't looked at them yet. And finally," Chris concluded by kicking a toe at two lone Bankers Boxes on the floor, "these are the D-Squareds."

"The what?"

"The *Doubly Deads*. That's what RCE calls them; various odds and ends, over-sized maps, the crap RCE couldn't find a better place to stick. I doubt you'll find anything in them, but who knows? We want to make sure that we don't miss anything. Believe me, Bill Carlyle is not a fan of surprises."

"What you mean to say is that I'm still being tested. That's why he grilled me back there."

"No," Chris corrected. "You passed the test. You said everything he'd hoped you'd say. So did you, Michelle," Chris emphasized with a wink. "Bill gave me the nod before he left." Chris then erupted into that infectious hacking cackle of his.

"What is it? What'd I do?" Michelle begged, raising a hand to her face. She was laughing so hard along with Chris that she started to tear.

"You should have seen your face when he asked you to sign his copies of your books. You turned more shades of red than an agitated octopus on one of those nature shows." Chris accentuated the quip by pulsing his fingers open and closed and making angry gesticulations with his face. Controlling his laughter, Chris's face darkened. "In all seriousness, there's a reason why we're all down here on this case and that Bill Carlyle's leading the charge—that's why he challenged you."

"Go on," Nick prompted.

Chris glanced at his watch. "That, my friend, is a story better told over a beer. I'd better get going if I'm going to catch up with Smitty. Tell you what, change of plans. Whataya say I come over around seven? I'll bring over some pizza and beer. We can chill out and shoot the shit while I fill you in on the case."

Nick looked to Michelle; both shrugged. "Why not?" Nick replied. "Besides, I'm not sure that we're ready to go out just yet. "Maybe later to a sports bar for a night cap if we catch our second wind."

"Yeah, sure. I know of a few nice places down along the waterfront. Until later, then," Chris said, taking his leave.

Chris arrived as promised shortly past seven, toting two pizzas and a mixed case of beer from a local brewery. "Picked them myself," he boasted, as if he'd culled the beverages from his own private biergarten. Nick relieved him of the pizzas, and they took both food and beverage to the kitchen where they cracked opened a couple of cold ones. Nick filled a party bucket he found in a cupboard with ice and a handful of Chris's select craft brews. Trudging his way upstairs to the balcony, Chris asked where Michelle was. "Never mind," he followed, answering his own question. The sound of shower spray and the pleasing scent of shampoo gave away her location.

Nick forced an amused sniff. Over his shoulder he remarked, "She must be having a midlife crisis. Get this; she took up in-line skating. You no sooner leave and there she goes, rolling her way down the sidewalk to that lake. Most people buy a 'vette. Hell, she coulda bought me one with all her cash, but no! Instead she takes her chances in a pair of shoes propelled by eight tiny wheels. I kept waiting for the paramedic's siren the entire time she was gone."

It was a comfortable evening to watch the post-workweek traffic make its way up the street while draining beverages on the balcony. The subject of conversation varied, but for the most part focused on catching up on what each had been up to since they'd last collaborated. Chris accepted a fresh beer that Nick fished from the ice bucket. "Thanks," he said, popping the top, taking a swig. "Coast Brewing Company makes some pretty good stuff. They're from right here in Charleston." Nick grabbed one of the same.

They sat in silence savoring the moment. A garrulous sort, the charismatic Chris Orrey had dominated much of the dialog to that point, leaving Nick to struggle to interject his own thoughts. That's why, when the moment of silence lasted a little too long, Nick shifted his gaze from the dive-bombing mockingbird they'd been watching to Chris, whom he observed staring fixedly at something down on the street. "What are you looking at?" Nick asked.

Chris didn't answer, his attention remaining fixed on the street below. "Nothing. It's nothing." Another lull ensued, and finally, after a long drag on his bottle, Chris said, his voice a low croak, "I've been thinking about something for a while now. My workload's been increasing and, quite frankly, I've been run ragged."

This caught Nick's attention. "Uh-huh."

Without breaking eye contact with whatever had him fascinated on the street, Chris lolled his head to the side to say with nonchalance, "I was wondering if you'd be interested in firming up our relationship."

Now this was something Nick didn't expect to hear: a business proposition. "Hmm," he hummed. He was certainly interested, this much was true. Nick very much enjoyed the legal casework Chris had thrown his way, and the pay was fantastic, but could he really afford to give up even some of the professional freedom he enjoyed as a sole proprietor? "You're asking if I'm interested in working for you—or perhaps going into business together?"

"I dunno," Chris said, still staring at the street below. "Something like that, I guess. I haven't thought about it too deeply, but yeah. I think we work well together, and I have complete confidence in what you bring to the table. I think you know that." Nick agreed. "Think about it," Chris added, his interest on the street-side mystery having run its course. "Let's see how it goes while you're down here. If you're interested, we can talk about something mutually agreeable."

Nick mulled the proposition over. "Sounds like a plan," he answered. He also requested that they keep the subject between themselves for the time being.

"Of course. No problem. That's great. Now whataya say that we go back inside. I don't know about you, but I'm getting hungry."

The boys had tapped deeply into the pizza by the time Michelle made her way downstairs. "Hi Chris!" she said from the hall leading into the kitchen. "Sorry it took me so long. I was on the phone with my mom. I just *had* to tell her all about this gorgeous house."

Something in the way Nick and Chris were looking at her piqued her curiosity. "Now what? You two look like you're up to something, besides eating pizza."

"Oh, nothing," Chris said, the hitch in his voice about as awkward as Nick's lame shrug. Michelle eyed them with suspicion long enough for Chris to create a diversion. "Tell me why after all these years you decided to go back to Ghost Creek. I have to admit that I'm a little surprised." Instead of launching into an enthusiastic discussion of her latest book project, Michelle blanched and Nick grimaced. "Alright, what did I miss?" Michelle's posture softened. She smiled. Michelle explained how the project had come about and her plans to root out how the community and some of the minor players in the original book recovered and moved on with their lives. "What's the problem? That sounds like a great idea."

"She plans to go back inside the mines."

"*Oh!* That explains it. You think Calamity Girl here will find a way to get herself into trouble," Chris said to lighten the mood. Nick grumbled under his breath. The best Michelle could offer was a meek smile. "Come on, the two of you. I understand that you're going with Garret's sister and will be meeting with some camera guy, right? Am I correct? Besides, I can't imagine that you'd be allowed to go inside the mines without representation from that conservancy group, right?" Michelle's face tightened, prompting Chris to press further. "It seems to me that you should be plenty safe. Has there been any other trouble out there since the late eighties?"

"Not that I'm aware of," Michelle lied.

"And you're not having any reservations about how you or Garret's sister might react when you set foot back inside the mines?"

"You mean emotionally? No," Michelle said truthfully. "Melanie either, from what she's indicated to me. Actually, it's Nick who has reservations." They looked at Nick who gave a subconscious tug at the closely cropped beard that covered the scar Garret inflicted on him that final day.

"Stop your worrying, then" Chris said with finality. "Michelle, you go and enjoy the experience. Stay focused on what you need to do and be careful. If you or Melanie has reservations about going back inside the mines, don't go. Let the camera guy go. Better yet, ask that land trust group, or whoever they are, if they have any photos you can use. I'm sure they must. Honestly, it would add a whole level of creepiness to the book if you *couldn't* make yourself go back inside. Just imagine," Chris emphasized, waving his hands about like a movie director, "the Curse of Coronado still at work, casting its spell over the place where so much tragedy has occurred over the centuries—Badger Heart's spirit still running amok inside the mountain."

Michelle blushed. Chris could give Connor Lewis a run for his money when it came to pitchmanship. "You're right," she agreed. So long as they stayed together, there was no reason for her to be overly concerned. And no, she didn't need to go back inside the mines. Michelle noticed that even Nick couldn't offer a rebuttal to Chris's provocative suggestion.

"Have you come up with a title yet, or is that something you think about later in the writing process?"

"I was thinking of calling it *Reckoning at Little Bear*," she said, unable to shake the flush from her cheeks.

"So you *do* want to test your resolve and go back inside the belly of the beast!"

"Thank you, Chris. I promise we'll be careful. By the way, you'll have the chance to meet Melanie. She's arriving here Tuesday evening." No sooner said than a nervous wave crossed Michelle's face. "I didn't think about it. We're not leaving until Thursday. She can stay here with us, can't she? I kinda said she could. I didn't think about it."

"No worries. It's fine. Strictly speaking, those who stay here first need approval from HR. This is, of course, a special case, and Bill Carlyle has been known to make exceptions, not to mention he's one of your biggest fans. I don't think he'll have a problem. I'll ask Smitty to talk to him to make sure."

They retreated to a screened-in section of porch that looked out over the yard to talk about the case. Michelle was glad that they heeded Chris's advice and did not sit outside on the balcony because a thin veneer of bugs, attracted to the interior lights, soon coated the screen. Nick and Michelle plopped down in matching papa-san chairs positioned just so to collect the down-draft from a slowly oscillating paddle fan suspended from the wood ceiling. Chris remained standing. He amused himself wandering back and forth across the length of screen, flicking a finger here and there to agitate insects into flight.

"This is my fourth time working with these guys," Chris said, finally turning to the reason they were all together enjoying such a fine Charleston summer evening. "A few years back I got a call out of the blue from Ainsley MacDonald. Never heard of him or his firm before that. Turns out he knew someone working for a former client of mine who recommended me to him. Ainsley said he needed someone to head the technical group for a non-disclosure case in Virginia. M&C's client was suing the former owner of a property for damages because the guy failed to disclose that he hadn't properly abandoned a buried heating-oil tank on the property. Just so happens the tank was a leaker. Our client further claimed that the closure documentation wasn't provided to the proper authorities."

"I can imagine what happened next," Nick groaned.

"Yeah," Chris grumbled. "Problem was, it was a cash deal. Otherwise, a lending institution would have required the Phase I that should have revealed the issue prior to sale. Our client knew that the tank was there and that it had supposedly been abandoned-in-place, but of course he buys the property without first asking for the closure report, which—surprise, surprise—doesn't exist. Fast-forward a few months and our client decides to remove the tank completely as part of a building expansion project, and guess what? They break ground and find contamination everywhere. And did I say that the Virginia DEQ was never notified of the release?"

Nick groaned again. Michelle sighed; the legal mess that must have uncoiled like a ball of snakes was all too clear.

"Tell me about it!" Chris clucked. "It was a comedy of errors. The former owner claimed ignorance and, as you also might expect, Billy Bob and his backhoe was nowhere to be found. It was a sticky case. Ainsley's other two cases followed not long after that and were somewhat like our current one, determining liability for an area-wide plume of groundwater contamination. Suffice it to say we won each case. Unfortunately, the consulting firm numbskulls I had to work with made things challenging." Animated as always, Chris screwed his face into a tight knot. "Idiots!" he griped.

Nick and Michelle watched with delight when Chris snapped a forefinger against the screen, sending a clumsy June bug hurtling off into the night. "What happened?" Nick chuckled.

Chris contemplated how best to summarize his frustration with technically gifted colleagues, consultants and lawyers alike, between swallows of beer. "Successfully navigating a legal case, particularly one that involves a jury, is an art form. It requires the lawyer to blend a healthy dose of manipulation and trickery supported with the right amount of factual information to sway the jury to his way of thinking. It's a beautiful thing, really. Trust me, most of the time the jury has no idea just how much they're being maneuvered into agreeing with a side whose evidence may be little more than a collection of half-truths window-dressed by a spin doctor in a pin-stripe suit. The way I see it, there are two weak links in most environmental legal cases: the quality of the supporting evidence and the courtroom awareness of the tech heads called upon to testify."

Reading between the lines, Nick shifted uncomfortably. "I wasn't aware that you planned for me to provide testimony."

"No worries, mate, I'm not—you're not. I'm not sure why they called me down for that first case. I was really handcuffed." Chris fluttered a hand. "Let me rephrase. I should say that they didn't have a good idea what to do with me. M&C's process was jumbled, and their consulting firm geologists and lead engineer were too narrowly focused. Needless to say, we didn't see eye-to-eye."

Nick and Michelle rolled their eyes at the understatement.

"As for the tank case, Ainsley's boys did a good job except for one thing, failing to review all of the documents at their disposal. The geologists discovered that most of the property had contaminant hotspots, accumulated over years of commercial and light industrial uses. The abandoned tank in question was actually located smack dab in the middle of several overlapping oil plumes probably derived from when the property was used as a machine shop. Even if the tank didn't have a leak of its own, there was no way the former owner shouldn't have known there was a problem, considering that one of their guys was there to monitor the abandonment process. We uncovered proof of that. Billy Bob or no Billy Bob, the former owner should have known. It seemed like a slam dunk, only the defendant wouldn't back down, so we proceeded with our prep for court.

"I didn't do much except sit around with a thumb up my ass for a while. There was nothing they really needed my help for, and yet the defendant refused to back down. Their attorney said our client had all he needed to know, that our claim was baseless."

"Sounds fishy. Did anyone ask what that meant?"

"Yes. Our client said that he had no idea what the defendant was talking about. Something kept bugging me, though, and since no one wanted my help, I asked if I could look through the legal documents related to the sale. Buried deep in a stack of email copies, I found one from the defendant allowing our client to perform any 'testing or inspections deemed necessary' by a pre-determined date prior to the sale. Basically, our client was given an out or the chance to negotiate a sale price based on what he found. By doing nothing he agreed to buy the property 'as is.' Of course, our client claimed he never saw the email, even though it was printed down from his server and was contained in a file in his office."

Nick groaned again. "M&C should have picked up on that much, much earlier."

"Someone should have, and certainly not me, but no one did—except me!"

"Did you still have a case?" Michelle asked.

"After trying to figure out whether or not the email was a legally binding document, our client decided to proceed and we changed tactics, claiming that the former owner willfully withheld information by virtue of his representation on-site at the time of the half-assed tank closure. We also played up the email as backhanded, because an invitation to perform due diligence prior to sale should have been forwarded by formal means. The jury ultimately sided with us, though at a fraction of the settlement we asked for. They held our client's negligence to keep tabs on his own correspondence against him."

"I bet they were glad they had you," Michelle said.

Chris paused to catch his breath, as much as to refresh their drinks. He returned with a slice of pizza held cross-wise between his teeth.

"Yes and no. The client certainly was. I caught his oversight in time for M&C to rework their argument and avoid further embarrassment. As for Ainsley, I'm not so sure. I could tell he didn't like the fact that it was me and not their guys who made the catch. That's why I was surprised when he called me back. Unfortunately, Ainsley again let his consultants take the lead, though I was given a little more latitude the next time around."

"How'd that work?" Michelle asked.

"This time we represented two adjoining light-industrial-facility clients, both of which used chlorinated solvents for metals degreasing. They were being sued by the local municipality for contributing to a region-wide plume of groundwater contamination that was being pulled into the community public water-supply system, a cluster of wells about five miles from the two sites. How's that for irony?"

"Seriously," Nick said. "Sounds like you paved the way for our representing PSTRE against Athens."

"You could say that. Bill Carlyle took notice," Chris said with a greasy smile. "The solvent plume had no definitive source and was impacting the deep bedrock aquifer that the public supply wells were drilled into. The municipality cast an area-wide net and named each facility with a reported chlorinated solvent release as a defendant. It was up to the defendants to prove that they weren't involved. M&C represented both firms after the legwork was ironed out, which allowed both facilities to share information. By the time I got involved, both clients were ready to sink a ton of money into drilling more wells, including a number of nested well pairs, the deeper ones going down between four and five hundred feet—pretty deep shit for monitoring wells. Mind you, both sites already had a number of monitoring wells. I took a look at their groundwater data. Neither situation appeared that bad, not serious enough to justify all the extra drilling work, and certainly not bad enough, or extensive enough, for the contamination from either site to be caught up in the supply-well capture zone."

Listening to Chris was like experiencing a lively theater performance. His use of motion and voice inflection was nothing short of riveting. "That was still an educated guess. *And?*" Nick said expectantly.

"You're right, I was working off a guess. Something again seemed out of whack to me. It wasn't like we were on a tight timetable. I thought Ainsley's consultant was being too aggressive with spending our client's money, so I took a page out of your book and thought outside the box."

Nick gave Michelle a whataya know look of satisfaction. "I'm all ears."

With the same greasy smile, Chris boasted, "I asked one of their hydro guys to run a very conservative groundwater model for both properties. I told him to apply the highest detected contaminant value in the existing shallow wells to both the shallow and deep groundwater-bearing zones beneath the property, even to the locations for the deep wells that weren't drilled yet, and to assume that the bedrock between the two units was leaky—you know," he explained for Michelle's benefit, "where fractures in the rock allow dirty groundwater from above to migrate down to the water-bearing zone beneath and contaminate the aquifer that provides the community water supply."

Michelle thanked him. It was what she thought but wasn't sure.

"I asked him to assume that the fracture orientation was on strike with the well field and to use highest transmissivity values for the rock type. I did my best to show a model-predicted, worst-case scenario. I really tried to provide a free and easy path for the contaminants on both properties to be captured by the public supply wells.

"As for the rest of the team—you'll like this—I asked them to comb through the public records and find all sites in the area with a documented chlorinated solvent release, and to pull out plume-limit maps, groundwater modeling results, and the ground-water-flow direction for each property. I also asked them to look for capture-zone maps for the public supply-well field—and for crying out loud, a map showing the limits of the regional plume of groundwater contamination that all the defendants supposedly contributed to. The municipality didn't offer one; do you believe that? How could a defendant demonstrate that it didn't contribute to the regional plume if it didn't know where the plume was? What bullshit. *Lawyers!* I took what M&C's consultant gave me and asked their GIS folks to throw everything onto one large map that included the municipal well field."

"*Ahh!* You remembered!" Nick said, reflecting gleefully back to a similar piece of evidence chasing he did a long time ago. "I haven't thought about that in ages."

"Yes, back when we worked for Wyatt."

"No kidding. That wasn't long after we came back from Oregon. What'd it show?"

"That our client's plumes were very small and came nowhere close to the regional plume, let alone having the potential to reach the well field. In fact, very few defendant plumes, we discovered, had the potential for capture by the well field cone of depression.

Further, the sheer size, geometry, and chemical signature of the regional plume suggested that it was related to a much larger release from elsewhere. We showed our data to the municipality. After a few legal rigmaroles, our clients were off the hook."

"Ainsley had to appreciate that," Nick said, beating Michelle to the punch. "You saved both clients a ton of money, not to mention all the stress. Nice work!"

"He seemed so outwardly, though I'm sure he and his consultant were not happy being shown up again. The clients were another story. They still had their own contamination issues to attend to, but they were thrilled. They thanked us profusely for getting them out of harm's way in the way of fines and chipping in to pay for the O&M costs on the well-field stripping tower." Chris shrugged his shoulders in an *all a day's work* manner and flicked another finger against the screen.

Nick reached into the box for another slice of pizza.

"I gather things are going to be different this time around? I take it you're actually in charge of the technical team?" Chris nodded. "That's what I thought. How then do we," Nick said, motioning to Michelle, "fit into the web of judicial brilliance you plan on spinning?"

"Glad you asked!" Chris responded with that squeaky cackle of his. "I'm not sure if Ainsley MacDonald fully appreciated what I did for him. He's a close-to-the-vest kinda guy. That's why I wasn't too surprised to get a call from Bill Carlyle instead. Like I said before, I did impress him. He made it a point then to say so. When I told Bill that I only did what you'd done before on those well-field cases, he wanted me to get you on board."

"Oh, wow. That was really nice—and thanks!" Nick said as modestly as he could. "That really means a lot." Michelle patted Nick's foot.

"Don't mention it. Bill's an entirely different animal than his partner. He's methodical, a real deep thinker, mentally always on the move. He may be looking at you, but he's really looking through you, around at you, probing, constantly interpreting what you've

Rick Ley

said and where you're going with your thoughts. He really puts me through my paces, and that's saying something. And don't let that Norm Peterson mug fool you," Chris emphasized with a wave of a finger. "Bill has a rapier tongue that he's not afraid to use. So if you don't relish the thought of a public undressing, you'd better be spot on or at least sufficiently convincing with your reasoning. Thus far I've been lucky. He's also the consummate host and probably one of the most genuine individuals you'll meet. This place, the firm, it has Bill Carlyle's thumbprint all over it. His name may come second, but he's the one really in charge."

The conversation wore on well into the evening, long enough to finish the pizza and work on a good buzz. Chris explained that their client, PSTRE, and neighboring Athens Petrolatum had a long and stormy relationship that dated to the late 1800s when both companies supported the telegraph communications industry. Athens treated the pine logs with creosote that PSTRE then sold as utility poles. Both companies were once related through marriage until a falling out between the families occurred nearly a century ago.

"I understand that descendants still work at their respective companies and that they still hold a grudge even though PSTRE and Athens no longer cross paths professionally." Chris explained that the bad blood resurfaced a few years ago when Athens refused an aggressive purchase offer from PSTRE, and that it was common knowledge that PSTRE had been vying for the Athens property for years. Speculation abounded that Athens declined PSTRE's overtures out of principle over the long-standing feud. Chris also explained that it was rumored that old man Merrill intended to mothball the Athens facility if he could leverage a sale. The tipping point in the melodrama happened when PSTRE discovered the yet to be identified 'oil' in the long forgotten supply well buried in the weeds in an overgrown area of parking lot behind the PSTRE manufacturing building. It was crucial, Chris said, reiterating Bill Carlyle's claim summary, that this well be able to meet the needs of PSTRE's expansion plans, hence the contention.

Chimes sounded faintly from the great room. "That's me," Michelle said. "I'm expecting a call from Mel. I'll be right back."

Chris used the disruption to finish explaining their roles in the upcoming case. "PSTRE is one of M&C's biggest clients. Bill and Ainsley hob-nob with the higher-ups at PSTRE; you know, do the golf thing, shit like that. Bill realizes that PSTRE's wrongful act claim is hazy at best, and he wasn't happy with how Ainsley handled the last cases I described. That's why he took this case on personally, why we're here, and why he named Smitty lead counsel. Smitty may be a stuffed shirt, but he's also sharp as a tack. As for Brant, he's a competent lap dog, a real do-whatever-you-want worker bee. Oh, and the bully act? It's just that. If you challenge him, he'll back down. Carlyle likes Brant because he's relentless. Need something and he won't stop until the job's done."

Nick made mental notes. He craned his neck to see what was keeping Michelle.

"I'll go over everything again when she gets back. What you really need to know is that I agreed to take on this case so long as Bill gave me the reins to lead all aspects of the technical support and be the one who actually provides the technical testimony if the case gets that far. Remember what I said about tech heads getting lost in the weeds and not knowing when not to say too much? That's not going to happen this time around. Bill also agreed to change consulting firms for this one. That's why you see the influx of RCE docs in the files I sent you."

"I'll bite, why?"

"M&C is an offshoot of Glenanne Engineering, the consultant on board for the other cases."

"They fired themselves?" Nick said, amused. "That mustn't have gone over well."

"You could say that. Glenanne is a consulting firm that's had a lot of interaction with lawyers over the years. Carlyle started there as a geologist before taking a leave of absence to get his law degree. Somewhere along the way, old man Glenanne hired Ainsley MacDonald and another lawyer whose name escapes me. The lines eventually became blurred: were they consultants or were they lawyers? So they made a strategic move and decided to split into two companies. Glenanne pretty much uses M&C for all its legal needs. I understand M&C uses several consultants, including River City Environmental. In my opinion, the problem we had before was the overly friendly relationship between Glenanne and M&C. It was difficult to make a decision without having to navigate through all the office politics. I'm still getting familiar with RCE, and thus far I like their work. Using them allows both parties to work unencumbered. RCE's working extra hard to impress, much more so than Glenanne, so Bill's cutting Glenanne out."

"I look forward to meeting RCE," Nick said. His smile widening, he quipped, "You know Chris, this place has got to be the most atypical law firm I've ever run across. It's like a good ol' boys club from the British Isles. Glenanne, MacDonald, Carlyle, Smitty and his sidekick Fetch, I have the urge to change my name to 'O'Kozlowski,' or something, just to fit in."

"Funny you should say that," Chris erupted with a spray of beer, "M&C's known around these parts as the 'Defenders of the *UK*,'" which he pronounced like 'duck' without the 'd,' and to which they shared a hearty laugh. Then returning to business matters, Chris said, "As for what I need you to do, besides becoming familiar with everything that we have, is to steer RCE in the right direction. Until I hear otherwise, you have full rein to make sure that RCE collects any and all data you think are necessary." Nick's already wide smile widened that much more. "I thought you'd like that."

"Fuckin' A," Nick said with the enthusiasm of child who'd just received a room full of presents. "I haven't had the luxury of an open budget in a very long time."

"You can get used to that with M&C." Chris's next words, however, were guarded, implying. "I also need you to let me know how much rope I have."

"Meaning?" Nick asked, observing the twinkle in Chris's eyes.

"Like I said before, there's a purpose for you being down here. Do you know what that is?"

"We think alike and hold highest expectations for others and ourselves," Nick answered as if he'd rehearsed for this very question.

"Exactly!" Chris said, raising his bottle in a silent toast. "Like me, you evaluate everything at a deeper level and challenge the industry standard line of thinking. You ask all the 'what if' questions that open up unexpected options. I need you to challenge the data that work for us just as hard as what doesn't. I also need to know my limits of credibility. I won't lie, but I'm not afraid to operate anywhere in between those bounds." Chris paused to scratch at the screen, this agitating a beetle-like thing to wave its long antennas back and forth in silent alarm. "Courtroom testimony is like a tennis match. Sometimes you're baselining it, exchanging bombs and long groundstrokes—you know, *mano y mano*, argument challenging argument stuff—then you suddenly change strategy to gain a tactical advantage with a little serve and volley misdirection, softening them up for the *how the fuck'd they figure that out?* kill shot that leaves them reeling. Get it?" Nick gave a satisfactory grunt. "Good. Remember, this is a court of law. Anything goes. Truth be told, I'd be most comfortable if we could simply bulldoze them with irrefutable proof, but I'm not holding out much hope of that. I expect the waters to be muddy at best and for that, we will need to be creative. I just need to know how far I can dance."

Her cell phone was silent by the time she retrieved it from the great room table. It had in fact rung only twice. Michelle jutted her lip in a pout when she saw the familiar area code. She walked to a window overlooking the courtyard, cell phone in hand, anticipating a return call from Melanie at any moment, the double ring suggesting that she'd gotten sidetracked the first time around. Michelle was staring at the silhouette of the magnolia tree when her phone dinged. She jumped. She'd become so pleasantly distracted by her new surroundings that she'd nearly forgotten about her troubles. Michelle reached the home screen with the swipe of a finger. The mail icon indicated that she had forty-three new messages, at least a dozen more than the last time she'd checked. She paused, afraid to click on the icon, unsure if she was willing to put herself through yet another restless night's sleep. Of course, if she didn't look, the dread of not knowing would keep her up all night anyway. *If only Melanie would call me back...*

Michelle used both hands to steady the phone. She waited for a wave of nausea to pass before clicking on the mail icon, hoping for a reprieve until morning, when she'd check again. No such luck. The reason for her distress was buried seven messages deep—Jodi.

Michelle gasped, then peered as indifferently as she could over her shoulder, thankful that her involuntary outburst went undetected. She took several steps toward the sunroom anyway, just to make sure, before trudging upstairs to read the email in private. Michelle was relieved to find her fear of Jodi's latest installment of forewarning partially replaced by curiosity by the time she reached the bedroom.

Michelle left the bedroom door ajar so that she could listen for the boys coming up the steps. Retrieving her laptop from her backpack, she took a seat at the vanity, where she found the WEP key for the wireless network written on a small piece of paper taped to a bottom corner of the mirror. Michelle couldn't help nervously twirling a lock of tawny hair around her finger to pass the idle moments while the computer did its thing. It seemed an eternity until she worked up the courage to click on the user name *Hiker-Chic* from the field of unread emails. Sounds of laughter drifting up from the sunroom below were a painful reminder that half a house away, Nick remained oblivious of the unknown ghosts from their past that she was about to reactivate with her return to Colorado.

Michelle clicked on Jodi's email, surprised to find only two words:

Read!—Jodi

Her eyes bounced around the screen until she found the attachment. She opened it. It was an article from the *Central Colorado Times* newspaper, dated from the previous week. The headline was chilling:

TRAGEDY STRIKES SIXTH ANNUAL
GOLD RUSH DAYS EVENT

This Michelle wasn't expecting. She squeezed her lip between a thumb and forefinger and started to read. The Gold Rush Days Event was a regional celebration held each year outside of Leadville to pay homage to the area's rich mining history. The event was also held to celebrate the summer tourist season—and no doubt to pay good riddance to the passage of another long winter. The opening paragraph expressed optimism for a successful summer and planted the seeds for a new fall gala to usher in the winter ski season. By the time she finished the paragraph, Michelle felt pangs of nostalgia for the happy times she and Nick spent at Huron's field station, where they completed the field work for their Master's theses. Such feelings were dashed in the following paragraphs, which described the mysterious disappearance of one of the festival's exhibitors, which brought the festivities to a solemn and untimely close.

> *"Police were summoned to the fairgrounds later that afternoon when 47-year-old William Laney from Centennial failed to appear for a 2:30 PM demonstration on gold assaying. Mr. Laney's booth was located at the north end of the fairgrounds that backed on the surrounding forest."*

Michelle twirled her hair more tightly around her finger.

> *"Mr. Laney, a high school teacher and adjunct professor of history, is a renowned authority on Western U.S. mining artifacts and memorabilia who consults regularly for private*

collectors and museums, including the Smithsonian. Several witnesses reported last seeing Mr. Laney, who was dressed in period clothing, speaking with two unidentified men at a concession stand near his booth around 2:00 PM. The witnesses, who wished to remain anonymous, agreed that although it did not appear that Mr. Laney knew the men, tensions soon escalated between them and Laney walked off 'in a huff.' 'That's the last I remember seeing him,' said the same witness. 'It was odd,' said another, 'I've gotten to know Bill rather well over the years at various exhibitions. He was easily the most likable person in the room. I can't imagine him having any enemies.'"

Michelle swallowed hard. *What does this mean? Why did you send me this?* Michelle heard the muffled whump of the refrigerator closing downstairs. Outside, a police siren screamed off in the night. The story took on a more ominous tone when it was disclosed that signs of a scuffle and several broken crucibles were found scattered on the ground behind his booth. The report went on to say that the police suspected foul play, and that a search of the area woodlands for Laney and the two mystery suspects had thus far produced no viable leads.

Distressed now, Michelle continued to read what proved to be a rather lengthy article that bounced back and forth between how the tragedy might affect the already strained local economy, Laney's ties to local historical groups, his personal accomplishments, and police efforts to find him. It was not until she reached the penultimate paragraph that the relevance of the article was revealed.

"Laney's disappearance bears a chilling similarity to the unsolved mystery of Dylan Streeter from the Panner's and Picker's Rendezvous event held near the former Climax fairgrounds in August 1982. Streeter, an expert in the appraisal and trade of Indian artifacts, was also attired in period dress when he, too, went missing."

Michelle couldn't bear to read more. She slumped back in her seat and rubbed at her face. *What have I gotten myself into?* Pride and the inordinate amount of effort expended on multiple fronts precluded her from backing out at this juncture. What she desperately needed was to talk with someone. She needed guidance on how to proceed. Nick was out of the question and so was Chris. She really needed to speak with Melanie. There was just one problem, like there always seemed to be of late. The late arrival of Jodi's emails and her fear that Melanie might back out precluded Michelle from informing her friend of the escalating situation. Michelle had wrongly hoped that the problem would just go away.

A change in the background noise distracted Michelle from her worries. Female intuition suggested that the boys were talking about her. She scampered out of the bedroom and back down the hall. "I'm still on the phone," she fibbed. Nick thanked her for the heads up and extended a hello to Melanie. He said Chris wanted to take them on a walk to see the city marina lights. Michelle said that she'd catch up as soon as she was finished, and waited for them to leave. She slid down the wall to the floor when she heard the door close. Resting her chin on her forearms, Michelle let out a sigh and said, "I need to let Melanie know what's going on."

CHAPTER 2

MONDAY

Palmetto State Transformer and Relay
Industrial Drive off U.S. Route 26, North Charleston, S.C.
9:27 A.M.

Chris arrived at Ashley House a little past eight to pick up Nick for their site visit. Michelle invited him inside for coffee. "It's the best I can offer," she said, adding that they'd dined out the entire weekend. Chris thanked her and said not to worry. He planned to take Nick to a great breakfast place near the site where they would talk over the day's agenda. "One of the perks of living on per diem," he went on to say, slicking back his still damp hair. Michelle commented on the floral aroma of his shampoo. She giggled when he continued attending to his locks with cat-like fastidiousness. Chris Orrey would always remain something of an enigma.

"Nick, where are you?" Chris hollered, tucking several persnickety hairs behind an ear. "Daylight's wasting."

Nick barreled down the stairs in an elephantine stampede of foot clomps that echoed off the woodwork. Chris tilted his head in Michelle's direction. "That's annoyed me for the past thirty years," she responded, matching Chris's bemusement.

"Ready!" Nick announced with childlike zeal when his feet landed on the floorboards. "You texted something about breakfast?"

They left not long thereafter. Michelle followed the boys to Chris's car where she wished them luck. She said that she would use the time while they were away to organize the files in the caretaker's apartment, which she affectionately called the in-law suite. Chris pulled away from the curb and drove north on Ashley to Calhoun. Several jogs later they reached the Crosstown Expressway and proceeded north on I-26. Nick relished the opportunity to finally enjoy the scenery. Chris entertained him with his incessant bitching, even where the traffic was light. They got off the highway at the I-526 interchange. Chris had wanted to eat at a place called the Sunflower Café but when he pulled into the empty lot, he recalled that it was closed on Mondays. Chagrined, he doubled back and pulled into an IHOP, where they talked shop over a hearty stack of pancakes.

They piled back into the car satiated and jacked on caffeine. "The site's just down the road," Chris said, turning back off of I-26 South before The Who song *Squeeze Box* had the chance to run its course on the Classic Vinyl station. This was saying something considering that it was a two minute forty-two second song. "We passed it, actually, on our way to the IHOP." Chris made a right off of the road they were following onto Industrial Drive, a strip of weathered asphalt that appeared to end at a gravel parking lot fronting the PSTRE building.

"You're looking north. Athens is on the other side of the building." Pointing left, Chris explained that, "Industrial Drive continues on around the west side of PSTRE's property, past Athens to the north, and eventually dumps back onto the main road we just turned off of." Chris parked in a visitor's spot near the main entrance.

Nick took in their surroundings while Chris scrolled through his contacts for the facility manager's number. The property didn't look at all like Nick expected. There was just one immense, non-descript building constructed of brick with at least three corrugated metal expansions. The parking lot was a deteriorated mess of asphalt covered by a thin skim of gravel. Apparently PSTRE didn't believe in landscaping or the rudiments of industrial hygiene, either. The trash cans near the front door were over-stuffed, and the bedraggled grass fronting the building was much in need of a mow.

"I was surprised, too, when Smitty took me on my initial drive around," Chris said, reading Nick's mind. Chris called the number and spoke to the facility manager. "Come on. We're a little early, but the guy's ready to give us the grand tour."

"Gerry Dawson, facility manager," the man grunted, extending a fleshy hand. "You can sign in over there," he said, pointing to a clipboard on the ledge in front of the visitor's window. Dawson looked them over. "Good. You got your safety gear. Follow me; the production floor is this way."

Dawson spoke loudly to be heard over the din of background noise. He made it a point to imply that he was taking time out of his busy schedule only because he had to. Chris countered his blustering by asking ice-breaking questions about Dawson's tenure with PSTRE. Chris whispered over his shoulder, "Tactical ops." Nick laughed. He gestured for Chris to get a move on if they were going to keep up with the surprisingly nimble Dawson.

The goosing worked. Gerry Dawson boasted about how the company had been in continuous operation since 1889 and that he'd worked for PSTRE for the past forty-four years, beginning in 1974, three years before the building expansion and name change reflecting the present mainstays of PSTRE's product line: transformers and relays. "That's really something, amazing," Chris encouraged. Nick was only half listening to Dawson's ramblings about the product line and its new bread and butter, railroad transformers for self-propelled railcars. His attention instead focused on the buzz of activity happening on the production floor, where small groups of men here and there were attending to row upon row of state-of-the-art equipment. "We make everything in-house—well, almost everything," Dawson said, fanning the room with a sweep of an arm. "We also have a business office near 52 and Columbus where examples of our current products are displayed. Perhaps you've seen it."

Chris lied and said that he had. Nick followed suit. "How long have you been in charge here?" Chris asked. "And what's that over there?" Chris pointed to an enormous structure on the far side of the building.

"We'll get to that. "Twenty-one years, to answer your first question. I was hired here out of high school, so you've got the right person to ask questions." Dawson said, warming to his task as tour guide. He escorted them up and down every row of machinery, explaining the purpose of each. "This here's an electrical relay," Dawson said, interrupting a jumpsuit-clad worker who acknowledged the intrusion with a flyboy's salute.

Nick looked over Chris's shoulder at a smallish piece of complicated-looking equipment, amazed as always by the miracle of human ingenuity.

"This one, like much of our production line these days, is dedicated to our railroad-construction project in India."

"India? Are you serious?" Chris asked.

"Yes," Dawson confirmed. "We had to revamp almost everything. PSTRE has other bids on the table over there, too; China as well. Heaven help us if we land another big contract," he whistled, expressing pride in their ability to meet the challenge.

Dawson moved on. Chris motioned for Nick to hold back. "This must be why Merrill's panties are in such a knot," he said softly, as if anyone else could hear them over the noise.

"Right," Nick agreed, the magnitude of PSTRE's expansion now laid out before them. And no, PSTRE wasn't planning an expansion; they were in the middle of it. The troubling question was why wait until now to ensure that the production well could provide the quantity and *quality* of process water required. It was a grievous oversight.

"I understand that if PSTRE can't get their water issue resolved in one way or another they'd be forced to start from the ground up elsewhere. That's got to shoot who knows how many deadlines right out the window," Chris added.

"Not to mention being cost prohibitive," Nick replied.

"You coming?" Dawson barked. They hurried to catch up with the facility manager at a rather large and interesting looking contraption. "This is a tap changer. It helps with voltage regulation in the transformers. And hey," Dawson said, breaking his train of thought, "I didn't mean to snap at you guys back there. It comes with the territory."

Chris assured him that no offense was taken and asked several questions about the production schedule for the Indian order, about which Dawson was all too happy to oblige. The delay in their tour enabled Nick to wander off to satisfy his curiosity about something. Nick paused in the central shop area to observe the company's industrial hygiene practices. He was satisfied with what he saw: no obvious points for contamination to migrate into the subsurface. The integrity of the concrete-slab floor appeared intact. The surface was coated with a clear epoxy finish to facilitate cleaning and—as far as Nick was concerned—preclude the permeation of spilled fluids. There was some limited staining on the floor around most of equipment stations, and the several fresh stains he did see were covered with oil absorbent granules; nothing out of the ordinary that required attention.

Nick took several pictures. He documented these and other observations in his field logbook. Along a nearby wall was a clearly marked chemical wash station that was secondarily contained to capture overspills. Nearby was a similarly placarded locked metal cabinet that housed the chemical solvents PSTRE used to degrease metal stock. *Good.* No obvious spillage there either. Nick made further note that the several workers presently performing chemical work were wearing respirators, and that a fume hood captured noxious solvent vapors that would have otherwise escaped into the shop area.

Nick did notice several floor drains on his way back in Chris's direction. This in itself wasn't anything out of the ordinary, but it did elicit several obvious questions. Nick was sketching their placement and spacing when he heard Gerry Dawson call to him. Nick looked up to find Dawson waving an arm about, drawing an imaginary map of the floor drain system. "Thanks," Nick said when he returned to their location. "Are they still in use?"

"Yes, follow me," Dawson said, describing the floor-drain network in further detail as they continued with the tour. "We wash the floor down once a week, or as needed. All wash water that doesn't flow to a drain is pushed to the nearest drain with a broom. Metal turnings are swept up and recycled; other debris goes out with the trash. The drains connect together and gravity feed to this oil/water separator." He pointed to a metal grate in the floor. "We're on a milk-run schedule with the disposal vendor, who also recharges our solvent and other chemical cleaning stations, which I think you noticed." Nick nodded. "We have other vendors that provide our bulk-chemical stock that's stored in aboveground tanks outside. Questions?"

"Gerry, to your knowledge, have you ever had any petroleum spills within the building?" Nick asked.

Dawson pondered the question. "Hmm, no. Small stuff we control with absorbents like you see there," he pointed to a small area covered with kitty litter on the floor beneath a drill press. "Happens all the time, like in all plants. If you're meaning something that made it to the drain system? No. We did have a PCB spill 'bout fifteen years ago. That was outside. I can show you when we're done here."

"How about the floor? Do you know how thick the slab is?

"Over there," Dawson pointed in the direction of the looming monstrosity Chris had observed earlier. "We removed that portion of the floor two years ago to increase the slab thickness to accommodate the additional weight. We took it from about eight inches to eighteen inches of reinforced concrete."

"Recall any soil staining or any other signs of a release?" Chris asked. This was a particularly relevant question considering that the slab work Dawson pointed to was done at the north, or rear, end of the shop floor not far from the impacted production well outside.

"Nothing I recall. We excavated dirt out, compacted, and poured the slab." Dawson shrugged. "Didn't see a thing—*Oh!* Almost forgot. I have pictures. Remind me later to dig through my files."

Chris and Nick acknowledged their satisfaction. The lack of obvious contamination from PSTRE that could account for the oil in the well was a good thing. Dawson, of course, could be lying, but for the time being they would accept the man at his word. Drilling exploratory borings through deep, reinforced concrete was no joy. "That's great, Gerry," Chris said. "Appreciated. This really helps us with our understanding of what's going on. One more question: you do use petroleum-based liquids besides mineral spirits, is that correct?"

"No, not really. Not anymore. Like everyone else we used to use a PCB dielectric fluid. In the late '70s, after the ban, we switched to a non-PCB fluid—that was the release I mentioned. We used that until very recently, when we switched to an environmentally friendly, halogen-free ester compound. The name escapes me. I was told to make you a copy of the MSDS sheets for all of the liquids we use. I'm sure it's in there."

"Thank you. Do you still keep any of the old dielectric fluid on the premises?" Chris then asked.

"Yes. We have a tank that's about half full out back. Management's always saying they're looking to broker a deal and sell it instead of paying to dispose of it, but nothing ever happens." Dawson gave a little chuckle.

Nick asked if they could get a sample of both the dielectric fluid and ester compound to compare against the oil found in the production well.

"We can do that," Dawson said with surprisingly little static, then moved on.

He stopped before the enormous object Chris had noticed on the far side of the shop floor. They were so close now and the equipment was so large that it appeared to be part of the building, and not a freestanding product of PSTRE's efforts. Chris and Nick gawked at the gigantic...thing. "What the heck is it?" Chris asked, backing up, as did Nick, so that they could get the entire creation in their field of view.

"A locomotive transformer. This baby's going to India," Dawson said proudly. "This is what we overhauled our entire production line for, including the floor on which you're standing." Dawson indicated that, in fact, the entire length of floor along the north wall of the building—all one hundred feet—had to be thickened to withstand the incredible weight. This was no small undertaking. "See the roof?" Dawson asked. Chris and Nick looked skyward. "We had to install those retractable panels just so we can use a crane to lift the transformer out of the building and load it onto a flatbed parked on the rail spur. It was cheaper doing it this way than rebuilding the rail line inside the building after we thickened the floor."

They followed Dawson outside to the aboveground storage tanks that stored the dielectric fluid and other bulk chemicals PSTRE used. Nick again liked what he saw. The tanks were all secondarily contained inside a large concrete basin designed to hold the lot in the event of a tank failure. There was no staining, therefore no releases. Nick made a note in his logbook to scratch this area of concern off the list.

"We used to keep our chemicals over there." Dawson pointed to a concrete slab mostly obscured by weeds growing out of cracks in the surrounding asphalt. They walked closer to take a look. The slab was considerably stained, particularly along the leading edge near where they were standing. "One of our laborers ran into a drum with the forks of his skid steer. What a mess and an even bigger headache for me. That well there," Dawson pointed to the flush-mount well cap that Nick was photographing, "it was drilled as part of the investigation and cleanup."

Chris commented that he'd seen documents concerning the well in the project files, and that there seemed to be an inordinate amount of attention paid to this singular incident.

"Chrissakes yes! Seems like every other year one of you guys is here to dig another hole or collect a sample. Just the other day a little girl from that firm working on the other side of the building—cute thing—asked me where it was so that she could sample the water."

"Gerry, did she mention if she noticed anything?" Chris asked, ignoring the disparaging remark. Nick looked for the RCE work crew.

"Do you mean like oil? No. Like I told her, you guys oughta just get a backhoe out here and dig the area up instead of pissing good money into the wind grabbing a sample here, another there, every time someone wants to know if the spill's been cleaned up."

"Was it?" Nick asked.

"Hell yeah. We dug it up. An environmental firm collected samples from the pit and drilled that well after it was backfilled." Dawson shook his head. "I understand the original report was lost and that's why you guys keep coming back—to find what I keep trying to tell you. Like I said, pissing in the wind." Dawson walked off, leaving Nick and Chris looking dumbly at one another.

They followed him to the northeast area of the property. "We used to stage our treated telephone poles here until the late seventies." Dawson pointed ahead to an area of crumbling asphalt adjacent to a second and now defunct rail spur leading into the main Athens building. Dawson explained that both spurs merged into a trunk line east of the site that ultimately wended its way to a switching yard to the west, near the Ashley River.

Beyond this second spur were three more rusted aboveground storage tanks. "We used to keep our chemical stock here," Dawson said, gesturing to the relict tanks. "If there's anything left in them, I'm sure it's sludge by now," Dawson opined.

Nick observed that all access ports were heavily rusted. The tanks hadn't been opened in decades. "And these?"

"That new environmental firm from Columbia drilled those last week," Dawson commented, gesturing to one of the three skinny sticks of PVC pipe sticking out of the ground—piezometer wells used for the recording of groundwater levels—in the vicinity of the tanks. When Nick asked where RCE was working today, Dawson pointed to several jumpsuit-clad individuals attending to additional piezometers drilled along the south side of the chain-link fence separating the PSTRE and Athens properties.

Their current position provided them with a good view of the east side of the Athens property. Unlike PSTRE, which had but one large building, Nick saw three structures; one large but not quite as immense as the PSTRE manufacturing building, and two smaller ones of similar size that flanked the north and south sides of the same spur along which they were standing. Supply sheds, Nick guessed. Along the south property boundary that Athens shared with PSTRE was the tank farm PSTRE was certain was the source for their production-well contamination. Nick counted eight gleaming white aboveground storage tanks, each about 10,000-gallons in capacity. "Do you know what they keep in those?" he asked.

Dawson waved for Nick and Chris to follow him. "Can't say," he said, skirting a weedy patch. "A friend of mine over there says they make specialty steel coatings—but you didn't hear that from me, right?" Chris and Nick assured him that his secret was safe with them. "Good. Management doesn't like us speaking with Athens. If it helps, I'm pretty sure they no longer use petroleum products."

Nick and Chris looked at one another. That was an interesting comment to make for an employee of the company in the process of suing its neighbor. Did Gerry Dawson hate *management*, or was he just overly honest?

The Athens tank farm yielded no surprises that could be seen from a distance. The tanks were secondarily contained, as they should be, within an asphalt berm that showed no evidence of external staining or disrepair. Based on this, the unblemished paint job on each of the tanks, and the lack of distressed vegetation in the foreground, there was nothing to suggest that a release had occurred, at least not recently. Across the way, Chris observed several Athens employees conducting their own spy games on them. He recommended they turn their attention to the production well so as not to raise too much interest.

The production well, the cause of so much turmoil, was a mere stub of non-descript steel casing poking out of the ground roughly equidistant west of the manufacturing building and south of the property line. Standing at the well and looking past the RCE work crew to the Athens tank farm beyond, Nick couldn't help but like what he saw. The number and spacing of the piezometer monitoring locations RCE had already installed, coupled with an assumed favorable groundwater-flow direction, should be more than sufficient to implicate Athens Petrolatum. It wasn't quite that simple, of course; the M&C team also had to demonstrate that the contamination wasn't the result of PSTRE's own doing. "Gerry. In your opinion, where do you think the oil in the well came from?" Nick asked. "I mean, is there any indication that it could have been sabotage?"

Dawson eyed him warily. It was one of those dangerous double-edged-sword questions that the facility manager thankfully took in stride. "No, not that I would say. I can't imagine where else it could have come from other than from the ground…from those guys." Dawson jabbed a thumb in Athens's direction.

There was apparently no love lost between Gerry Dawson and Athens Petrolatum, friend working there notwithstanding. Nick made another note in his logbook.

"Besides," Dawson made it a point to mention, "how would anyone have even known the well was here? Hell, even I forgot all about it. I don't even think it was ever used, at least not since I've worked for PSTRE."

"Really? That's good to know," Chris said, making a note of his own.

"As you can see, we haven't used this area of the property much in recent years and just sort of let it go back here," Dawson said. "In fact, one of my guys practically ran over it with the mower when I sent him out to find it."

Dawson had a point, Nick thought. The small forest of grass growing from the neglected asphalt made for excellent cover. One would have to know specifically where to go look for the well. Logic, therefore, dictated that the likelihood of sabotage was low considering the limited number of individuals who would know of its location.

A strange thing then happened. Chris must have looked contemptuously at the deplorable condition of the landscaping. The gesture didn't escape Dawson's attention. His reaction was immediate. "Look, this is a private company," he growled. "We don't get clients here, got it? That's what the retail store and corporate office is for. We work rotating shifts twenty-four-seven, and don't have time to cut grass or water flowers. If Stan Merrill doesn't care, then I don't either." Dawson's cell phone rang. "Excuse me," he said, "I gotta take this," and stormed off.

"Where'd that come from?" Nick said with surprise. "He seemed happy just a minute ago."

"Dunno. Just a bipolar asshole, I guess."

They shared a laugh when Nick commented how only Chris could stir the pot without saying a word. Watching Dawson trudge off, Chris asked if Nick thought Dawson was being level with them.

Nick mulled the question. "He seems genuine, though I've never come across a foreman who I thought was completely honest. There's always skeletons tucked away somewhere. I will say," Nick added, offering the mercurial Dawson the benefit of the doubt, "that I saw nothing to suggest that we should have cause for concern. Everything, save the lack of upkeep of the grounds, is impeccable for an industrial facility." Nick knelt by the well. He pointed out that the standpipe and locking cap stood only about four inches above the ground, and the unruly weeds that now lay cut to the ground around them in every direction could easily have concealed a rusty stub of steel casing from view. Then, pointing to the several drips of fresh oil on the ground and noting the lack of obvious older staining on or in the well, Nick surmised that the fresh oil was the residual drippings from the recent sampling event when RCE used a bailer, or similar device, to remove what oil they could from the well. Chris agreed with him that sabotage was unlikely. "Answer me this, Chris: what am I missing?" Nick asked after taking everything into perspective. "All that retooling, the concrete work, all of Dawson's grandstanding about PSTRE's grand plans; none of that's cheap. And how much does it cost to set up shop in a foreign country? Seems to me that the magnitude of even modest future revenues would far outweigh the cost to tie into the local public water supply to make up for a production shortfall. Is that cost really a deal breaker in the big scheme of things?"

Nick was surprised to find Chris thumbing through his notes for an answer.

"Public water? That is a problem. There are no feeder lines that run out here. I understand PSTRE checked into it, and the local provider said that there isn't enough development here in no man's land to warrant the expense of running the mile or so of pipe from the nearest trunk-line connector. I gather PSTRE doesn't want to front that cost, but I don't know for certain. I'll check into it. Good question."

"Perhaps there's also a snag in the permitting process," Nick offered.

"Yeah, maybe. I'll have to check."

Nick's face tightened. No simple public water option? That answer raised even more questions. He was about to say something, didn't, and instead said something else. "Where is their active well, by the way?"

"Inside their building," Chris said. "Dawson pointed it out to me while you were off looking at floor drains."

"And they haven't detected oil in that well?" Nick asked. Chris shook his head. "Doesn't that strike you as odd?"

"It does."

"How about the construction?" Nick then asked. "Are the two wells completed at different depths? Maybe the active well cases off the oily zone."

"RCE's looking into it, actually," Chris assured him.

"Good." After another moment's pondering, Nick then voiced the next obvious question yet left unasked, "And what is it exactly they need the extra water for?"

Chris ran a finger down a page until he found the entry he was looking for. "Here we go…a paper press. Besides the need for more water for whatever else they're doing, PSTRE also wants to manufacture electrical insulation paper in house, and that, Dawson said, is a water consumptive process. He says that PSTRE has several lucrative deals in the works in China and India, and Ireland of all places. As Dawson put it, PSTRE plans to reclaim as much water as possible to remain under what he said is a rather restrictive permit. Groundwater withdrawal is a serious issue down here."

"Yes. Saltwater intrusion. I take it they have a discharge permit in place?"

"Uh-huh," Chris said, "hence the urgency to get this issue resolved. Lots of money has been spent to push the NPDES permit through, not to mention what was incurred on the purchase of the paper making equipment. It's a *train* wreck waiting to happen if the planets don't align and we can't help them out of their fix." Chris laughed at his joke.

"They make *rail cars…train wreck*. Nice!" Nick said, sharing in Chris's humor. Nick leaned back on the legs he had folded beneath him. "Any idea where they're discharging to? I'd be interested to see if there's any petroleum reaching the stream via groundwater baseflow. Duh! That should tell us which direction the regional flow is heading."

"I can help with that," a voice called out. Chris turned; Nick struggled to his feet. Walking toward them was a member of the RCE field team. "Hi. I'm Jay Watkins with River City Environmental. Is one of you Chris?" Watkins asked, peeling a latex glove from his hand. "Sorry, my hand's clean but it is a little sweaty."

"That'd be me, and no problem," Chris answered, grasping Watkins's hand. "And this is Nick Kozlowski; he's helping us."

Watkins shook Nick's hand with even greater enthusiasm. "Pleasure!" Watkins said with a broad smile. It was an awkward moment made all the more so when Nick had to pull his hand away. Watkins glossed over the moment by answering the question. "The permit discharge? That would be to Noisette Creek. It's over there, about a half-mile to the east," he said, pointing to their right. "The permit calls for PSTRE to pipe conduit the discharge below ground surface to the creek." Watkins then unexpectedly apologized for Gerry Dawson's outburst.

"That was your fault? What did you do?" Chris asked. His phone rang. "Ah! It's your boss. Excuse me while I take this. We're to meet with Sam this afternoon up in Columbia. Sam? Hi, it's Chris…"

With Chris preoccupied talking with Sam Piersall, Nick and Watkins discussed the work in progress. Watkins said that RCE had already drilled and installed fifteen piezometers, including the six standing sentinel before them along the north property line. Watkins confirmed what Nick had already guessed from watching RCE's three other employees: that each piezometer would be sampled following development, and that the resulting data would be used to determine where a lesser number of permanent monitoring wells would be installed. It was all Nick could do to keep up with Watkins's arm waving and rapid fire staccato of information. Nick was sorting it all out, jotting down details to speak with Chris about before their meeting with Piersall when he sensed Watkins hedging closer. "Can I help you?" Nick asked, taking a step back to maintain his personal space.

"Are you two," Watkins swayed his head around like a dog wanting to be petted, eyes searching, "you know…" his question trailing off to nothingness.

"Oh! *Y-E-A-H*," Nick managed, amused by the off-topic question. Jay Watkins wanted to confirm his and Chris's own celebrity status resulting from the EcoGenesis affair.

Chris cleared his throat to catch their attention. "Sam asked if we'd mind bumping the meeting up to one."

Nick shrugged. At this point, he was more or less still just along for the ride.

Chris placed the phone back to his ear. "That works for us. Oh. That would be Nick—Nick Kozlowski. Yes, the one and the same,"

Chris rejoined, shaking his head at Nick. "Jay? Yes. He's here, too. We just met. Let me check." Chris pulled the phone away from his ear again. "Do you have time to show us around?" Watkins gave him the thumbs-up. "That's a yes. Uh-huh. Right, Sam. We're really interested in the distribution of the monitoring points you guys installed. Of course. We'll speak with Jay and let you know this afternoon if we see anything out of the ordinary. Okay, I will. Appreciated." And looking at Nick and Watkins both, Chris said, "You could say that. Everything started off well enough. Uh-huh. Jay did say that he had something to do with it." This time a longer pause ensued while Chris listened to Sam Piersall's account of RCE's first encounter with the facility manager the week before last.

"What is it?" Nick asked. He knew Chris long enough to tell when his temper was about to boil.

"You're kidding," Chris snapped, ignoring Nick and an increasingly nervous Jay Watkins. "I wasn't informed of this. When did you find out? *Ahh!*" Chris groaned. "Does Bill Carlyle know?" Another pause. "Never mind. I'll find that out and let you know so that we're on the same page. Great. Yeah, no problem. Thanks for calling. See you in a few hours." Chris pressed his finger hard, ending the call—and cursed.

"What?" Nick begged.

"There's a new player at PSTRE that I was not made aware of. His name is Hal Cole, the guy who instructed Dawson to cut all this shit down."

Watkins affirmed what Piersall told Chris on the phone for Nick's benefit. He explained how his struggles with the overgrowth when looking for a place for the drillers to set up led to Cole's reprimand of Dawson for letting the grounds become rundown.

"Meaning?" Nick asked. "Why do we care?"

"Because Stan Merrill brought Cole in as a new senior officer. He's the financier behind PSTRE's rebranding into the railroad business and, more importantly, the company's expansion into international markets," Chris elaborated.

"That means what?" Nick pressed.

"I don't know. That's the problem. I need to call Smitty before we leave to find out what the hell's going on." Chris's mood then softened. "So, Jay, whataya say you show us what you guys have been up to."

Watkins escorted them to the line of piezometer wells installed along the north property boundary. There he introduced them to Tricia Bell and Mindy Porter, two of RCE's field geologists tasked with developing and sampling the recently completed wells. Nick was anticipating this moment all weekend, the opportunity to finally see and *feel* the data for himself, and not just some symbol on a map. "This is PZ-5," Watkins said. It was the fifth of the six wells in the line and the second farthest from the tank farm.

Nick marked the location on his copy of the site map. His nose caught a whiff of a fetid petroleum-like odor. He peered into the 55-gallon drum used to collect the development water Mindy Porter was removing from the well via a peristaltic pump and length of disposable tubing. The discharge was almost clear. This indicated that any loose sediment trapped within the well and sand pack around the well screen was nearly removed. Nick stepped aside so that Porter could monitor the turbidity in the discharge coming from the purge tubing. "How long are you purging each well?" Nick asked.

"Up to one hour, or until we get a consistent reading of less than 10 NTUs, whichever comes first."

"Good," Nick said, making note of this in his logbook. "We want to remove as much sediment from each well as possible to make certain that the results for chemical testing, the metals in particular, provide us with a best representation of groundwater quality."

"Of course," Porter replied, letting Nick know that she was way ahead of him. "We'll make sure Athens can't challenge our sample-collection protocols." Porter flashed Nick a reassuring smile.

Nick smiled back, then looked again into the drum. He was pleased to see the rainbow swirl of a petroleum-like sheen on the surface of the water. "Hey Chris," he said, "Take a look."

"Alright! Now that's what we're looking for," Chris rejoiced, patting Jay on the back.

Nick elected to remain calm until he saw something more conclusive.

"How about the other piezos, Jay?" Chris asked, hoping for additional good news. "Any oil?"

Watkins curled his lips into a reluctant frown. "Sorry. I don't mean to be the bearer of ill tidings, but this is the only location along this portion of the property line where we found anything," he regretted to say. "We did find something over there at PZ-7, there's a thicker sheen and globules of some kind of heavier oil," Watkins said, pointing to a lone PVC stick-up located at the extreme northwest end of the property along Industrial Drive, "as well as down there in PZ-9, just beyond the production well." He motioned to a similar casing sticking out of the ground not far from the south edge of the PSTRE building. "I thought for sure we would have seen more along here, particularly in the three piezos that front the tank farm."

Nick shifted his line of sight so that he could take in the locations for all of the piezometers in his field of view relative to the tank farm and production well. "You found nothing in those piezos there?" he asked, pointing to piezometers PZ-1 through PZ-4.

"No," Watkins said, equally confounded. "Here, I'll show you."

Watkins stopped at PZ-2. The piezometer was located due south of the tank farm and was the monitoring point most likely to be impacted if Athens's tanks were leaking—*and* groundwater flow was preferentially to the south, as they hoped. Tricia Bell, who was preparing to collect a sample from the well, placed her bottleware aside to open a nearby drum so that Nick and Chris could inspect the development water, which, regrettably, was devoid of visible impact. The uneasy feeling brewing in Nick's stomach prompted him to tug at his beard. "And elsewhere?"

Was their conceptual model all wrong??

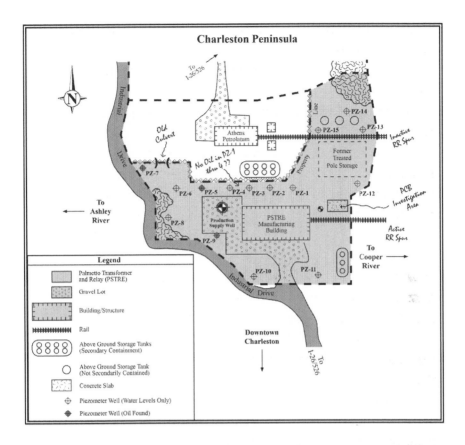

Watkins shook his head. "Nope, not yet, but that doesn't necessarily mean anything when you're working in the coastal plain. The subtle differences in lithology can be tricky and have a huge impact on contaminant migration. My bet is that if we drill a few more holes to fill in some of the gaps, we'll see something. We need to find the sandier zones that facilitate product transport."

A credible assessment, Nick told him. Viscous fluids like oil and creosote—which was essentially oil, only slightly heavier—have an easier time passing through the large pore spaces between sand grains, and all fluids, water included, will follow the path of least resistance. Pumping Watkins for additional information, Nick learned that each piezometer was screened to intercept a very shallow water table averaging 4 feet below ground surface, and that the lithology across much of the property consisted of a mucky assemblage of silts and clays with the occasional sand inter-bed thrown in here and there. It was a soil profile similar to that which Nick recalled from a recent drilling project back home near Buckeye Lake, in Ohio. Here, it was in the sandy zones in the PZ-5, PZ-7, and PZ-9 boreholes that RCE found evidence of oil. Watkins informed them that sandy soil was not found at the remaining twelve locations. He handed Nick his clipboard with the drilling logs for each location and promised to scan and email him a copy of each, along with his field notes, at the end of the day.

Watkins led them on a circuitous route around the remainder of the property, stopping briefly to observe a very old-looking culvert along the northwest property line. Kneeling down on his logbook so as not to soil his clothing, Nick inspected the ground. He used the flashlight function on his iPhone to peer into the pipe, the out-fall a barely visible half-moon mostly obscured by an overhanging thatch of grass. There was nothing telling beyond the earthy smell of the soil and vegetative matter plugging the opening. The feature must have been installed around the turn of the previous century, when relations between the two companies were amicable. The question was what purpose did it serve? Without a channel to drain into, stormwater management seemed out of the question. With no explanation forthcoming, Chris shrugged and suggested that they move on.

Watkins concluded their tour back near the site entrance, where he was installing pressure transducers into several piezometers to record long-term water-level monitoring data. The water-level data, Watkins said, would be recorded onto data loggers at 15-minute intervals per the project work plan and downloaded daily by the attending RCE field crew to be forwarded to RCE's Columbia office for processing and review by the project hydrogeologist. The pre-cision of the scientific equipment should have made it a snap to determine the prevailing direction for groundwater flow. *Should* was the operative word. Watkins frowned when he explained that the data they'd received thus far were…screwy.

"What's the problem, Jay?" Nick asked.

"I honestly don't know," Watkins said. "We manually collected two rounds of water levels from each piezometer, the first right after installation and the second four days later, in conjunction with the well-elevation survey. We calculated flow maps for both events and received conflicting data, some expected, some not. Tidal effects, of course, messed with the results for both events, and we had to make the necessary corrections. The data still looked whacky, though. We didn't make much of it at the time, considering simple recording errors by the field tech could have accounted for the discrepancies—the water table across the site is flat, you'll see, on the order of plus or minus a couple hundredths of a foot—and we were going to perform long-term monitoring anyway. We actually started long-term monitoring last week in these wells and the production well." Watkins pointed to several nearby casing stickups. "We did that as part of a test run and noticed that we were still experiencing interference after accounting for both lunar and earth-tide effects. What we're seeing is some strange jumpiness in the data, like a chattering or vibration. Like I said, whacky."

"Any quarrying or piling installation activities going on in the area?" Nick asked.

"Could be," Watkins replied. "We're looking into it."

"Good. Let us know what you find out. I'm sure it must be something like that," Chris said.

"As for the production well, now that one's really bizarre," Watkins continued.

"How so?" Nick asked.

"The well is several hundred feet deep and was completed in bedrock. At least we think so, based on what we know about the depth to rock in the area. The water level suddenly spiked and has remained that way until we stopped collecting data. That's what

I'm doing today, changing out the equipment—all of it—to rule out mechanical error. Hopefully this will resolve our issues."

They spoke a little while longer to confirm the field schedule and the expected turn-around time for the laboratory results from the groundwater samples RCE would be collecting. Satisfied that Jay Watkins was on board with the needs and interests of the case, Chris thanked him for the debriefing and let him get back to work.

Instead of heading out the way they'd come, Chris recommended that they continue following Industrial Drive behind the PSTRE and Athens properties so that Nick could see the surrounding grounds. "It'll give you a better perspective of the lay of the land," Chris informed him. They'd scarcely rounded the bend when Chris suddenly turned off into a pull-off designed to accommodate opposing tractor-trailer traffic entering the curve in the narrow road. "I'd better call Smitty about the new guy—Cole—I wasn't informed about," he said.

Nick was happy he did. Their location gave him an excellent view of much of Athens's property as well as the north half of PSTRE's. He could also see the RCE crew in action from his vantage point. It was remarkable how little space there actually was between the Athens tank farm and the production well. Perhaps the biggest take away, however, was the remoteness of the Athens/PSTRE complex from the bustle and distraction of everyday urban life. He could see how easy it could be for tempers to escalate, feuds to fester. Hell, it wasn't a reach to assume that even the truckers who made regular deliveries had likely taken sides.

Nick drafted questions to ask Sam Piersall until Chris finished his call. "Sounds like your spider senses were on to something," Nick said, tucking his logbook away. "Is something clandestine afoot?"

"You could say that," Chris said, remarkably composed for his typically high-strung self. "There is indeed a new player in the mix. According to Smitty, Stan Merrill and Hal Cole first met several years ago at a city function. Things escalated quickly from there, and PSTRE suddenly started refitting their operation to service the railroad industry."

Rick Ley

"So, who's this Cole guy? Where'd he come from?"

"That's still murky according to Smitty. Stan Merrill is selective in what he tells his legal team. Be that as it may, Cole was first billed as a business consultant, though it was common knowledge that the relationship was deeper than that. How so? Not sure. Smitty has Brant sniffing around. Cole was hired soon after and whisked through the ranks of upper management. He was recently made an officer. As Smitty understands it, Cole makes most of PSTRE's production decisions as well, and is in charge of the railroad side of the business entirely."

Nick made a humming sound. "Fishy. That had to piss a lot of people off."

"You could say that, if Gerry Dawson is any example."

They continued watching the RCE crew go about its tasks. Nick said that he liked Jay and thought that RCE had developed a sound plan for the investigation. When Chris then asked what he thought about the project in general, Nick was far less certain. He expressed his concern about the timing of PSTRE's lawsuit.

"Why's that?" Chris asked.

"I think Merrill's jumping into what well may be a very wrong conclusion. Why is he so hell bent on pressing a lawsuit when his real concern should be whether or not the production well is still serviceable and if his company is the one responsible for creating its own mess? I'm with Dawson on this one. Quit wasting time poking holes in the ground and get a backhoe out here and open up the ground. Get the information he needs, right now, before spending another dime on this overseas venture of his and pissing away good money chasing a lawsuit that might blow up in his face. Get the facts first and move forward, information willing, and let the investigation and lawsuit unfold in due course."

"I hear you," Chris said, sharing in Nick's frustration. Chris was staring past Watkins at the PSTRE parking lot when, in his peripheral vision, he saw Jay slip, then look quickly about to see if anyone saw him use the PVC casing as a crutch to keep from falling.

"What's so funny?" Nick asked, looking up from his notes.

"See Jay there rubbing a hand along that length of stickup? He almost fell and used it to brace himself. He's probably fretting about whether or not he cracked the casing."

Nick snickered, recalling some of his own clumsy field moments.

"Now tell me," Chris asked, still chuckling at Watkins. "What was all that about back there—while I was on the phone—was Jay hitting on you, or what?"

"No, it was nothing like that," Nick snorted. "Jay recognized who we are from the whole Oregon thing."

"Ah, yes! Fifteen more minutes of fame for *The Boy Who Lived* and his sidekick, Ron Weasley."

The Harry Potter quip was intended as a joke, only Nick didn't take it that way. Chris's comment resurrected his concern about Michelle's upcoming folly with the mines.

"Hey man, I didn't mean anything by that. You know that, right?"

Nick sighed. "I know. I know, Chris. I'm the one who should be apologizing to you. That was funny. This whole trip thing, it still bothers me. Something's up. Michelle's been acting really goofy the past couple of weeks. Goofy even for her."

"Like I told you before, do you blame her? Think about it. She plans to call her book *Reckoning at Little Bear*, right? And she's going without you. I'd think that there'd be something wrong with her if she wasn't acting a little goofy."

Chris was right. Nick thanked him for the support. "I've been too critical of her. The fact is, Chris, her mettle is much stronger than mine. Garret nearly killed her and she's still willing to go back there, *in there*. I couldn't do that. I wouldn't do that." Nick hesitated, thinking how best to accurately relay his feelings. "No, it's not that that's bothering me; not entirely. It's her preoccupation with her phone that has me concerned. You've had to notice how she's constantly looking at it, rubbing it as if she expects it to go off at any time. She's worried about something."

What he said should have elicited a response. When it didn't,

Nick found Chris distracted by something. "What?" Nick said, in response to his friend's devilish smile. "What are you looking at?" he then asked, following Chris's line of sight to PSTRE's parking lot.

"See the red car next to that silver pickup?" Nick nodded. "They're watching us."

"*Really?*" Nick said, leaning forward, eyes drawn to a squint. "How do you know?"

"I saw that car before."

"When?" Nick asked. Inside, he saw movement and a glint of light. "What the hell—"

"I count two of them, one black and one white," Chris said. "Not sure when they got here. I first saw their car last Friday when we were on the balcony at Ashley House. That's why I wanted to go back inside."

Another glint of light.

"They're passing a pair of binoculars between them."

"Sonofabitch," Nick said, still squinting. "Who do you think they are? They're not from Athens, are they?"

"Mmm," Chris purred. "I'm banking on it. I think they're Athens's legal spies. Let me call Smitty and see if he or Bill wants to rattle some cages, then let's get out of here and see if they follow us."

———

Ashley House
Ashley Avenue, Charleston, S.C.
2:47 P.M.

Michelle worked into the early afternoon hours sorting through and then cataloging the small mountain of documents she pulled from the file cabinets in the caretaker's apartment. It was a daunting task, considering that Chris, despite his comment to the contrary, had provided only a fraction of the available files, reports, and loose papers she was tasked with combing through. Had she stacked up everything identified as belonging to PSTRE, Michelle was certain she could climb the paper trail high enough to peer right into Mrs. Mockingbird's nest out there in the magnolia tree. At least the filing kept her mind off the chilling newspaper account she replayed over and over in her mind all weekend in an ultimately failed attempt to decipher its relevance to her trip.

In an odd way, Michelle found the sorting effort not too unlike the infamous and now humorous mud-bogging debacle that disrupted the camping trip she, Nick, then boyfriend Garret, and best friend Tracy went on one weekend back in college. They were at Nick's uncle's farm when, in a moment of faulty logic, Garret—with Nick's encouragement, no less—decided to drive his station wagon through a mucky-looking area to get to *the high ground* Nick promised was the best camping spot on the property. Defying the girls' insistence that it would be wiser to carry the camping gear across the soft ground, Garret did one of those stupid things boys were apt to do and gunned the engine…and promptly buried the car to the axles. Several mud-caked hours of bitch-filled toil later, the car was finally inched to firmer ground. Needless to say, special favors were not given that night.

The similarity lay in the overwhelming discouragement that Michelle felt at the beginning of the sorting process, when the sheer number of files to process seemed insurmountable; this was followed by moments of progress punctuated by more bogging down in the document mire. It was reminiscent of the fits and starts of progress they experienced that evening once the moment of helplessness when the station wagon had bellied out in the mud had passed, only to bog down again. Who would have thought that incident thirty years ago would help to prepare her for this undertaking? Undaunted, Michelle continued to plug away, and, come early afternoon, had gained traction and was able to quickly sort through the remaining files, even the stack of wayward chicken scratches she'd placed in a box on the floor to keep them out of the way. At this point, the task was no longer a work project but a prolonged victory lap, her opponent in the final throes of resistance.

By gosh, it was like finishing out a winning hand of solitaire, when it was obvious that all remaining cards in the discard pile soon would have a new place to call home.

Michelle leaned back from the work table to relieve the kink that had formed in her back. Peering at the fruits of her labor all laid out in neat piles before her, she was pleased to find that, save for some recently obtained Athens data that she and Nick hadn't seen yet, there really were very few surprises. Chris was right after all. In fact, there had been a remarkably limited history of environmental activity for the amount of paperwork generated over the one hundred thirty-odd years of continuous operation. By far the most voluminous was the several file drawers full of documents related to PSTRE's air-emissions permit and facility-waste management. Skimming through the files as she sorted them, Michelle learned that PSTRE was both a large and small quantity generator, meaning that the company used and properly disposed of varying amounts of chemicals as part of its operation. In these documents, she stumbled upon references to several rectified clerical violations. By all accounts, PSTRE was in regulatory compliance, and had been for the past seven years. This information, though not germane to the needs of their case, did provide evidence that the company was not a slipshod operation. Michelle penned a few notes to that effect on the sticky note she placed on top of the pile containing the most recent compliance records.

She also found documentation for the removal of three underground storage tanks and the replacement of several above ground counterparts. Here, Michelle placed sticky notes on those documents she was sure she hadn't seen. A rather sizable report prepared for one of the above ground tank replacements looked particularly juicy because it contained a lengthy soil-investigation report in one of the attachments. Nick will be eager to see this, she thought.

Michelle also found the documents Chris had given them about the PCB spill. She was no expert but was surprised nonetheless by the dearth of documentation about the event. It was a reportable release to the South Carolina Department of Environmental Health and Environmental Control, yet the information consisted only of routine groundwater monitoring reports—an after-the-fact record of on-going groundwater-quality monitoring performed after soil cleanup had been completed. Missing was all of the intervening *good stuff* she expected to find…like a discussion of the cleanup effort, for crying out loud, among other pertinent information. She would talk to Nick about this once he and Chris returned.

Lastly, Michelle stumbled upon an exceptional number of due diligence reports. These were completed at the behest of PSTRE's lending institution to limit the bank's liability in the event PSTRE defaulted on its loan or became entangled in an environmental lawsuit. In short, the lending institution doesn't want to be stuck with an environmentally distressed property it can't unload. All told, Michelle counted four full Phase I environmental assessments and two environmental-transaction screens, dating back to 1997.

Michelle learned from working with Nick that considerable information about the potential environmental condition of a property, in other words how "clean" or "dirty" it is, can be gleaned from a Phase I. In addition to the site walk and review of state and federal regulatory compliance databases, a Phase I includes a summary of findings from a rigorous scrutiny of the operational history of the property and reports of completed investigations and cleanup actions. It's not as good as having results of chemical testing of samples collected from a boots-on-the-ground Phase II investigation, but it is certainly better than having nothing at all. The big question was whether the recent uptick in due diligence reporting correlated with an increase in site activity that might explain how the oil had gotten into the production well. For PSTRE's sake, she hoped the answer was no.

Her task complete for the time being, except for figuring out what to do with the small mountain of duplicate copies that complicated matters during the sorting process, Michelle scuffled her way to a cane-backed rocking chair on the outdoor porch overlooking the courtyard. There she propped a foot onto the railing. It was a beautiful day, the sun warm, the air refreshingly dry, or as she liked to call it, *thin*. Subtle wafts of nectar drifted her way from the red flowers in the hedge behind the house. It didn't take long resting in a very comfortable chair to realize just how exhausted and grimy she felt after only several hours schlepping files. She mused that somehow she could compete against *kids* half her age in the Dayton to Cincinnati in-line charity skate yet be whipped shuffling papers. Clearly, she wasn't in clerical shape.

Michelle twisted out a few more kinks before slumping deep into the rocker and closing her eyes. A sun worshipper at heart, she relished the soothing warmth that whisked the air-conditioner chill from her bones. Her mind drifted. Around her, the soothing sounds of everyday Deep South suburban life spoke to her: occasional voices, singing birds, the whoosh of the cars travelling up the street. Off in the distance, she could hear the muted roar of the many car engines from the city proper. Just like back at the rest stop, it wasn't a stretch to pretend that she was listening to the sound of waves crashing on the beach.

Yelling on the street below interrupted her reverie. On the far side of Ashley Avenue, two young men were in conversation, one from the stoop of a house who was yelling to the other standing on the street. Michelle became annoyed when neither man made any effort to walk toward the other so that they didn't have to shout. It was moments like this when she wished she had Nick's BB-gun. At least the hoodlum with no regard for sidewalks was worth looking at save for the baggy jeans that hung way too low on his ass. When the obnoxious conversation carried on for too long, Michelle decided she would fight fire with fire and play music from her phone—loudly, thank you very much! Whether the men responded to the not so subtle suggestion to shut the hell up, or had just said all that there was to say, she couldn't tell. Regardless, they soon waved one another off and the one on the street walked away, the man on the stoop calling out an afterthought to his friend who he called Jordy. The similarity to *Jodi* stimulated an involuntary tightening in Michelle's throat.

Michelle forced herself from the rocker. She still needed to clear her mind from her work and went back inside for a drink. She returned with a cup of water and an apple from the fruit basket replenished that morning by M&C's custodial service. Pleased to find that the street-level noise had returned to its pre-interruption din, Michelle settled back into the chair to dwell on her looming venture into the unknown. Thankfully, she wasn't getting cold feet again. To the contrary, since the initial shock of Friday's Jodi post, Michelle found her fears slowly replaced with curiosity. More remarkable, she found her conflicted self actually *wanting* to hear from Jodi. There were so many questions she wanted to ask, answers she needed to know before she and Melanie arrived in Colorado, the most important of which was the meaning behind that dreadful article. Even the fact that she still had to have her little talk with Melanie didn't overly concern her. This was not to say she wasn't still apprehensive; the throat tightening reminded her of that.

Michelle reflected on the first time she contacted the Tarry-all Mountain Foundation. She spoke with a man named Teddy Monroe, who introduced himself as an official with the Conservancy. She recalled Monroe as distant, guarded. Michelle thought that one of her worst fears had come to fruition, that *Ghost Creek* had evoked a lingering resentment at how she'd portrayed the Breckenridge community. It would take several minutes of parrying with Monroe to pry from him a not so subtle request to "Just let the past go." Undaunted once she realized that she hadn't necessarily offended anyone and that it was Monroe who didn't want to be inconvenienced and not the community at large, Michelle presented the scope of her project, along with a sincere promise not to do anything intentional to open old wounds. Monroe relented when Michelle requested that the Conservancy serve as her escort. Monroe said that he would think about it and call her back.

But he didn't call her back. Several weeks would pass before Michelle summoned the nerve to again pick up the phone and call, thanks to the insistence of her agent, who encouraged her not to give up so easily. This time a woman named Bethany Stockwell answered the phone. In contrast to Teddy Monroe, Ms. Stockwell, as Michelle first called her, was a friendly and engaging conversationalist. By the time their first talk ended, they were on a first name basis, and although Ms. Stockwell—Beth—remained noncommittal, she promised to speak with the other trustees about her proposal. Michelle thought that she was making some real progress.

It would take several more weeks of frustration before the Conservancy agreed to lend its consent. Michelle had called at least once each week and really just wanted to finally hear a definitive "*No*," so that she could tell Connor Lewis that she'd tried, when, to her surprise, Beth called her back with good news. Elated, Michelle said that her schedule was open and asked if she could visit the following week—in mid-December. "Honey," Beth said politely, "we've several feet of snow on the ground. Don't even think about it until at least May, perhaps June. Besides, there's some paperwork that needs to be squared away before you can come." And so began the legal odyssey that would take half a year and much in the way of personal fortitude to complete.

Michelle was asked to prepare a written proposal describing her book project, outlining the specifics of what she planned to do while in Colorado. In essence, the Conservancy wanted to know the extent she planned to use their resources and what liability the organization might incur. It was a reasonable request, Michelle thought, and by early February, the first of ultimately four drafts of her proposal was mailed from her publisher's legal department.

Michelle found the proposal process a godsend. It helped her define a possible structure for the future manuscript, forcing her to focus on all of the fine points that her book project might encompass. This included everything from who she wanted to interview and the questions she wanted to ask to that all important detail the Conservancy wanted to know most: where she planned to visit on the former Huron College research-station grounds. Michelle found the legal process fascinating; all the wrangling over injury liability, the haggling over confidentiality agreements, the hashing over copyright law when she said that she wanted to use some of the informational pamphlets Beth said the Conservancy had published about the mines. Naturally, Michelle wanted to include photographs of both mines, only to find out that the Conservancy actually didn't own the photos. Then there were all the Conservancy regulations that she needed to contend with. Thank goodness it was the lawyers who were tasked with handling most of the tedium.

Remarkably, the Conservancy barely flinched at her request to walk the Sacred Lands portion of the property, so long as she was escorted. The Conservancy, she discovered, didn't actually own the mines either; like the photos, a shell company did. Because the shell company was fine with the tour arrangements, so too was the Conservancy. *But aren't they really one and the same?* It was all so confusing. So long as she abided by the wishes of her Conservancy escort, she was free to explore the grounds as she saw fit. Most important was the rapport she developed with Beth Stockwell, through whom Michelle gained valuable insight into the Conservancy's hierarchy. Beth, as it turned out, was instrumental in the Conservancy's procurement of the Alpine Lodge Field Research Station tract from Huron College following the Ghost Creek disaster.

Sure, there were some minor details that still needed ironing out, like the degree to which she could actually explore the mines. These issues, Beth assured her, would be squared away by the time she arrived. With the groundwork for her book project all but complete, and with a supporter in Beth Stockwell awaiting her arrival, Michelle found herself at ease for the first time in a very long time. She couldn't wait to jump into the car with Melanie and begin the long ride to Colorado.

Everything inexplicably changed a little over two weeks ago, during what should have been nothing more than the next routine conversation with Beth. The call started off well enough with Beth informing her that she was making headway on obtaining a copy of the engineer's report on the structural integrity of the two mines, the original having been loaned out or misfiled. This document, she said, specified the limits to how far Conservancy staff could safely take Michelle and her party into the mines during the underground portion of the tour. The conversation digressed from there into a rambling discussion about the Tarryall Mountain Foundation's on-going stewardship projects. Michelle found particularly interesting a project to reintroduce the Colorado pikeminnow—the new and *enlightened* common name for the erstwhile squawfish, a giant, voracious minnow capable of reaching six feet in length—into some area rivers.

The problem started when Michelle said that she would make it a point to stop into the Fish and Wildlife Service branch office when in Denver to learn more about what Beth explained was a collaborative effort between the Conservancy and the department. She was going to Denver anyhow, to inspect local archeological society records about the old skeleton she'd literally fallen onto back in the summer of '88, in the weeks leading up to Garret's mental implosion. Michelle had expected Beth to jump at the opportunity to rehash the discovery of *The Body* that had created such an electric, albeit brief and unceremoniously ended commotion. Instead she was greeted with silence. Alarmed, Michelle assumed that she had breached one of the provisions in the access agreement. Beth assured her that she had not and abruptly changed the subject. The call lasted several more minutes, and although Beth remained cordial throughout, there was no mistaking the strain in her voice.

Michelle was scrolling through her emails the following morning when she noticed one from *HikerChic@RMTC.com*. She didn't recognize the address and summarily deleted it as spam. The last thing she needed was another unsolicited outdoor-apparel or health-bar-connection eblast to clog up her inbox. She then picked up the phone to call Beth. Connor Lewis, the excitable sort he was, had peppered her with so many questions about the lost engineer's report earlier that morning that Michelle couldn't recall whether Beth had said there still were any hiccups about mine entry.

It was a little past eight in the morning local time when she made the call. Beth Stockwell answered on the second ring. Michelle was pleased to find Beth back to her old self. Whatever invisible line she'd crossed the day before had passed and Beth was eager to answer all of her questions. Michelle jumped back onto the Internet a short while later to send Melanie a message about what clothes, and most important, what shoes to bring. Per usual, she first looked at her inbox, and there, three emails down from the top, she saw it again, another communication from *HikerChic*. This time she clicked on it and received the following cryptic message:

It's not what you think

The missive was signed by a person calling herself "*Jodi*."

Michelle stared at the odd message. <u>*What*</u> *isn't what I thought?* she mouthed back at the screen. With no reference to go by in the subject line and not familiar with anyone named Jodi, she assumed that the message was received in error and deleted it.

Beth called her the following day to say that she'd found the engineer's report and that there was nothing precluding entry to either mine to depths of 250 feet and 325 feet below ground surface, respectively, for the Little Bear and Big Bear mines. Below these depths, the engineer deemed the mines to be unsafe. Michelle jotted down the depths, circling the 250-foot depth over and over while she spoke with Beth. This was the level on which the disaster had taken place in that little, mined-out room in Little Bear. Could she actually set foot again in that horrific place so far underground? She had to admit the thought made her queasy. More importantly, could she actually find the exact room after so many years?

As always, the conversation came around to her itinerary for the trip. Michelle explained that she and Melanie would be arriving either late that Friday or early the Saturday morning before their Monday meeting to take in some of the sights in Denver. A ping

Rick Ley

from her computer informed her that she'd received an incoming message. How fortuitous: she was expecting to hear back any time now from her photographer, Mark Boone, about his schedule. Beth had been asking for this information. Michelle unfortunately hit a wrong key and her computer did whatever it did when such things happened. Angry with herself, she was only half listening when Beth said something about a Joe Hayden and the mine tour. "I'm sorry, did you say Joe Hayden?" Michelle asked.

Beth confirmed the name, then repeated once more about the mine tour.

Michelle, though, remained distracted. The email wasn't from Mark Boone; it was another message from *HikerChic*. Against her better judgment, she opened the email.

They know u'r coming! —Jodi

That's when she understood that the message was meant for her...and thus set into motion a fifteen-day period of gut wrenching turmoil.

"Hello? Michelle? Ms. Snow?"

"Huh? Oh!" Michelle said, shaking her head, the haunting message having caused her to forget that she was still on the phone. Michelle did her best to explain away her distraction while deleting the message. Beth then apologized, saying that she had to cut the conversation short to address a timely office emergency only she could manage. They hung up. Michelle retrieved the message from the trash and said to herself...*They know u'r coming!*

Three days later, she received her fourth email from Jodi, and this time the message was much more personal.

You need to watch u'r back! Do you understand?!?

The message was chilling, a warning. *What does that mean? Who's watching me?* Intuition told her it was the Conservancy. Beth, though, had given no indication that anything was wrong. Sure, she acted strangely the other day, as did the evasive Teddy Monroe before that. Neither, however, implied that she had to keep an eye out for trouble. Besides, if the Conservancy had concerns for safety, why the parsing out of cryptic information? Why not just tell her she needed to be careful or back channel such concerns through her publisher's attorneys? The Conservancy could have also refused to cooperate—which they did not—or require that her inquiries be conducted solely over the phone. She was reading too much into it, of this much she was certain. It was probably some system glitch causing her network to hi-jack someone else's mail…this giving her pause for a new concern—that there might be someone else out there in trouble.

But what if there wasn't? What if the messages were meant for her, and it wasn't some hacker looking to incite random fear, or worse, a slime-bag scam artist trying to engage her in an electronic conversation to encrypt malware or spyware or someotherware into her computer? From what she knew about scammers, they usually tried several times to encourage a bite before moving on to easier prey. Feeling up to the challenge, Michelle thought she'd put speculation to the test and searched the *RMTC.com* address. She wasn't sure what she expected, or wanted, to find out. What she did find, however, did nothing to allay her concerns. RMTC stood for Rocky Mountain Telegraph and Cable, a local service provider different than the one used by the Conservancy. The address wasn't bogus. RMTC was a legitimate Colorado-based entity, and that meant—at least to her—that there was a quasi-anonymous third party, not necessarily related to the Conservancy, who didn't want her meddling in…*something.*

Anxiety gnawed at her after that. She could have, should have, said something, didn't, her lack of action triggering dreadful night-mares and bouts of profound exhaustion that left her at times feeling lost in a zombie-like haze, all because she didn't want to cause a stir that might somehow come back on her. Battle-hardened or not, there was still some of the old Michelle left in her, whose weak-nesses would continue to plague her. The bitch of it was she knew that Connor Lewis wouldn't allow her out of her predicament. She was quite certain that he would jump through the phone and kill her himself if she didn't capitalize on the journalist's dream unfolding around her. It was real life Jason Bourne cloak-and-dagger stuff. The problem was she wasn't some danger-seeking journalist or a Lara Croft super heroine. She was just Michelle Kozlowski, a.k.a. Michelle Snow, a.k.a. Calamity Girl from the rural outskirts of Cincinnati, who wrote children's books and the occasional best seller. She never went looking for trouble. Trouble always found her.

Michelle became increasingly preoccupied waiting for the next contact from the mysterious Jodi. She caught herself more times than she cared to remember reaching for her phone, wishing for a ping, yet fearing that Jodi just might have something even more portentous to say. Two days later she received not so much a message but a string of numbers.

39.2522.03 106.0306.14

Michelle didn't recognize the numbers for what they were until the following morning when she was listening in on Nick's conference call with Chris about RCE's forthcoming field investigation. Chris asked whether Nick wanted RCE to record GPS coordinates for the drilling locations so that they could be plotted on a Google Earth map, or if he preferred to wait until the points were surveyed professionally and located exactly on the GIS base map they were working from.

Survey coordinates…

Looking over Nick's shoulder at the notes section of the oversized print he was working from, Michelle noticed that survey coordinates were listed next to each corner point of the PSTRE building. Looking from the print to the email she called up on her phone, Michelle started to count—and then smiled. Jodi's numerical message consisted of seventeen characters, the same number of characters for the two sets of numbers comprising each building corner point on the drawing. Using a crib sheet to reconfigure Jodi's message to account for the missing degrees, minutes, and seconds notation, and then adding a negative sign for longitude west of the prime meridian, Michelle arrived at the following:

Latitude: *39° 25.22' 03"* Longitude: *-106° 03.06' 14"*

She waited until Nick's voice trailed off to jump onto the computer and find out what was so special about this particular location. She opened Google Earth, and without a better reference point to start with, typed in Breckenridge, Colorado and clicked on the spyglass icon. Michelle watched expectantly as the eye in the sky zoomed in to a hovering view 60,000 feet above the Summit County town. She remarked how the innumerable long ski runs, so beautiful during winter, looked like a bunch of bald scars on the landscape in the late September imagery. As she suspected, the town proper was several minutes of latitude north of the location Jodi provided. Michelle clicked on the screen and used the little hand cursor to pan her way south along the mountain slope that bounded the west side of Route 9. She couldn't help drawing an involuntary breath when her quest halted several miles south of Breckenridge at a location roughly half way up the slope. It had to be on the defunct field-station grounds. Reflecting back to the haunting memories of Garret's decades-old journal entries, Michelle came to the realization that Jodi was summoning her home to contend with *(or was it to avoid?)* an unsettled aspect of her past.

The spot that Jodi identified was unremarkable. Zooming in didn't help either; there were just too many trees. If only the imagery was taken just one month later. Maybe then she might have been able to see something after the scattered aspens had dropped their leaves. It was as if the forest had swallowed everything up in one great expanse of green.

Two more days passed when she received a bizarre message to look up a story in the *Central Colorado Times* newspaper:

U need to Read: C.C. Times 8/23/82

The lead story was about the mysterious disappearance of Dylan Streeter during the *Panner's and Picker's Rendezvous* event held in the Lake County mining village and ghost town of Climax, Colorado. The article described the unfortunate timing of the tragedy. At one time, the article reported, Climax was the world's leading producer of the metal molybdenum. The mine had since fallen on hard times, and the community was looking to reverse flagging morale by sponsoring a festival. The article, unfortunately, was but a snippet of a larger piece. Missing was any discussion of the then ongoing investigation into the fate of Mr. Streeter. A little digging revealed that the *C. C. Times* was archived in the newspaper's parent-company collections in Denver.

Like clockwork, she received her next installment two days later: *Don't Come Alone.* This was followed the next day, Monday, with: *U Need To Get Help!*

What disturbed her most about the most recent messages was that she hadn't spoken with or received any emails from the Conservancy or its attorneys in over a week, yet the warnings kept coming. Something beyond her control was happening half a continent away. Like she did after receiving every post, Michelle emailed Jodi back asking for clarity, only to be ignored. And finally, on Friday, after four excruciating days of waiting, she received the latest communiqué from *HikerChic* about William Laney.

Gazing contentedly into the magnolia tree for Mrs. Mockingbird, Michelle contemplated what it all meant. Taking a crunch from her apple, she was comforted to find the mystery finally taking on a semblance of order. Yes, she was certain the Tarryall Mountain Foundation was involved. Exactly how remained to be determined. She further concluded that her involvement in the mystery, as inexplicable as it may be, was somehow related to the similar disappearances of Dylan Streeter and William Laney. Lastly, and more to the point, Michelle realized that if she planned on figuring out how she was involved, she needed to tread lightly and remain vigilant.

CHAPTER 3

TUESDAY

Ashley House
Ashley Avenue, Charleston, S.C.
1:15 P.M.

"C helle, would you mind downloading what's on this and print out what looks useful?"

"Sure. What's on it?" she asked. Michelle saved her work and plugged the flash drive Nick handed her into her laptop.

"There's an updated base map and graphs for the water-level data RCE's collected thus far. Chris said there's other stuff as well."

Michelle was working in one of the two repurposed bedrooms at the rear of the caretaker's apartment when Nick returned from the site. He was in more of a hurry than usual, breezing in and out of the room, giving orders, barely saying hello. She intended to ask how it went; instead she had to settle for a trailing rejoinder.

"There should be photos, too. Can you check? I understand there's a good one that shows the row of piezometers and Athens's tank farm. It has PSTRE's production well in the foreground. Make me a copy—*P-L-E-A-S-E!*" Staring at the preponderance of PSTRE files Michelle had so kindly laid out in tidy stacks three rows deep on the work table, Nick ran his fingers through his hair, wondering where to start the daunting task of wading through them. He couldn't help venting his frustration. "I also need you to mark up the new map with all of the historic sample points and other relevant features you can find while I start plowing through this crap."

"You don't have to yell," Michelle said. Nick jumped, not realizing that she was standing behind him. Michelle jumped in kind. She placed a hand on his shoulder to curb his agitation. "What's going on?" she asked, her voice fluttery. "You're running around like your hair's on fire."

Nick explained Chris's conversation with Smitty. "Something has legal in a tither. Smitty got Chris riled up about some new sugar daddy at PSTRE who's calling the shots. The long and the short of it is that legal had a knee-jerk reaction and is coming here this afternoon for a sitrep, and I haven't had the time to get a handle on… this." Nick panned an arm over Michelle's handiwork. "I was hoping to get through all of this between today and tomorrow. I should have done this by now." Nick was speaking so fast he struggled to complete his sentence. He took in a great lung full of air and exhaled.

Michelle waited for him to recover before holding up the small stack of papers that was the answer to his prayers.

Nick squinted at the facing page. It was the detailed chronology of PSTRE's and Athens's environmental history. "No way!" he gushed, hugging her.

"You don't remember asking me to do this, do you?" she said smartly, this time with a pat on the back. "What do you think I've been doing up here the past two days?" Michelle fanned through the summary and twenty-odd pages of supporting information for Nick to see. "Here's everything worthwhile that I could find. This should get you through the meeting."

"Yes," Nick said, embarrassed. "I did forget. Thank you!" When Michelle then pointed to several of the closest stacks on the worktable and explained that she'd segregated them chronologically by activity, he positively beamed. Kozlowski's *associate* once again had his back. "Can I keep this or do you still need to add stuff?"

"It's all yours," she said. "I'm done and made a copy for myself. With any luck I can have the map updated by the time M&C arrives. Do you have any idea when that might be?" Nick shrugged. "Okay, I better get to work." Michelle trudged off back to her office space. Nick settled in to matching her chronology to the document stacks.

Michelle was horror-struck. Nick had somehow managed to scatter all her neat piles across the table and floor in the short time she was gone. In fact, he was kneeling on the only portion of floor not covered by the dishevelment. All her hard work was…

"I know, I know," Nick panicked at the scorn on his wife's face. "I know where everything goes! I promise to straighten things up before Smitty and Brant arrive."

"You'd better," she warned.

Nick decided it was wise to move to safer ground. "Whatcha find?" he asked, lowering an eye to the markup in her hand.

"I have a question about what to call the new exploratory borings and surface-soil samples that were done yesterday. There's a sketch but no ID labels. I need to know what to call them."

"Sure. In my logbook, there on the counter. I made note of what RCE intended to call them. Memory serves that RCE planned on seven borings."

"Yep. That's what I counted." Michelle retrieved the logbook and flipped through the entries. "Good. Here they are. By the way, where's Chris?" she asked. "I thought he was coming back with you."

Nick made a little snorting noise. "You know him. He couldn't wait. He went over to M&C to ferret out what's going on about the new guy. He'll be here soon."

The sound of footsteps tramping up the exterior staircase announced Chris's imminent arrival. Nick was putting the final touches on restoring the documents to their original order when Chris barged through the doorway without so much as a knock. "Whoa!" he said. "That's impressive."

"Michelle did all the work. It's a good thing you arrived when you did," Nick confessed. "It wasn't a pretty sight in here a few minutes ago. I kinda had everything all messed up."

Chris laughed his approval of his buddy's housekeeping skills.

"Hi Chris," Michelle greeted him. "I thought that was you I heard coming up the steps."

"You heard correctly! Nice work by the way," he said, complimenting her on the orderly, if not overcrowded tabletop. Michelle smiled in silent appreciation.

"What did you find out?" Nick asked from his perch behind a stack of air-permit compliance records.

"Nothing," Chris said, dejected by his thwarted quest to find an answer to the Hal Cole question. "Everyone was holed up in one of the conference rooms. Even Bill Carlyle was there. He was supposed to still be out of town. When I tapped at the glass, Smitty waved me off." Chris raised his arms in the air and shrugged. "He did send me a text when I was already in the car to say that he'd explain when he got here." Chris looked at his watch. "They should be here within the hour." And with a treacherous grin he then announced, "Makes me wonder if it has anything to do with the fact that we're still being watched."

"What? *Right Now?*" Nick croaked his surprise. He leapt to his feet and rushed to the window.

"What are you two talking about?" Michelle asked. "Nick? Chris?" With no explanation forthcoming, she demanded their attention with a forceful, *"GUYS?"*

"You didn't tell her?" Chris said, speaking past Michelle to Nick, who was peering out the near side window. "What are you doing?" Chris scolded him. "Don't be so obvious. Go over there and peek around the corner." Chris pointed to the main window, which offered a more discreet view of the southerly length of Ashley Avenue. He explained that a different car, a gray sedan this time, was parked down the street.

"Nick?" Michelle pleaded—first her issues with the Conservancy, and now this? She butted her way in front of Chris when Nick didn't answer her right away. *"I said, what's going on?"*

"Yesterday we saw two men in a red car watching us while we were at PSTRE, and last Friday night I saw what I think were the same two watching us when Nick and I were on the balcony."

The revelation didn't sit well. Arms plastered to her sides,

Michelle screeched, "*Here?* I've been alone here…and neither of you thought that I should know?"

She was so angry that her hair danced a quarterback's cadence independent of her shaking. Nick stepped away from the window to settle her. "It's okay, really. Chris thinks it's Athens trying to find out what we're doing, what we know—you know, in the event the case goes to court. They're following Chris and me, not spying on you. Right, Chris?"

"Sure," Chris answered, his response less than convincing. Michelle glared at him. "No, really, Michelle," Chris said in a vain effort to reassure her. He rustled his fingers through his beard like Nick did when he was nervous.

"But you don't know for certain?" she pressed.

"Well, no…but I think so," wisely adding, "You're right. We should have told you."

"So what's your excuse?" Michelle then asked of her very much in trouble husband.

"I didn't want you getting overly concerned and start peeping out the window every other minute, wondering what those douchebags are up to."

"Is that right?" Michelle tested him. "I don't like this at all. They could be listening in on us. Am I right? They can do that? Invade our privacy? My privacy?"

"Yes," Chris admitted on Nick's behalf. "Smitty's aware of what's going on and he spoke with Bill. They both agreed that we should keep tabs on them for the time being, and we thought—I should quit while I'm behind and just tell Smitty to have Carlyle put a stop to it."

"That would be a good idea," Michelle warned the two of them before taking her leave.

⸻

Chris was in agreement with Nick that proving liability in a court of law would not be as simple as demonstrating that there was oil in the subsurface stretching from the Athens property line to a long forgotten production well some fifty feet away. There were just too many variables to contend with, between the complex hydrogeology and the long and partially conjoined relationship between adversaries. They decided that disentangling the combatants' operational histories was the most logical place to start. Deciphering the screwy groundwater data could be RCE's problem for the time being. Nick selected the Phase I report with the most detailed historical land-use summary to start with. Chris paralleled his reading by scrutinizing the finely rendered line drawings on the Sanborn fire-insurance maps contained as an appendix in the disassembled report. The drawings presented the area property-use history dating back into the late 1800s. They had no sooner started when Chris cursed.

"Uh, oh!" Nick said. As so often happens, the subject area was tucked away in the coverage periphery, in this instance, the upper left corner of the earliest maps. Chris grumbled because the map coverage cut off just beyond Athens's north property boundary. Coverage to the west of both properties was also cut short. A quick peek through the remaining Phase I documents revealed that, each time, the consultant used the same view area. "Don't worry about it," Nick said, "I was planning on traipsing over to the municipal buildings in town later this week to look for historical coverage not likely found through the conventional means. Still, you would've thought that at least one of these bozos would have asked the vendor to expand the search radius."

"No kidding," Chris groused. "Sloppy work. Let's hope we don't find any more surprises."

PSTRE, they did know, was founded in 1889 as Palmetto State Electrical Supply on 59 acres of former farmland located between the Ashley and Cooper rivers. The property was purchased from the Middleton estate, the Middletons being a prominent family in early Charleston. Chris confirmed Nick's findings on the 1884 and 1888 map coverage: *"Farm Land (Middleton, et.al),"* was printed in neat script across the space. PSTRE then purchased and moved the Georgia-based Athens Creosote Company to the property in 1891. Two years later, the northern 27 acres were parceled out from the existing property for Athens's use as a separate corporate entity. Chris noted the property split on the 1902 map. "Check this out," he said, spinning the map around so that Nick could see. A *"Pole Storage Area"* was identified on the PSTRE parcel, and *"Oil Barrels"* were identified next to a rather large collection of tiny circles at the northern limits of the coverage, just above the words *"Athens Creosote."* The existing northern rail spur that they presumed was used for creosote delivery to Athens was also present, as were various structures called *"Wood Cribs,"* along with other unlabeled structures strewn hither and yon across both properties.

"Fascinating," Nick said. Revealing the secrets of a property's former use was one of Nick's favorite parts of the investigation process, particularly when the site had a long and rich history like PSTRE's and Athens's. In many ways, Nick thought of a property as a living entity, its cultural dynamic ever changing along with its owners, most of whom never knew that the others existed.

In 1902, the Athens building was a much smaller wooden structure identified by the letters *"Whse,"* short for *warehouse.* "Huh, did you notice that most of the creosote was stored on the northern half of Athens's property?" Chris indicated that he did. "Wonder why? One would think it would be kept much closer," Nick continued, noting that the creosote barrels were stored well away from where the treated utility poles were stored. Chris shrugged. "And these?" Nick added, pointing to several linear features with slightly curved ends, just beyond Athens's north property boundary at the upper limits of the source coverage.

"I saw those as well," Chris acknowledged.

Nick made a mental note to figure out what the features were when he made his foray into town. Nick then flipped ahead to the next fire-insurance map, from 1944. Land use on both properties had changed dramatically over the intervening forty-odd years, and the features, to his regret, were now gone. They were also absent from the earliest aerial photography coverage, from 1937. Nick had a little luck in one of the other Phase I reports. In it, the consultant said that there were ponds north of Athens's property. This made sense since the former Middleton estate was once a farm that encompassed much of the central portion of the Charleston peninsula, now bisected by I-26. Nick amused himself at the thought of clouds of mosquitos hovering above the watering holes each evening, talking over dinner plans before sallying forth on that night's blood-letting raid into town.

Reading aloud, Nick explained that a name change occurred in 1927, when the utility-pole operation was sold and the name of the company was changed to reflect a subtle shift in business: Palmetto State Electrical Supply ceased to exist and Palmetto State Transformer was born. The text went on to describe how PSTRE had become increasingly involved in the manufacture of electronic components along with the sale of pre-treated, vendor-supplied utility poles. Finally, in 1977, the name was changed to Palmetto State Transformer and Relay, to reflect the new focus on the manufacture of transformers and related appurtenances and, of course, self-propelled railcars. The text didn't explain the difference between what they were doing then versus now.

Maybe then they were making only parts and now they made the whole shebang???

"What about Athens?" Chris asked, flipping through the later fire-insurance map and aerial photography coverage.

Nick scanned ahead, moving his head back and forth like a typewriter. "In 1927, they made a switch to light petroleum lubricants. There's no real description of what they did with the stuff. Didn't Dawson say the feud started around then?"

Chris chewed at his lip. "He might've. I don't remember."

"Remind me to ask Smitty," Nick continued. "Maybe he knows. Okay, let's see…what else they did. In 1963, Athens started producing medicinal petroleum jelly. That's weird. They got away from that by 1992. Since then it looks like Athens has been making *synthesized material*—whatever the hell that is—for use in plastics and specialty steel coatings. Now that's an interesting product shift. Whatever you gotta do to maintain a niche, I suppose." Nick pondered the text description. Something didn't add up. Rather, something obvious was missing.

"What is it? I know that look," Chris said.

"The report doesn't make any clear mention of where the old pole-treatment pits and other whatnots were located." Nick grabbed the remaining stack of Phase Is, scanning several at once. "I take that back. In this one here, the consultant said that pole treatment 'occurred on the north part of the PSTRE property.'" His voice trailed off to a raspy whisper, the meaning behind the passage hanging heavy in the air. They exchanged glances. "That's not good," Nick said with a hard swallow.

"That's an understatement," Chris agreed. "If that's the case, it's likely that PSTRE did contaminate its own well."

"I thought PSTRE only stored the treated poles on their property and that it was Athens that did all the dirty work."

"That's my understanding as well. What am I looking for?" Chris asked, looking more closely at the earliest aerial photograph, from 1937.

"The untreated poles would have been placed in some kind of pressurized container full of creosote; or, if the operation was more primitive, rolled in a pit dug in the sand. They would have also used tanks or barrels to recover the used product and to capture condensate and rinsate from equipment washing."

Chris retrieved a magnifying glass from his satchel.

"Also look for evaporation pits where the sludge was collected and areas where the poles were allowed to drip dry. See anything like that?"

"Hmm. I'm looking. If I remember correctly, sludge pits used to be unlined. That should have left quite a mess behind," Chris said casually, squinting through the lens from the photo to the turn-of-the-century fire-insurance map. "No, nothing, other than the pole-storage area on PSTRE just where Dawson said it was. As for Athens, ah, I see nothing. Now that's odd. I should be seeing something." Chris sat up and, rubbing at his eyes, sighed. "Either we're missing something, or we're looking at this all wrong. Simple logistics implies that log treatment would have been where Athens's tank farm presently stands, right? I mean, from what I see they most always had some form of tank or barrel storage at that location, and yet I don't see anything suggestive of a pit or treatment operation. Tell me I'm wrong."

"No, you're right. Maybe the operation wasn't as large as we think, or maybe the treatment operation took place under roof in Athens's warehouse. Another mystery to add to the pile."

"Anything jump out in the deed search?"

Nick flipped to a table that presented the title history for both the PSTRE and Athens facilities. "Very good...well, sort of." The information was jumbled. Separate tables would have been better, Nick thought. The consultant must have had trouble separating the two entities so he discussed them in tandem. Complicating matters, the table referenced not two properties, but three: Parcel A (PSTRE), Parcel B (Athens), and a third and confusing Parcel C (identified as 'Lands sold by PSTRE to City of Charleston, 1929'). Parcel C was a mystery. In fact, the site-location map made no clear distinction between the PSTRE and Athens properties besides an unlabeled property-boundary line denoted by a series of dots and dashes, and PSTRE Parcel C wasn't identified at all. Adding further insult, Nick was dismayed to read the small print in what proved to be an otherwise irrelevant footnote that described Parcel C as: '...being part of 487 acres of additional lands in the greater Charleston area acquired from the Middleton estate in 1889.'"

"Give me a break!" Nick grouched, dropping the report onto the table.

Chris was amused by the tantrum. When Nick summarily retrieved the document, flipped to the executive summary at the beginning, and then to the conclusions at the end, Chris couldn't contain himself. Nick's face turned a deep crimson by the time he'd finished and again threw the document, this time to the floor in a flurry of loose papers when the binder clip lost its purchase in mid-flight.

"This piece of shit doesn't answer any of the obvious questions that we, let alone a lending institution, need to know. Where did the operation take place? How can *not* knowing information on where the raw logs were treated *not* be flagged as a recognized environmental condition? And—oh, here's a good one—where the *fuck* is Parcel C?"

"Is this a bad time?" Michelle interrupted from the short hall threshold, measuring the tension like one does when investigating a strange noise in the night.

"Not at all," Chris said, waving her over. "Are we still in the dog house?" he ventured only after he was certain she appeared less annoyed than before.

"No," Michelle said, pleased to find that she still had them buffaloed. "So long as whoever *they* are go away and you two promise to think about me next time."

"Agreed!" Chris said.

"Yeah, deal!" Nick concurred, hoping to ride on Chris's coattails.

Michelle mocked him by feigning exasperation. She would let Nick stew a little while longer.

"Your timing is impeccable!" Chris followed. "You have something for us?"

"I do," Michelle said, her vibe suggesting that their blunder was behind her. "But first, why were you swearing?"

Nick explained their Phase I issues.

"I'm sorry to hear that," she said. Maybe this will help." Michelle handed them a copy of the updated base map. She explained that it was an Adobe mock-up of the map Nick gave her earlier. "It includes everything I found when organizing the files, which you might have seen in the packet I gave Nick."

"I did," Chris nodded in approval. "That is a big help." Turning to the new handout he asked what the colors meant.

"Sample locations and activities are color-coded by event type. There was a PCB spill; tank removals; the well associated with the PCB event I made another color because it's sampled about every time there's a consultant out there doing something. Stuff like that." She pointed to the legend.

"I see. Excellent. Tell you what, Michelle," Chris said, tearing off a scrap of notebook paper. "Send a copy of what you made to Brandon Butler at RCE." Chris scribbled down Butler's email address on the slip of paper and handed it to Michelle. "He knows you're helping us. We've talked and he's playing with the base map again as we speak. Ask him to add what you found."

"Again? Why?" Nick asked.

"Modify the base map? This one's too cluttered. I think we need to strip it down, and then use that to create successive figures, each showing specific information like historical aerial photography and property-use coverage, soil type, and geologic contact information—shit like that—on something less busy."

"Great idea, Chris" Nick said. "We can also have him create figures that show groundwater flow and contaminant-plume coverage."

"That goes without saying," Chris crowed, reveling in his visionary moment. "I've been known to be useful from time to time. You'll do that, then?" he asked Michelle.

"Of course!" she answered. "I'll do that right now. Let me know if you guys find anything else you want to add and I'll send that along as well." Michelle returned to her cubbyhole to carry out her assignment. In the excitement, she didn't once think about the corporate spooks lurking on the street below.

⸻

Michelle dashed an email off to RCE. With an anticipatory click she now checked her inbox, not so much for another post from Jodi but for a response from Aero-Recon, the database vendor Nick used to obtain historical mapping information. Chris's mention of aerial imagery reminded her that she had ordered a suite of aerials covering the area surrounding Jodi's cryptic latitude and longitude coordinates. Michelle scolded herself for not having placed the order until yesterday after her call to Beth. Finding that she'd received nothing yet, she called her account representative at Aero-Recon, who assured her that the electronic files should be received at any moment. A hard copy would be expedited at no additional cost, to arrive tomorrow afternoon in time for her trip, as compensation for the inconvenience. What service! Michelle found the gesture thoughtful even if it wasn't necessary. She was the one who waited until the last moment.

The aerial coverage dated to the mid 1950s, pretty much as expected. What she didn't expect for such a remote area was a whopping fourteen images, recorded every five to ten years, the most recent flyover performed in 2013. Such attention, she reasoned, must be needed for urban planning purposes related to the area ski and tourism industries. The extensive coverage was a good thing because most of the photos were either too blurry or shot at too high an altitude to be of use. Seeming peculiar was the absence of the Big Bear and Little Bear mountains, formidable obstacles on the ground that, when viewed from the air, were reduced to hillocks drowned out by the flattening effect of the dense forest cover. Without a prominent physical feature on the hill slope in the vicinity of the Alpine Lodge grounds to use as a point of reference, Michelle used the familiar twists and turns in Route 9 south of the Goose Pasture Tarn water body to gain her bearings. She aided her search by queuing the coordinates Jodi provided into Google Earth.

The first thing Michelle noticed was that the landscape in the 1956 photo appeared much different than the picture on her computer screen, not to mention how she remembered it looking in the mid '80s during her field-camp days. So, too, did the forest cover in the three successive photos. She used the Google Earth hand icon to hover over the coordinate location on the computer screen and compared the

Rick Ley

current and improved Route 9 to the goat-path of the 1950s to find Jodi's mystery area; but it wasn't until she reached the fall 1979 coverage that Michelle realized something she should have surmised all along—that whatever it was Jodi wanted her to see was located in the forbidden Sacred Lands north of the former field-research station. A knot formed in her stomach. The location was near where she remembered the Little Bear mine should be, and certainly not very far from where legend claimed that fur trapper turned prospector John Parker stumbled upon the mutilated remains of a murdered Indian prophet over one hundred and twenty years before. Worrying anew, Michelle couldn't prevent a gasp from escaping her lips.

Nonsense! Quit letting your mind play tricks on you! she scolded herself. *Focus!* Michelle did just that and realized that the early photos appeared different because a sizeable portion of the photo coverage, including the field-station property, was clearcut and, by the 1950s, was in a stage of successional regrowth.

She saw nothing telling in the successive photos, save for portions of several field-station roofs poking through holes in the foliage. "Oh, well," she huffed.

Wait! What's that???

Her heart fluttered. Michelle sat forward in her seat. There was a tiny blue-green blip in the right general area on the 1989 photo, which happened to be taken in false-color infrared and not the standard black and white. Color infrared photography offers a different way of looking at the landscape. Agriculturalists and foresters use the images to gauge vegetation health. Similarly, geologists like Nick use color infrared to look for signs of stressed vegetation—places where the plants were adversely impacted by contaminants taken up by their root systems. Michelle wasn't exactly sure what she was looking for, but it was something. She snatched the photo from the table and held it side by side to the Google Earth imagery. "No way!" she cheered softly, so as not to disturb the boys in the other room. To her amazement, the little blue-green spot lined up pretty much smack dab with Jodi's coordinates. *Okay, now what?*

Michelle squinted at the image. The surrounding foliage was a strong red, the river black, and Goose Pasture Tarn milky green. She recalled from her brief stint as a practicing biologist that this meant that the vegetation was healthy, save for a small patch of trees farther up slope that was a light pink, probably a blight. The black color of the stream indicated that its water was clear, free of entrained sediment, while the tarn—a slow flowing pond within the river—carried a moderate load. This left the little blip of a spot, which stumped her until she recalled that a blue-green expression was indicative of moist silt or loamy soil. *An excavation?* There was one other color infrared photo in the lot, dated from 1993. The blip in this photo was slightly larger and teardrop shaped, had diffuse edges, and was a dark blue-green. This suggested that erosion had enlarged the possible excavation, and that the vegetation was healing the scar from the outside in.

So what was so important? Obviously, the feature was related to something that had happened back about when she was at the field station. Michelle frowned. Did it have something to do with Garret? Did he actually find John Parker's grave, or perhaps Badger Heart's? *Oh, stop it,* she laughed at the silly notion. That's stupid. *Or was it?* In his journals, Michelle discovered that Garret did look for and thought he found Badger Heart's grave, though there was no mention of him actually finding bones. The real question was why Jodi wanted her to know about this particular location. What could Jodi possibly expect her to find after so much time? If it was a gravesite, it was surely robbed by now. How did she know this? If Jodi knew it was there, others certainly did as well. No, that couldn't be it. Besides, the grave of a long dead Indian, prophet Badger Heart or otherwise, would only help the Conservancy's bottom line through the sale of gift-shop trinkets to all those occult worshiper whackos, or through donations from curious sane people interested in area folklore, right? No, something else happened there that the Conservancy—or someone—wanted to hide.

Much like yesterday, Michelle was confused. The answer had to be staring her in the face. If only the collection of emails made sense. And why, if Beth Stockwell was in fact Jodi, didn't she just spell everything out if she was contacting Michelle through an alternate IP address? Thinking through this new information, Michelle was now not only certain that the Conservancy was involved, but that it had something to hide that was—okay, probably—somehow involved with the two missing historians. "Jiminy Christmas!" she said loud enough to interrupt Nick and Chris in the other room. "Sorry!" she yelled through the wall, and they continued about their business. So, was Beth's revealing the location a preemptive warning not to go there, *or* a tantalizing suggestion to shed her escort long enough to investigate?

Forget about it and get back to work, she demanded of herself. Excited now that she'd made some real progress to follow up upon, or better yet the excuse to elicit another communiqué from Jodi, Michelle was reassembling the aerials into their chronological order when she made a second discovery in as many minutes. The field-camp-area grounds had been burned, not logged as she suspected, the edges of the burn area scalloped and not shorn straight like they would have been when the loggers reached the limits of the prescribed cut. Moreover, the burn area was fan shaped and roughly centered on either side of the Ghost Creek valley, fanning outward to what Michelle guessed was at least a mile in width by the time the blaze raged up the mountainside to the tree line. With haunting recollections of places past, Michelle noticed that the fire appeared to have started where Ghost Creek meets the Blue River at the source of so many nightmares—Satan's Lair.

"Good afternoon, gentlemen," Smitty announced. Nick and Chris stood. "Please, don't get up on our account," he urged and the boys sat back down. Smitty let himself inside. Brant followed close behind and closed the door. "My apologies, I didn't see you standing over there," Smitty added when Michelle popped her head up from behind the kitchenette-cum-refreshment dispensary and present resting spot for the two boxes of miscellaneous files that Chris called the Doubly Deads. Michelle said hello back and Smitty pulled out a chair beside Chris and collapsed into it. He commented that the file stacks reminded him of a crude diorama of a city skyline. With no further preamble, Smitty said that they, too, saw the gray sedan. "It pulled away when we parked. Our inquisitive friends are not as discreet as they should be."

Michelle placed an ice bucket filled with bottled water on the worktable. She pretended not to show any interest in Smitty's remarks.

Brant jockeyed a chair next to Nick. "We're rather certain they know that they've been made. They gunned their engine after turning onto Bull."

"About that," Chris said to Smitty, "We need Athens to call off their dogs."

Smitty didn't seem at all put off by the request. He looked instinctively at Michelle still standing over the table. His lawyerly powers of observation read the discomfort in her body language. He looked to Brant.

"Consider it done. Be my pleasure," Brant replied, rubbing his hands together with anticipation.

"Thank you," Michelle said. Nick echoed her appreciation.

"You should never have been made to feel uncomfortable in your own home," Brant said, his voice uncommonly kind. "Which, by the way, you've taken great strides to improve. I speak for Smitty and the firm when I say that we wish all our guests took such care of the accommodations. Hospitality, unfortunately, is too often taken for granted." And spreading his hands apart to encompass Smitty's model city, added expressly for Michelle's benefit, "I understand that we have you to thank for this as well. Your efforts are much appreciated." Brant then did something else most unexpected; the grim-faced junior attorney asked her to join the meeting.

Michelle was elated. She was now an official member of the team, someone of real significance and not just Nick's helper. Equally important, Brant Sutherland was no longer the brutish sidekick she thought him to be. For that matter, she no longer considered Smithson Griffin the boorish snob he appeared to be during their first encounter last Friday. One small reintroduction later and they were now just Smitty and Brant.

"Where should we start?" Smitty asked. "Do we have some things figured out?"

"Not really," Chris answered truthfully. "We've got nothing. At least nothing concrete." Nick agreed. Smitty was already splayed out unlawyerly in his seat like a prize fighter who'd barely made it back to his corner after a hard fought round. When he sagged that much farther, Chris was quick to redirect, "We were hoping that you were going to bring *us* some good news."

Smitty chuckled. "Good news? How about indeterminate news? Athens wants to meet with their lawyers this Friday afternoon, like Bill suspected they would."

"You don't think they're looking to settle, then?" Chris asked.

"No, at least not yet. But it is progress. They're at least on a fishing expedition to see what evidence we have. We'll see. Now, what problems do we have?"

To Nick's surprise, Chris passed the question on to him. Nick collected his thoughts. "For starters, the field data are thus far inconclusive. You are aware of that." Smitty and Brant indicated as much. Nick watched Brant unroll a blueprint-sized copy of the base map, updated per Chris minus Michelle's additional modifications. "Wow, that was fast," Nick said, a satisfied crook curling his lip. He asked Brant to look at the line of piezometers installed along the property boundary south of the Athens tank farm. "We expected to find impact in any number of these. We didn't. There was just a sheen on the discharge here at PZ-5." Nick pointed to the small circle near the end of the line. "We also found evidence of a petroleum-like impact here and here." Nick pointed to the randomly located PZ-7 and PZ-9 near the west property boundary and PSTRE production well, respectively.

"Assessment?" Brant asked, tapping a finger on PZ-5. "Nothing anywhere else along here? What about PZ-2? I would have expected we should have seen something there."

"No, nothing."

Brant asked for copies of RCE's field logs. Nick extended his copy of the rough field notes. Brant waved him off. "I don't need to see them now. I'll wait for a scrubbed copy. You've looked at them?" Nick acknowledged that he had. "What do they tell you?" Brant asked, continuing his hawking over the map. "I presume that groundwater is within a few feet of ground surface?"

"More or less," Nick said. "The lithology is very tight, a mix of silt and clay with some sandy zones, if you can call them that. Jay, the RCE field geologist we spoke with, indicated that the oil appears to be confined to the sands."

"You don't sound convinced?"

"It's not that. It's just that what he calls sand, I call a non-homogenous mix of fine to very fine mixed sediment that I find hard pressed to allow a light-end petroleum product, let alone a heavier oil or creosote, to pass through. I might be wrong. Just saying."

"I see. We're not observing widespread contamination coming off the Athens property like we hoped," Brant said in summary. He countermanded his former comment and grabbed Nick's copy of the field logs. "Try looking at field descriptions from the contaminant's perspective and not how you perceive it should travel through the substrate. Make sense?"

"It does," Nick said. "That's a good idea, Brant. RCE did a good job recording estimated percentages of the fines. I'll see if I can identify a preferential pathway."

"Please do that." Then stubbing his finger on the Athens tank farm, Brant asked, "What do we know about these borings?" Brant was referring to several soil borings that Athens's consultant had drilled during a tank-replacement action performed several years before.

Nick had yet to review the Athens documentation. In fact, he didn't realize that M&C was aware of this work. It was an addition from the earlier version of the map that he and Chris had. Nick deferred the question to Michelle.

"They didn't find much of anything," Michelle said, happy to add to the discussion. "They noted a little petroleum odor, that's all. I don't recall them finding any oil in the ground. There was also nothing in the soil-sample summary table to suggest an exceedance of state or federal standards. The borings didn't go very deep, though."

"That doesn't matter," Brant said. "Contamination would have migrated from the top down. The consultant would have—should have—reported any issues, which you say they didn't, beyond odor."

Michelle appreciated the explanation. She then ventured to ask something that had been bothering her since last Friday's meeting, something that she had since heard Nick and Chris hash over several times amongst themselves. "Can I ask why we're here? I mean we don't seem to know anything about what's going on. We're not even sure which way the groundwater is flowing."

"That, Ms. Kozlowski," Smitty said, "is the question, now isn't it? We've been asking ourselves much the same since this fire drill started. I have some answers that should appease you, the both of you as well," he said including Chris and Nick in on his answer. "Might I start with a question for you, however: do you know who Stan Merrill is?"

Michelle nodded. "He's PSTRE's president.

"That's right. Stan Merrill is, how should I say, an impatient man?"

Brant's amused snuffle echoed his colleague's assessment.

"Stan's become increasingly frustrated with Athens's refusal to sell. I don't know how much Chris or your husband has told you, but PSTRE is positioning itself to greatly expand operations abroad in the rail-service industry. To do this, PSTRE needs to expand its footprint, hence their interest in the Athens property."

"I thought they only needed more water," Michelle said.

"They need both, actually."

"Hold on!" Chris interrupted. "Since when?"

Smitty cooled Chris's jets with the lift of a hand. "We've suspected as much for some time. This is more than a simple blood feud for Merrill. Our suspicions were confirmed yesterday afternoon in a conference call between Bill Carlyle, Stan, and some of the other PSTRE officers. I was informed last night. In its current configuration, PSTRE's property simply doesn't meet its expansion needs—which begs the question why Merrill decided to move ahead with the costly expansion. My guess is that Cole has something to do with that. I also think that Stan underestimated Athens's resolve and found that he couldn't throw enough money their way and coerce a sale."

"This complicates things," Chris said.

"We're still proceeding with the case, right?" Nick asked, unable to conceal his disappointment if they weren't.

"Yes. Proceeding as planned as if nothing's changed. In fact, Bill's working on a backup plan with our real-estate attorneys as we speak, and he's called in a couple of favors with his political connections in Columbia to see if we can't expedite a brownfields cleanup on an idle property that meets PSTRE's infrastructure needs. If he can get the authorities to wave some environmental requirements in lieu of getting a derelict property back into service, we might be able to make PSTRE's space and water issues go away altogether. We do need to work quickly, however, because PSTRE isn't the only player looking to exploit the Indo-Far East market."

"What about surrounding properties?" Nick questioned. "It's undeveloped in all directions."

Smitty's expression suggested that he had fielded this question before. "Expansion east or west is complicated by wetlands, and Industrial Drive is problematic to the south. PSTRE would have to jump through all kinds of hoops to get the road rerouted, even if they could acquire that property."

"I see," Michelle said, still confused. "But the land and water issues do become moot if PSTRE convinces Athens to sell. Is that correct?"

Smitty responded with a little laugh. "Yes and no. The land part yes, the water…maybe. Local complications require that PSTRE, at a minimum, have the combined water output from both of their wells *and* possibly Athens's production well to serve as a booster. Of course, we won't know what PSTRE's production well is capable of producing until the contamination is removed and a pumping test is completed. We also don't know what Athens's well yields. The situation is, as they say, complicated."

"You're saying that even if Athens does sell, PSTRE isn't home free," Michelle persisted.

This brought a smile to Smitty's lips. "Now you got the picture. The first hurdle is to hem in our client, whose aggressive posturing has ushered in a new round of hostilities. Putting it kindly—and you didn't hear this from me—Stan's a bully used to getting his way. He doesn't realize, or refuses to admit, that he doesn't have leverage yet over Athens, nor does he appreciate the gravity of his well issue. This 'environmental stuff,' which he's wont to dismiss as an irritation, is outside his bailiwick. Add to the mix a new company high roller who stands to lose much and might pull out at any time, and PSTRE has one very big problem. We can only collect all the data we can to guide him, let Bill handle things on his end, and hope that sooner rather than later he gets it. Until then, I'm afraid Athens is only going to dig their heels in deeper."

"It's a real pissing match," Brant commented over the boring logs he held in front of him.

"This Hal Cole guy. Any new information on him?" Chris asked.

"Nothing new," Smitty regretted to say, taking off his glasses, this time to clean them with his tie. "We're still looking into his background. So far, he comes as advertised, a venture capitalist looking to make money."

"Hold on," Nick said. "Can't we drill several deeper exploratory borings on PSTRE's property and convert one or more of those into a production well? Or does this fall into the realm of 'local complications?'"

Smitty punted the question to his colleague. "Brant? Care to handle this one?"

Brant explained that North Charleston's newly ratified water budget, which mirrors the plan currently in place in Charleston proper, placed very conservative freshwater-withdrawal limitations within the municipality. Excessive pumping, he explained, had depleted the city's freshwater reserves, causing saltwater intrusion into the public water-supply system and costing the city millions in infrastructure repairs. A moratorium was also imposed on the drilling of new withdrawal points within city limits until it was determined that the aquifer system was sufficiently recharged. "What this means is that North Charleston has declined PSTRE's request to tap into the public water supply."

"I thought they couldn't tie in," Chris said, scribbling down notes.

"That depends on *who* you are. Money talks. Merrill has some pull. We recommended he try, in the event that their well isn't salvageable. We told him to offer paying for the public line extension and perhaps sweeten the pot with a generous charitable donation."

"It didn't work," Nick said.

"No," Brant smirked. "City do what city does," he said, shaking his head. "Unfortunately for our client, PSTRE's needs come at a bad time."

"Their needs do meet the new withdrawal limits, right?" Nick expected Brant to say yes. His treacherous smile said otherwise.

"I don't understand," Nick said. He looked to Chris for an explanation only to find him equally perplexed.

There was no mistaking Brant's joy when he informed them that, "The limitations apply only to public water use and new wells, which presently can't be drilled. A loophole in the regulations allows for unlimited pumping from *preexisting* wells. It's curious how the threat of losing political contributions can affect how legislation is written. Good for the few and screw the rest."

Brant's comment got Nick thinking. "What if we deepen the existing well, then? We could case off the upper impacted zone and extend the borehole to the next adequate water bearing zone or zones. I don't see why pumping from multiple zones within the same well couldn't make up any supply shortfall."

"A great idea," Smitty said, shaking with relief. "Brant?"

"I'll check right into it," Brant responded in a flurry of movement.

Michelle forewent formality to pat Nick on the shoulder.

Perplexed by his own brilliance over this timely if not obvious overlooked solution, Nick built on his savior status by offering one more salient thought. "Would this not then provide PSTRE with leverage? Think about it. If we suggest to Merrill that PSTRE can engineer around the contamination issue, he might consider upping the ante on a purchase offer in lieu of pursuing a lengthy lawsuit. Seems to me this would be a win-win."

"I love it!" Chris applauded. "Now that is some good news. It has a certain devious quality about it. That's something I would think of."

"Okay, everyone," Smitty said. "Let's not get our hopes up too much yet. But this is good. Real good. Brant, you check whether the legislation says anything about modifying existing wells. Now, are there any other issues that we need to be aware of?"

"Now that you mention it," Chris said, couching his and Nick's earlier findings, "we have some concerns after our review of the property-use and ownership history. Nick, if you'll do the honors?"

Ashley House
Ashley Avenue, Charleston, S.C.
8:20 P.M.

Michelle was passing through the great room when Melanie pulled to the curb. She scampered across the cypress hardwood to the adjoining parlor room and announced, "Mel's here!" to Nick and Chris, who were inside watching a Braves game.

Ever since the meeting ended, Michelle found herself waiting with increased anticipation for Melanie's arrival because, for the first time in nearly a year, she was in the enviable position of having absolutely nothing to do. Now that all of the planning was finished, the reins to the project files handed over to Nick, and the game of cat and mouse with her elusive guardian angel was in stasis, her mind was finally free to relish the moment—her moment.

"You're staying here? It's beautiful!" Melanie chimed her approval from the curb. "It's even prettier than the pictures you sent me."

Michelle bounded over in greeting. Her heart danced when Melanie replicated her approach, bags in tow, with her own gleeful scurry. They met with an embrace that melted away the years since they'd last met. Michelle held her friend at arm's length when they separated and for a profound moment, found herself staring into her past.

"Is something wrong?" Melanie asked.

"Heavens no!" Michelle said, struggling to contain her emotions. "To the contrary, I'm just so happy to see you!" And with that they hugged again. Wiping a tear from her eye, she grabbed one of Melanie's bags and said, "Come on, let me show you inside."

They walked arm-in-arm along the stone walk through the courtyard, engaged in rambling gossip. The camaraderie was interrupted when Nick yelled his welcome from his perch against a porch column.

"Nick!" Melanie hollered back and, with a repeat of her reunion with Michelle, took off across the remaining expanse of walkway and up the wooden steps where she leapt into his arms. "It's so good to see you again!"

"Great to see you too. Safe travels?"

"Yes, thank you. It was a nice ride, no problems. I was so happy when Michelle invited me down. I've never been to this part of the country." Melanie stepped beside Michelle, who'd just made it up the steps, to take in the grandness of the porch and entranceway to Ashley House. "I'm so happy for both of you," she said, leaning into Michelle. "I mean, who wouldn't want to *have* to work in South Carolina and stay in a neat place like this? It's magnificent."

"Come on inside, then, and let me introduce you to the person responsible." Inside, they found Chris in the parlor room organizing his satchel, getting ready to leave. "Chris, you don't have to go," Nick urged. "Please stay." Chris stopped his fumbling and stood. "Melanie, this is Chris Orrey, the one who finagled our client into letting us stay here as their guest. Chris, Melanie…Sutton. I'm sorry. It is just Sutton now, right?"

"Yep, just Sutton. No more yada yada," Melanie said, bubbly as always. She thrust out her hand. "Please, call me Mel."

Chris grasped her hand and with his best attempt at Southern hospitality said, "Well, 'Please call me Mel,' you may call me Chris." The gesture was entirely out of character for Chris, his voice tinny and constricted. Melanie curtseyed with exaggerated formality. Chris offered a goofy smile in return.

Michelle giggled at the exchange, which she likened to the courting dance of the whooping crane.

"So, Mel," Nick interrupted. "Have you eaten? Chris and I were about to put a couple of steaks on the grill. There's always room for one more. I can also rustle up some shrimp if you prefer."

"That would be great if it's not too much trouble. I am rather hungry. I'll have shrimp if there's enough."

"No trouble at all," Nick said, turning to Michelle to keep from laughing at Chris who was staring dumbly at Melanie, oblivious to the spectacle he'd become. "How about you?" he asked her.

Michelle said that she too wanted shrimp and would take a bite of his steak. Michelle then whisked Melanie upstairs to her room to unpack.

"What was that all about? I didn't know we were having dinner."

"Could you have been any more obvious?" Nick cracked.

"What?" Chris said, drawing his beer to his lips.

Nick gave him the once over. "Uh, huh. I hope you don't melt like that if we have to go to court." It was a not so secret fact that black-haired, dark-complexioned women were Chris's kryptonite. "Does the Lady Lumberjack Competition ring any bells?"

Chris shot beer out his nose. "Really?" he cackled, wiping the wet spots off the floor with his shoe. "Again?"

"You were going down that road." Nick said, shaking his head. He was referring to the near fight Chris caused back in their Oregon days with a burly woodcutter over his ogling of a shapely, young Siuslaw woman wearing a plaid flannel shirt tied off at the midriff, who was carving a likeness of Bigfoot out of an inverted pine log.

"He was a big sonofobitch."

"Quite," Nick admitted.

"How was I to know she was his girlfriend? Come on, chicks with chainsaws? You can hardly fault me there."

"I'll give you that. She was gorgeous, though you should have figured that one of those bags of sawdust standing around us was her old man."

Chris stole a quick look upstairs and whispered, "In my defense, you should have warned me that Michelle's friend looks like Catherine Zeta-Jones. What a hottie. And those eyes! I could fall right into them. They're so dark and liquidy."

"Tell me about it," Nick said. "I thought that I was looking at a ghost. Garret had eyes like his sister. I'd forgotten how much they resembled one another, only Garret didn't have Mel's hair color or skin tone. Memory serves she's the only one in the family to exhibit their Spanish lineage."

"How could I forget? The Curse of Coronado connection." Chris's demeanor then turned serious when he asked if Nick was fine with her staying at the house.

Nick took in a deep breath. "Yeah, I'm fine. You know, Chris, I don't think I'll ever be over him. I still miss Garret, sometimes. I really do. I miss the Garret who was my best friend. It's a little awkward, but I'm glad she's here. Mel's a positive reminder of all the good times we shared before it all went to hell."

Laughter upstairs chased the melancholy away. "Come on, Chris," Nick said with a start, "let's fire up the grill and get you better acquainted with Miss Melanie."

The boys went to the caretaker's apartment garage to rummage through the clutter for the grill and propane tank. "You don't think I made a bad first impression do you?" Chris asked.

"Not at all," Nick managed through his struggle with a stand of obstinate beach umbrellas that refused to remain standing. "She didn't realize a thing."

"*Ex-Cellent!* Do you know then if she's seeing anyone?"

Chris's near social blunder set the stage for a spontaneous evening to remember. As it turned out, there weren't enough steaks to go around, and only a paltry number of previously rejected shrimp remaining in the freezer, so the boys made a dash to the grocery store, where they filled two baskets with gulf-side surf and per-diem-sized turf to go along with a small mountain of vegetables, two more six packs, and several bottles of wine. It was a perfect evening for grilling out, and afterwards, a relaxing walk through the residential neighborhoods and a loop around Colonial Lake. Played out, they settled in to gossip on the balcony where soft music played from Michelle's iPhone and the resident insect population made bug sounds off in the night.

Melanie Sutton was the life of the party, with her ability to command every situation and her infectious personality that made everyone feel they were the center of attention. It was as if she were the host. It was like October, 1990 all over again, when Melanie appeared on Michelle's doorstep, a ray of much needed sunshine when her life remained mired in the physical and emotional horrors inflicted by Melanie's twin two summers before. Sure, she added to the conversation here and there, but mostly Michelle enjoyed listening to Chris and Nick answer Melanie's questions about their line of work.

Melanie impressed with her knowledge and passion for environmental matters. She piqued Nick's interest with her participation in a clean water activist group that worked with Michigan state and local officials to rehabilitate surface water contaminated by a century-plus years of copper mining in the Keweenaw area. She impressed Chris with her description of the wolf relocation projects she co-sponsored. It just so happened Chris was wearing a t-shirt with a large wolf's head screen printed on the back. Nick gave them all a good laugh when he asked if the shirt was made special for an Orrey family reunion; the resemblance was uncanny. Mostly, though, Melanie was interested in Chris's vagabond lifestyle, living wherever the legal realm took him, which gave them much in common. Michelle winked at Nick and he at her: a budding romance perhaps? Michelle thought they looked good together.

Melanie further fueled Chris's interest by engaging him in a lively discussion about her recent working trip to Idaho, where, she was proud to say, she volunteered her time to photograph gray wolves to raise public awareness about the indiscriminate killing of wolves on public lands. Michelle was intrigued at the effortless manner in which Melanie exposed Chris's personal side. He was quite the endearing speaker when he wanted to be. It was during this revealing moment that Michelle realized that the answer to her literary impasse was sitting beside her. Melanie was the perfect foil to what gave every indication of becoming another dark story. Conner Lewis, Michelle was certain, would approve.

Success isn't always what it's cracked up to be. Take book reviews, for instance: they work both ways and at times can be downright irksome. While it was true *Ghost Creek* was well received, certain critics couldn't keep themselves from taking what in Michelle's opinion were undue liberties with her work when describing the book as too dark, too brooding, and—Yikes!—too depressing. The climax, one critic went so far as to say, was too graphic and fraught with gore.

Michelle argued that the remarks were cutting, unfair; that such opinions were just plain dumb because these so-called experts certainly skipped the epilog. Simply put, *Ghost Creek* was a coming-to-terms piece, written during her convalescence as a disaster survivor so that she could be reborn. The book was dark because it was factual and needed to be…and, oh yes, it *was* uplifting at the end. What didn't they get? Well skilled in the art of coddling client egos, Connor Lewis said that she was too protective of her work. "The people have spoken," he encouraged, "and they loved it! A heavy read, however, isn't for everyone. With this new book I want to see conflict meted out with an equal dose of inspiration, not added on like a condiment at the end." Whatever. Point taken.

This was easier said than done. From the moment she'd chosen the foreboding title, Michelle struggled to devise a means to balance out the many possible gloomy elements sure to litter the book's pages. Sure, she promised to give the Breckenridge faithful their due to atone for making the ski haven out to be some western version of Burkettsville, a mecca for Blair Witchesque flatlanders seeking to check a demon or ghoul off of their bucket list. But what if they were still resentful? And who knew where her inquiry into the lost skeleton might lead? And then there was Jodi to contend with. Why not throw in an earthquake or mine cave-in and make it a real hoot.

Still missing until now was the special interest story Connor Lewis had mentioned way back when the project began, a parallel focus on something that was uplifting. Melanie was the epitome of the feel-good story of triumph over despair she needed—the perfect counterweight to whatever moldy old Badger Heart had up his sleeve. Michelle closed her eyes and continued to listen to Melanie and Chris delight in one another's company.

Michelle flinched at a cold sensation brushing against her cheek. It was Nick. He was amusing himself and the others by touching her wine glass to her face. "Hey! Cut it out," she demanded. Laughing along with the others, she explained that she was thinking, not dozing.

"Care to share?" Nick asked. "You were staring at me and didn't even react when I got up to refill your drink."

"Or pay a lick of attention to a word we've said," Melanie teased. "About our trip, I hope?" she begged, fists clenched in childlike anticipation.

"You could say that," Michelle said. "Fill you in later," she said, smiling. "And no, Nick, it's nothing worth mentioning, except to Mel. It's a girl thing. Now what did I miss?"

"Well!" Melanie answered, "I was about to explain to Chris that I am a photographer and that's how I ended up working in Idaho."

"Yes!" Michelle interjected, relieving Nick of her wine glass. "Her pictures are beautiful! Chris, you must check out her web site."

"Do tell," Chris said coyly. "I'm a bit of a photo buff myself."

"Really? What kind of camera do you have? " Melanie asked.

Nick struggled to keep from choking on his beer. Chris had no photographic skills whatsoever and was succumbing again to kryptonite's pull. "Here we go," he said hoping that Chris would take the hint.

No, of course not. Instead of rallying himself, Chris dug himself a full shovel's worth deeper when he answered with a nonchalant, "Oh, it's a Nikon. I shoot whatever strikes my eye," and, sealing his fate, he framed his hands into the shape of an imaginary camera and used an index finger to pretend snapping pictures. Nick found a reason to excuse himself. Michelle put a hand to her mouth to stifle whatever might escape.

Melanie sat up arrow straight in her papa san, pinched her eyes to a tight line, and for a tantalizing moment, scrutinized Chris and his trigger finger as it gasped out one last, lame click. The jig was up. Her liquidy eyes steeped with mischief, she challenged, "So you're a point and shoot kinda guy?"

It wasn't so much what she said but her delivery and Chris's response when she touched his knee that made Nick and Michelle burst with laughter.

Chris recoiled like a cat whose foot had just slipped into water. "It has a really big lens," he babbled, his fingers now formed into a great circle.

"Uh-huh," Melanie retorted with a "what the hell's that supposed to mean?" look that turned Chris into a crimson-faced ball of mush.

Nick rescued Chris from himself. "It does. I'm not kidding. Big honking thing that manages to capture at least one finger in every frame!" He clapped Chris on his shoulder, shunting the focus back onto Melanie by saying to him, "In all seriousness, Ansel, you have to check out her web site. Mel's photos are remarkable."

"Thank you! And I like the reference. Ansel Adams is my inspiration," Melanie admitted, her face becoming as ruddy as her dusky complexion could allow. At Nick's urging, Melanie explained her niche within the U.P. artisan circle. "I'm old school. I use a standard camera and develop the film in my own darkroom."

"That's refreshing," Chris commented. "I thought everyone uses a digital camera these days. Do you have a specialty?"

"Landscape photography. My medium of choice is black and white. For the most part, I still use the first camera I ever bought. It doesn't have many bells or whistles, but do you know what's funny? It takes much better photos than any of my higher-end cameras."

"That's interesting," Nick grunted.

"Isn't that crazy?" Melanie agreed, slapping her hands on her thighs.

"Black and white? Fascinating," Chris said. "I have to ask—"

Versed at responding to the question, Melanie tapped on the link to her web site and passed her phone to Chris. "*Oh!*" he said.

"Yeah," she said, admiring her own work. "I find black and white soulful, much more so than color. I don't take a black and white photo for the picture's sake either," she said with pride. "Does that make sense? That's what my digital is for. Professionally, I only shoot scenery or situations that move me. Something about the subject has to move me, stir emotion, so I wait until the moment presents itself. You probably think that's artsy-fartsy."

"Not at all," Michelle said in defense of her friend. "I can tell from looking at your photos that you see the world at a whole other level. That's why they're so good."

Melanie accepted the compliment in stride. "It's the power inspired by the moment that makes a photo great."

"Like the impact of that photo of Muhammad Ali standing over Sonny Liston," Chris said.

"Exactly!"

This time when she tapped Chris on the knee, he didn't so much as twitch. Rather, he stared across at Nick with an *I'm cured!* mien that set Nick off again.

"What's so funny?" Melanie asked.

"Never mind those two," Michelle said with a frown. "They're behaving like children."

"Right," Melanie deadpanned, raising a brow of her own. Keeping with the sports theme, she expanded on Chris's comment. "I was thinking of *The Goal*, actually."

"Ooh!" Nick said with reverence. "Bobby Orr's game winning overtime goal in the 1970 Stanley Cup finals."

"Get out! You get a star, too!" Melanie praised her *other* child.

This time it was Nick who sat straight in his seat to give himself a self-congratulatory pat. Chris responded with a Bronx cheer that charmed a laugh from the girls.

"What makes that photo great," Melanie explained between giggles, "is the euphoria on Orr's face as he's flying through the air. It's the embodiment of how a great moment should feel. It's that kind of emotion I hope to capture in my photography."

"Is this a special one?" Nick asked, referring to her web page background, a striking black and white photo of a group of daisy-like flowers in front of a split rail fence. The photo was so crisp that even the silver-gray shafts of sunlight appeared three-dimensional. Nick picked the phone up from the ottoman. He tilted the tiny screen in Michelle's direction before handing the phone to Chris.

"Yes, it's my favorite. My first and best client, the one who enabled me to become a full-time photographer in the first place—bless his heart—is a Civil War buff. He's originally from Maryland and commissioned me to go to Sharpsburg to photograph some of the famous landmarks from the battle of Antietam. I was reluctant at first. I'm not a war buff by any means and couldn't wrap my head around what I should be looking for that would suit his interest. I mean the war's been over a century and a half, right? I called him to back out of the offer and found myself invited to a business lunch where he showed me this book about the battle. The destruction was horrifying. He wanted me to create a collage of then-and-now photos based on the ones taken by Alexander Gardner, who documented the aftermath within days of the battle. In his words, he wanted to 'honor the blood shed on the terrible September day.' He challenged me to 'capture time in a bottle on the bloodiest day in American history for future generations to marvel at the sacrifices made in the name of human spirit.' I remember that because I made him say it again so that I could write it down. I still wasn't sure exactly what he meant, nor if I'd recognize the moment when it presented itself."

"Looks to me like you nailed it," Chris praised. "What does this one represent?"

"I call it, *Hope for the Future*, in honor of the men who fought at the Sunken Road for three and a half hours on September 17, 1862. The results from that project are by far my best work."

"What happened?" Nick asked.

"I was standing on this paved country road. Above, on the steep bank to my left, Union forces of the Irish Brigade shot at Confederate troops from North Carolina on the opposite bank. I swear there was no more than fifty feet separating those closest to the front. The fighting was so terrible that the section of road I was standing along is also called Bloody Lane."

"*Eeww!*" Michelle shuddered.

"Tell me about it. Something like five thousand of the sixteen thousand men who fought on that area of battlefield became casualties."

"Wow!" Chris said. "That's horrible."

"Incomprehensible. I climbed the embankment to where the Confederates fought and that's where I saw these," she said pointing to the flowers on the phone screen. "I just got this really creepy feeling, an otherworldly sensation that I was both there and here at the same time. I could hear the appalling roar of gunfire; men shouting, others screaming, still others moaning where they fell while their comrades fired volley after volley at the Federals across the way. There was this frenetic energy of just trying to stay alive churning all around me, and yet there I was standing alone on a hazy summer morning that couldn't have been any more delightful. It was a total contradiction. And there they were, this little grouping of black-eyed susans poking out from the long grass along a split rail fence. That's when I knew that, if I could capture the essence of what I was feeling at that particular moment through those beautiful flowers, I would have time captured in a bottle."

Her spellbound audience stole wide-eyed glances at one another.

"Those flowers, they spoke to me. I saw in them all of the emotion, all of the blood poured out on that battlefield so long ago in the name of god and country—in the name of freedom. The flowers represent the men themselves, a reminder that even in the worst of times a better future, a stronger future, lay ahead so long as we want it to be."

"You're a powerful speaker, Mel," Chris said solemnly.

"You're not going to cry, are you?" Nick teased him, discerning the choke in his voice. Chris scratched the end of his nose with his middle finger.

The conversation meandered after that until well past midnight. It concluded with what Michelle had on tap for her and Melanie come morning. Mere mention of that party killer tempted a yawn from Melanie and, for Chris, a look at his watch. He regretted to say that it was already morning and that he had better take his leave if he and Nick were going to be worth anything in the day ahead. Nick walked Chris to the door. Melanie said that she should turn in as well. Michelle waited for the boys to take their closing discussion outside when she turned to Melanie and said, "I need to talk to you about something upstairs."

CHAPTER 4

THURSDAY

U.S. Rt. 70
St. Louis, Mo.
8:37 P.M.

The girls awoke before sunrise to the sound of Mrs. Mockingbird's morning ritual of jumbled bird noises. To and fro they scurried about Ashley House like a couple of kids, grabbing every conceivable something that might prove fun, or necessary, on their journey. Nick gave up offering advice the night before during the first round of last minute desperation packing. He wrongly assumed that purchasing any forgotten items at the local Wal-Mart was a good idea.

Michelle dropped two armloads of luggage at her feet behind the rear hatch and stretched her arms toward a cloudless sky. Melanie shuffled along behind with a load of her own; and behind her, Nick strained with much of the rest. It was still early, much too early for the morning traffic into the old port city to build. Michelle closed her eyes to revel in the moment. She snapped her fingers as a physical reminder to jot down her thoughts in the notebook stashed away in her daypack on the back seat before they drove off, so that she could recount them later in her book.

"*Aww!* Look at the kitties," Melanie gushed, pointing across the street to where Jordy with the low-slung pants and his friend had disrupted Michelle's file-sorting project days before. There, three cats basked in the warmth on adjacent porches, watching the goings on up and down Ashley Avenue.

Michelle promised to capture that moment as well.

"Holy shit, you two brought enough footgear to outfit a third-world nation," Nick groused, dropping his burden into the rear compartment of the SUV. "Why on earth did you bring all this inside?"

Michelle gave him her annoyed look. "How are we supposed to know what to wear?"

"It's South Carolina in the summer," Nick countered. "How many choices can there be?" The hairy eyeball he received in return was all he needed to know that there was no sense in trying to make sense of the matter, so he did what was expected and went back inside to fetch a second load. It was a good thing Michelle rented an SUV for what he thought was supposed to be an interview and note-taking mission. They would need all the room that the vehicle could spare.

The Highlander pulled away from the curb not long thereafter. Michelle waved goodbye into the rearview mirror. Nick waved back until the war wagon with "Colorado or Bust" fingered into the hatch-window dust passed out of view on Bull Street.

The first call to order was breakfast. Michelle wanted to reenact her mid-eighties maiden voyage to Colorado and stopped at a McDonald's near the interstate. She ordered her standard fare back then, a bacon-egg-and-cheese sandwich on a biscuit, a hash brown, and orange juice. "Oh, I almost forgot," she said, amending her order, "can I also have a small coffee with two creams and three sugars?" Melanie thought the idea cute and ordered the same, minus the extra sugars. On the walk back across the lot, Michelle recalled the euphoria she felt at the time.

"Sounds like you're reliving a life moment. I wish I could've been there to share it with you," Melanie said, opening the passenger-side door.

Happy in one another's company, it wasn't until the outskirts of Hendersonville, North Carolina loomed on the horizon, some four hours and a half tank of gas later, before they noticed that the sand and palmettoes had been left behind in favor of mountains and oak trees. For Michelle, this was the first time since she and Tracy went on a spur-of-the-moment weekend getaway to Bermuda several years back that she had the pleasure of another woman's company for an extended period. She delighted at how easy it was speaking with Melanie about the lively happenings of that heady summer field session in 1985. If Melanie was at all uncomfortable, she didn't show it. To the contrary, Melanie was grateful to learn a little more about the brother she had lost.

They stretched their legs at a travel plaza west of Knoxville. Verbally spent from the hours of non-stop talking, they spoke little from the time Michelle turned on the blinker to pull off the highway to when Melanie sidled up beside her in front of the travel kiosk back outside the facility. The necessities taken care of, they sized up their progress on a sun-bleached travel map. Michelle traced the course west from their location to St. Louis, their destination for the evening. "Only several more inches. That isn't so bad," Melanie commented.

Michelle uttered a mirthful chirp when she caught her friend stealing a strained look at the mileage chart.

"I'll drive for a while," Melanie offered.

Michelle declined. "Maybe after the next stop."

The conversation resumed where it left off several miles later when Michelle, in a mischievous moment, remarked about the freakish collection of humanity milling about the travel plaza. Melanie was thinking the very same and burst out laughing, this precipitating an epic fit of juvenile digression. They laughed until their sides ached and tears rolled down their cheeks, right up until the moment was interrupted by the startling *WHOOP* of a police siren. Frazzled, Michelle looked into the rearview mirror, and then to Melanie who was jabbing at the air for her to look to her left. Michelle turned in slow motion to find a young statie in an unmarked squad car in the passing lane, instructing her to slow down. Michelle thought she actually saw the officer smile before he blew past. "We still got it!" Melanie applauded their youthful appearance, as Michelle took her foot off the gas.

"He looked like he was twelve," Michelle replied. And once the adrenaline rush had passed reminded Melanie, "You could be his mother!"

"*T-r-u-e*," Melanie said, drawing out the word, "but I'm not getting any younger, you know."

The exchange facilitated a fresh round of joking that lasted until the post-adolescent deputy was safely out of view.

Melanie used the diversion to again thank Michelle for letting her tag along. "I'm having the best time."

"Heavens, the pleasure's all mine. You can't possibly know how much this means to me, considering that little bombshell I dropped on you the other night." Michelle had sprung the *Jodi saga* on Melanie Tuesday evening after Chris had left. She tested the waters again yesterday morning over breakfast, before they embarked on an epic shopping spree along the King Street strip. At best, she expected Melanie to be angry with her for not being forthcoming. To the contrary, Melanie found the danger factor enthralling.

"Of course I still want to go," Melanie reassured her. "Like I already told you, I want to put this behind me once and for all. My life, my family's lives—yours and Nick's too—they've all been turned upside down by what Garret did, and now this, whatever *it* is?" Melanie collected her thoughts. "I understand why you have to do this, Michelle. I also appreciate Nick's position, and why you couldn't tell him about this Jodi person. That's why I would never let you go alone, let alone pass on the opportunity for closure—and, well…some excitement. I finally get to be *you*!"

Michelle thanked her for the compliment.

"By gosh," Melanie said, stomping her foot, "we'll get to the bottom of this Jodi thing together! You know, Michelle, it seems to me that your book is writing itself."

That's interesting, Michelle thought. Melanie was right; it was. Still, she had trouble seeing herself as a heroine, though the idea was growing on her.

Melanie's thoughts spun off in another direction. Fear-factor excitement or not, the cryptic emails bothered her. "You said that Jodi's emails started about two weeks ago, after you first mentioned wanting to find out what happened to that old skeleton you found, right?"

"Rather, I fell into," Michelle corrected in a way that made light of her misfortune.

"You also said that you've been talking with the Conservancy for months now, and that there aren't any issues, other than visiting the mines…and that the lawyers worked those details out."

"Uh-huh. Why?"

Melanie disregarded the question. Drumming her fingers on the armrest, she asked, "You've spoken to everyone who works there?"

"Most, I think, the important ones, anyway. There's Teddy Monroe and Bill Clay. I've spoken to both of them once. I gather they're somewhere in the middle of the command food chain. And Beth Stockwell, of course, she's my primary contact, and the one who I think is Jodi. Beth's also mentioned a Joe something or other—Hayden. Joe Hayden—who they all report to, if I got it right. I've not spoken to him…and a Bud Walker—he's up there in the food chain as well; I haven't spoken with him, either. I've also heard other voices in the background from time to time when speaking with Beth. They sounded young, perhaps junior staff or maybe they were just visitors. Why? What are you thinking?"

"That none of this makes any sense. I don't get it."

"Tell me about it," Michelle lamented.

"Seriously. Think about it, Michelle. You say that we're going to have an escort."

"Right."

"What then are we possibly going to find out? What's the chance of running into that one remaining someone who just *might* be able to recall anything about a skeleton that vanished without a trace decades ago? The land trust people? I don't think so. Likewise, if it's something else, we're not going to find out anything about that either. They're only going to tell us what they want us—*you*—to hear."

Chris had pretty much said the same thing the other night. "You think I'm wasting our time," Michelle said coolly.

"No, silly!" Melanie replied, frustrated that Michelle didn't get it. "I think something's up, and that this Beth person, if she is Jodi, wants you to figure out what's going on."

Michelle's face erupted into a broad smile. "That's exactly what I was thinking," Michelle said, relieved that she was not alone in her opinion. "You can't imagine how happy I am to hear you say that."

"So you do think something's up. Why didn't you say so before?" Melanie asked, giving Michelle a shove.

"I wasn't sure what to think," Michelle said honestly. "I thought you might think that I was crazy." This prompted a burst of laughter that ended in a deep, resonant sigh that spoke volumes. Michelle then asked if Melanie thought the emails were a call for help.

"Perhaps. It could be that, too. Then refining her thought, she said, "Yes, I do. There must be a reason why she can't go to the police herself." Thinking a little more, Melanie added, "And if they—Tarryall, I mean—are hiding something, they can't say or do anything too obvious that might jeopardize their position because—"

"I'm the one writing the book," Michelle rejoined, this time completing her friend's thought on cue. "Huh!" Michelle clucked. "I'm the one who's actually in control. I didn't think about it that way."

"Exactly! That's my conclusion. At least that's what it seems like to me. Michelle, you are in control, and Jodi is hoping that you'll piece all the clues together and unravel the truth."

They drove on. Michelle ruminated on their breakthrough in the Jodi conundrum. If it was a call for help, the focus of her new book had just taken a juicy turn.

They passed a billboard shaped like a giant percolator that read, *"Keep alert and out of the dirt. Stop at Coffey's for a cup of Joe!"* The corny propaganda sparked a funny-bone response that churned

Rick Ley

off several more miles. Their good humor waned when the oblique reference to danger teased Melanie to comment about how one minute they were hoping to avoid trouble, and the next they might be diving headlong into it. "Now I can see why you decided to write children's books."

Michelle replied with a not so facetious, "Ha!"

"Oh, no! What happened?"

"I can't win for losing," Michelle said with a deprecatory chuckle. "I'm not sure if I told you, but we're only here because my agent brought up this project while I was working out a graphics issue with my latest children's book."

"*Really?* How so?" Melanie slouched against the passenger door, staring back with a curious look, waiting to hear all about her hero's next journey into happenstance.

Michelle blew a curl away from her face to reveal that there actually could be a sinister side to children's literature. "Only I could incite a riot at a children's-book signing."

"Do tell!" Melanie dared, having now adjusted herself into a cross-legged position without so much as unfastening the restraint.

"I should back up," Michelle said with a small huff. "The riot and graphics snafu were not part of the same children's-book project, though they rather rolled into one another."

"Got it!" Melanie said, more intrigued than before.

Michelle trilled her lips. "I was promoting my latest book at a local nature center this past Mother's Day weekend. It's one of those places where they have educational classes for both kids and adults. The center is located in a park that has walking trails and a stream that feeds this gorgeous pond. The group running the facility approached me a while back and asked if I would write a children's book about how outdoor hobbies can teach kids about the world around them. It was part of a bigger push in the area to promote physical education. You know, to get kids away from video games and back outdoors."

"That's a great idea," Melanie said.

"It is. And it's working out much better than anyone anticipated. The nature center started with a few interactive classes to bring parents and their children together to learn about nature in their own backyard, making decisions that limit environmental impact and promote habitat diversity, things like that. Heck, they now have a full slate of classes that includes everything from making observations while day hiking to learning about insects and wildflowers to rock collecting and making a fall leaf collection."

"I'm impressed!"

"Seriously," Michelle agreed. "They were conducting the first stream study of the season the morning that I was there. You should have seen how much fun the kids had flipping over rocks, looking for bugs clinging to the undersides."

"Ooh! I used to love to do that!" Melanie clamored. "I can remember the first time my brother Brad showed me a crayfish. He called it a crab and threw it at me."

"*Boys!*" They chimed in unison.

"Some things never change. It must be hard-wired into them. I was supposed to be helping out with the identifications, but ended up spending most of my time saying things like '*Stop splashing*,' '*Now, go wash your hands*,' '*Leave that alone*,' and '*Quit throwing things at your sister.*' It was a real educational experience—*for me!* The girls were no trouble whatsoever. No wonder I never had kids; I might have had a boy. I've had enough of my own problems."

Melanie agreed, whole-heartedly.

"The book I decided to write was about conservation and fishing. How many kids do you see fishing these days?"

Melanie shrugged.

"When we finished with the stream study, the nature center served complimentary snacks and I started my program. I signed a few books and was finishing a discussion about how creel limits and size limits not only maintain the resource, but can greatly improve the quality of the fishery, when this man didn't just interrupt the program, he started yelling at me!"

"No!" Melanie gasped.

"It was frightening. *'You should be teaching them to leave the fish alone, not KILL them!'* he ranted. *'You should be ashamed of yourself...teaching kids to be MURDERERS!'* I'll have to show you a video tape of the seminar." Michelle got so worked up she started to fume, her knuckles turning white from her fingernails digging into the steering wheel.

"What did you do?"

"Laid into him, is what I did. I practically flipped the table over, I stood up so fast. First I gave him hell for his behavior; then I hammered him on the absurdity of his position. Ever since the EcoGenesis fiasco, I've had it up to here—*Ouch!*" Michelle jammed her fingers into the headliner with her theatrics.

"Are you okay?"

"Yeah," Michelle said, flexing them. "What I was trying to say is that I've had it up to here with people who can't tell the difference between a salmon and a sailfish trying to brainwash people with their bullying tactics. We're stewards of this planet and shouldn't be made to feel guilty about using its resources, all to meet some idiot's self-aggrandizing agenda. Is there a time and place for voicing one's opinion? Of course there is, but there, in the middle of the presentation—in front of the children like that? No way. Some people need to be taught a lesson in respect and decorum, so I let the jerk have it."

"You go, girl!"

Calming down, Michelle continued. "Ban fishing—or hunting for that matter—and you lose a lot of people who understand and care about the very environment that the preservationists want to protect."

"You're saying that people won't support what they can't enjoy."

"Exactly, Mel. The very resource you're trying to protect becomes at risk of neglect or exploitation because those who care eventually lose interest if they can't appreciate their passions first hand...in the field, so to speak. You end up with not enough people with the means or power to fight the fight. That's what those people don't get."

"I see your point," Melanie said. "What happened to the guy?"

"As you can probably imagine, he didn't take kindly to someone like me shoveling his shit back at him. When I reminded him that he didn't pay attention to the part about catch and release because all he was interested in was hearing his own gums flap, he lunged at me."

"You're kidding? Tell me somebody stopped him."

"You could say that!" Michelle trumpeted. "The moment he came after me, several dads rushed in to restrain him. One held him down with a foot on his back. Of course, all the kids were crying at that point. It was a mess. Thankfully, a police cruiser was making a pass through the park at the time. He settled everyone down. As for the guy, the officer arrested him for disorderly conduct and aggravated assault."

Melanie was speechless. Michelle gave her a *'See what I mean?'* look. A bump in the road later, Melanie changed the subject. "So, what's the name of your latest problematic children's book?"

"Ramón the Rascally Remora."

The silence was deafening. Melanie wanted to burst, but was curious to learn more. Michelle felt the tips of her ears grow hot.

"It was a big misunderstanding," Michelle explained. "The artist's name was Mike and I thought he made Ramón look…too Hispanic."

"Too Hispanic?" Melanie snickered.

"Ye-ah!" Michelle said, laboring on the word. "The last thing I wanted was for parents to think that I was some kind of bigot or racist."

Another snicker.

"I asked Connor, my agent, if he would talk with Mike and ask him to tone it down a notch. Connor asked and Mike got all upset. Get this! He thought I was being prejudiced against Latinos.

"No way!"

"Way!" Michelle said, in *Wayne's World* fashion. "It turns out that his given name is Miguel. When I saw his picture on his web site, I realized that Miguel made Ramón look like himself, sombrero

and all, just like in his studio publicity still…Artists! I could've died. Connor talked him off his artist's ledge, and I apologized. I told Mike that I meant him no offense and would keep Ramón in all his Pancho Villa likeness. See what I mean? Trouble has a way of finding me."

"You told him that he looked like a Mexican mercenary, or whoever Pancho Villa was?"

"No, silly! Of course not."

Melanie waited to hear more. Michelle pushed her over the edge when she described her character's appearance. "Wait until you see the little fella. Ramón's so cute with his under bite and pencil-thin moustache."

"You're too much! My sides are killing me," Melanie panted, bending forward, fanning at the air.

"No kidding," Michelle said, laughing alongside. "My stomach feels like I just did a hundred sit-ups! I haven't laughed this much, for this long, in ages."

Melanie got a hold of herself and asked what the book was about.

"It's about symbiotic relationships among ocean creatures, like how two organisms that should lead a predator-prey relationship live side-by-side for some mutually beneficial purpose."

Melanie's eyes wandered as if they were following the amblings of a fly. "A remora, what are they, exactly?"

"They're those skinny fish that attach themselves to sharks and other large fish and sea turtles."

"Yes! Yes! I know the ones you mean. Sharks don't eat them?"

"No, they don't; hence the symbiosis. At least no remora has ever been found in a shark's stomach, as far as I've read. The remora saves energy being pulled around by the shark and feeds on the scraps of food drifting about that the shark leaves behind. In return, the remora cleans parasites off of the shark's skin."

Relieved to hear that Ramón's living kin were safe from becoming sushi, Melanie asked, "I take it that there's a shark in the story? Does it also have a name?"

"Yes. His name is Timmy—Timmy the Tiger Shark. He's twelve feet long and is proud of his pretty stripes. Timmy and Ramón are BFFs."

"That's so sweet!" Melanie fawned. "Where do they hang out when they're not hungry?"

The girl talk waxed and waned as the morning turned into afternoon. Somewhere in the reaches of southwestern Kentucky, Michelle's cell phone rang, breaking up a lively conversation about, of all things, the upcoming fantasy football season. It was Nick. "Hi Nick! Great, we're having a wonderful time. What's up? Uh-huh. Where are we? We just passed Paducah. Yeah, we're making really good time. Michelle pulled the phone away from her ear. "Nick says hi. Mel says hi back. What? Really? A little bit ago, you say. Uh-huh. That's super! You'd better! No, you go! Thanks for calling." Michelle signed off.

"What's happening?" Melanie asked.

"Nick said that they just found more oil on PSTRE's property."

Melanie had gained a working knowledge of the rudiments of the case from listening to the others over the past several days. "That means that they got them, right?"

Michelle mulled this over. "Not necessarily, though it is a good sign. Nick and Chris are heading to the site now." Excited by the news, Michelle yammered on about how Nick was enjoying the high stakes realm of environmental litigation consulting, working alongside Chris. It was important, she said, for Nick to put on a good showing for both Chris and their client so that he would be invited back for future work; preferably in another nice place like Charleston. She also prattled on about the rejuvenation she'd felt since delving back into the real world for the first time in over two decades. Melanie, though, didn't seem to share her enthusiasm. Finding Melanie staring off into the distance, Michelle asked what was wrong.

For a while, Melanie said nothing. Fixated by the rolling waves of corn, the tops of which forming a stark line beneath the angry blush of clouds from a distant storm, she thought how best to ask a very personal question that was important to her. It was a question about Michelle's relationship with her deceased brother. "Do you think of Garret often?" she asked when she was ready. "I mean, do you ever think what it would've been like if things were different? Like, if Garret wasn't who he had become? What it would have been like if the two of you had stayed together and gotten married?"

There it was: the question Michelle had prepared herself to answer ever since she and Nick married and moved on with their lives. The funny thing was, Michelle couldn't think of a thing to say.

"I didn't mean to pry. Forget I even asked," Melanie backpedaled.

Michelle kicked herself for her brain's failure to recite what should have been an automatic response. "Oh, Mel! It's no problem at all. Yes, I do think of him often. Particularly this past year since I've been working so much with Nick. It's hard not to. I will *always* carry a piece of him in my heart."

"Thank you," Melanie said. "That means a lot. All my life, I've wanted to believe that Garret was a good person. I hope that he made you happy…at least to some point."

Michelle forced a sigh. A sniff was heard coming from the passenger's seat. Michelle and Melanie looked briefly at one another with glistening eyes. "My, yes," Michelle said. "There were times when he was just the most tender-hearted person."

"Can you share one?"

Michelle smiled. Keeping one eye on the road, she leaned in close and said, "He serenaded me once."

Melanie placed a hand to her mouth. "He didn't!"

Michelle crooked her lip. "It was a beautiful spring afternoon. We were down at the frat house. The windows were opened wide, the air as fresh as could be. Everyone was in a good mood. I was helping Garret clean his side of the room he shared with Nick—which, by the way, was atrocious, except for Garret's school stuff. That he kept neat as a pin."

"I can see that. I kinda remember him being much neater than me."

"Garret always was a neat freak. Anyway, Bad Company was my favorite band at the time, and I had this mad crush on Paul Rogers. I got Garret into listening to them. He put one of their cassettes into his boom box. When *Seagull* came on, he started singing."

"Oh, no!"

"Oh, yes!"

Melanie stared back, goggle-eyed. "I have to ask."

"It was the kindest, most horrible sound you could imagine!"

And that set off yet another round of giddiness. "He pretended to have a microphone in his hand and started swaying back and forth, singing into it—to me—bellowing away like a bull moose calling to his cow. I was sitting on the edge of the bed, cracking up the entire time."

Melanie prodded for more examples. She reached behind the seat for a bag of granola while Michelle searched her memory banks. Michelle thought of the perfect one, and in her excitement bumped Melanie's arm, causing the bag to spill. Peering to the floor, Melanie announced that if there were a mouse down there, he'd be well fed for quite some time. And then looking to Michelle, said, "Think of anything else?"

"Yes, but let me preface it by saying that it's a sad story with a fairy-tale ending."

"I'm all ears."

Michelle asked if Melanie minded if she used her microcassette recorder to document their conversation. Melanie said that was fine and set up the machine for her. Michelle began when she saw the sprocket spokes turning. "The summer after my sophomore year through spring of my junior year in college were hard times for me and my family. My dad passed unexpectedly after school let out sophomore year, and then my boyfriend at the time dumped me. If it weren't for Tracy, I don't know what I would have done. The return to school for the fall semester and leaving mom alone at home was also hard, even if it did provide the distraction I needed. That fall, of course, I met Garret, and for a couple of days felt like a carefree teenager all over again until—well, you know."

"How could I forget? I'm so sorry," Melanie said softly.

"Thanks. You may also recall that I went home to recuperate after the doctor stitched me up. Mom was so happy to see me. I really needed her. I was a real mess. Maybe that's why I didn't see it. I was so stupid. Mom asked if I'd like to stay with her, and not to go back to school. I remember looking at her strangely. As much as I needed my mom, the last thing I wanted to do was stay home to dwell on dad's passing. School was my escape. It kills me to this day that I didn't give it a second thought that maybe I was *her* escape. Mom made no further mention of it, and I didn't know what to say, so I said nothing and went back to Huron for the rest of the semester. That was a mistake. My knee responded slowly to therapy, and I was afraid to see your brother so soon afterward. I had no idea what I'd done to make him so angry with me."

"You poor thing." Melanie offered some granola.

"Appreciated," Michelle said, taking a handful. "Things didn't change much over Christmas break. Tracy was there for me, though she was madly in love with Nick at the time. She did her best to juggle the opposing emotions—to be with her boyfriend or to be there for me."

"I can imagine that being very hard for both of you."

"It was awkward. I didn't want to dampen her mood, so I— we—kinda pretended that Garret didn't exist, that the event never happened. Then, just before New Years, mom came to my room in tears. I always knew that we weren't a family of means. I just didn't know how much so."

Melanie tensed. "I don't think I like where this is going."

Michelle dabbed at her eye. "I'd gotten some scholarship money to go to Huron, but apparently that wasn't enough to cover the out-of-state tuition and room and board. Now that we were receiving less without dad, mom said that she could only scrape enough together to pay for the spring semester. After that, I would have to transfer to one of the state schools back home. I felt so guilty. I offered to leave Huron then and there. She surprised me and said no, that I needed to be with my friends; that she would think of something."

Melanie sniffed. "You must have felt like you were drowning."

"I did. It was like the world was caving in around me. The idea of being separated from Tracy was unthinkable. Then, remarkably, the semester started and things began going my way. Beyond my wildest imagination, I got back together with your brother from the get go, and that set off the weirdest, most exhilarating period of my life," Michelle said, with a lilt that fell in step with her reversal in fortune. "Our first brush with romance ends in colossal failure, and there we were again. We fell head over heels in love, yet were scared to death of each another. Does that make any sense? I was afraid that Garret would lash out again, and I think he was petrified that I'd run away if he did anything cross, which he didn't. I can honestly tell you that Garret was embarrassed, truly embarrassed, by what had happened in Canada."

Melanie's heart glowed.

"Not long after we reconnected, fliers went up on the zoology department message board about the annual writing competition. First prize was five thousand dollars. I was a good writer and thought that if I could win, it would help mom with my tuition. That year's topic was on environmental heritage. I wrote about something that was near and dear to me—the significance of tall-grass-prairie habitat across the Midwest, which was all but gone from places like Michigan and Ohio. I was psyched. I knew that I had a good chance of winning."

"Did you?"

"*No!*" Michelle said emphatically, deflating the emotion bubble she'd created. "I didn't even place. I was crushed. They were looking for topical environmental issues like acid rain, farm-field erosion, soil compaction, stuff that was all the rage at the time."

"What did you do?"

"I went back to my dorm and cried my eyes out. I wanted to get away from everyone. I was angry, embarrassed, and, most of all, humiliated for letting my mother down. I fell asleep at some point. I awoke feeling well enough to call home. The phone was a common one hung on the wall out in the hallway. We barely said hello and I started crying all over again. We must have talked for an hour, with me all huddled up and facing the wall with a finger plugged in my ear, trying to ignore the other girls who sneaked past like I had the plague, or something."

"That's so sad," Melanie said.

Michelle caught Melanie using the heel of her hand to wipe away a tear. Instead of joining her, Michelle spun the emotional dial around, and with a return of that familiar lilt, said, "What I didn't know was that Garret had come to see me while I was on the phone. He stopped when he heard me sobbing. I didn't know he was there. About the same time, a girl who roomed several doors down from me scurried past. She later told me that she gave Garret a crazy look and pointed for him to turn around and go the other way. Thank goodness he did. The last thing I needed was to scare him off now that we had something positive between us again."

"Aww!"

"Like two days later, I was walking into the dorm when the RA on duty said that a package had arrived for me, that I needed to see the RD. That was odd because personal deliveries were always held at the RA's desk, so I went down to the resident director's suite and knocked. Plain as day, I recall Sylvia saying, 'Boy are you lucky!' before she stepped aside, and there, on an end table, was this gorgeous purple and white orchid. The stalk and flower were so delicate that the RA was afraid to keep it at her desk where it could be accidently broken. I was stunned, speechless. My hands were shaking so much that I was afraid to touch it, let alone reach for the card."

"It was from Garret!" Melanie said, scooching her way closer.

Michelle closed her eyes and smiled. "He said, '*I hope this makes you feel better—Garret.*' It was short, sweet, perfect!"

"*YES!*" Melanie shouted with joy. This was the side of her brother she'd always hoped existed.

"It was a very expensive flower. It cost him like thirty dollars. Remember how much that was back then? When we were in Sudbury, he remembered me mentioning how much I liked orchids and that lavender was my favorite color. I never dreamed he would remember. Garret said that he called a local florist who, in turn, called around until she found one as close to lavender as she could. Garret actually skipped his classes one afternoon to drive all the way to Detroit to buy it. How he ever got it back without breaking the stalk, I'll never know. I got all weepy and shared a big hug with Sylvia, thinking that I was the luckiest girl in the world."

"You have no idea what it means for me to hear you say that," Melanie said. "So much about Garret has focused on the negative that it's hard to remember the good little boy I knew. I just knew that there had to be goodness inside of him. Beyond my earliest memories, I've had to piece together what his life was like. To be able to experience how he had found love—*found you*—is priceless. I can only hope that he treated you as well as he could and that, for a while, the two of you shared true love."

"Oh, my yes!" Michelle assured her. "We did for a very long while, and it was wonderful." Michelle remembered something. She craned her neck about and looked to the back seat. "Grab my pack, if you would. There's something I want to show you."

Melanie pulled Michelle's daypack between the seats and placed it on her lap. She unzipped it. "What is it?" she asked.

"You'll see." Michelle glanced into the opened pack. "There," she pointed.

From the bag, Melanie retrieved a clothbound book with a decorative floral print on the cover. She drew in a breath. "Your diary? Are you sure you want me to see this?"

"It's fine. There's nothing to hide…well" Michelle added playfully, "maybe a few things! Flip to the page I tabbed for you to read."

Curious, nervous, Melanie dared to peer into the innermost secrets of another woman's private life. It was a passage from the early days of Michelle's relationship with her brother; a snapshot in time when the writer's life was turned on its head in the throes of young love. "Are you really sure?" Melanie asked again. Michelle tapped her finger on the page and Melanie started to read:

"His eyes fascinate me. They're incredibly dark, without definition—mystical, I think! They're bright and have this devilish twinkle about them that makes me want to dive right in. I'm not sure yet what to make of him. I can't ignore that he hurt me, or the fact that he's apologized to no end…and I believe him. If I could only get Tracy, my great protector, to like him the way I do!"

Then, a little further down, Melanie found a second comment, this one penned in pink instead of green:

"His eyes are dreamy. If I could only crawl inside and take a look around. There's something very strange about them; they draw me in without my even trying (I cannot keep away!). I don't want to either…All the same, there's something disturbing about Garret I cannot deny. I know what I said before, and I kinda see why Tracy doesn't trust him like I do…To me, his mystique is like a hot knife and I'm a stick of butter. Where she sees lifeless eyes hiding inner rage, I see something totally different…a million and one little secrets hidden in those sexy, haunting eyes begging to be set free. I just hope that I'm the one to whom he hands the key!"

Melanie glossed over Tracy's repeated reference to Garret's dark side. He had made Michelle happy; that's what was important. "You had one of those clicky pens with all colors, too!"

"I did!" Michelle laughed. She said that she'd written the entries when she returned to her dorm room following the semester kick-off party at the Chi Zeta Rho fraternity house, where Garret and Nick shared their room. It was the same party where she and Garret officially reconnected. As expected, the diary entries launched an emotion-filled, roller coaster of a discussion about that evening. They touched on just about everything from what Michelle was thinking to the fraternity brother who introduced them to the Ghost Creek legend, to Tracy's long-standing distrust of Garret. The discussion even dabbled about the periphery of the time when, much later during their relationship, Michelle realized that she and Garret were no longer lovers but two ships passing in the night.

Remarkably, thankfully, no matter where the conversation took them, Melanie remained unflustered; her eagerness to learn more about the brother she barely knew was insatiable. In fact, it was Melanie who demanded to hear the truth about some less than savory *what if she asks* questions Michelle hoped to avoid. Kerry might be the psychiatrist in the family, but Michelle had no doubt that Melanie could give her sister a run for her money in the therapy game.

They chased a waning sun that eventually slipped below the horizon. Their day concluded not long thereafter at a Holiday Inn Express near the St. Charles historic district outside St. Louis. Michelle chose the destination as much for its quaintness as its proximity to Trailhead Brewing Company, where they shared a much-anticipated pub-grub dinner over a lively discussion about some of Melanie's fondest childhood memories of Garret.

MacDonald & Carlyle Law Firm, LLP
Broad Street, Charleston, S.C.
2:55 P.M.

Nick spent much of the morning on and off the phone with Sam

Piersall and Mindy Porter. A convenient opening in RCE's schedule enabled Piersall to respond to Chris's call following Tuesday afternoon's pow wow with M&C and mobilize a field crew to PSTRE to complete a punch list of loose ends in advance of tomorrow's meeting with Athens's lawyers. Nick liked working with RCE, the affable Piersall in particular, who embraced his support role on the case. "Can't stand lawyers," Piersall explained to Nick's amusement. "Now, you guys?" he was quick to add, referring also to Chris, "You two I can work with until the cows come home. Let me know how I can be of assistance." That was Piersall's closing comment to every technical discussion.

"Gotta love that Southern hospitality," Nick quipped to Chris during one of Chris's war-room flybys to see if they'd received the final revised base map. The constant manipulation of certain figures, only to come back around to a previous iteration, was something ingrained in environmental consultants that has frustrated graphics departments everywhere since the dawn of the industry.

With Chris and the lawyers busy elsewhere, and because there was nothing demanding his immediate attention, Nick decided he would take a stab at determining the groundwater-flow direction across the site, having tired of waiting for RCE's hydrogeologists to spit out the official computer-derived versions that Porter told him might not happen until the morning. Nick would use the pressure-transducer data from yesterday that Porter had forwarded to him. Granted, PSTRE wasn't obligated to share its findings just yet. All the same, there was nothing like waiting until the last moment to be assured that their case remained valid. This Nick could do without the latest iteration of the map.

Nick was proud to consider himself a member of the old guard, one who liked to get his hands dirty the old fashioned way, without the assistance of an off-the-shelf algorithm. *Feeling* the information, using a calculator and engineer's scale to crank out computations and then draw a sketch of what the water table looked like clarified his ability to interpret what might be going on in the subsurface in a way that technological conveniences never could. Connecting the dots to derive a series of equal elevation flow lines enabled him to think about the nuances that might affect flow, contaminant flow in particular, through the mix of fine-grained sediments, in what was blandly described in the geologic literature as *terrace deposits*.

He would use the water-table elevation data for all fifteen piezometers to create separate flow maps for five distinct times over the previous twenty-four-hour period: 2:00 A.M., 8:00 A.M., noon time, 4:00 P.M., and 10:00 P.M. These times bridged the lunar high and low tides for Charleston for yesterday. Nick omitted the production well from his maps when Porter told him that the transducer data for that well were still acting screwy. The mysterious chatter and wonky variations in the water-table elevation in the well continued to defy logic.

Nick started by jotting down the 2:00 A.M. water-level elevation next to each piezometer on a fresh copy of the base map. When finished, he looked at the distribution of the data and whistled. Groundwater elevations across the site were flat, incredibly so, varying by no more than four-hundredths of a foot, or 0.04 feet, between locations in any given direction. Not too surprising, the data revealed a broad flattened area across the central portion of the property. Because PSTRE and Athens occupied an area of the peninsula about midway between the Ashley and Cooper rivers, groundwater in the area was trapped in physical purgatory against the force of gravity: subtle nuances between pore size and pore pressure between soil grains; the gentle pull of the low, slow meandering streams; man-made alterations to the land; and, of course, owing to its proximity to the coast, the tides. These factors and any number of others combined to influence which way the groundwater flowed. Nick was starting on what promised to be an interesting, perhaps even daunting task. At least he had a goodly number of monitoring points scattered across the property from which to work his magic.

Nick selected the two piezometers along the east property line with a maximum difference in water-table elevation between them from which to begin calculating where the lines of equal elevation would fall. These were PZ-14, located north of the Athens rail spur, and PZ-11 along the south PSTRE property line near Industrial Drive. The distance between them was approximately 205 feet, and the difference in elevation a mere 0.03 feet, about the length that the average fingernail grows in two and a half months. Nick used a straight edge to draw a line connecting the two locations. Next, he laid his engineer's scale along the line and used the 20-scale on the rule to determine that there were 68 increments, or tics, between them. Using his calculator, he divided the elevation difference by the number of tics to determine that the space between each tic on the ruler represented 0.0004 feet on the ground. "Yowzer that's flat," he whispered. It was a nearly imperceptible hydraulic gradient, a fall in elevation from north to south of 0.00015 feet per foot, or roughly half of the diameter of the average human hair. Even more remarkable was the fact that this minute change in water-table elevation was a veritable hill when compared to other elevation differences across the site.

Nick repeated this process over and over between points, making little tic marks, then connecting the dots with his pencil wherever an even 0.01-foot distance—the contour interval—was encountered, until he worked his way across the map. As expected, he found that there weren't that many calculations to perform because of the large expanses where the groundwater appeared not to flow at all, as there were no contour lines to plot. Regardless, the results were telling. In a PSTRE-perfect world, groundwater flow would be north to south—from Athens toward PSTRE. It wasn't, but it was close enough for argument sake: groundwater flow was to the southwest, toward the Ashley River. Now, if they could demonstrate that a release had occurred in the general vicinity of the Athens tank farm, this map would prove that contamination *had* flowed onto PSTRE property in a direction that could be intercepted by the production well.

So much for small victories: the 8:00 A.M. data told a different story. The lines of equal elevation showed a contrasting flow component to the southeast toward the Cooper River. "Fuck," Nick said louder than intended. "Hold on!" He smacked himself for reacting without thinking. He checked his notes. "Huh!" The first high tide occurred yesterday morning at 1:08 A.M., and the corresponding low followed six and quarter hours later at 7:20. "There are tidal effects," he mumbled, drumming his fingers. This was good; great, actually, because what he had hoped was happening *was* happening. They were that much closer to building their case. Nick worked quickly through the remaining data, belting out a sigh of relief when finished. Chris and the M&C boys would be pleased. Groundwater, he determined, wandered restlessly back and forth across the bottom half of the compass dial, flowing from southwest to southeast and back again at the whim of the tides. This meant that contaminant-laden groundwater originating from pretty much anywhere on Athens's property eventually encroached onto PSTRE's. This simplified things immensely because now all they needed to do was rule out PSTRE as a source.

"Don't you look like the cat that ate the canary? Tell me you got something."

Nick looked up from his doodles. It was Chris. He was yelling from the opposite side of the war-room glass, his quirky smirk creating a crooked jag in his beard. "Got great news!" Nick hollered. "Athens's crap *does* flow onto PSTRE's property. It should be a slam dunk if Jay can give us some supporting data."

"That's great, Nick!" Chris replied, striding into the war room. "I'll do you one better. What if I said, he just did?"

"What are you talking about?"

"When I spoke with RCE about getting a survey crew out there post haste, I might have mentioned being eternally grateful if they could kick some driller in the ass and scare up a drill rig."

"Go on," Nick said.

"Sam called in a favor. He's had a crew out there since lunchtime. He didn't mention this to you?"

Nick shook his head.

Chris shrugged. Then, as if it were an afterthought, said, "They found some oily material near where they drilled those tank-farm-area piezometers."

Preoccupied with trying to figure out why Sam hadn't mentioned anything to him about having a rig on-site, Nick was slow to respond.

"What are you waiting for?" Chris demanded when his technical lead failed to jump to attention. "Let's go!"

They took Chris's rental. In their rush, Nick forgot his work boots and they had to loop around the block to his car. He waited until they reached the interstate before giving Michelle the good news, promising to fill her in with more details once they had more information.

It was pushing a quarter past four when they reached the site. The moment they rounded the corner of the PSTRE building, their ears were assaulted by the down-winding ratta-tat-tat sound of the drill string being direct-pushed into the ground. Jay Watkins acknowledged their presence with a wave. "Your buddy's happy to see you," Chris teased. Tricia Bell was tending to the previous soil-core sample at Watkins's feet.

"Be right with you," Watkins shouted over the din from the idling rig. Chris waited for him and Bell to finish their examination of the fresh core lying within the acetate liner just removed from the business end of the drill string.

Nick meanwhile snooped around. He checked on their progress by looking for other small drill holes in the ground.

"Anything?" Watkins asked his partner. Bell, who was scanning the soil core with a photoionization detector for telltale signs of petroleum vapors, shook her head.

"Nothing, huh?" Chris asked.

Watkins tucked his clipboard under an arm and pulled off a surgical glove with a loud snap. "Nope. Nothing here…or there… but there, yes." He pointed in the direction of the PSTRE building. "It's a real puzzler. Sure you guys didn't find anything in the old reports about what PSTRE did out here?"

Chris said that they hadn't. Nick edged up beside them, extending his hand in greeting to Watkins, and then Bell, who had just finished her work. He watched while the driller decontaminated the downhole tooling. "You only found impact there?" Nick pointed to the same unlikely hole in the ground that Watkins just alluded too. "What'd it look like?"

"We'll show you. Tricia?"

"Samples are over there, in the cooler." she led them to RCE's field vehicle, where she pulled the cooler from the opened hatch. She opened the cooler and reached inside to pull out a glass jar labeled B-1. "We found this at the first place we drilled." She handed the jar to Chris, who looked at it briefly before handing it off to Nick.

"Smells tarry," Nick said, wrinkling his nose when he opened the lid. A dark, nearly black liquid was weeping from the plug of fine sandy soil in the sample jar. He closed the lid and handed it back to Bell. "How far down?"

"Oh, my bad," she said. I should have written it on the lid." She flipped through her notes. "Five to five and a half feet. Groundwater was encountered at four point six feet."

Nick again asked Bell for the jar. "The sample is from below the water table. Pretty sandy." Looking to Watkins, Nick commented, "You said that product was found only in the sandy zones." Watkins nodded. "Where were they again?" Watkins pointed to various disjointed locations across the property. Nick matched those spots on the ground to the pink highlighted locations on the map he was holding in his hand. "Interesting," he said, looking from the map to where Watkins had pointed.

Jay read his mind and refreshed Nick on the site lithology. "The sandy zones are anomalies in an otherwise mucky soil profile. They can be rather thick, too, like over there, at PZ-9. The sand's something like four feet thick. Am I right, Trish?" Bell confirmed his thoughts. "Who knows how the sands finger in and out around here. By the way," Watkins said, asking about their meeting needs, "was Mindy able to give you what you wanted?"

"She did, Jay, thanks," Nick said, making the mental leap to the pressure-transducer data dump Porter provided that morning. Noticing that Watkins was craning his neck to see what was on the loose sheet he was holding, Nick handed him a rough sketch that summarized groundwater's tide-induced daily swing through the subsurface. "Tell Mindy that she was a big help. Depending on timing, I might ask her to get Brandon to pretty this up before the meeting."

Watkins sized up the effort involved to mock-up a meeting-ready graphic of Nick's sketch.

"I can do that," Bell offered. "We're going out after work. How about I ask her to call you in the morning?"

"Appreciated," Nick said to them both. With Bell also taking an interest in the sketch, Nick described his findings. Bell agreed with him that the sketch was telling. Watkins said he wished he could be there at the meeting to see how Athens tried to talk away the incriminating evidence that tidally-influenced groundwater had to be in one way or another responsible for the off-site transport of oil onto PSTRE's property.

"I wouldn't go that far yet," Chris reminded them, playing the role of devil's advocate. He pointed out that if groundwater oscillates back and forth like it no doubt does, then where was the smear zone where the oil was being dragged back and forth to create a much wider-than-should-be area of contamination? This they were not seeing. Chris then reminded them that all they still had were a few scattered spots of contamination, and that this just-found B-1 contamination, owing to its *inland* location, away from the property boundary, didn't necessarily help their cause. Opposing counsel would argue that it was a yet unidentified PSTRE problem. No, they needed more proof. The round of eye rolling that followed was enough said. "I see." Rallying the troops, Chris urged that they get a move on and find proof. "Where are we now?"

"We're ready to move to B-4," Watkins answered. He then briefly changed the subject to the whacky production well water levels. "Before I forget, something funky is still going on with the pressure transducer in that well. We were dicking around with it for a while before we started drilling. That's why we're only on the fourth boring."

Nick said nothing. His mind was stuck on unraveling the smear-zone riddle. *Product preferentially moves through the sand, following the path of least resistance with groundwater that's affected by the tides. It's here but not there, meaning that the sandy zones are—*

Chris was another matter. "Now what's wrong, Jay?" he groused in frustration over the faulty equipment. The tense crackling sound of his voice broke Nick's train of thought.

"I know what you're thinking, but it's not a mechanical problem, from what we can tell."

Chris gave him a demanding look.

"The water level in that well has been exceptionally high, right?" Jay asked.

Chris nodded.

"People back in the office tell me that it suddenly dropped by almost twenty feet before rebounding again. The equipment, however, continues to pass all of our diagnostic checks."

Chris was unconvinced. "There's nothing wrong with the equipment?"

Watkins reminded him that RCE had switched out the equipment several times for equipment that worked elsewhere on the site. Only in the production well did the equipment *not* work.

Chris huffed. "That makes no sense." He looked to Nick for an explanation.

"There's always Occam's razor."

"You're going with that again?" Chris chuckled, his mood lightening.

"It's better than anything else we got, which is nothing," Nick said.

"Point taken."

"What's that…whatever it is you said?" Watkins asked.

Chris extended a hand in Nick's direction.

"Occam's razor is an investigation tool. It basically says that you should select the hypothesis with the least assumptions."

Watkins absorbed this. "You're saying—"

"That we should believe the data," Bell completed her mentor's thought.

"Correct," Nick said. "The idea's hung around for centuries because it works. We should be looking at the problem from the other way around. Instead of arguing the many ways that it could be an equipment problem—which, Jay, you say is not the issue—we should accept the data at face value and figure out what natural phenomenon might be causing the fluctuations to occur."

The drilling subcontractor tapped a hammer against the side of his rig. He was ready to move on.

Chris rolled his eyes. One problem at a time, he reminded himself. "Where to next, Jay?"

"There," Watkins said, pointing to a spot near the property-line fence, about equidistant between the B-1 and B-2 borings.

"Nick?" Chris asked.

"It's as good a place as any," Nick said. "You said this one will be B-4?"

They watched the driller retrieve the B-4 soil core from the ground, hoping, wanting, only to be disappointed. No contamination. The same held true at B-5, drilled in the opposite direction, away from the property line; the subsurface held fast and refused to yield its secrets. At least they caught what they thought might be a whiff of a fetid petroleum-like odor at B-4, but that was all. Chris shook his head. They were fast running out of time and places to look.

Nick was frustrated as well, although not for the same reason as Chris. He had seen this situation before, only he couldn't remember where. Was it in Ohio or Indiana? *What the heck did we figure out was happening there?*

"Ideas?" Chris asked him.

"Huh? Oh." The others were looking at him for a suggestion. "We haven't tried there yet, Nick said, pointing to the former pole-storage area.

"Are you sure that we want to do that?" Chris asked. If PSTRE was the source for the impact, the pole-storage area was the logical spot.

"Do you see any option that *doesn't* include drilling in the most likely location? We'll have to do it at some point."

Chris reluctantly agreed. "Yeah, I know we will. Let me speak with Brant or Smitty and first see what they say. If they give us the go ahead and don't like what we find, we can blame them. How's that sound?"

Nick approved. "Passing the buck works for me." Watkins and Bell agreed.

"Spoken like oft-beaten messengers!" Chris placed the call. He explained to Brant what they'd found and didn't find. When asked if they should drill beneath the pole-storage area, Brant told him to wait while he flagged down Smitty. This took some time. In the interim, they hashed over alternate drilling locations. Chris turned away from an increase in rig noise when Smitty got on the line. "You're okay with that? Right. Exactly. Will do." Chris hung up. "It's a go! Smitty says that we won't share any negative findings with Athens until M&C works on an exit strategy, should it come to that."

Much to everyone's relief, the dreaded pole-storage area turned out to be another Capone's vault. The B-6 boring was drilled near the southwest corner of the feature. Beneath eight inches of gravel and crushed brick was a half-inch-thick layer of dark gray stained soil that yielded to eight feet of non-impacted muck beneath. That was it. The same held true at B-7, drilled catty-corner on the northeast side of the former staging area; only there, there was no staining at all. They had exonerated the only known PSTRE source. Moreover, a legal monkey was excised from PSTRE's back. High-fives were passed all around.

Taking charge, Nick instructed the driller to move the rig to the south side of the Athens rail spur and work his way in a southerly course along the shared property line, placing borings five to ten feet apart until they found something. Pay dirt was achieved two borings later. Chris was on the phone with Brant, filling him in on the pole-storage area news, when Tricia Bell pointed excitedly at the tarry substance clinging to the outside of the drill rods at B-9. A moment later their olfactory senses were assaulted by the rank, sweet smell of *creosote*.

The feeling was electric. They had hoped to find at least one more piece of damning evidence, and they had done that! Irascible old Stan Merrill was right after all. Fugitive product had migrated from Athens, and once again it was confined to a layer of sandy soil. Even sourpuss Gerry Dawkins, who had stopped to inform them that they were running up on quitting time, was excited. He relented to Nick's urging that he spare them some extra time to chase out the product-bearing layer. All told, they would drill three more impacted borings that could be correlated to one another and B-1. Satisfied, Chris told Watkins to start tearing down and placed another call.

"Who are you calling?" Nick asked.

"Bill," Chris said with a lofty smile. "Smitty told me to call him directly with the news."

CHAPTER 5

FRIDAY

U.S. Rt. 70
Hays, Kans.
3:18 P.M.

"That's too funny!" Melanie said, slapping at her thigh. "I can just picture him doing that. Who drove then?"

"I did," Michelle giggled. "Speaking of which, hold on." Michelle put her foot on the accelerator to pass a convoy of trucks. They were making their way through central Kansas, gossiping about what else? Michelle's magical summer of '85 ride to field camp. The reminiscing resumed when she returned to cruising the *slow* lane at a tepid seventy-five.

"He was really mad?" Melanie asked, making no attempt to conceal her amusement.

"Nick was *so* mad," Michelle insisted, "that he sulked for I don't even know how long before Jamie Mason eventually punched him in the arm and told him to quit being a puss. I didn't know what was happening. One minute we were talking about everything under the sun, shouting over the music and the roar of the air pouring in through the windows, and the next the car goes screeching off onto the shoulder. And there goes Nick, storming out of Garret's beater station wagon. I can still hear him yelling at me to '*DRIVE!*' as he rounded the front of the car. We cracked up when we realized the reason why he was so upset, and that made him all the madder."

"He didn't even make it out of the state? Too much!" Melanie laughed even harder when Michelle explained that Nick had taken the wheel at the first opportunity upon leaving Missouri. "Was it somewhere around here that he pulled over?"

Michelle looked over the rolling countryside, zoomed out the GPS view screen. "I honestly don't remember. I guess I don't blame him. Kansas did go on like, *F-O-R-E-V-E-R.*"

"Then what happened?" Melanie asked.

Michelle blew a curl from her mouth. "He sulked some more until Jamie punched him again and, well, boys became boys."

"It sounds like you guys had so much fun. Jamie's the kid you picked up on the way, right? How'd he get invited?"

Michelle was enjoying the trip down memory lane perhaps a little too much.

"You're blushing! Okay, *spill!* He was cute, wasn't he?"

"Gorgeous!" Michelle gushed. "Knew it, too. He had flowing curls and these little dimples that creased his cheeks when he smiled. It took Garret and Nick a good while to warm up to him."

"They were jealous?"

"Good lord, yes. It was cute. Tracy and I found it endearing. Jamie went to Indiana University. Our field camp was open to anyone, so it wasn't uncommon to have kids from other Great Lakes area schools attend. We begged the boys to stop on our way south through Michigan to look for this rare type of warbler. They weren't too happy about bird watching, so we agreed to stop at a place of their choosing. They wanted to collect rocks—imagine that—along this road cut on the highway south of Bloomington where IU is located. Jamie had sent a letter to the geology department at Huron asking if someone could give him a lift, so it was on the way. It was Garret's idea to pick him up."

"Really? That was nice."

"It was. I was surprised. Nick was the social planner. Hey, do you mind if I change stations?" Melanie agreed and she dialed the Sirius station down to *'80s on 8.* "To get us in the mood," Michelle said, tapping her fingers to a Richard Marx tune.

"I like it. It takes me back."

Another clunk. Michelle asked Melanie to flip the tape. "Talking about all this stuff is really helping me think about what I want to include in my book."

"It's helping me, too. Now tell me more about this sexy boy."

"You're old enough to be his mother," Michelle teased, like she did the day before over the man-child trooper.

"Not when you were going to field camp, I wasn't," Melanie reasoned.

"Well played! I suppose not." Michelle placed a hand to her mouth; said slyly, "He certainly was cougar worthy."

Melanie snickered. She wriggled herself again into a cross-legged position.

"I don't know how you do that." Envious, Michelle failed in her effort to lift her non-driving leg and place her foot on the dash. "I think I did this once when I was like sixteen. I never was that limber."

Another laugh.

"Anyway, Jamie was definitely hot by any age standard. One can only hope that he aged gracefully."

"Have you checked to see if he's on social media?"

Michelle frowned. "No…I never thought about it."

"Wanna check when we get in tonight?"

The idea was tempting. "Let's do it!" Michelle said, to which Melanie applauded with a light clap. "I have to say," Michelle warned her, "our first encounter left much to be desired."

"Not good?"

Michelle shook her head. "Not by girl standards. It was dark when we got there. The frat house was this old mansion, much like Ashley House, only in need of a makeover. The porch light was out and had these unruly yew bushes that practically overran the place. Plastic cups were littered everywhere. It stunk, too, like stale beer or pee depending on where you stood."

"*Eww!*"

"It was disgusting. Oh, I almost forgot!" Michelle recalled, patting her hand on the wheel, "The porch steps were rickety. Tracy lost her balance and fell over the side."

"She did not!"

"Right off the side and into the yews she went," Michelle described with a sweeping motion. "She was so mad. Nick and I were struggling to pull her out when the front door opened, and standing in a shaft of light coming from the foyer was *Thor*. Jamie looked so tall, blonde, and built from our vantage point... right up until we saw him up close and realized that he was just a skinny kid who only appeared ripped because he was wearing a wife-beater t-shirt. He also wore those skintight eighties short shorts—remember those? If he wasn't blonde, he could have been mistaken for Billy Squire. Tracy and I were speechless. It was hard not to be attracted to him. Nick and your brother were so jealous, and we just played to it."

"As you should," Melanie said, approving of Michelle and Tracy for exercising their womanly rights.

"He showed us inside. There, Jamie introduced us to a few of his friends. He asked if we wanted something to drink. Garret and Nick of course said yes. Jamie then showed us to this once lavish ballroom, since reduced to the demilitarized zone they called their party room. It was so sad. In the middle was this humungous fountain. I have no idea where they stole that from, or how on Earth they got it inside."

"*In-ter-est-ing*," Melanie said, drawing out the word.

"I hate to admit it, but it kind of was. The centerpiece was this tall thing surrounded by all these stone cherubs."

"*Oh, no!*" Melanie cringed, guessing at what the cherubs did. "They didn't..."

"Oh, yes, they did," Michelle affirmed with a resigned sigh. "Jamie flipped a switch and beer started flowing from where they peed."

Melanie scrunched her face. "I'm not sure if that's funny or disgusting."

"Trust me, it was the latter. Of course, just one look at beer spewing from their little things and the boys were enamored. Then and there, Jamie Mason was elevated from enemy suitor to way too cool dude."

Now it was Melanie's turn to sigh. "Boys are so simple." On a more serious note, she broached her brother's mental state. "If I remember correctly, you mentioned in *Ghost Creek* that Jamie helped Garret. Did you notice him slipping away then?"

Michelle had mulled over this very question on many sleepless nights. Still, she struggled with an appropriate answer. "In hindsight, yes…then, no. Garret was passionate about many things; grades were one. Knowledge grounded him. It was the one constant in his life that he could control. He also carried a heavy class load. Lord knows I played second fiddle to several grueling lab classes that kept him late at the science building on most evenings." Thinking some more, Michelle added, "I could tell that something was bothering him, like maybe he wasn't going to get the grade—or should I say the level of grade—he was anticipating. The thing was, it spilled over into the weeks that followed after school let out, right up to our ride to field camp. We didn't know at the time what was bothering him. I was afraid to press; so was Nick. Your brother didn't take well to prying. What I can say is that his mood brightened considerably after Jamie joined us. Jamie Mason was one of those annoying friends who knew how to get you out of your funk even when you didn't want to be let out."

"I know the type. What'd he do?" Melanie asked.

"Oh, nothing specific. This or that, little things mostly—like he would prod at Garret about things Garret would yell at the rest of us for." Michelle gave her head a shake. "But not Jamie. Garret never snapped at him. Jamie had a way of forcing a smile out of Garret. You know, I think Garret needed Jamie as much as we needed Jamie because Jamie Mason added the spark that made that trip special."

"That's nice to hear."

"As for him slipping away? Let's just say that in my opinion, certain events that school year resurrected memories from his past that conspired against him. So, yes, even then I think Garret was fighting a losing battle."

Melanie looked as if she was about to cry.

"I'm sorry. Mel?"

A tear trickled down Melanie's cheek. "There was so much I wanted to say to him over the years and didn't because it was convenient not to."

"Perhaps. But I do know that Garret appreciated every time you did. It made him happy."

"Thanks," Melanie sniffed. "I wish I'd done so more often. I really hoped that one day we would reconnect." Failing to contain an angry sob, Melanie said sharply, "I hate it when I get this way!" and ground the heels of her hands into her eyes. "There were so many times when I was angry with him for what had happened to our family. I even hated him at times. Those days thankfully passed. Deep down, though, I always loved him"

"You feel responsible for letting him founder?" Michelle asked.

Melanie deflected the question with a soul-bearing declaration. "This is going to sound cold, but in some ways I think Garret was the lucky one. He was able to escape. Is that a terrible thing to say? Me, I've lived every day trying to repair that part of me that stopped growing when I was a little girl."

Michelle had no idea that Garret's actions affected his sister so deeply. A few decades before, Melanie was the pillar of strength she and the others needed in the wake of the Little Bear disaster. "Please explain," she urged.

"Trust. Abandonment," was Melanie's brusque response. "Everything that was a constant in my life changed after our parents' separation and mom's breakdown, yet through it all I held out hope that one day we would be reunited as a family. First it was our parents, and then we were sent our separate ways."

"If you don't mind my asking, why didn't you stay with your dad?"

Melanie's chin fell until it rested on her chest. Lifting it, she said, "It wasn't in him. Our father may have been crusty and resolute on the outside, but beneath all his bravado he was afraid—it was all a façade. He had no idea how to raise a family. That was mom's job, and she'd become incapable. At least we had family to take us in."

Saddened by the tale, Michelle said nothing and listened.

"Dad promised we would be together again soon. Us kids, we started drifting apart when this didn't happen. Fortunately, Kerry and me had each other for support. Who I really missed, though, was Garret. We were allowed to see him only when the situation demanded. He was the family mistake we were encouraged to avoid. I felt so sorry for him. The grownups? They didn't help matters. They blamed Garret for everything that went wrong with their lives after that; we were a burden after all. Kerry calls it stress transference. Aunt Joan and Uncle Terry took in Kerry and me. They were nice enough, and they did provide us with all of the material things we needed. All the same, we were treated different from their own kids. This fostered a degree of separation between us and our cousins that exists to this day."

Michelle continued to listen.

"Don't get me wrong. They didn't intend to treat us different, and I would never admit this to them because I'm sure they'd be devastated. But they did, and I handled it poorly. I saw us as the neighborhood kids with the scarlet letter who the other kids and their parents talked about. Do you know the worst of it? We were told not to talk about Garret in front of others because of the negative reflection this might cast on the family. That was horribly unfair."

"Why?"

"Why I thought it was unfair?"

"Yes," Michelle persisted.

"Isn't it obvious? What aren't you telling me?"

Michelle navigated the mounting strain. "I don't mean to pry. It's for the book," she said evenly. "I want to get to the root of everything."

Rick Ley

"Of course. That's fine." Then with less defensiveness, Melanie said, "I know what he did. It just wasn't him."

"You're saying that you don't think Garret was responsible for his actions?"

Melanie stared back, a look of puzzlement in her eyes. "I don't," she said with conviction. "What is it?" she demanded when Michelle's face reddened.

Michelle maintained her evasiveness. "Oh…nothing," was all she would offer.

"O-kay," Melanie said glumly when Michelle refused to elaborate. She continued to fill Michelle in on the details of that life-altering period from her childhood.

"We were a collection of castoffs the others were stuck with. That hurt. We saw even less of Garret than we would have because he was dumped on Aunt Carol's doorstep. She wasn't well liked by our other relatives. I think Garret was as much her punishment as she was his. It was a double whammy that Kerry and me had to deal with."

"You did write to him. That was good."

Melanie appreciated the encouragement. "I did a lot at first. That slowed, unfortunately, as our situation wore on. I wrote to him now and then through high school and a few times after that when he went to college. He didn't write back often, but I savored each time that he did. I still have his letters."

Michelle tapped lightly at Melanie's shoulder. "It's a good thing your brother made for a better girlfriend than I did," she said playfully.

"What do you mean?"

"Grab my pack if you would. There's something I need you to see."

Melanie reached behind the seat, and with a repeat of yesterday's effort, lurched the heavy daypack onto her lap. "Your diary?"

"No. Garret's journal." Mere mention of it stopped Melanie mid-motion.

"Are you serious?" Melanie asked, staring wide-eyed into the pack. "His journal?" She resumed her rummaging with a hasty scramble.

"I brought two of them. They're blue cloth. See the one with the frayed corner? Grab that one and open it at the green-colored tab. I don't think I ever showed you these."

"No, you didn't." Melanie opened the cover and gulped at the sight of Garret's name and school address printed on the flyleaf. She began flipping through the pages, stopping several times to feel the indentations made years ago by pen on paper. "This is the closest I've been to my brother since I don't know how long," she murmured. Melanie continued her flipping until she reached the tab. She looked at the date. Only then did she realize that this particular journal captured her brother's final entries, the last one written the very morning of his death.

Michelle waited for the ramifications to soak it in.

"I see what you mean," Melanie said, unable to formulate a more appropriate response. "His notes are meticulous. Where?" she asked, again feeling the reverse Braille-like indentations with her fingertips.

"Around there," Michelle pointed. "You must have written to him not long before...*you know*."

Melanie was shocked by what she read. The entries were dark, angry, written by an irrational mind that had clearly lost its battle with the demons tormenting it. Melanie was stunned at how far her brother had slipped away at the end, but seeing was believing, and it was horrifying. Michelle's depiction of her brother in *Ghost Creek*, her own distant remembrances of his troubles when they were children, the increasing detachment she sensed in his infrequent letters, they did nothing to prepare her for what lay bare before her. "Why are you showing me this?"

"Keep reading. There!" Michelle said, stealing a glance away from the road. She directed Melanie to the opposite page.

Crammed between two rage laden entries was one dated May 17, 1988, written in response to her final letter. Melanie was thunderstruck. It was the redemption she had long been searching for. Cutting to the part that mattered most, she read out loud:

"Melly was always there for me when the others turned their backs. She's the one person I can always trust, the only true friend I ever had."

The passage was written in a moment of clarity when sanity emerged from gripping psychosis. Did her letter conjure positive memories from his youth? Did her others? Melanie was overwhelmed; this time the feeling was all good. *"I did make a difference..."*

"Yes you did! That's great, Mel, really great. I couldn't wait to share this with you."

Melanie read and then reread the passage again to make sure she made no misinterpretation. *"No... Yes... Oh no!"*

Michelle's telepathic powers correctly deduced Melanie's reaction as a sign of distress about Garret's one true friend comment. "Don't worry, Mel. I'm fine with what he wrote. I always was."

"Are you sure?"

"Absolutely," Michelle assured her. "What's important is that Garret always loved you because of who you were. Living through it all, after reading his journals, I realize that I could never compete with you, nor would I wish to. And so you know, a part of me still loves Garret. We—Nick, Tracy, the others—just got caught in the way of what he'd become after he lost the ability to control... *It...* the Scary Man."

Melanie appreciated the candor. She found herself wanting neither to bawl nor shout out in joy. While Garret's rage-laden rants were devastating, this was no longer how Melanie wished to remember him, and she had Michelle to thank for showing her the way. She had spent a lifetime running away from her past: enough was enough. Hereinafter, Melanie would focus on the contentment she was feeling, knowing that in her small way, she had lessened her brother's suffering. Melanie leaned over and gave Michelle a peck on the cheek.

"You're welcome! I was hoping that you would take it that way." Michelle said. Melanie further rewarded her by saying that her trip—

her life for that matter—was now complete. Michelle responded in the only way she felt was right and offered Melanie Garret's journals to keep when she was finished researching her book.

They drove on, two women lost in a transcendental moment of discovery. Bliss was interrupted by the untimely needs of a demanding microcassette recorder. The cassette tape swapped out, they pushed on, conversing about nothing in particular until Michelle risked ruining the moment by asking how Melanie's family fared following Garret's death.

"I don't mind your asking at all," Melanie encouraged, "especially after what I know now. Shoot."

"That's a relief," Michelle confessed. "Let me start by again saying how composed you were when we first met in Colorado, and then afterwards when you helped us through our recovery."

"Me? Please make no mistake, that wasn't me. That was all Kerry. She's the one who gave me strength. I must have covered my issues well because inside, I was a mess. I was the one who broke the news to the others. Telling our parents was the hardest thing I ever had to do. And my divorce still wasn't final. That wouldn't happen until after you and Nick had moved to Oregon. It was an awful time for me, just awful."

"*Oh!* Right. I'd forgotten about that. I can't even begin to imagine what you must have gone through. You seemed to take everything in such stride. We will be forever grateful."

"I did my best to keep myself in check—but boy, it sure wasn't easy." A keen observer and even kinder friend, Melanie relieved Michelle of the burden of asking some of the more delicate family questions. "It was about as bad as you can imagine, telling my parents. Mom took it very hard. She did recover for a spell, and we almost got back together again. Like I said, his passing was a relief of sorts."

"I imagine it would have relieved a lot of stress."

"It did. As tragic as his death was, it provided finality to a lingering situation that was never far out of mind. We could finally move on. Unfortunately, our father's stubbornness prevented that. He still carried resentment toward mom's inability to control Garret when we were children. This brought back her feelings of failure, and that was that. I was so angry with him, we all were, and then dad got sick and that added yet another burden."

"I don't know what to say."

"There's nothing to say, Michelle. Whatever comfort Garret's death provided was gone. There would be no happy ending. Dad's gone now and mom's barely hanging on emotionally; she's been beaten down for so long. She manages the situation through avoidance. That, too, has been difficult. Garret's the brother—the son—that never was."

Saddened by Melanie's family story, Michelle offered to change subjects. Melanie, though, remained steadfast in her desire to put the matter to rest and jumped to the topic of her ex-husband. "His name was Kyle, right?" Michelle asked. "Did he help you through any of this? Was Garret the reason for your divorce?"

"That would be no…and no. We had already broken up, but Garret's death did complicate things later." Melanie adjusted her position. "There, that's better. My leg was falling asleep."

"How did you two meet?" Michelle asked.

"I met Kyle at Michigan Tech. It was one of the few bright periods in my life. Much like you, I used college as a means of escape. There, I could just be me, whoever that was. I met Kyle at a bar. I went with a couple of girlfriends and an off-duty bouncer we knew who snuck us in under age. We were drinking Long Island ice teas when I saw this really cute guy sitting a few tables away. I couldn't take my eyes off him. I kept sneaking little peeks in his direction. All the while, my girlfriends kept pushing for me to go over to him. Then a waitress dropped off a drink and said 'compliments of the young man over there,' or something like that. She pointed and he flashed the dreamiest smile. Well! I'm not sure that I got up, as much as I was shoved out of my chair. That night was the best night of my life."

"Sounds magical…did you?"

"*Michelle!* I won't tell you everything!"

"I'll take that as a *yes!*" Michelle kidded. "Then what?"

"I fell head over heels in love. It was wonderful, liberating. For once, I was like every other girl." Pausing, Melanie thought, then said, "We sure are a lot alike, aren't we?"

"I'll say," Michelle concurred. "The similarity is uncanny."

"Yeah, crazy. Kyle was my first real boyfriend, and we were in the same year. He asked if I would move with him to Racine, Wisconsin after we graduated. He said that he was offered a partnership in his father's pool business. Naturally, I thought we were going places, the perfect couple."

Michelle frowned. "I sense a *but* coming,"

"Kyle's 'partnership' turned out to be running a register and stocking shelves. He was also paid like any other worker. His father said that he needed to learn from the bottom up, that he was grooming him to take over the business *some day*. Kyle expected to start in a top-level capacity right away. They started to fight, and then we started to fight."

"Hmm," Michelle said, solemnly.

Bitter, Melanie explained that her husband forced her to quit her job because she was making more money than he was, and would be for the foreseeable future.

"That's awful!"

"I discovered much too late that Kyle was just like dad, old school. It was a pride meets principle thing for him."

"It's regrettable that women still have to fight the chauvinism fight."

"No kidding. It was pig-headed bigotry, even for then. When was Title IX passed? 1972? I thought I'd finally found myself, and Kyle tries to take a piece of that away. I didn't mind struggling to make ends meet until he worked his way through the ranks. He did. I finally had enough and left."

"Where did you go?" Michelle asked.

"Kerry was still in school in Madison, so I moved there. I got a job pretty much right away. That was good. I needed that. I was really feeling down on myself. Thank goodness for my sister. She had taken up psychology for obvious reasons. I was sort of her test subject. Kerry insisted that I find a distraction when I wasn't at work. She suggested I dive right back into dating since I would have a better idea of what to look out for, but that wasn't for me. Not yet at least. I didn't want to set myself up for another fall. Then she recommended I join a gym where I could mete out social dabbling with men at a safer place, where flirtation played second fiddle to a good work out. That idea I liked. Besides, I had been seeing Kyle for so long that I needed to work on my singles skills again."

"She's good. I know where you're coming from. I felt much the same before I met Garret."

"Yes, she is. And it worked. I met a woman named Erin Marten who was in line ahead of me when I went to sign up. We got to talking and soon became close friends. We decided to room together when Erin's lease was up. Like Kerry, Erin was convinced that I needed to get back into circulation if I wanted to get over Kyle and move on. It wasn't even a week after that when I met Danny— Danny Schaize. We hit it off from the start." Taking a purposeful breath, Melanie said that, "Everything was going fine…right up until I started having premonitions of Garret's death."

"*Oh, boy!*" Michelle gasped, recalling where this part of the story was going.

"How could you forget is probably more like it."

Michelle nodded. She swerved to avoid a piece of truck tire. "I wish they had to clean up their mess," she groused.

Melanie snickered at her irritation. "I tried to make it work, but I was afraid—afraid for me, afraid for him."

"You didn't know that they—the premonitions—were about Garret at first, right?"

"That's right. They were just shadows, gray indistinct images of someone in trouble. I was certain, though, that it was someone that

I knew. Don't ask me how. The premonitions were intermittent at first. I had one maybe every other week. Then they started to come more frequently, also during the day. Those were the worst. I didn't know when they'd happen or where I might be. I was afraid to go to work, afraid to go out in public, afraid to tell anyone except Erin and Kerry."

"And you couldn't tell Danny because you didn't want him to think you were crazy."

"That's about the size of it. It was far too soon to drag out the family's dirty laundry."

Michelle found the summation amusing. "I don't blame you," she empathized. "But why Erin?"

"How could I not? She couldn't avoid knowing about them. She was the one who came running into my room when I woke up screaming in the night."

"That must have been dreadful," Michelle said.

"It was, believe me. Then they became worse, much, much worse."

"How so?" Michelle struggled to suppress that tremulous quaver her voice often did when she became excited. Garret had written numerous journal entries describing his own dreams that were eerily similar to Melanie's.

"The shadows soon started taking shape—a boy wearing a ball cap." Melanie started to tremble. "There was someone else as well, a human-like figure that terrified the boy."

"*The Scary Man*," Michelle said soberly. "Were you seeing your psychiatrist at that point?"

"Yes. Again, that was Kerry's idea. He kept probing, pushing, trying to get me to think about my past to riddle out the who and the why."

"I'm not sure that I follow," Michelle said. "He did think that the two were related—Garret and your premonitions, I mean."

"Yes. Only I couldn't put it together. It's so obvious now. If I had only acted then, perhaps I could have done something. As for Danny, I tried to dump him as gently as I could, but he kept coming around. He wouldn't take no for an answer. He said that we could work out whatever was bothering me together."

"Sounds like he was a very considerate young man."

"He was. That was the problem. Danny didn't deserve someone like me with all of the baggage I was carting around."

"Did Danny know that you were seeing a psychiatrist?"

"I don't think so. He did know that I was going to the doctor, a lot. If he put two and two together, he didn't let on." Melanie raked her fingers through her hair. "The poor guy. It all came to a head at a restaurant. We were double dating with Erin and her boyfriend. We'd just ordered our meals and Danny was talking to the boyfriend when I felt another premonition coming on. I tried to fight it, couldn't, and that's when it happened…Garret's face was revealed, and I just shrieked. I made a real spectacle of myself. I can still see Danny's face, Erin's face, the faces of the others at the tables around us, they were all staring at me."

"What did you do?"

"I ran right out of the restaurant. Erin followed. She must've asked for her boyfriend's keys because she offered to take me home. I said that I needed to go to the airport instead, where I bought a ticket to Colorado, only it was too late. If I just had the chance to talk him down…"

Michelle chose her words carefully. "In all honesty, Mel, I'm not sure if there was anything that you or anyone could have done at that point. Garret had pinned himself into a corner. Even if you did trigger his mind to return to a rational state, I'm certain he would have reacted like a desperate man with so many people hunting him between the mine and field-station grounds. Any wrong action on his part and he would have been shot."

Melanie stared fixedly into the distance. "What a waste," she said after some time. "If it weren't for Kerry, I don't know what I would have done after Garret died. She made time between her coursework to be there for me. She also convinced me to continue seeing my therapist. That helped. Tackling what happened head on enabled me to become comfortable with talking about the tragedy instead of letting it eat away at me. I was somewhere in that process when I first called you."

"We certainly had no idea," Michelle again complimented her. "How did what happened affect Kerry? It's good that she was able to keep up with her schooling."

Melanie nodded. "Thankfully, she had very few problems. She held fast, steady as a rock. I guess a year's development must mean a lot when you're a toddler because she doesn't remember Garret's earliest troubles. She didn't make the same connection between what had happened then and what happened when we were in middle school like Brad or me."

"You two were a year and a half apart?"

"Yes, just about eighteen months. She used to ask Brad and me a lot of *why* questions: 'Why did Garret do this?' 'Why is he so bad?' Because of that, she had an easier time accepting the circumstances of our life growing up than I did. Don't get me wrong; what'd happened did affect her, only not to the same degree. I did my best to shield her from the ugly family matters. In my opinion, Garret was more of a curiosity to her. When I called to tell her that I thought Garret was in trouble, and then, following what happened in Colorado, that Garret was dead, she reacted with sad detachment. It was as if she expected that outcome. Kerry always was an analytical thinker. I'm sure that's why she went on to get her doctorate and become a psychiatrist. Whether she realizes it or not, psychology was her coping mechanism."

"She wanted to find explanations."

"I think so. The structure of academia and the objectivity that detachment provides allowed her to process what happened better than the rest of us. Because of that, she's led a mostly normal adult life. She's amazing, the consummate listener and life coach."

"And you were the consummate student, if how you helped us is any indication."

"And I thank you!" Melanie said, finally realizing that indeed she was a lifesaver. Tapping a finger against her lip, she then steered the discussion to a relevant and parallel topic, "You know, Michelle, we also have a lot in common in another way. We've both carved out a nice niche for ourselves. It might have taken me a little longer than you, but hey. In fact, if it weren't for all of those dreadful things that happened in our past, none of what we've become would have ever happened. We'd never be here, right now. How's that for irony!"

Michelle practically slammed on the brakes. "I never thought about it that way. You're right. If it weren't for what happened to me, first at Little Bear, and then what those bastards did to me in Oregon, I might have led a normal, boring life. Speak of privileged misfortune!" The revelation put Michelle's mind into overdrive. The structure of the personal-interest-story side of her book was unfolding in her mind with each new insight into the lives of Garret's family, about how his actions had affected them—*and her.* "Does Kerry have a specialty?"

"She works with special needs cases, mostly those with dissociative identity disorder," Melanie replied in a most casual manner, as if DID was a commonly diagnosed malady.

Michelle couldn't believe what she'd just heard. *"You mean like split personalities?"*

"That's right," Melanie said, unfazed by Michelle's bewilderment. "She rather stumbled into it, actually, and not by design as you might think. She was doing her residency at a Madison-area clinic that also consulted to local hospitals. There, she learned that the clinic was asked to evaluate a woman being held at a mental institution, pending trial for homicide. The woman's lawyers argued that it was one of her personalities that surfaced only when she was in an altered state of consciousness that had committed the crime, and not *her."*

"Like Sybil?" Michelle could just pinch herself. Kerry's vocation, her own recent astonishing discoveries about Garret, they fit hand in glove. The timing was impeccable. Michelle resisted the urge to jump right in to her great reveal.

"Yes. Sybil's real name was Shirley Mason. That movie about her hit home with our parents when it came out in the early seventies. We were too young to see it and couldn't understand why our parents forbade us from talking about the movie, other than it having something to do with Garret."

"They knew then?" Michelle asked, even more amazed.

"I don't think so. I think they saw the character in the movie as just another crazy person with mental issues like Garret, and not another individual with the same problem. I rented the movie one night when I was in college, back in the good old days of VHS. I honestly don't remember Garret acting like the Sybil character in the movie. Not to say that he didn't. The movie was frightening, nonetheless, and brought back many bad memories."

"I'd say so."

"Kerry says that dissociative identity disorder is a contentious diagnosis, which many in the psychiatric fraternity dismiss as fantastical. Those who don't believe in the disease assume that the patient is suffering from something less controversial like schizophrenia or post-traumatic stress: one person, one mind. To claim that an alternate personality did *whatever* is too convenient. We just don't know enough yet about what happens inside the human mind. Kerry also said that the clinic was reluctant to handle the case because the ramifications of taking on one so controversial could be severe. Neither the clinic nor the doctors directly involved wanted to risk sullying their reputations. I give her credit. Kerry asked if she could read the patient's files, anyway. She discovered a number of behavioral similarities between Garret and this woman based on what us kids told her about Garret when we were very young *and* after reading your book."

"*Ghost Creek? Really?*"

"Yes, really!" Melanie insisted. "Kerry holds you in highest regard. She hasn't said so directly, but from the way she talks about you whenever your name comes up, I can tell that she's grateful for what you've done to help launch her career. Talk about something to include in your new book!"

Michelle was speechless. The road ahead blurred into one great, oversized lane.

Melanie sipped from her water bottle. "Kerry was open-minded about the disorder. When she read your descriptions of Garret's actions, she just knew the woman had some underlying disorder. Kerry basically forced the clinic to take the case."

Humbled, but proud, Michelle said she was touched. "What was the outcome?"

"The clinic won because of Kerry's efforts. The woman was committed to a high security psychiatric institution where she could get proper treatment. That case and the notoriety coming with it made Kerry's career. She's since moved to Seattle to be closer to a male patient who, she says, is being used as a pawn in some old-money family squabble. I gather from what she can tell me that the family wants the patient removed from the facility so as not to undermine another family member's political ambitions. Kerry believes the man is mentally too unstable to leave the facility."

"It sounds like your situation all over again. I feel bad for her patient."

"Apparently so," Melanie said irritably. "Hide the family skeleton and hope nobody finds out."

Michelle deflected Melanie's irritation by asking if Kerry was certain that Garret had dissociative identity disorder.

"She won't go that far."

"Why not?" Michelle was confused.

"Because she didn't evaluate him for herself. But, between you and me," she then continued with a hushed voice, "I'm pretty sure that she does think so."

"For what it's worth, it's reasonable to me that Garret did have the illness, or one of those similar ones. You weren't there that day in the mine, Mel. It wasn't him. He was an entirely *other* person, one moment yelling at some invisible someone, and the next seeking encouragement from the same someone or some other imaginary thing or being. Then there was the moment in that room…just after he killed our friend Dave, and before he attacked me. Garret was maniacal." Michelle shuddered. "I'm not sure if that's the right term. But, it was the most frightening thing I ever saw—far worse than at Sudbury." Michelle again pointed behind the seat. "One more time if you would? There's more I need you to see."

Familiar with the drill, Melanie elected to forego another struggle and left the heavy pack where it sat. She turned around instead, knees on seat, and reached behind the center console.

"The other journal," Michelle instructed. While Melanie searched, Michelle described Garret as different from others, different from them. And with that she changed the course of their discussion away from the problem-child Garret to the misunderstood brother.

"How do you mean different?" Melanie asked.

That wasn't so bad, Michelle thought. Melanie's response was inquisitive. This was good because she was maneuvering the conversation into troubled waters. Michelle took further solace when Melanie hugged the keepsake of her lost brother's thoughts. "See that slip of paper sticking out?" she asked. "Yes, there. Open it. I'd like to ask you a few questions about what he wrote."

Melanie perused the journal, stopping when she reached the slip of paper.

"You know that he was smart," Michelle said; adding, "I mean really smart," to grab Melanie's attention. "And not just book smart. Anyone can be that. Garret didn't apply what he'd learned the way the rest of us do."

"*Right.*"

"His mind processed things in a manner far beyond what others are capable of. It was maddening, really. I can't begin to count the times he'd outpace us, making connections between things beyond our comprehension."

"What are you talking about?" Melanie asked.

Michelle paused. She had deliberated as long as she could. It was time to press the issue of the Sutton patriarch and his treatment of them as children, brother Brad in particular. Michelle took her eyes off the road to point to one of the open pages. "Read this," she said. Melanie did, bristling as expected, her demeanor then softening by the time they passed the next mile marker. "Am I right?" Michelle asked when Melanie again rubbed at her eyes. "Do you mind talking about it?"

"This is unbelievable," Melanie said softly. The understated way in which she responded by no means countered the shock registered by what Garret had penned one evening during an introspective rant early in his college days. One look at the impassioned entry and Melanie was overcome with angst-filled affinity for her brother. *"He felt sorry for him,"* she mouthed.

Her astonishment provided Michelle with all that she could have hoped for. Recognition that all little Garret wanted to do was help, only to have his older brother turn him away over an unfortunate misunderstanding.

Melanie sniffed. She reached into her purse for a tissue. "I never thought that the issues between dad and Bradley could be a reason for what Garret did. We'd just assumed that Garret was sick. That's what we were told."

"Was your father that hard on Brad?" Michelle asked.

"He was. Dad was demanding. He had to be. As a supervisor in the mines, discipline went hand in hand with managing hardened men. He also had to defend his workers' production to management, with whom he often didn't see eye to eye. Unfortunately, he often brought his work issues home with him. He'd be angry. I vaguely recall asking him one time why he was so mad. Being a girl, that was all it would take and he'd soften and become dad again. And Kerry, she was his little darling. I don't remember him ever being upset around her. She had this way of making him melt into a puddle."

"Aww!"

"Yeah. That's how I like to remember dad, the loving father, and not the hardboiled disciplinarian." Melanie's tone darkened. "It was different for Brad. Being the oldest, and a boy, dad was really tough on him. He was like my ex after we moved to Wisconsin, the epitome of old school. Domestic issues like raising the kids were beneath his concern; that was mom's job to handle—and Brad's because he was the man of the house when dad was at work. If something didn't go right at home, dad would vent his frustration on Brad."

"But why? He was just a child."

"To toughen him up. We were like the Walton family of Ontonagon," Melanie mused. "Dad came from a poor family. He had to work his way up through the ranks in the mines, and though we weren't poor, we had little beyond the necessities. He didn't want Brad's future family to go through what he did, to live like we did, so he pushed him. Kerry thinks he was grooming Brad to be a little version of himself. The problem was, being daddy's little house general wasn't in Brad's makeup. He'd cry, dad would get frustrated, and round and round it went." Melanie rested her head against the passenger's side window. "You were right, Brad was just a little boy who wanted to be a kid."

Michelle was feeling about as depressed as Melanie sounded. "That's a huge burden. I can see how that would affect Brad—and Garret for that matter, when he was exposed to such tension."

Melanie thought this a fair assessment.

"He never hit your brother, did he? Would Garret have witnessed that?"

Melanie blinked. She brushed off her discomfort at the invasive question. "I know he did. We all got smacked from time to time, if that's what you mean. Once I was swatted with one of those orange Hot Wheels race-track things for sticking our dog's ears together with a piece of gum because I thought it was funny. That really hurt. I learned my lesson and didn't do it again. It's what parents did, at least where I grew up. Why?"

Michelle's heart fluttered. She didn't answer her and instead asked, "Can I presume that Brad had his own difficulties?"

"You could say that," Melanie replied, having resumed her scrutiny of Garret's journal entry. "Oh, Bradley! You really need to see this. Mom, you need to see this, too."

Michelle watched Melanie as she tried to draw more meaning from Garret's words by passing her fingers across the indentations like a record needle teases music from the grooves of an album.

"Brad blamed Garret for everything. He still does. The last straw was mom's breakdown. Aunt Beth and Uncle John took him in. We didn't know them as well as some of our other relatives, and didn't see Brad all that often. This changed some as time went on, and I did make it a point to see him as often as I could after I went to college."

"That's nice," Michelle said.

Melanie drummed her fingers. "It was, but not like you think. We were always glad to see each other, of course. Brad, though, had fallen in with the wrong crowd. This changed his attitude, the clothes he wore. He became difficult to be around. I could never visit for very long. He also got into drugs, and that led to a minor criminal record—nothing serious—just enough *not* to land a dependable or well-paying job."

"I'm sorry to hear that. Did he eventually straighten himself out?"

Melanie grimaced. "Last I heard, he was running equipment at an area mill. Brad never escaped the confines of Ontonagon—not that there's anything wrong with where we grew up. It's just that he let his hatred for Garret and our misfortune eat away at him to the point that I don't think even he knows how to lift himself from the depths he's put himself into. I've sure tried to help…but now I know that he was wrong; that we all were." Her mood brightening, Melanie patted the journal. "You know, maybe this is just the boost he needs to forgive and forget, to move on—to pick himself up and start living his own life instead of dad's for a change. Believe me, Michelle, when I say that this, too, is the best news imaginable. Thank you so much for sharing this with me."

"I wish I'd picked up on it before. I certainly would have told you."

"I know you would have," Melanie reassured her, stroking the threadbare cover.

"Tell me this, then," Michelle challenged, "is it possible that Garret's problems started *before* the conflict between Brad and your father?"

Melanie extended a halting look. "I don't see how. Why?"

Michelle said nothing. She didn't have to.

"You're bursting to tell me something. *Out with it!*" Melanie implored, with a return of that effervescence of hers.

Michelle did her best to match Melanie's enthusiasm. "I am! I've been dying to show you this as well for weeks now. I would have called you, only it's something that needs to be shared in person." This time Michelle did the honors and reached behind the seat to retrieve a three-ring binder from her daypack. She handed it to Melanie, who placed it on her lap beneath the journal. "I could be wrong," Michelle cautioned, "but I think Garret responded in the only way he knew how to. How old were both of you when his troubles started, three? Four?"

"Something like that."

"Perhaps the breaking of things, his tantrums, the lashing out—violent as it may have been—was his way of saying '*Hey!* I don't like what's going on with daddy and my big brother,' or maybe, 'this is scaring me,' only it backfired. Everything went terribly wrong when his call for attention was turned onto him."

"Mmmm," Melanie hummed. "I'm not sure what you're getting at."

"That it was he who'd acted out, only it wasn't him, not the Garret you knew—or thought you knew. Does this help?"

"I think so. Wait! Dad didn't hurt him did he?" Melanie answered in a panic.

"Heavens no!" Michelle apologized for the misunderstanding. "I didn't mean it that way, Mel. I found nothing in any of Garret's journals to suggest that your father hurt him physically in any way. To the contrary, I think he might have *said* something instead, something to you all—inadvertently mind you—that might explain everything."

Melanie was chewing on this when the reason behind Michelle's beating around the bush, and her questions and interest in Kerry's career crystallized. She felt so dumb. Putting the journal aside, she picked up the binder and said with profound surprise, "Tell me you

Rick Ley

found something suggesting that Garret had dissociative identity disorder?"

"I think I might've," Michelle was excited to share. "I think Garret experienced something so powerful when he was very young that *it* manifested whenever he became overly emotional, like when your father's aggression toward Brad became unbearable."

"*It?*" Melanie questioned, looking from the binder to the journal she just stuck between the seats.

"There are many entries in Garret's journals suggesting that even at a very young age, he knew that there was something wrong with him. He alternately describes the Scary Man and John Parker as friend or foe, depending on the situation. He describes them as coercive elements in his life."

Melanie recoiled at the irrepressible chill that made her shiver in spite of the day's heat. "They were just characters in a story—the legend," she managed, stumbling over her words in false denial.

"But what if they weren't?" Michelle speculated. "What if these entities were much more than that? The more I read through his entries, the more convinced I am that they were very real to him—real to the point that the characters had become a part of him, buried in his subconscious, awaiting the appropriate time to emerge."

Melanie fought off a wave of nausea. "You didn't make them up in *Ghost Creek*?"

"No. The legend and its characters are based on fact—fact in the sense of what has been passed down through time. We probably will never know how much of the story was based on truth. I wasn't sure how everything tied together until you mentioned Kerry's specialty. It…" Michelle let her statement hang in the air for effect; "all makes sense now, considering what I have in there." Michelle pointed to the binder. "DID *could* explain everything. What if Garret had alter egos, or whatever they call them?"

"Identities," Melanie answered. "Kerry says they're called identities, or dissociated personality states. You think it was an alternate identity in Garret's mind—one of the characters from the Ghost Creek legend—that performed those terrible things?'

"Yes, that's exactly what I'm saying. Just like Kerry's patient whose dissociated personality committed murder."

"But how? You said that the first time the two of you heard of the legend was in college, at a fraternity party."

"Again, what if it wasn't?" Michelle placed a hand on the binder on Melanie's lap, and, with a satisfied smile, asked her to look inside.

The sound of an approaching siren made them jump. Melanie whipped about. Michelle jerked her head to look into the rear-view mirror. A squad car blew past. "Whew!" They said in unison, thankful that they weren't the objects of the officer's attention. "How fast was he going?" Melanie asked. The squad car was already a gray smudge in the heat ripples ahead. Michelle did a double take. She was doing eighty-five. "Well over a hundred, has to be." Rolling along, they giggled about what might have happened had they gotten pulled over. Ahead, the reason for the high-speed pursuit was revealed in the form of a bright yellow sports car that had been pulled over. "I never saw him pass us," Melanie commented. Michelle shrugged.

Getting back to business, Melanie opened the binder. "What am I looking for? Oh, wow!" she reacted with a start to the collection of documents tucked neatly into separate plastic sleeves inside. Some were news clippings, while others were notebook pages with Garret's writing on them. Still others were crib sheets written in Michelle's hand, summarizing the telephone calls she'd made. There was even Melanie's last letter to Garret. "He saved this?" she said, stunned in the happiest possible way. "You collected all this? It's all about Garret?"

"Yes," Michelle said proudly. "It's my research notes from when I wrote *Ghost Creek*, along with a bunch of newer stuff I found while researching this project. I thought I'd done a thorough job investigating that first book. I read Garret's journals, spoke with I don't know how many people, got copies of whatever was published in the local newspapers. Boy was I wrong!"

"What did you do differently this time around?"

"What else? The Internet," Michelle replied, admitting to the cyber equivalent to John Henry's steam-drill nemesis.

"You Googled it?"

"I did, and voila! There was a lot, actually, much more out there on the subject than I ever imagined. What'd happened back in 1988 made national news. Most of the printouts toward the back of the binder are various newspaper accounts. It took a bit of digging to get everything because many Internet hits only provided a summary or partial article. Suffice it to say, I had to buy a lot of newsprint."

"You mean archived newspapers aren't public domain?"

"They are, and some are free, though most come with a fee of some sort."

"I guess that makes sense." Melanie paged through the sleeves. She whistled. The newspaper mastheads spanned the continent from North Carolina to Washington state and Hawaii. Melanie found funny the thought of a steady stream of paperboys with out-of-state plates on their bicycles littering Michelle's driveway with newsprint each morning.

"What I didn't expect to find was accounts of the Ghost Creek legend dating to the 1930s. And some of those were reprints from even older mining-company-related newspapers from the 1800's. That got me thinking. I did a little checking into the U.P.'s mining history and found something." She asked that Melanie turn to the last sleeve.

Inside, Melanie found a packet of copy paper stapled together and folded in half. "What do we have here?" she dramatized, as if opening a present she feigned not to be expecting, her fingers trembling as she first removed and then unfolded the print-out.

Michelle smiled when Melanie drew a deep breath. It was a copy of *The Porphyry*; the tag line read: *"Bringing You Mining News From Keeweenaw's Copper Country Since 1837."*

Melanie tore through the pages like a mad woman until she found what she was looking for: *Tales from the Dutchman*, an entertaining column about mining folklore. "The Dutchman! I haven't thought about this since I was a little girl."

"Thought so!" Michelle laughed. Still, Melanie didn't seem to get that there might be something relevant about this particular copy, the Dutchman column in particular. "I had to look up the meaning of the name of the newspaper. It's some kind of rock that they mine for copper."

"Uh-huh," Melanie offered in vague recognition. She wasn't listening. Curiosity drove her to continue flipping through the copy pages. She stopped when she reached a spread of advertisements that brought back a flood of nostalgic memories. Above an ad for the latest in state-of-the-art washer and dryer technology was a feature article about the discovery of an overlooked vein of high-grade copper extending beneath Lake Superior that promised to revitalize the industry.

"Ah, Mel? The Dutchman?"

Melanie lolled her head with "stupid me" daffiness. She turned back to the Dutchman column and recited with fond remembrance how she used to sink into the crook of her father's arm when he read each new macabre account. Reliving the distant echo of her father's showman's panache for the dramatic, Melanie read the columnist's words out loud, until she reached the subject of this latest installment…when her mouth fell agape:

"This week the Dutchman takes us to the windswept slopes of Breckenridge, Colorado where over 400 years ago an Indian…"

"Look at the date," Michelle urged. The article was dated Thursday, March 9, 1967.

After a pause to scan the article, Melanie stammered, "It's your story!" Fluttering her hands about, she continued, saying, "You know what I mean…the Ghost Creek legend." Hesitation, blinking, comprehension settling in. "I must have heard it before. This means—"

"That Garret did, too."

Melanie took to fidgeting. "We were only three. You think that hearing this story led to what Garret did?"

"In a manner of speaking. As a coping mechanism, yes," Michelle contended. "Bear with me on this. I think the story made a powerful impression on Garret. According to Nick, he always had a fascination with the supernatural."

"Like bigfoot."

"Yeah, like bigfoot," Michelle said, to which they couldn't avoid sharing a laugh. "If that's so, then it's not much of a leap to reason that he could have been taken in by the Ghost Creek tale as well. Along the way, he's tormented by what's happening between your dad and older brother, and somehow, for some reason, Garret's mind adopts the creature he calls the Scary Man from the legend as an alternate identity."

"But why him...*It*?" Melanie pleaded. She continued reading the article.

"Comfort maybe? Perhaps as a protective barrier or some excuse for his acting out on Brad's behalf. I don't know. Garret doesn't explain why—Perhaps he never knew why, exactly."

Melanie thought this made sense. "Who's Jack Parsons, then?" she asked, referring to an unfamiliar character in the Dutchman article not included in Michelle's book.

"He's John Parker. I've also seen the character called Jim Perkins and John Parry. I used Parker because it was the name used in the only sources I had to work with when I was writing *Ghost Creek*. I believe Garret's mind took on John Parker as an alternative identity to compensate for everything that was bad about the Scary Man. Parker's carefree lifestyle offered Garret's mind an alternate place of escape. In his journals, Garret explains Parker as the imaginary friend he leaned on for advice and protection when the Scary Man identity became unbearable."

"Fascinating."

"You sound like Nick! That's something he would say." Michelle twirled a finger in her hair. "The shame of it all," she said sadly, "is the strength it must have taken him to control his alternate identities. Garret mentions in a number places his struggle to keep them reined in. To think that he was shouldering all of this, and we didn't know it."

Melanie broke the heavy reflection that followed by asking if Michelle thought Garret was a good person.

Michelle found it refreshingly easy to say that she did. "He did terrible things, don't get me wrong. But I'm convinced that life as it unfolded when you all were very young created the demons that haunted him to the end. Garret all but says that he did the Scary Man's bidding because he *was* the Scary Man. Some of his later journal entries reveal that he was confused about who he was when certain events occurred, and like I just mentioned, he was aware of his alternate identities. Therefore, I think Garret was a tortured soul with a serious medical condition that went undiagnosed. This I am sure of."

Melanie found Michelle's analysis insightful. "And the end, the last stage of his illness, it manifested itself on the Sudbury trip?"

Michelle fought the urge to cry. "I think it did. There was something about that crystal that set him off." She scratched vacantly for the pendant she no longer wore around her neck. John Parker, she explained, sold his soul to find the gold buried in the hills of the Ghost Creek valley. "Garret did, too, in his search for the crystal's source. And then there was that night at the frat party, a later lecture by one of his professors about abandoned mines, the allure of finding one's own mine at field camp. It was all too much for him."

—————

They crossed the Centennial State line with hearts uplifted in the shared belief that Garret Sutton was not a monster. Michelle declared her former boyfriend an unfortunate victim of circumstances. Melanie, in her own right, was comforted by the realization that her brother's actions were ultimately beyond his control.

Michelle promised that soon the rest of the world would know that Garret had not only loved his sister, he had stuck up for his big brother and fought his affliction to the bitter end, until he had no will left to give.

Melanie amended her comment of the day before and pronounced her life now definitely complete—unless Michelle had something even more profound to share. Michelle said that she didn't and put the matter to rest by pronouncing that this was the *real* Ghost Creek story. What more could they possibly learn in Colorado?

A strange vibration touched off a brief scare that they'd suffered a flat. Not to worry, it was only a rough patch of road that just as soon passed, returning them to the same trouble-free glide to which they'd become accustomed. The perturbation did have the benefit of pressing the reset button on their conversation to a lively discussion of fun anecdotes that Michelle was all too glad to relive from her field-camp days. She interspersed her tall tales with a rundown of all the places she wanted to show Melanie, Satan's Lair—the serpentine stack of granite boulders at the confluence of Ghost Creek and the Blue River—in particular. "Legend has it," Michelle warned, "that Satan serves as guardian to the Sacred Lands located farther upslope, past the former field station. The stones are really creepy."

Melanie also enjoyed listening to Michelle's excited retelling of the Ute prophet Badger Heart's murder at the hands of Coronado and his men, which gave rise to the legend. "I have a confession," Melanie announced when Michelle had finished. "I don't mean to be a kill joy, but I've been having nightmares about Garret ever since we firmed up our plans." When Michelle remained silent, Melanie asked, "Do you think it's possible that I might be having some kind of flashbacks because of the Ghost Creek legend we heard from the Dutchman story when I was a kid?"

Isn't that something? Michelle wondered. Melanie was thinking about the same question she had been asking herself. "I've been having nightmares, too," Michelle admitted, finding solace in the knowledge that she was not alone. "They started—"

A ding. They reached for their phones.

"Not mine," Melanie said.

"Must be me, then," Michelle said cheerily. "Would you mind checking?"

"Of course," Melanie said, grabbing Michelle's phone from a drink holder.

Michelle pushed her hands against the steering wheel and stretched her shoulders. "Anything?"

"Ah, Michelle?"

"Don't tell me something's fallen through," Michelle said with concern that some last minute legal wrangling had derailed their plans. *Wouldn't they have called instead?* "What is it?" Michelle asked, resigning herself to the fact that the news was going to be bad.

"It's not that." With apprehension in her voice, Melanie informed her that it was another email from *HikerChic*.

Michelle froze. It had been a week since she received her last communiqué from her virtual pen pal.

"Michelle?"

"Read it!"

Melanie did, her voice shaking. The message, composed in capital letters and italicized for effect, read:

STOP AVOIDING ME!! THEY WIL—

"Will what?" Michelle demanded with a matching tremor.

"What do you think?" Melanie replied sarcastically. "She must have been interrupted. Here, look."

Melanie turned the phone for Michelle to see. Michelle frowned. "Yeah, but who are *they*?" she said with a hollowness that underscored the implication of the final two words of Jodi's message. There was no mistaking that a malevolent undercurrent was still swirling about the Conservancy, the mines, the Sacred Lands. The curse of Coronado was alive and well.

"It's a threat," Melanie said, not liking to be toyed with.

Exasperated, Michelle said, "That's it! I have to call Connor and tell him we're not going through with this. I should have informed him from the get go. This is ridiculous."

"*No!*" Melanie insisted. "You should call him, but I want to put an end to this as much as you do," and with that she placed her phone to her ear.

"Who are you calling?"

"My sister. Kerry will know what to do."

O'Reilly, Kreider, Ftorek & Gare, Attorneys at Law
Broad Street, Charleston, S.C.
3:07 P.M.

"You about ready?"

Nick glanced at his computer. "Jeez! You're right," he gasped, looking at the time. "Where'd the afternoon go?" Chris was right. He'd better get his ass in gear. At least they were only going several blocks farther down the Murderer's Row of legal firms along Broad Street to meet with Athens and their attorneys. Nick made a last pass through the dozen copies of the exhibit packet he'd prepared and whisked out of the building to catch up with Chris and the others on the street below.

Nick was in high spirits. Yesterday's findings clearly demonstrated environmental malfeasance by those evildoers north of the PSTRE border. All other nagging details aside, like explaining that persnickety water-level abnormality, were small potatoes in light of finding contaminant encroachment from Athens. The science was sound, their kung fu strong.

They had capped off the day before over brisket and beer at the Southend Brewery & Smokehouse on Bay Street, in the city's French Quarter, where he and Chris spent PSTRE's money discussing how Smitty and Brant might present their bombshell at the forthcoming meeting. For fun as much as usefulness, they conducted a point-counter-point of the questions Athens might try to undermine the credibility of their findings. Not one to regard others' personal time when there was work to be done, Chris had no qualms with calling Jay Watkins at home to confirm RCE's adherence to proper sample-collection procedures. Watkins put himself back on the clock after the third call and joined them at the pub. Watkins's input and barrel-full-of-monkeys personality added much to what turned out to be an enjoyable and productive evening. Chris was satisfied with the thoroughness of their preparation. His only concern was the growing list of figures and tables that had yet to be properly QA'd before distribution at the meeting. This was Nick and Jay's charge.

RCE completed its part of the assignment by mid-morning, when Nick received the first of several emails from Watkins. Jay and his peeps had been busy, Nick mused, upon seeing the fresh stack of lithologic logs resting on the printer tray. The batch, all scrubbed through for consistency and looking pretty, even included the logs for the dozen borings they completed yesterday. By the time he finished clicking the print button, Nick was also the proud owner of a hot-off-the-presses collection of piezometer-well construction diagrams, a GIS-rendered copy of the generalized groundwater-flow map he took with him to the site, and a small stack of computer-prepared groundwater-flow maps. Excited by his own findings, Nick asked RCE to up their game and work up a corroborating map for each of the five times he had selected to bridge Thursday's tidal cycle.

Nick took his haul back to his desk to sort. "Ah-ha!" he congratulated himself when he compared the flow maps. Man and machine had worked independently to achieve the same result once again: groundwater in the vicinity of PSTRE and Athens flows north to south with an east-west swing imparted by the tides. Red pen in hand, Nick made a few last modifications to his generalized map for clarification purposes and fired off a scan copy of his doodling to buddy Jay—yes, after last night he was now just Jay—for his thoughts. Jay then handed the mock-up off to Brandon Butler to perform his magic. Butler scaled back the opacity on the finished product so that only the salient points stood out.

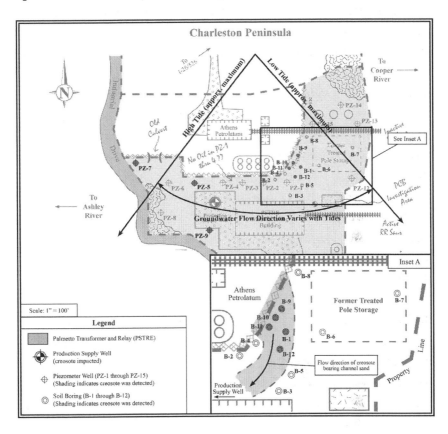

A flashing icon announced the arrival of another email from Jay. It was the results for the fingerprint analysis of the product sample collected from the production well. At long last, the answer to that all-important question: *what is it?*

Nick skimmed the data package and Jay's read on the results. "Creosote confirmed!" was Jay's opening line. Jay said that he consulted with the laboratory manager and Sam Piersall, and that they all agree that the findings were consistent with coal-tar creosote, based on the high concentrations of polycyclic aromatic hydrocarbons, or PAHs, in the sample. The chemical fingerprint was far more complex than that of the heavy oils commonly used for heating or industrial purposes.

This was fantastic news. Everything was coming together perfectly. Their defense was bordering on bulletproof. Nick stood to take a victory lap around the office and inform Chris, only to be confronted by the dumbfounding question of what *is* creosote? He would be remiss not to know what it was, exactly, considering the nature of their case. Beyond his understanding that there were two types and that the sweet smelling gunk was used to preserve utility poles against infestation and rot, he knew next to nothing about it. This was the first project in all his years as an environmental consultant where creosote was the principal contaminant of concern.

Nick returned to his desk and typed *creosote* into the computer search engine. Coal-tar creosote, he learned, is comprised of a complex assemblage of up to several thousand compounds, and mostly PAHs like naphthalene, phenanthrene, 2-methylnaphthalene, fluoranthene, acenapthene, and phenanthrene; compounds derived from the high-pressure carbonization of bituminous coal. These same compounds are also common in oil, which makes sense considering that coal and oil are ultimately derived from the decay of ancient plant material. Important to the identification of coal-tar creosote is the phenol content, which is generally less than one percent by volume. By contrast, wood-tar creosote, the Internet source explained, is comprised of between eighty and ninety percent phenolic and cresol compounds. The practical uses for and chemistry of wood-tar creosote were also inconsistent with the sample results and operational history of PSTRE and Athens. Wood-tar creosote is the soot that lines chimneys and the antiseptic in smoke used to cure meat. Nick was amused by the thought that the bag of jerky tucked away in his computer satchel was creosote-cured beef.

So, coal-tar creosote it is.

There was something else pertinent in Jay's email that he'd glossed over. The sample did not contain pentachlorophenol, or

PCP, which became the preferred alternative to creosote after 1950. "Holy shit!" The creosote sample submitted for analysis was that of a long obsolete product, the only reasonable source for which was contained in the three relict tanks that probably hadn't been opened in ninety years. "Gotcha!" Nick said, murmuring Jay's tag line. These pieces of timely new information also exonerated PSTRE of sabotage.

Nick called Jay to hash over the product-analysis data. He bounced several last questions off him for concurrence purposes, the most important being the reasonableness of their argument that residual creosote had found its way into the production well via a shallow breach in the steel casing and surrounding grout seal. Nick was certain Athens's consultant would jump all over this. "No worries," Jay said, allaying his concern. "If the casing is damaged, it would have happened near ground surface. Happens all the time on busy industrial sites with heavy equipment moving around, you know that. It's nothing we can't confirm with a little downhole-camera work. Besides," Jay then reminded him before signing off, "I seriously doubt that will come up. I think Athens has bigger problems to worry about, don't you?"

Nick thanked Jay and told him that he had better get a move on if was going to be ready in time for the meeting.

Nick followed at a short distance. His senses told him something was amiss. Smitty and Brant were engrossed in a tension-fraught huddle with Bill Carlyle, whose unexpected presence gave Nick pause for concern. Also odd, Chris was not included in their conversation. Nick flagged him down. "What'd I miss?" Nick asked.

"Merrill tried playing hardball. He wasn't going to show up," Chris replied.

"He is coming, right?"

"Yes," Chris said. "Reluctantly. Cole, Merrill's new lackey, said that he'd make sure Merrill would be there."

They followed the M&C team across Church Street to the following block.

"This apparently has been brewing for several days. Carlyle's pissed, which is why he's here," Chris said between breaths.

"I see," Nick said, his concerns put to ease.

Chris stopped short. "So you know, Bill's not fully up to speed yet with what we got. That's why Smitty's going to lead. Brant and I will follow. Bill's only here for extra insurance."

"Thanks for the intel."

"No problem. Bill also wants to make sure that Merrill, the obstinate sonofobitch, doesn't add fuel to the fire. Come on, let's rock Athens's lobster."

"The B-52's? Nice!" Nick quipped, impressed with Chris's timely reference to the *Athens*, Georgia-based band. "How long have you been saving that one up?" ·

They walked through the doors of O'Reilly, Kreider, Ftorek & Gare at precisely five minutes of three. Inside, they were greeted by a paralegal named Claire Underwood and a younger man who, Nick gathered, was an intern. "If any of you need a restroom, they're that way down the hall." Underwood pointed to their left. "If there's anything else you need, like to make copies, stationary, or to place a private call, Henry will show you the way. No?" she said when there were no takers. "Very well then, please follow me."

Ms. Underwood led them up a winding staircase every bit as grand as M&C's. Nick, relishing the thought of having no specific duties at the meeting, allowed his mind to drift. He found himself somehow standing just behind Ms. Underwood at the head of the line. Realizing his blunder, Nick slunk his way back to his proper place in the pecking order. The others were fortunately too preoccupied with their surroundings to take notice. A gracious Ms. Underwood instructed them to wait near the second-floor landing until she was assured that the conference room was ready and that Ted Carlson, Athens's lead counsel, was notified of their arrival.

A tall, impeccably dressed man strode in from one of the closer conference rooms.

"Ted, a pleasure to see you again," Bill Carlyle announced. They met with a genteel hand over forearm handshake reminiscent of Tom Cruise meets Kevin Bacon in *A Few Good Men*. Nick fought the urge to laugh at the thought of them challenging one another to a game of one-on-one when the meeting was over.

"I take it you had no trouble finding us?" Carlson asked, demonstrating his humorous side. "Smitty, Brant, a pleasure as always." Carlson then greeted Chis and Nick in turn.

So far so good, Nick thought. Chris appeared to think so, too.

A commotion coming from the direction of the bank of conference rooms caught their attention. It was Claire Underwood. She was struggling to manage an armful of empty water bottles and beverage cans left over from a previous meeting. "I'm sorry Mr. Carlson, this was supposed to have been cleaned up."

"No problem, Claire. "We're in no particular hurry."

There was no mistaking the bobcat glare she flashed at poor Henry. Nick couldn't help but feel sorry for the kid. Derelict in his duties, Henry withered like a plant doused with weed killer.

"Sucks to be him," Chris whispered over his shoulder.

"Since we're both still waiting on a few people, what do you say that everyone make themselves comfortable." Carlson led them to a lounge area. "I trust there are plenty of refreshments to go around?" Henry was on the ball this time. "Very good. Bill, a moment?"

They broke off into small groups. Claire Underwood soon returned to say that the conference room was ready. Chris recommended that Nick go on ahead and pass out the exhibit packets.

"Will do," Nick acknowledged.

"Tell you what," Chris called after him when Nick started to leave. "I need to talk to Brant and Smitty about something. Can I bring you any refreshments? It's on their dime!" he said with a sly smirk.

"Sure," Nick remarked with a matching chortle. "Grab me a water and one of those pastry things over there," and slipped out of the lounge.

Nick took a seat at the far end of the conference table near a window with a commanding view of the street below. Might as well make the best of it. *Damn comfortable chair*, he commented to himself. Nick retrieved the dozen exhibit packets from his satchel. Admiring the high gloss finished cypress table and yellow pine paneling he wondered if all the legal firms in Charleston shopped at the same place.

Nick passed out the exhibits, stopping when he reached the chairs he assumed Stan Merrill and Athens's counsel would take to thumb through their copies one last time to make sure that all of the pages were in order. He kept an ear tuned to the mumblings going on in the hall to gage the weather there. Chris was talking softly with Smitty and occasionally to Brant, the trio having migrated to near the doorway. Beyond, Bill Carlyle was engaged in a lively conversation with Ted Carlson. Nick thought that he heard them share a laugh. *Good!* Everything was going as planned.

His cell phone made an angry buzzing sound in his pocket. Nick jumped. He remembered to switch his phone to vibrate, but not to turn down the volume. It was Michelle. Melanie must be driving, he thought. Nick read Michelle's message and chuckled. *Remember Kansas?* the text read, followed by a winking emoji. The message stirred a painful, fond remembrance of his failure to drive all the way from Lawrence to Denver—so much for best intentions. "Man, what a miserably hot afternoon that was," Nick texted back, glad to see that they were enjoying themselves at his expense. He then added that the meeting was about to start.

A change in tone and tempo of the goings on in the hall interrupted his reflection on days past. An older, grumping man—Stan Merrill, no doubt—was occupying the attention of the PSTRE contingent, which now included a tall man attempting to cajole him—likely Hal Cole—and, to his surprise, Gerry Dawson. Along the far wall, between the lounge and second floor landing, Ted Carlson was greeting two unfamiliar faces that Nick supposed was the balance of Team Athens.

"Nick! Come and let me introduce you to a few people," Bill Carlyle shouted over the nonsense, taking control. The attention now shifted to him, Nick stopped what he was doing and stepped into the hall.

"Stan, this is Nick Kozlowski, Chris's geologist confidante I told you about. Nick, Stan Merrill." They shook hands. Carlyle then introduced him to Hal Cole, and Athens's consultant, Jim Cresson. Nick was left to make his own reacquaintance with the PSTRE superintendent, who responded to the snub with a dissatisfied grunt. The remaining unknown face was still in discussion with Carlson along the far wall.

They filed into the room. Dawson sat beside Nick. Jim Cresson sat to Dawson's left, and Chris to Nick's right. Gerry Dawson inadvertently grabbed the exhibit package that was meant for Cresson. Nick obliged Cresson by handing him a copy from the pile of extras. The Athens consultant thanked him and Nick sat back down. "Why's he here?" Nick whispered in Chris's ear, referring to Dawson.

"Tell you later." Chris nodded toward the head of the table, where Ted Carlson was observing his audience for the appropriate moment to start the meeting.

"Gentlemen, let's say we get started," Carlson announced when the chatter settled. "And may I introduce some of you to Mike Dodd. Mike is the president and CEO, and Mr. Merrill's counterpart at Athens."

Nick, as did Chris, watched closely the interaction between Cole and Merrill. Cole, a big man of Carlyle's stature, was patting the withered frame of Stan Merrill. The rigidity of Merrill's posture suggested that he was anything but settled.

"I think we all know why we are here today," Carlson began.

"I'll tell you why we're here," Merrill griped. "It's those sonsob—"

"Stan!" Carlyle silenced Merrill with a stern command.

"What I think Stan meant to say," Cole intervened, "is what are you and your client planning to do to rectify our little problem?" Cole spoke for the PSTRE patriarch in a sugary manner that verged on the embarrassing.

"That's what we're here to talk about," Carlson answered evenly. "In a civilized and professional manner. Mr. Merrill?"

Stan Merrill pushed himself away from the table. He crossed his arms, scowling like a petulant child.

Nick observed a smug Mike Dodd delighting in Merrill's discontent.

"Dodd's an old-guard family member at Athens," Chris whispered.

Nick lifted his head in acknowledgement. Odd, Cole had a similar expression on his face. Beside him, Chris was compiling a running list of adjectives to describe the attitude and mannerisms of Cole and Merrill, along with the Athens attendees.

"May we proceed?" Carlson asked.

"Yes, of course," Carlyle answered before Cole or Merrill could open their mouths.

"Very well. We understand that oil was found in a well on PSTRE's property?" Carlson directed the question at Carlyle.

"That's correct."

"And this occurred about a month ago?"

Carlyle deferred the answer to Smitty.

Smitty cleared his throat. "That is also correct, Mr. Carlson. Creosote, not oil. We have the analytical results here." Smitty pointed to a clipped copy of the data in front of him. Brant raised his pen in agreement.

This news teased a subtle rise out of Dodd and Carlson. "Creosote you say," Carlson responded, making a note on his legal pad. "Now, this well, a production well I understand, its located behind PSTRE's shop. Was the well tampered with?"

"No!" Merrill growled.

"And you know this how?"

Merrill and Cole both looked across the table to Gerry Dawson. Dawson fidgeted with his fingertips. "It was locked when I was asked to find it."

"Who asked you to find it?" Carlson probed still deeper.

"He did," Dawson said with indifference, jabbing a thumb in Cole's direction.

"I see," Carlson said, making more notes. "Creosote is a readily obtainable product. How do we know that someone, a disgruntled PSTRE employee perhaps, didn't pour some creosote down the well and reseal it? Tell me, Mr. Dawson, what was the condition of the ground when you found it? Perhaps there was material spilled on the ground, at the well?"

Dawson shrugged. "Not that I recall."

Carlson made several notes. "Fine." Turning to Merrill and Cole, Carlson then asked evenly, "If this well was that important, it goes without saying that PSTRE should already know where it is. Why did Mr. Dawson have to go looking for it?"

At that, Merrill lurched forward, sneering at Dodd. "You bastards contaminated my well! You know I need that well—"

"*Enough!*" Carlyle demanded. "Stan, you've been warned. Hal, please take Mr. Merrill outside."

They watched Cole escort an agitated Stan Merrill from the room.

"You made me be here in the first place!" Merrill grumbled back as Hal Cole ushered him through the doorway. "PSTRE did nothing wrong. *They* did!"

With Merrill gone, silence filled the room. Nick found the exchange revealing. Now he understood the reason for Gerry Dawson's presence. He was nominated as PSTRE's de facto representative until Bill Carlyle weighed in. Nick wasn't surprised to find Chris, the muckraker that he was, enjoying every moment.

Bill Carlyle spoke. "Ted, we both know why we're here, so if you don't want this meeting spiraling out of control at every turn, I recommend sticking to the point and asking what proof we have, and you explaining how Athens is not responsible for the contamination in PSTRE's well. And another thing," he said, shifting his beefy frame to make certain Cole and Merrill were out of earshot, "I insist that you call off your surveillance. Do I make myself clear?"

Carlson was dumbfounded. Mike Dodd also appeared to be caught off guard.

"*They don't know!*" Chis whispered into Nick's ear.

"*Who then?*" Nick whispered back.

Chris shrugged.

Nick glimpsed at Chris's legal pad. Beneath the underscored *Doesn't Know*, which he was idly circling with his pen, the list of adjectives used to describe Cole was growing: *Gladhander, Mollifier,* and *Slimy*. This was interesting because Nick was thinking much the same. Hal Cole gave the appearance of one of those overly kind, insincere management types that corporate peons loved to hate. As for Merrill, Chris described him as *Disruptive, Disinterested, JA,* Chris's pet acronym for jackass. Nick stifled a laugh.

"I know nothing of this," Dodd responded to Carlson's demanding glare.

Nick watched Chris scribble *Sincere* beneath Dodd's name.

"Who was followed? Since when?" Carlson asked.

Chris raised his hand and waved his pen back and forth between he and Nick. "Last Friday," Chis said. Nick concurred and they proceeded to provide witness to the various times, places, and the types and colors of the cars used by the surveillance tail. The common thread between each observation was the description of the two men: one a large African American male and the other a Caucasian male of medium build with light-colored hair.

"You will look into this?" Carlyle demanded.

"Of course," Carlson promised. Dodd added that the description for either man didn't necessarily pertain to any of his employees, the large black man in particular. Continuing, Carlson promised that M&C would be the first to know of any improprieties conducted by Athens or anyone connected with his law firm.

Carlyle sounded his approval.

Carlson followed his promise with a telling remark, "As you will soon find out, we have no need to be following your people around."

"Uh-Oh!" Nick mumbled. *Missed Something!* Chris wrote, and then underscored and circled on his tablet. Even Gerry Dawson was roused from his torpor.

Carlyle pursed his lips, gave his counterpart a long, penetrating stare. "We'll be interested to hear what you have to say."

"What d'you think they know?" Nick whispered.

Cocking his head in Nick's direction, Chris said, *"I wish I knew."*

The meeting resumed after Hal Cole escorted an arguably subdued Stan Merrill back into the conference room. Cole promised that there would be no further outbursts. Carlson respected Bill Carlyle's wishes and focused his questions on RCE's findings. Oddly for a technical discussion, it was the lawyers who did most of the talking. Carlson and the M&C boys exchanging compliments and gripes over the relevance of the findings presented in the exhibit packet. Curious as this was, Nick hoped that their volleying would soon lead somewhere. It had better because Stan Merrill was tiring of the techno babble and started to fidget. Nick didn't have to know the man to know the type. A mental implosion was imminent.

"I don't understand," Jim Cresson, Athens's consultant, interrupted. "What's not understood? We explained that Athens never housed creosote in the tank farm, or elsewhere on the property. How then do you consider Athens to be the impact source?"

This was a dubious comment at best, Nick thought. Cresson should have been more concerned with the validity of his client's assertion that Athens was innocent. Something didn't add up. Chris's restless shifting told him that Chris was eager to challenge Cresson's assertion.

Chris had no sooner called out Cresson's name when Brant overode him. "We've traced fugitive creosote residuals coming from your property onto PSTRE's," Brant said, tossing his copy of Nick's mock-up in Cresson's direction. Looking from Cresson to Carlson, Brant warned, "How much do you want to bet that when we analyze the product found in yesterday's borings the results will be a match for the substance found in PSTRE's well?"

Nick's throat tightened. Even Chris had a look of surprise. The proceedings were heating up more rapidly than either of them had expected.

Cresson scrutinized his copy of Nick's work, pushed it aside, then said haughtily, "Surely, you must know that PSTRE stored both treated logs and creosote raw stock on *its* property."

Brant picked the diagram back up. He looked at it briefly, flicked a finger against it, and gave a snort.

Cresson took the bait. "I didn't realize that I said something funny?"

"Mr. Cresson," Brant said slowly, "you apparently fail to see that we've done a lot of poking around and have found no evidence of a historical release anywhere near the pole-storage area, or in the vicinity of the rail spur where virgin material was once received. May I also remind you—*again*—that creosote operations were *never* performed on PSTRE property, and that Athens was relocated from Georgia to continue with its former business practice—*the creosote treatment of logs*—on property sold to it by PSTRE. Our work demonstrates quite convincingly that creosote contamination extends from your client's property onto PSTRE. To quote your own words, 'what's not understood,' Mr. Cresson?" Three chairs to Brant's right, Stan Merrill couldn't resist the temptation to spout a devilish guffaw of approval.

Cresson remained unfazed. On the contrary, he glared back with a patronizing smile.

"You've got something different to offer?" Brant asked, annoyingly picking at his thumb.

Nick had a bad feeling about where this was going. So did Chris.

"How can you not know?" Cresson questioned, spreading his hands in disbelief. He looked to Dodd and Carlson for their approval to continue.

"Indulge us," Carlson urged.

Rick Ley

"I'm at a total loss," Cresson said with feigned shock.

Chris tapped the end of his pen against his tablet.

Nick followed the pen to its cap where Chris had written: *They're scripting this!!*

"What are you driving at?" Smitty snapped, speaking for the first time in minutes.

"How can Mr. Merrill not know that Athens never performed creosote operations on *its* property?"

The subtle inflection and personal accusation was cause for confusion. Nick looked to Chris, as Brant and Smitty did to Bill Carlyle. Everyone from the Athens contingent to Hal Cole then turned to Stan Merrill who, bristling with anger, leapt his withered frame from his chair.

"Stan! Let us handle this," Carlyle warned. Cole settled him back into his seat.

"That's bullshit," Merrill erupted, itching for a fight. "Dodd you conniving sonofobitch. You goddamn well know that slipshod operation of yours contaminated my well!"

"Whoa!" Dodd recoiled, exposing his palms as if warding off a rabid dog. "We did no such thing."

Nick watched the debacle unfold with mounting trepidation. They were missing something. Next to him, Chris was speaking with a rapid whisper into Brant's ear. Only Hal Cole appeared amused by the tension. *Why?* Cole stands to lose a small fortune in the India venture if this meeting, their case, goes badly...*Or does he??*

Merrill threw his arms up in disgust. "If you didn't, who the hell did?" he shouted.

"You did, you ignorant ass. PSTRE did!" Dodd was only too pleased to announce.

All hell broke loose: the meeting devolved into chaos. Dumbfounded, Nick was rendered helpless. His skin prickled. The only thing certain was that the problem had to come down to their understanding of the property history. Chris just so happened to be sharing the same concern with Brant. Beyond them, Smitty was attempting to calm a suddenly furious Bill Carlyle, who was simultaneously trying to quiet Merrill before he said something they would regret, while insisting that Carlson explain the ambush. Around the horn, Mike Dodd and Jim Cresson watched with amusement; and to his left, Nick saw that Gerry Dawson appeared as if he could give a shit.

"That will be enough, gentlemen." Carlson spoke over the clamor. He brought the meeting to a head when the room fell silent. "Mr. Merrill, I find it regrettable that you do not have an understanding of what happened on your property—*all of your properties*—in the past."

Stan Merrill glowered at Carlson. He was literally shaking. Hal Cole resumed his shoulder patting.

"Whatever are you talking about?" Cole responded on the old man's behalf. "Stan, here, has been associated with PSTRE since he was old enough to work. He has made it his mission to ensure that everything performed under his watch was done with best intentions to meet industry standard practices and all environmental regulations, as they exist."

"Be that as it may," Carlson conceded, speaking past Cole to Merrill, "you still are responsible for the sins of your forefathers." Then reading from a sheet of paper he retrieved from his briefcase, said, "Mr. Merrill. We therefore expect PSTRE to: 'make full monetary reconciliation to Athens and the Dodd family for environmental damages incurred to Athens's property from the historical release of creosote from a former PSTRE property, when said former property was used by Athens, under PSTRE direction, for the preservation treatment of wood logs in support of the communications industry.'" Carlson slipped the sheet back inside the folder. "Furthermore," he said, this time speaking to Merrill through Carlyle, "PSTRE will also pay in full, any and all revenue losses incurred from the disruption of Athens's business during cleanup."

"You're filing papers?" a bewildered Carlyle asked.

"Yes, against PSTRE *and* the City of Charleston."

"The city? Explain?" Carlyle demanded.

Fortunately, Stan Merrill was too much in shock from the bizarre turn of events to muster a response.

A disturbing thought surged through Nick's mind. He grabbed Chris's arm hard enough to make him wince.

"Jeezus," Chris said with a jerk. "What is it?"

"*Parcel C*," Nick whispered. "Has to be."

"If you please?" Carlson interrupted. "Now, Bill," as much as I regret your client pressing this old family vendetta without knowing all of the facts, PSTRE has left Athens with no recourse. The information your client needs is public knowledge—PSTRE forced my client to look it up. I'm sure that you'll find Athens's concerns are legitimate. May I suggest that you have your consultant and Mr. Merrill do a proper due diligence? In the interim, I'll have a copy of Mr. Cresson's report forwarded to your attention. Have your people review it and we'll talk again. Agreed?"

"Fine," Carlyle capitulated. "Gentlemen," he said to his charges through gritted teeth. "We're done here."

Rising from his seat, Chris turned to Nick and said, "Imagine that, we're the ones being sued!"

CHAPTER 6
SUNDAY

Dinosaur Ridge National Natural Landmark
Morrison, Colo.
Saturday, 1:36 P.M.

Saturday was a far cry from Friday afternoon when they were still reeling in the wake of Jodi's threat. Help was on the way. Michelle even allowed Nick's PSTRE debacle to simmer in the back of her mind for the time being. What plans she had made for the days ahead Michelle cancelled in favor of allowing the weekend to unfold on its own accord. With so much stress behind her and more certain to come, it was time to take advantage of the down time and relax. Locating the Central Colorado Times archives and getting a leg up on several nagging project-related loose ends could wait until Monday.

Kerry had returned Melanie's call within the hour on Friday, and for the first few minutes was anything but sympathetic. "You're telling me that you don't know who these people are, what you've stumbled onto, or what you might be getting yourselves into. In other words, you don't know anything." When Melanie attempted to mollify her sister by explaining the arrangements, Kerry astutely noted that they were placing their safety in the hands of a perfect stranger. "And have you told this person?" she pressed. "Does this *camera guy* know what he's signed himself up for? Do the two of you really expect him to protect you if push comes to shove?" The resounding silence that followed was all Kerry needed to snap, "Don't do anything until I get there."

Rick Ley

Kerry was right. They were needlessly throwing caution to the wind. Regretting her poor planning, Michelle asked that Melanie assure Kerry that they would stay in public places where others would see them. Kerry agreed that was a good idea and promised to meet them in Breckenridge by Monday evening.

Michelle followed Melanie's lead and called her agent later in the afternoon and explained everything. True to his word, Connor Lewis called Michelle back Saturday morning, not long after they had awakened from a troubled sleep. Lewis informed her that he had spoken with the publishing-house attorneys, who in turn contacted their counterparts at Tarryall. Michelle was mildly amused to discover that indeed there was an issue with the Conservancy that fell completely within and *outside* the realm of expectation. Tarryall's servers, Lewis explained, had been hacked by a special interest group, angry over the Conservancy's plans to turn an undeveloped tract of forest land into, of all things, an environmental park. Lewis chuckled. "It would seem that you again find yourself caught up in some eco-wing-nut propaganda mongering."

Swell. Here we go again. Experience told her that Lewis was on the other end of the line, rubbing his grubby hands together like an overgrown leprechaun, salivating over the pot of literary gold that awaited. Michelle chewed at her lip. She pondered the plausibility that the EcoGenesis affair might actually be repeating itself.

"Tarryall's been receiving threatening emails. They're working with local authorities to resolve the issue. It doesn't sound like there's much you need to worry about. All the same, I'd be careful."

Mixed signals notwithstanding, Michelle was relieved. She even allowed her agent to rope her into one of his verbal salads about how to work the eco-crazy angle into her book. She placated Lewis by insisting she would consider his suggestions. Lastly, she thanked him for assuring her that Mark Boone, her photographer, had been briefed and was fine with the situation. "He's happy to be on board and is looking forward to meeting you," he told her. Then with slightly less zeal, Lewis mentioned in closing that the Conservancy, in response to the *hacking thing*, had again become skittish about mine access, until he reminded them of the binding agreement that was in place. "They came around," he asserted. "Still, I wouldn't do anything to upset them when you're out there."

Satisfied that big brother Connor was watching and little sister Kerry was on her way, Michelle felt a sense of normalcy settling in, even if she wasn't completely at ease. "You wanted to know what it was like to be me?" Michelle reminded Melanie. "Well, welcome to Calamity Girl's world!" They shared a laugh and decided to forego the hotel's continental breakfast and be waited on at a family diner across the parking lot, where they would plan the day's agenda.

It was a thin Saturday morning crowd. They were seated right away. The waitress showed them to a booth with a nice view of the distant peaks shrouded in a light blue haze. She returned soon to take their orders and place a fresh carafe of coffee on the table.

"You look perplexed," Melanie commented between bites of her Western omelet, the temptation to do the *when in Rome* thing too irresistible to pass up. "You've hardly said a word since we sat down."

Michelle stirred a second cream into her coffee. "I don't know," she said slowly, teasing out the words. "There's something about this hacker story that isn't sitting well. I can't put my finger on it."

"You think the Conservancy is lying?"

"I dunno. Probably not. It's just that the nature of the emails doesn't seem consistent with something a hacker who's got a problem with the Conservancy would do. The messages seem deliberately directed at me. How would they know that I'm coming?"

"Their server was hacked, right? Whoever they are might have intercepted your correspondence as well. Maybe the messages were sent to you, but meant to cause problems for the Conservancy. We don't know the whole story." Melanie asked if Michelle was worried.

"No. Forget it. It's just me being my crazy, paranoid self. If my publisher's spoken to them, I'm sure we have nothing to worry about, now that the Conservancy knows we're watching. All the same, I think Connor's right. We should keep our wits about us."

"Good idea," Melanie agreed.

Michelle smiled. "I think we should pretend that nothing is out of the ordinary and just go about our business; see if anything—and I hope nothing—unfolds. We'll call Connor and your sister the moment we sense any danger…like if we find that Jodi is a real person and she's been reaching out to me as a call for help." Comforted to see that her words were calming them both, Michelle put their Jodi concerns aside and said, "I can't believe that your sister's also a private investigator."

Their waitress passed by and asked if they owned the maroon SUV with its lights on in the parking lot. Michelle stood, confirmed that it was hers, and started for the car.

Melanie stopped her, saying that she needed to go to the car anyway to get something she'd forgotten. Melanie returned several minutes later and had begun to say something when she realized that Michelle was on the phone. Melanie placed a finger to her lips in apology and sat down. She rubbed at her arms while she waited, to ward off the chill of the air conditioning.

Michelle turned the phone away from her mouth to whisper, "It's Nick." She made a shivering gesture in recognition of the cold.

Melanie picked up her fork and continued to pick at her meal.

"You're okay, then? Good. Let me know if you catch anything. Love you, bye." She rang off and slipped the phone into her pocket.

"How's Nick doing?" Melanie asked.

"Better this morning. Their boss called Chris last night. He told them to take the weekend off and regroup. That Bill Carlyle—he's a good man. Nick said they're going fishing with the subcontractor who's helping them."

"That sounds like fun. He's not in trouble, then?" Melanie asked.

"I don't think so."

"That's good. *Oh,* here," Melanie then said, placing printouts of the places she thought they might want to see on the table.

"Sure!" Michelle promised. Michelle took several bites of her breakfast. "Kerry. Tell me more about why she became a private eye."

"We never did finish, did we?" Melanie slid the papers aside, rolling her eyes. "She got her P.I. license so that she'd know how to properly collect forensic information whenever she got all full of herself and stepped outside of her clinician's box."

Michelle gave a little chortle. "You said that first case of hers was almost thrown out of court."

"Not exactly. The woman's case never went to court per se, but the perpetrator's did."

"I see."

"Kerry wasn't happy about the lack of support the woman was receiving from the authorities. She empathized with her because of Garret. Curious, she got to poking around and discovered circumstantial evidence that the woman was provoked into committing murder by the plaintiffs, which included the surviving perpetrator and the family of the deceased. This was key because the clinic was already convinced—unofficially mind you—that the woman was unstable, but, as I told you yesterday, was reluctant to get involved. Kerry provided the nudge the clinic needed to get on board and help."

Michelle shifted uncomfortably. "The poor woman. She was lucky to have your sister in her corner."

"She was. Kerry's findings implied that the deceased and his accomplice *knew* that she had mental issues; they'd grown up in the same neighborhood with the woman. They believed she witnessed a crime that they committed and were trying to bully out of her what she knew when the woman snapped. The problem was that the murder was committed in the victim's house and the woman was holding the weapon when the police arrived. There was also some confusion as to how the woman ended up in the victim's house to begin with, and how the gun ended up in her hand. Kerry said that the plaintiff's case was shaky, based on the victim's criminal history, only the woman's lawyers needed an alibi for her actions. What they wanted was definitive medical proof or a formal consensus from her doctors that she was mentally impaired and, therefore, not responsible for her actions. Insanity cases, however, are notoriously hard to prove in court."

"Was it Kerry who actually figured out her mental condition?"

Melanie lamented that she couldn't remember some of the specifics. "She was part of the team that went so far as to say that the woman was sick. It *was* Kerry who later championed DID as her condition when the woman became her first patient following her residency. It was also Kerry's early findings and persistence that forced the clinic and the authorities to look at the case in a new light."

Their waitress dropped off their bill, along with courtesy cups of coffee for the road.

"It's amazing that Kerry did that, change the course of an investigation. That took a lot of nerve on her part. I would have been a nervous wreck."

"Believe me, she was. She must have called me every day, just to hear my voice, until it was over, and that took over a year. Her problems started when the focus of the police investigation shifted away from the woman. Now faced with defending his clients, the perpetrator's attorney attacked Kerry's evidence collection methods."

Michelle groaned. "I'm feeling sick just thinking about that."

Melanie dabbed at a spot of coffee on her shirt. "If the proceedings had played out differently than they did, Kerry's findings, some of them at least, would have been deemed inadmissible. Kerry told me if that had happened, she would have been fired and her medical license possibly revoked. That scared her, so she studied to become a private investigator so she wouldn't make those mistakes again." Her demeanor brightening, Melanie elaborated that Kerry probably would have been fired anyway if her findings weren't the basis for a landmark ruling regarding mental health. "She helped bring validity to dissociative identity disorder as a disease. And to think…if you hadn't written that book about Garret, her career path would have taken another direction, the woman probably would have been convicted and sent to jail for a murder she didn't commit *in her right mind*, and a thug never would have been brought to justice."

"Now I really feel like a goof," Michelle remarked about the trouble she'd caused. "Some role model. I owe your sister an apology for my getting us into this mess."

"Believe me, I'm the one who'll hear about it. She considers me the risk taker in our family, even more so than Brad."

The last thing either thought they would be doing this fine day following their cross-country excursion was sitting behind the wheel, and yet here they were driving aimlessly around the city. Michelle had planned a casual day of taking in some of the cultural sites in town, only to find much of the central business district cordoned off for a bike race that thwarted their every turn. So much for the natural history museum and several artisan venues Melanie wanted to see. "Maybe on the way back," Michelle hoped. Begrudgingly, she hopped onto the closest expressway to go wherever providence took them. Strange as it might seem, they didn't mind the ride. In fact, they quite enjoyed it, what with gleaming skyscrapers competing with a Rocky Mountain backdrop to grab their attention. Melanie took out her camera to take pictures of the cityscape framed by majestic Front Range peaks. Driving, they discovered, was altogether different without the pressure of trying to get somewhere.

A youthful resurgence invigorated Michelle's middle-aged bones. It was an infectious feeling that spread to Melanie, who reveled in sharing with Michelle the tricky art of taking non-blurry photos from a moving vehicle. Michelle could hardly keep her hand steady on the wheel, she was laughing so hard, when Melanie said, "Watch this," and leaned way out of the window to snap photos of some cows in a far off pasture at the lightning fast shutter speed of 1/1000 of a second. "You fall out and I'm not telling your sister!" Michelle shouted over the roar of the wind.

Fate found them on the west side of Denver in the community of

Lakewood, on West Alameda Avenue, the one Denver-area roadway Michelle remembered from her field-camp days. "Mel! Look up dinosaur tracks on Alameda," she said, excitedly. "You have to see them. They were so cool. I hope I can remember where they are."

"Around here?" Melanie questioned, confused by the urbanness of their surroundings.

"Yes," Michelle replied. "They're the neatest thing, right there along the highway. Tracy and me used to stop to look at them when we needed to get away to Denver for a little retail therapy."

Melanie scrolled away on her iPhone. "Let's see. Okay…it looks like there's a visitor's center… with trails. Yes, let's stop," she said, sharing in Michelle's excitement.

"How do we get there?"

Melanie tapped her way back to the visitor's center home page and found the directions. "Ahead should be an exit for I-470. Take it and make a right."

"Wow! This sure wasn't here back in the day," Michelle said, marveling at the well-appointed visitor's center. I would have remembered this." The frenetic energy provided by the throng of tourists was overwhelming. Bright colors and prehistoric animation vied with wood and glass to create a balance between theme-park showiness and rustic ambiance. Children scurried everywhere. And just beyond a protective railing, defended against the travesties of man, was one great sublime step back in time to the Mesozoic Era.

They backed away from the rail to allow a group of kids and their guardians to pass. In her backing, Melanie bumped into an attractive younger man passing behind her. Melanie excused herself for stepping into his path. The man did likewise with a broad smile that exposed a set of gleaming teeth.

Michelle wondered if it was here that she'd stopped. Things looked very different than she remembered. Then again, that was a long time ago when she was not so apt to pay attention to her surroundings. Noticing her friend's distraction, Michelle followed Melanie's line of sight and watched as the younger man continued to walk away. "If I didn't know any better, I'd think you still had Jamie Mason on your mind!" Michelle whispered in her ear.

Melanie snapped about in a quarter turn to face the outcrop exhibit. Using Michelle as a shield so that others did not hear her, Melanie spoke in a rapid whisper, "Did you see him? He's *gorgeous*. He looks like Bruce Springsteen."

Michelle stole a quick peek. Melanie was right; he could pass for a body double on the front of that album cover.

"You wouldn't think that dinosaurs would cross the highway and walk up a rock like that," Melanie giggled, trying to change the subject. "And look at that one," she continued, pointing at a set of tracks imprinted into the bedrock at a seemingly impossible angle. "It had to have been leaning way in like this just to keep from falling on its butt."

Muffled chuckling was heard from several nearby patrons.

"Now that would have been funny to see! If only Dinosaur Ridge was here at the time," an authoritative voice commented behind them.

Startled, they wheeled around to find a park-service ranger with an uncanny resemblance to Eddie the Eagle Edwards, the iconic—goggle-less—English ski jumper from the Calgary Winter Games, looking expectantly. "Hi," Melanie said, embarrassed. "I kinda knew that. I was just kidding."

"Of course you were!" the ranger said. "Have either of you been to Dinosaur Ridge before?"

"No," Melanie said clumsily. Whether he was a real park ranger, or a volunteer who liked to dress the part, was beside the point. The man's square-jawed uniform-refined appearance made him the epitome of what a park ranger should look like. Melanie suppressed the urge to look at Michelle who, likewise, found the ranger's near comical persona amusing. A glimmer twinkling in her liquidy dark eyes, Melanie replied, "I haven't, but Michelle has."

"So it was you I heard speculating about whether you were here before. How wonderful!"

"That's right," Michelle managed, face flushed.

"Welcome back, then! My name's Rick."

Michelle was again hit by the urge to burst. *You can't be serious...
Ranger Rick?* She sought safer ground by introducing herself and
Melanie to keep from inadvertently joking about his name.

"Good, very good," the ranger continued, his intonation inquisitive. "You know," he said, reading her mind as he cast a wary eye
about before leaning close to speak in confidence, "Between you
and me, a name like *Ranger Rick* goes a long way around here," and
with that, he gave her a wink. Below them, around them, children
scurried, chased by corralling parents.

"I'm so sorry," Michelle said, taking a step back to share in
Rick's laugh at his own expense. The reference to the park ranger's
hat-adorned raccoon cartoon caricature from the children's informational nature magazine was simply too much to ignore. Nor
was it missed by the small huddle of intrigued parents and curious
children, who stopped to take in what the man of the moment had
to share. "I wasn't expecting...you know," she said, the ruddiness
in her cheeks having concentrated into rosy buttons.

"Not a problem in the least." He paused for others to gather.
"Well then, it's Ranger Rick at your service." He bowed to his con-
gregation and concluded his introduction by grasping his hands
before him in a gesture of appreciation for everyone's attendance,
enjoying fully the spotlight that his given name and chosen profession afforded. "Now tell me, when were you here last."

"Almost thirty years ago, back in the eighties." Michelle's voice
trailed off with *am I really that old?* dejection.

"Why, there's nothing wrong with that. Much has changed since
then, as you can see. Were you passing through with your parents?"

"And I thank *you!*" Michelle said, welcoming the compliment.

Rick's flattering remark prompted a *"Hear, hear!"* from another
fiftysomething standing beside her daughter—and *granddaughter*.

"I was a zoology student," Michelle explained. "We shared a field
station with the geology majors at our school near Breckenridge,

and came here when we could to look at the dinosaur tracks. Would I have been right here before?" she asked, looking from the ground at her feet to the highway beyond.

A flash of something red and familiar caught her eye as she did so. It was Melanie's Springsteen doppelganger interest. He was standing behind them and to their right, near the back of the crowd. No wonder Melanie was attracted to him, Michelle thought. He was attractive in a refined, yet scruffy way, with dark curly hair that protruded from the bottom edge of his worn ball cap, distinguished gold-rimmed glasses, and a pleasing, angular face with prominent cheekbones. He was staring back at them. Michelle nudged Melanie's arm. She made a subtle gesture in his direction only to find that he was gone by the time they looked.

Who *was* still paying attention to them was the park ranger.

Accustomed to such distractions, Ranger Rick picked up where he had left off. "The answer to your question is, not exactly. That's why things might look different to you. The park service worked with numerous volunteers and the Friends of Dinosaur Ridge to expose these particular tracks when the grounds were developed, beginning in the early nineties. We needed to protect the remaining tracks from vandalism, or being removed altogether."

"That's right!" Michelle said, excited with recollection. "I remember some being jackhammered out."

"Correct. Very good. Now tell me, what else do you remember from your school-trip days?"

Michelle's face took on a sheepish look. "Not much I'm afraid."

A small boy materialized from the tangle of legs. No sooner had Ranger Rick asked if the child liked *Jurassic Park* and the boy said yes, than Rick launched into a whirlwind history of what he affectionately called *Jur-taceous Park*.

They were standing on approximately 60 million years of history, right at the height of the dinosaur's reign during the Jurassic and Cretaceous periods, a time when true giants walked the Earth. Semi-arid and rimmed with mountains now, this area of

Colorado, Rick explained, was a low, lush plain cut by lazy rivers, the climate warmer and more humid. "It was a great time to be a dinosaur!" he announced with a vivacity that rippled through the crowd. Michelle strained to catch every word. She had to because a murmur of heated chatter behind her was making it difficult to listen to what he had to say. Michelle was irritated at the inconsiderate behavior. She decided she would make amends for her part by asking a question she hoped would force those in the periphery to quiet down and listen.

"What kind of dinosaurs, you ask? Well," Rick said, directing his answer to the child before him, whom they learned answered to Billy, "instead of deer and squirrels, imagine there being the 70-foot long *Apatosaurus*, the even longer *Diplodocus*, *Camarasaurus*, and the beefy, plate-backed, spike-tailed *Stegosaurus* plodding along the ancient shorelines, feeding peacefully on the leaves of long extinct trees…and especially for you," he added to appease Billy's plea for a *T-Rex* or *Velociraptor*, "we had *Allosaurus*, and it was a terror to behold in the Late Jurassic."

Little Billy's eyes came alive. "It lived here?"

"Absolutely! If you visit the Dinosaur Bone Site on the other side of the park, you can see *Allosaurus* in the flesh, or should I say *in the bone*, for yourself."

The boy's wonderment turned to joy when his parents said they would take him there on the next tour bus.

A round of applause interrupted the presentation. Children begged their parents to visit the gift shop to buy a toy dinosaur, or visit the Bone Site. Michelle whispered to Melanie that she, too, wanted a stuffed dinosaur. Certain parents followed their children to the gift shop while others assessed their schedules and moved on. The majority, along with a few new recruits, milled about to hear the rest of Rick's informational. Melanie said that she was thirsty and took advantage of the break to set off in search of a water fountain. Michelle said she would stay back to keep their place.

The interlude allowed Michelle to take stock of the rude mumblings that had resumed behind her. The crowd having thinned, Michelle spied a tallish man in all his puffed out arrogance, expressing his literalist diatribe to a woman with two small children who was having none of his nonsense.

Jesus would be appalled were the kindest words Michelle could think of to describe the man's lack of courtesy. This was neither the time nor place to force one's beliefs on others.

The man's persistence was not lost on the park ranger, who spoke over the crowd, requesting him to refrain from disrupting the patrons. If he had something to say, Rick promised they could meet afterward to discuss his views in an appropriate manner.

Michelle couldn't help smirking. The unspoken words she imagined Rick wanting to say were, in a *civilized* manner. Interesting, Michelle thought as she watched the crowd begin to re-form. The uncomfortable exchange was either missed or ignored. Across the way, she saw Melanie merge with a small group of returning patrons. Michelle used the remaining time to snap a few pictures of the building and grounds. She might include color plates of some of the interesting sites she and Melanie visited in their quest to bring the Ghost Creek story to rest.

That's when she saw him through the view screen of her phone, the curly-haired man, standing alone just inside the facility. Michelle was certain that he was watching her—and talking to someone. Melanie, in fact, had just walked past when the Springsteen look alike, observing her pass, again said something to no one in particular. The sight rose her hackles. Michelle continued to observe him through her phone, pretending to fiddle with the zoom with her fingers, when he melted out of the frame and into the depths of the visitor's center.

"Did I miss anything?" Melanie asked.

Michelle explained the situation, saying that she thought they might be being stalked. This got Melanie's attention.

"Are you sure?" she asked, taking a nervous glance in the direction of the visitor's center. The man was nowhere to be seen.

Michelle admitted that she wasn't certain. It just seemed to be too much of a coincidence that he would keep popping up in whatever direction she was looking. When Michelle mentioned that she saw him speaking to an unseen accomplice the moment Melanie passed him, Melanie countered that maybe he was on a call and wearing one of those *ear things*. A valid point. "Yeah, maybe," Michelle replied.

The talk resumed when a sufficient crowd had reconvened. Ranger Rick talked more about the various creatures that lived both on the land and in what Rick called the Cretaceous Seaway. The footprints in the angled slab in front of them, he explained, were made in soft sediments by a dinosaur akin to *Iguanodon* that once walked along the ancient shoreline where they were now standing. "We call it *dinosaur freeway*," he said with pride. "Fascinating."

Even more fascinating was what happened next.

"Everything was low and flat, lush and green, and then in a 30-million-year blink of a geologic eye, a great period of mountain building, the Laramide Orogeny, lifted the Rocky Mountains to heights arguably equal to those of the Himalayas. The seabed tilted to an angle of 45 degrees and volcanic activity covered much of the area in ash. After that came a 40-million-year period of intense erosion that chewed the rocks away, leaving the more resistant ones behind as long chains of ridges, or hogbacks, like Dinosaur Ridge. Everything stayed pretty much the same, the ancient tracks hidden away, until the construction of Alameda Parkway in 1937 unlocked these wonders of the Mesozoic world for all to see!"

The discussion wandered about at this point, ultimately making its way to where it always did when the topic was dinosaurs: their extinction. It was here that trouble was rekindled. "*Yeah!* They all died," called out the troublemaker in an indignant voice from the back of the crowd. The murmurings his response elicited quickly escalated to a heated exchange between the troublemaker and a concerned Samaritan, who came to the defense of the woman with two small children, who remained the focus of the troublemaker's badgering.

Michelle whispered to Melanie that this was a carry-over from what she'd missed when she left to get her drink.

"What a jerk."

"Tell me about it."

When Rick attempted to divert the troublemaker by working in how they died, the jerk's outbursts became louder. Rick asked the man to settle down and motioned for assistance from several facility personnel already on their way. The jerk quieted down at seeing the converging force.

Continuing the presentation, Rick explained how spectacular changes in climate, brought on by a one-two punch of massive outpourings of flood-basalt lava in India and the Chicxulub asteroid that struck the Yucatán Peninsula in Mexico approximately 66 million years ago, and the erosional processes that followed, had wreaked havoc for life both on land and in the sea across the planet. Greenhouse gases were released during these events, then swallowed up via erosion-induced chemical reactions—these prompting global temperatures to rise, then suddenly cool; the oceans becoming acidified in the process. At this, the jerk once again became agitated.

It was Melanie who saw him first. She thrust an elbow into Michelle's ribs.

The curly-haired man was walking with purpose in their direction.

The girls looked nervously about. They couldn't be in a more secure place, yet felt utterly unsafe.

Even the easygoing ranger was losing his patience. With firm politeness, Rick asked again that the man refrain from disturbing the patrons. The reminder worked for only so long as it took Rick to discuss how wildly changing weather patterns over the million-year period leading up to the dinosaur's asteroid-impact demise had greatly diminished their numbers. The jerk had had enough and started to talk over him.

…And in a reprise of Michelle's Mother's Day fiasco, an ugly confrontation ensued.

A swarm of well-intentioned men and the angry mother converged on the jerk. Push came to shove and a few errant shoves and a stray punch later, tempers boiled over. Michelle wanted no part of this and moved away from the mob to distance herself, Melanie following close behind. Michelle would have urged that they leave altogether had she not noticed the curly-haired man closing fast from the direction of visitor center.

What was he going to do to them? Michelle looked for a means of escape. Regrettably, there were no safe havens. All available authority figures were busy separating the horde's combatants, and the remaining bystanders had scuttled away.

He was almost upon them. The girls huddled close.

"What do we do?" Melanie pleaded.

There was nothing that they could do. An island between storms, they were out of time with no place to go.

Grim, dour, the curly-haired man was a mere step away when he extended an arm in their direction. And that's when the unexpected happened…in a sweeping motion, he politely asked that they step aside.

It was so obvious. They had allowed their Jodi concerns to imagine a Conservancy thug where one did not exist. The curly-haired man was nothing more than a concerned handsome bystander. He had been watching the situation unfold. It just so happened that each time Michelle saw him, she and Melanie were standing between him and the jerk. If there was anything odd about his actions, it was the manner in which the horde reacted to his sudden intrusion. The fracas broke up within moments of his arrival. They had no idea what was said; just that one moment he disappeared in the crowd, and the next the combatants disbursed, leaving them all to watch the handsome stranger follow the jerk toward the parking lot.

It didn't take long for a sense of normalcy to return. Ranger Rick saw to that by redirecting his audience's attention. Experience taught him that idleness following such disturbances has a ripple effect that often spawns still other arguments, like a smoldering fire not fully quenched.

Interestingly, it was as if the disturbance hadn't happened at all. Rick's presentation followed a logical and uninterrupted progression about the end of the dinosaur's reign and how natural forces modified the climate and terrain at Dinosaur Ridge over the ensuing 65 million years, right up until highway construction and manifest destiny of progressive minds created the visitor's center to slake peoples' curiosity and preserve history. Of particular interest to Michelle, and a fortuitous tie-in to her book project, was Rick's sidebar discussion about NASA's Planetary Defense Coordination Office and Center for Near Earth Object Studies, where all kinds of information could be found about the over fifteen thousand identified asteroids and comets—or NEOs, as he called them—that have been cataloged. It was during that fate-filled fall-break Sudbury mineral collecting field trip in 1985, after all, that she first fell for Garret while picking over pretty rocks from the erosional scar of a billion-plus-year-old meteor-impact crater. No need to wonder when the next *big one* was going to pass close enough to Earth to create widespread damage. "You can go to the web site and find out for yourself when the next one will whiz by." He further promised that none have yet been identified that we need to be concerned about in our lifetimes.

And so they continued to listen to their engaging orator until the Dinosaur Ridge Trail tour bus returned on schedule to the visitor's center. Ranger Rick bade them all a fond farewell and strode off in search of his next group of unsuspecting listeners. Michelle and Melanie decided to forego the tour. Instead, they tramped off on their own to explore the park trails. Exhausted, they spent the remainder of the afternoon resting their oxygen-depleted bodies by driving around and admiring the scenery, stopping here and there for Melanie to take pictures. It was, by all accounts, a fantastic impromptu day. They had had so much fun that Michelle decided they should spend their last guaranteed worry free-day at Garden of the Gods Park, where she promised Melanie some incredible photo ops.

———

Garden of the Gods Park
Colorado Springs, Colo.
Sunday 11:41 A.M.

"Finally!" Michelle announced with relief after being stuck in I-25 traffic for nearly two hours, much of it ensnarled in an ungodly stretch of road construction nowhere close to completion. "Highway improvement? Tell that to my bladder," she kidded Melanie in the midst of a tire-screeching turn off into the Garden of the Gods Visitor & Nature Center parking lot. Inside, they shook off the rump rot, perusing the exhibits and browsing the festive gift shop, before stepping back outside into the sun. Michelle commented on the thinness of the rarefied mountain air of their Front Range foothills surroundings, even at the comparatively low elevation of 6,400 feet.

"The air, it smells so...I can't quite place it," Melanie remarked, opening her arms wide to soak in the rays.

"I know what you mean. There's something about dry climate and conifers that gives the air that pleasant spiciness." Taking a look around, Michelle mused that in the non-jaded days of her youth, she would have been appalled by the glitz and glam of the golf club and pretentious housing development that lined the bluff overlooking the visitor's center. The nature defiling atrocity now didn't look quite so repulsive. She went so far as to say that they should look up the management office before leaving to see if there were any condos or timeshares available.

———

"Are you coming?" Michelle urged, casting an impatient glance for Melanie to get a move on.

"Hold on!" Melanie answered in a fluster. She was rummaging through her daypack, which doubled as her camera bag, for all the right lenses, filters, and whatnots to handle anything *the Gods* could throw her way. The task would have been much simpler if she weren't shaking with anticipation at capturing on film the grandeur of the finlike slabs of rock jutting into the air.

They were in a burgeoning parking lot off Juniper Way Loop, at the north end of the Central Garden area of the park. Michelle checked her messages, swatted at a bug. She wondered what Nick was up to and sent him a text, explaining where they were and that all was good. Around her, a swarm of other flat landers, some decked out in all of the latest high-end trekking gear, readied themselves for an afternoon afoot. Michelle watched as a young family assembled a buggy-like stroller with over-sized wheels. Mountain strolling: Michelle was jealous. She would have loved to be pushed around in such a contraption when she was little.

Across the lot, Michelle noticed a casually dressed, field-ready man rooting around in the back of his car. A smile came to Michelle's lips when she thought of Nick getting ready to dash off the beaten path in search of some neat new specimen for his cabinet of curiosities. Michelle then checked again on Melanie's progress. She was still futzing around, now with her daypack, checking pockets, testing the zippers. She sighed; she was tired of waiting and getting antsy. Carrying nothing more than a notebook and a phone, it took her no time to prepare. There was so much she wanted to see and share with Melanie.

Michelle couldn't help looking back at the man who, like Melanie, was adjusting the straps of his own pack. There was something familiar about him. Perhaps in his mid-thirties or a little older, he was tallish, skinny, and wearing tattered jean shorts that were every bit as bedraggled as his faded t-shirt and the tattered bandana tied loosely around his neck. His hair was shaved close to the temples and rose to a tall hive of curls bunched on the top of his head. Glacier glasses rounded out his appearance. Michelle likened him to a young version of Lyle Lovette with panache. Finished, or perceiving that he was being watched, the man abruptly stopped his pre-hike check, closed the rear compartment hatch of his vehicle, and walked off toward the trail.

Michelle watched him shrink away into the distance while shuffling her way back to their car to urge Melanie along. Distracted by his familiarity, Michelle narrowly avoided walking into the path of a pedestrian hurrying to catch up with his party.

"What were you looking at?" Melanie asked. "You almost ran into that person."

Michelle pointed sheepishly at the young man, who had just turned onto the trail. "Him. He's parked over there," she said.

Melanie looked from the car to the man Michelle was pointing at. "You checking him out? Wait 'til I tell Nick."

"No, I'm not checking him out," Michelle frowned, hands on her hips. "And don't you dare! He looks familiar."

Melanie looked again. She caught a fleeting last glimpse of the man before he disappeared from view. "Sexy. Where do you know him from?"

Michelle racked her brain. "I don't know," she said, still frowning.

They followed the walking trail on a southerly course that paralleled the immense slabs of rock. Beginning at the Tower of Babel, they passed North Gateway Rock and the Kissing Camels; Signature Rock was to their right. The stony monoliths were beautiful in the late morning light.

Even with Melanie stopping every few moments to snap pictures, they soon passed many of the glacially slow pedestrians who thought the trail was their own private garden path. "This used to not be paved," Michelle snapped in response to a particularly obvious heavyset man who used his bulk to block others. At this latest impasse, Michelle reached an arm out in front of Melanie, motioning for her to wait for the man to slug his way forward and still others behind them to pass. "Trust me?" she asked, and when no one was looking grabbed Melanie's arm and, together, they backtracked until they came upon a break in the split rail fence, at which Michelle led them off the trail and into the scrub.

"Do you know where we're going?" Melanie asked, huffing, trying not to trip over the uneven ground. More times than she cared, she had to pause to tug at her pack, which kept getting caught by gnarly branches that seemed to go out of their way to grab at the plastic buckles and webbing straps.

"*Shh!*" Michelle urged. They were standing in a copse of scrubby oak trees out of sight of the other pedestrians. When she was sure that no one was following, Michelle answered Melanie's question. "Pretty sure. I had to get away from all those people. *There!*" she pointed to a cluster of tall rock spires not far from their present location. "We want to go there. I'll tell you why when we get there. Come on!"

"We're not supposed to be doing this, are we?" Melanie asked, nervously hoping that they weren't breaking some federal law by leaving the trail.

"Maybe," Michelle said uncertainly. We didn't get in trouble back in the day." With a glint in her eye, she then challenged, "I didn't see any signs, did you?"

Melanie wasn't sure. She decided to play dumb and blame Michelle if accosted by a park ranger.

"Look at that. Aren't they beautiful?" Michelle commented, directing Melanie's attention to a cluster of pinnacles. "I think those are called the Three Graces, and those the Cathedral Spires…or maybe it's the other way around."

Melanie copied Michelle's lead and looked skyward to the tops of the spires. "What are you looking for?" she asked when she realized that Michelle was searching for something.

"It's nice to see that some things haven't changed after all these years," Michelle replied. A flock of pigeons flew in slow, coordinated zigzags between and around the middle reaches of the spires. Every few seconds, Michelle looked from the pigeons to the tops of the spires some distance above. There it was! Michelle pointed skyward and said, "Look! Get your camera ready, Mel."

"What am I looking for?" Melanie asked, sliding her pack off her shoulder. Michelle asked that she grab her camera with the fastest lens. Camera in hand, Melanie shielded her eyes and searched until she found the object of Michelle's attention: a dark, slender shape perched atop the tallest spire. "Is that what I think it is? *Shoot!* Hold on. I'm going to need Gus for this," she said, blindly groping inside the pack at her feet, pulling out a much larger and expensive looking camera.

Melanie didn't have to wait long for the shape to shift fully on its perch, and with logic-defying speed dive-bomb a trailing pigeon, the small bird erupting into a puff of feathers upon impact. The peregrine falcon then continued on its swoop, alighting on a lower crag to spy where its dinner had fallen.

"That was incredible!" Melanie gasped, astonished by the bird's aerial precision. "It had to be doing at least a hundred miles per hour." She scrolled through her photos.

"Did you get a good one?" Michelle asked. She looked over Melanie's shoulder. "Wow!" Michelle remarked with glee. Melanie had captured the entire encounter in a series of several dozen crisp shots. "You'll have to send me those. I'll commission you to have that one framed." Michelle chose a frame clicked the moment just after impact—the falcon looking behind as if checking on its success, the pigeon dropping away; both predator and prey partially obscured in a shroud of gray and white plumage.

They walked deeper into the park. Michelle remarked about the first time she saw a peregrine falcon on the hunt during that first summer field session. A little farther along, Michelle again held her arm out for Melanie to stop. "My, gosh!" she gushed, exhilarated at the sight of a decrepit old tree hanging on by its last root. "That tree there, it was here when I was here! I remember it. There was this guy in our program. He was such a doofus, the kind of person things just happened too. I was standing right about here and saw him walking under that tree, which looked quite lively back then, when a raven took off from the ground beside him. There was more scrub at the time as I remember. Neither realized the other was there until the bird took flight with this croaking squawk. And get this," Michelle said, slapping Melanie on the arm, "it clipped him on the back of the head, knocking off his hat. He stumbled and the bird, equally bewildered, flew into that branch and fell back to the ground."

"Was he okay? What about the bird?"

"Both were fine," Michelle assured her. "I'm not sure what was funnier, the bird bouncing off that branch, or the guy—I wish I could remember his name—spinning around like a startled cat, wondering what had just happened."

The land started to rise, affording them a good view of both the ground ahead and the hummocky valley beyond the back side of Juniper Way Loop. Melanie halted their travels when she spied an attractive flower growing from a crack in the bedrock. What made this photo op perfect, she said, was the majestic view of one of the red sandstone ridges in the background, which just so happened to be the new temporary hangout for the flock of pigeons, minus one. Michelle loitered about a step or two behind, admiring the scenery, so as not to get in the way. She bent over and picked up a cream-colored rock with some rosy mineralization on one side. Rolling the eye-catching rock around in her hand, she succumbed to temptation and slipped it into her pocket.

"That's a federal offense, you know," a masculine voice called out, frightening them. Michelle pulled the rock from her pocket and threw it to the ground.

It was the man from the parking lot. *No, wait!* Michelle strained her eyes. They grew wide when the man took off his glacier glasses... it was the curly-haired man from yesterday, only he appeared to have had a complete makeover. Michelle tensed. They were in the middle of nowhere, off the beaten path, and yet here he was... stalking them. "Who are you?" Michelle demanded.

Melanie, who had to shield her eyes as she looked up from her camera-op position on the ground, recoiled when she recognized him.

"I didn't mean to startle you," the man said. "I'm Kris. I remember you two from yesterday. Funny we should meet again. And you are?"

Michelle maintained her guard. "I'm sure you do. You were watching us. Why?" Not allowing Kris time enough to respond, Michelle offered a terse introduction that left no doubt that she was wary of his presence.

"Well hello Michelle, Michelle Koz-lowski," he said, mimicking the hiccup in her voice. "Ms. Sutton. I'm Kristian Fletcher. That's Kris with a '*K*.'" Noticing that both women remained apprehensive, Fletcher apologized. That jerk at Dinosaur Ridge had annoyed him, and the girls just happened to always be standing between him and the jerk, as Michelle suspected. "That wasn't right," Fletcher said with regard to the inconsiderate ass. "Nobody needs to hear that. See?" he said, flashing the same disarming smile that had caught Melanie's attention to begin with, "I don't bite. Hey, is that an Olympus?" he then asked Melanie, gesturing to the camera hanging from the strap around her neck.

The subterfuge worked. Melanie double-checked what camera made it out of the bag to shoot the flower. Michelle's posture softened.

"Oh," Melanie said awkwardly. "Yes. It's an OM-D E-M1 Mark II. I'm a photographer." She extended her camera for him to inspect.

Fletcher declined. "I should have known," he said with another, softer smile. "That's a serious piece of hardware," he commented, admiring the camera from a distance. "It would be great for catching some of the peregrine falcons in flight. Are you—"

Melanie cut him off. She obliged their new friend with a recounting of their recent experience. She stepped closer and scrolled through her photos.

"Impressive. Incredible. Look at the intensity in the bird's eye!" Fletcher slipped his pack off his shoulder and took out his own camera. "Suffice it to say, I'm not that good. This Canon, though, serves me just fine." He handed it to Melanie. "Honestly, the poor thing is in need of an operator who knows what to do with it. What?" he said in response to her excitement.

Melanie searched inside her pack and pulled out an identical model.

"I'm sensing a connection, here. What's the chance?"

His comment incited dimple crescents to form at the corners of Melanie's cheeks.

The flirtation was working. Kris Fletcher had an endearing quality that complimented his scruffy good looks. He seemed safe enough, Michelle thought. And the way he was fawning over Mel's camera and her response to his interest suggested that there definitely was a connection.

Still, Michelle wasn't ready to let her guard down completely. For all she knew, the Conservancy or that eco group her agent warned her about could have sent Kris Fletcher as a wolf in sheep's clothing to gain her trust. That's when the realization hit. She had done exactly what Kerry and Connor Lewis told her not to do: she had led herself and Melanie away from the safety of a public place... only to be accosted by a perfect stranger.

"Is there a problem?" Fletcher asked.

Michelle gaged Melanie's expectant look as a sign that she did not share her concern. Michelle tested him anyway. "What are you doing here?" she asked, observing Fletcher from head to toe, nodding to the rock pick hanging from his belt.

"I should be asking you the same thing," he countered. Then realizing how his sudden presence could have been taken as a threat, he took a step back. "Again, I'm sorry. I didn't mean to make you uncomfortable." Tapping the holstered pick against his leg, Fletcher explained that he and his partner were collecting samples of one of the rock formations in the park. "Our goal is to settle a dating issue." He looked for his partner. "She's around here somewhere."

Michelle smiled. "Of course. I should have figured as much. That would also explain why we saw you yesterday at Dinosaur Ridge."

"In a manner of speaking, yes. I was there with my brother and his family. My nephew's entered the dinosaur phase." Shaking his head, Fletcher said, "I'm glad nothing came of that idiot. I followed him to his car to make sure he didn't intend to cause any more trouble. Afterward, I took the family for a drive around the ridge." Then, rubbing a hand against the side of his bandana-covered head, jovially added that he had his "ears lowered after that," in reference to the trim job that tamed some of his wilder curls.

"That was a nice thing you did," Michelle said with a little laugh. "Things could have gotten really out of control—trust me, I know!" Melanie nodded her agreement. Kristian Fletcher—Kris—had passed the test. "I've had more than…never mind. It's not important. You look like a professor. Do you work for one of the area colleges?"

"You had every right to ask. And, no, I don't work for one of the colleges. That, however, is a story you might find interesting," Kris said with a smile. "I work for Infinity Research Group. It's a private sector mineral-resources company turned think tank. Back in the 1950s, our geologists did some of the siting work for those guys." He pointed to a mountainous protrusion rising off in the distance.

"That's Cheyenne Mountain, isn't it?" Michelle said, framing her answer in the form of a question.

"You've heard of it? You would know that," Kris corrected, recalling her discussion yesterday with Ranger Rick.

"What happens there?" Melanie asked.

The corner of Fletcher's lips curled into a mischievous smile. "Cheyenne Mountain is a point of local interest, the kind of place that tickles the conspiracy theorist's fancy."

"How so?" Melanie asked again.

Michelle found it amusing that Melanie was absentmindedly fondling her camera strap.

"It's the home of NORAD, the North American Aerospace Defense Command,"

"Oh. What does that mean?" Melanie persisted. Her camera strap was now curled tightly around her finger.

Convinced she had sufficiently vetted Kris Fletcher, Michelle was free to think of him in a different light. She thought he and Melanie would look good together, even if he was a little young for her. The question was whether he was oblivious to or uninterested in Melanie's geeky overtures.

"NORAD," Kris was pleased to say, "was created during the Cold War as a three-story underground nuclear bunker. The bunker is supported by springs to cancel the effects of earthquakes and, of course, nuclear explosions. It also has its own power plant in the event that the country goes dark. NORAD still has some functions there, but most day-to-day surveillance operations are performed at a nearby Air Force base, also here in Colorado Springs. It's interesting when you think about it," he said after taking a drink from his Yeti bottle, "the Cold War's over, but NORAD's function is probably even more relevant today, to safeguard against electromagnetic pulse destruction of our computer systems and critical sensors."

"EMPs? I thought that was a thing that only happened in the movies," Michelle said.

"Afraid not. There's a whole new world of terrorism and warfare out there that's far less costly, and in many ways much more devastating. Imagine everything electronic connected to a power grid ceasing to function at once. Most people wouldn't know what to do. How frightening is that?"

Michelle and Melanie didn't respond.

Kris allayed some of their concerns by saying that their cell phones might survive an EMP attack. "An increasing number of cell networks worldwide are converting to solar power, partially for this reason."

"That makes me feel a little better!" Michelle answered for her and Melanie both.

Having trouble reconciling her disconnect between the hammering at outcrops and high defense countermeasures, Melanie asked, "What does that have to do with looking at rocks?"

"Nothing really," Kris said honestly. "Over time, Infinity Research has evolved into a multi-faceted science and engineering catchall. We still support NORAD and the military, but more often than not these days we find ourselves working the private sector. Infinity also receives grant money for outreach projects. Take here, for instance. We're collecting rock samples of the Lyons Formation sandstone—that's what makes up most of the hogback ridges in the park. They're called hogbacks because the sharp arches of rock look like the humped back of a wild boar, or razorback. What?" Fletcher said in response to Melanie's unexpected pushing at Michelle.

"Told you so!" Michelle said, giving Melanie a playful shove in return. "We had a debate about where the name came from."

"Your professor would be proud," Kris complimented Michelle on her memory. "Where was I? Yes, our client wants to settle a debate about the basal age for the formation—that is, when the Lyons Formation sediments started to accumulate into what would later become the sandstone rock. Is it Late Pennsylvanian or Early Permian?"

Melanie frowned. "Someone actually cares about that?" she let slip without thinking. She lifted a repentant hand to her mouth.

Humored, Kris said, "Someone does. And somebody else at Infinity thought the client's proposal worth tossing money at to solve. I have to admit," he clarified, "answering this particular question is a tad outside the norm of our typical work. Who knows? Maybe some senator wants to give his kid a leg up on the next science fair."

"That's too funny!" Michelle giggled. "I take it you're using radiometric dating?"

"Pollen, actually."

"You're a palynologist?" Michelle was surprised. Stringy, his clothing tattered and dust-covered Kristian Fletcher fit the mold of most every other geologist she'd ever met. Whatever a pollen specialist was supposed to look like, Kris Fletcher missed the mark.

"I am. My partner Amy, she's the geologist. We're interested in the pollen unique to the Paleozoic windborne desert sands that formed the Lyons Sandstone, as opposed to the pollen in the river-derived sediments that formed the underlying Fountain Formation, or the muddy marine limestones of the Lykens Formation above." Kris checked the time. He regretted to say that he'd better get a move on if he and his partner were going to accomplish their agenda.

They were disappointed. Kris with a 'K' had provided an unanticipated bright spot in their day—and yes, yet another sidebar for Michelle's book.

"Again, I didn't mean to frighten you." He looked around. Addressing Michelle, he reminded her why she was nervous earlier. "You two should be careful. Being off the beaten path like this might not be the best thing. Besides, the terrain can be tricky." Kris pointed to a nasty looking scab on the side of his calf.

Michelle promised that she and Melanie would head straight for the trail.

"Good. Maybe we'll run into each other again." He reached for his wallet and pulled out a business card. He scribbled something on the back with a pen he took from the leather field case hanging from his opposite hip and handed it to Melanie. "If you need anything, please don't hesitate to call. That's my personal cell on the back." Kris gave them a departing smile and started to walk away. He stopped after several steps and asked for the card back.

Michelle and Melanie were already reading what he had written. The card read: "Thanks for the conversation! Kris." Melanie handed it back to him.

"I was thinking," Kris said, retrieving the pen once more from his field case. "I hope that I'm not being too forward, but Amy and I plan to head into the 'Springs when we're done here for a drink and bite to eat. I'd like to introduce you to her. I think you'd hit it off. I can tell you some more about what we're doing here in the park and would love to hear your story. And perhaps you could give me a few pointers," he said, gesturing to the camera hanging from her neck. He scribbled something else on the card and handed it back to Melanie.

It was an address.

"Amanda's Fonda is a great little Mexican place just down the road on West Colorado Avenue. You can get there by heading south on Juniper Way Loop."

"We were just on that, right?" Michelle asked.

"We're both parked just off of it," Kris answered. He again looked to his watch. "It's about one now. We should be done in a few hours. If you're interested, say we meet there around four?"

Michelle looked at Melanie who was hoping that she would say yes. Michelle thought about it. This was something totally outside of her character to do. Still, she found Kris Fletcher interesting, and an added female presence was comforting. It didn't take further urging from Melanie for her to again throw caution to the wind and say *yes*.

"Excellent!" Kris said. "We hope to see you there," and he walked off in the direction of a rise between two great vertical sandstone slabs.

Ashley House
Ashley Avenue, Charleston, S.C.
Sunday, 8:07 P.M.

Nick leaned back and rubbed at his face to shake off the malaise that had returned following a second day on the high seas on Sam Piersall's boat. Opening his eyes, he watched cobweb tendrils make eel-like movements in response to the gentle turnings of the overhead paddle fan pushing warm summer air around the caretaker's-apartment file room.

At least he wasn't being held accountable for their *Black Friday* disaster. That distinction, Chris had informed him while en route to the Cape Island fishing grounds, was reserved for Bill Carlyle himself. Carlyle, Chris explained, had specifically requested everything Stan Merrill knew about the property ownership and operational histories of PSTRE and Athens weeks before. Merrill assured Carlyle that everything M&C needed to know was contained in the Phase I documents, which obviously wasn't the case. In essence, Carlyle had wrongly taken Merrill at his word and failed to react proactively when first made aware that important details were lacking.

Still, Nick felt that he had let them down. He should have listened to his inner voice and better prioritized his time. Had he made the short jaunt to the Recorder of Deeds office like he told Chris he would, he could have warned them of what might be coming. Time...there's always time, at least in retrospect.

Nick picked up his cell phone and called Michelle. They hadn't spoken since yesterday morning and had lots to catch up on. Besides, if there was anyone who could pull him out of his funk, she could. As it turned out, he had called at a good time. She and Melanie were getting cleaned up following their day afield and impromptu dinner.

They spoke for nearly an hour, good therapy for them both. Michelle was particularly chatty. She missed him, Nick could tell. He delighted in hearing all about their weekend adventures, the chance encounter with the handsome scientist who took an interest in Melanie in particular. From how loud she was speaking, it was obvious Michelle was sharpening cupid's arrows as they spoke. Nick then had Michelle in stitches when trying to convey Chris's bewilderment when, during a cast, his bait was snatched out of the air by a big ugly bird Sam called a shearwater. Chris, Nick said amidst his own hysterics, staggered about the cockpit like a drunkard, first reeling the bird from the sky and then from the water where it splashed down, only to be pecked until bleeding as they tried to release it.

When Michelle asked if he was still heeding his boss's advice to take the weekend off, Nick said of course he wasn't. He'd been plowing through every sheet of paper in every folder of every file cabinet during every free moment when he wasn't fishing. Before him, he told her, lay the remaining pile of folders. When she then asked if he had gotten anywhere, Nick reluctantly said no. He did concede that he planned to take a short break to order in a pizza, after which he would go through the remaining documents and throw in the towel. "I'll need to take a walk and enjoy the night life to clear my head." This relieved her.

She told him not to work too hard and signed off with a few parting words of wisdom. "Don't fret about it. Do you really think that you could have justified taking the time to go into town with all that was happening last week?"

"Not really," was his honest answer.

"See!" she said wisely. And in conclusion said, "The answer will probably come from some place you least expect, and that, I'm sure, you wouldn't have had time to find before the meeting."

Nick gathered the armful of remaining files from the table. Using his feet, he scuffed the two boxes containing the Doubly Deads toward the caretaker's apartment door. Outside, he parked himself in a metal chair on the second-floor porch, where his pizza and a bucket of beer awaited him on the patio table. Settling in, Nick retrieved the top-most folder from the neatly stacked collection of manila files at his feet and propped a foot up on the railing.

A flash of movement grabbed his attention. Mrs. Mockingbird made a twilight dive-bomb at an orange tabby in the courtyard below. Nick reached for his phone, but the cat was gone before he could snap off a picture of the distressed animal low-riding its way between the gaps in the Ashley House veranda lattice. *Bummer, Michelle would've loved to see that.*

He flipped through the folder, and then another and another one after that. Nothing. Nick reached for his beer. The remaining files thus far consisted of general correspondence generated over the past year, none of which was relevant to the case. He was in the clear at this point and knew it. Time was not available to perform this level of review of non-target files. While comforted to know that he hadn't missed anything obvious, a part of him did want to find something that would focus his search in town come morning.

The clicky whoosh of a car spitting road grit as it moved north along Ashley switched his mind to the spy games Dodd and Carlson promised Athens wasn't playing. A silver sedan passed through the intersection and kept moving north. Another car soon followed, this time a red something or other. Weren't they the colors of the cars that were spying on them? Nick continued leaning forward until he saw that car, too, roll through the Bull Street intersection. "Idiot!" he'd fallen for one of Chris's conspiracy theories. He grabbed a bite of pizza and resumed his task. "Just a few more," he said to the tabby cat now poking its head out from the latticework.

The remaining folders were equally non-rewarding. RCE was also right, the Doubly Deads did come as advertised—a hodgepodge of whatnots that defied proper filing but that somehow avoided the axeman's purge. Despite their randomness, Nick noticed that RCE did a good job of creating order by organizing them categorically by decade from new to old, with technical items followed by dated correspondence and plain old junk. Nick always found combing through a company's older records, even the D-Squareds, a useful nostalgic endeavor, the peeling back through time every bit as much a history lesson as it was a mundane review for events that might have left a chemical signature to be reckoned with.

He further enjoyed the exercise because it gave him a chance to reminisce about his own career and the stories his father and grandfather told about their days working the copper mines and timber mills of his Upper Peninsula Michigan home. His father worked a variety of mostly white-collar jobs for the mines, while his grandfather rendered much of the wood he felled into the furniture used by the miners' families. The diversity of their experiences, recounted so colorfully in the stories they told, reminded him of the bygone era represented in the D-Squared records.

Nick had never told this to anyone, but he often imagined himself as the preparer of the document in hand, in this case a purchase order for treated logs dated, December 10, 1942. He imagined himself sitting at an executive work desk in PSTRE's administration office, Glen Miller playing on the radio, the starched sleeves of his white cloth button down cuffed above the elbow and a cigarette wafting lazy curls of smoke skyward, while he scrutinized the order. The quantity on the slip of paper suggested that PSTRE ran a formidable and—as the results for the drilling program implied—remarkably clean operation for the time. Were that many logs going to support overhead utility service to a new area of expansion? Or perhaps the order was made in support of the war effort. Silly as the process might seem, the exercise did help him glean that much more from the records. Besides, it was fun.

It was also a journey down technology road. First up, coming from D-Squared box number one, were files mostly generated in the 1980s, during the early days of laser printing. The record here was surprisingly thin, quickly yielding to that lost time of dot matrix before it, and finally to a bevy of folders from the 1970s and 1960s containing files prepared by that old workhorse, the typewriter, and Nick's favorite means of duplication, the mimeograph machine. Here, his sleuthing slowed as he allowed his mind to linger on his middle school days, with fond remembrance of Mrs. Allen, in the AV room, rolling off copy after copy of their next social studies exam. Nick recalled like it was yesterday how the process permeated the air with that soft, sweet smell of mimeograph ink. He even imagined that he caught a whiff of that long forgotten aroma while prying apart the pages of a rusty-stapled piece of legal correspondence from 1967. Alas, by the 1950s, the PSTRE record trail thinned again, yielding to an increasing amount of pieces written in longhand.

Turning to the second box, Nick retrieved the limited remaining file folders that RCE identified as ">1940s," which also included a limited number of pre-depression-era documents. He was overcome by an unsettling feeling while holding the oldest record, a 1919 inter-office memorandum written in cursive with browning ink on onionskin paper when the company operated under its original moniker, Palmetto State Electrical Supply. It was the height of the Spanish flu pandemic, when Word War I was still a terrible and all too recent memory. Did this guy, whose name was written in fanciful looping script, contract the disease? If so, were viral residuals still adhering to the tiny undulations of the page? Nick shuddered and quickly slipped the page back inside its folder.

He thumbed through the contents of the files, working systematically from front to back. Looking up to the magnolia tree where Mrs. Mockingbird was calling merrily away into early night, Nick pulled a two-page piece of correspondence from a folder titled *'Legal Documents'* that, to this point, had failed to live up to his expectations. The pages were sticking. "Huh!" he chirped in response to the small crumb from an ancient executive pastry that sloughed off one of the pages when he peeled them apart, leaving behind a small smudge of grease. *Breakfast anyone?* He mused. Nick skimmed over the facing page, expecting nothing, when his eyes locked onto the words *'tar pipe,'* about two-thirds of the way down the page.

Oh shit!

Reading in earnest, Nick discovered that it was prepared by a Charleston legal firm and was addressed to a Calvin Pearcy, then president of Palmetto, about a pending real estate transaction. The date on the document was August 27, 1928.

Of course! Nick jumped to his feet. He dashed inside to retrieve his laptop. Returning to the porch, he queued up the spreadsheet containing the chronological history for PSTRE and Athens that Michelle pulled together before she left. He compared the 1928 date on the letter to the information contained in the table, then smiled. The correspondence was about the former PSTRE entity's sale of what had to be Parcel C to the City of Charleston in the coming spring—the city still owned the property, hence their inclusion in the lawsuit. Following the thread of the letter, Nick observed that it was written in response to previous discussions between PSTRE and its legal counsel concerning preparations for the sale. What made the document particularly intriguing was counsel's urging that Palmetto address previously identified environmental issues prior to closing. *What issues?* Nick wondered. The language was remarkable, considering that the birth of the environmental movement was still over twenty years away.

Reading still further, Nick discovered that the letter was prepared in response to a singular, multifaceted issue that, as far as PSTRE was concerned, remained regrettably at the heart of the contention going on today. Summed up in three lengthy bullets that spilled over to the following page, the first urged Palmetto to:

> *"Seal off the 'tar pipe' at the northerly boundary between Palmetto and Athens Petrolatum to prevent creosote tars and stormwater overflow from the former 'Pit 5' on Athens property from discharging to Palmetto's property."*

Nick felt a queasy spell coming on. This information could be good *or* bad. They *did* perform creosote operations on Athens property, but at whose direction? There were suddenly more questions than answers. He became downright nauseous after reading the second bullet, which in part stated:

> *"At the same meeting, we urged Palmetto to seal the same pipe at the boundary separating the Palmetto North Property and Athens Petrolatum prior to the sale of the North Property to the city. Furthermore, it was strongly recommended that all remaining pits on the North Property not already having been so, be filled to grade with clean soil capable of supporting grass. It is our understanding that neither action has yet been completed..."*

"No! No! No No! No!" Nick rattled, his mind reeling. "What pits? Why was this never discussed in any of the reports? Surely Merrill knows about this."

Mrs. Mockingbird chattered angrily at Nick's outburst.

And for the *coup de grâce* that flooded his system with nervous excitement, Nick shook his head in disbelief when he read the start of the third bullet:

> *"In our opinion, your comments expressed last Tuesday that Palmetto bears no future responsibility to Athens for damages stemming from the past use of creosote tars on Athens property remains doubtful if you cannot provide written proof of the terms of the gentleman's agreement made between—"*

"Come on!" Nick moaned. Apparently there was a third page, now missing. The staple holding the document together still clasped a tantalizing corner fragment beneath one tooth. A frantic look through the remaining papers in the folder he was holding, and again through the contents of the Doubly Deads, was fruitless.

Michelle was right again: talk about finding something where you least expected it. *Geez!* He was hoping for a miracle to justify M&C's keeping him on the case. Well, he found one, and then some: a catastrophe ninety years in the making.

Nick went back to Ashley House. He changed into a fresh t-shirt and was getting ready to go for that walk to think how best to break the news. A good place to start, of course, was with Chris. Nick grabbed his phone from his shorts pocket and dialed. Chris answered on the fourth ring. "Chris? Nick. You'll never guess what I just found."

He was in their bedroom, slipping on a sneaker when he heard a noise like muted chimes. Nick looked about, opened a window, the phone still pressed to his ear. "Sorry, I thought I heard something. Chris, you'll never guess what."

There it was again, only this time, the chime was repeated. "Hold on," Nick said, annoyed. "I think someone's at the door."

He walked downstairs, opening it without so much as looking out the side window. To his dismay, he found himself looking up at an immense, impeccably dressed Black man in a dark suit. The man was one of the same two men he and Chris had observed following them over the past week. The man glanced at Nick and into the house. He then looked over both shoulders to the street behind him and, without saying a word, reached inside his suit jacket. Startled, Nick jumped backward.

"Nick? You there?" Chris's voice carried off into the air.

The man lifted a hand, and with the other extended a business card in Nick's direction. He then revealed his badge and credentials and said in a booming baritone, "Nick Kozlowski? May I come in? We need to talk."

"*Ah, Chris?*" Nick managed. "You better get over here."

CHAPTER 7

MONDAY

Cordilleran Media Resources
Colfax Avenue, Denver, Colo.
9:07 A.M.

"Is that it?"

"I think so," Melanie replied with reasonable certainty, glancing from the street-view app on her phone to the buildings beyond the passenger-seat window. "I don't see an address, but that has to be it."

Michelle pulled into a nearby parking garage, from which they retraced their course, here and there bumping into one another along the sidewalk like a couple of urban geocachers, following the lead of Melanie's cell phone, in search of Cordilleran Media Resources. They stopped in front of the same building they had peered up at from the car. With no other cues to go by, Michelle shrugged and headed up the marble steps toward the bank of glass doors.

They meandered through the morning foot traffic to a directional marquee on the far side of the entranceway. The object of their information sleuthing was located on the eighth floor, along with a number of other journalistic media outlets and public-relations firms. Equating her tribulations with the Conservancy over the specifics of the mine-entry access agreement to the limits of journalistic license so in question today, Michelle joked that it was probably not a coincidence that the seventh floor was dominated by law offices.

They stepped off the elevator and followed direction signs down an exceptionally wide and tastefully decorated hallway that, to their surprise, opened to a galleria dominated by a sky-lit glass atrium filled with metal art butterflies and tropical plants. The upper floors clearly had been remodeled, like M&C's, only on a much greater scale. Michelle tugged at Melanie's shirtsleeve. She had heard that Colorado—Denver at least—was a state living on culture's cutting edge, but this was just plain weird. Professional offices competed with retail shops and eateries for floor space. It was like so many of the vogue-chic airport concourses she'd become accustomed to wandering through while passing the time during her book-tour connector-flight layovers. Michelle pointed across the indoor courtyard to a set of double doors that identified Cordilleran Media Resources. On either side were offices for Ajax Communications and Terrabyte Recovery Systems, and on either side of these were a computer-repair shop and a camera-supply store that caught Melanie's eye.

On second look, Michelle realized what this place truly was. With few exceptions, the courtyard tables were occupied by smartly dressed professionals peering intently at their computers, speaking into their smartphones or Bluetooth devices, or conversing with one another over a coffee and pastry. Elsewhere, still others huddled in loose groups around recharging stations where electronic lifelines were being energized to meet the day's challenges. This was no attempt to appease the materialistic demands of the next genera-tion of urban professional. No, it was a gathering place where work was performed outside of the office space, an interactive gathering place where those in the media trade could share ideas or eavesdrop on the latest gossip. Michelle found the concept brilliant. What a wonderful, effective way to remain engaged in one's work. The big question left unanswered was where everyone was getting those scrumptious pastries?

They found a similar attention to comfort inside Cordilleran's office. Artistically adorned half-walls and lounge chairs were placed just so to cordon off the room into what Michelle guessed were a dozen or so sections that provided a sense of enclosure while still maintaining a pleasant open feeling. Warm-hued wooden tables, each supporting a computer terminal and printer, were conveniently placed throughout each section; a gas-log fireplace along one wall awaited the first chill of the season. Olivia, the woman on duty at the help desk, informed them that Cordilleran owned sixteen local and regional newspapers from Wyoming to New Mexico and Arizona. Olivia bragged that, "The company caters to the intellectually curious adventurer. We select and promote our publications based of their uniqueness." When Michelle asked what that meant, Olivia was eager to oblige. "Say you're visiting Winter Park and want to know more about the mining history of nearby Hot Sulphur Springs, or you want to go on one of the area's famous wildflower hikes, then the *Grand County Informant* can help you."

Olivia's spiel was honest and heartfelt. She was clearly a woman who loved her job. Michelle said that she was interested in researching the Climax area and wanted to see the *Central Colorado Times*. Olivia complimented Michelle for doing her homework and escorted the girls to a corner area near the stacks of bound print, where they dropped off their things next to a desk overlooking Colfax Avenue.

"Everything's arranged geographically," Olivia explained, motioning to the stacks. "This area covers central Colorado west of Denver to Durango and Montrose." When Michelle asked if it was fine if they could keep their coffees and pastries while they worked, Olivia gestured around the room. Almost everyone was enjoying some sort of refreshment. She then gave Michelle and Melanie a tour of the stacks and a tutorial on how to access newer information on the computer. "Don't be shy about asking for assistance," Olivia offered, before returning to her post at the help desk.

Michelle followed Olivia's instructions to access the *Central Colorado Times*. Melanie meanwhile leafed through one of Michelle's notebooks to find the appropriate Jodi reference. Michelle was wowed by the full-color, interactive nature of the computerized archives. The *C.C. Times*, she was pleased to find, was available electronically from its inaugural printing in 1978. Michelle perused the most recent edition as Melanie continued her search.

The *C.C. Times* was an eclectic, weekly publication. Each issue consisted of four feature articles ranging from adventure to local history to the local artisan scene. Along with the stories came news recaps from around the region and a bargain-hunter section where people could buy and peddle their junk. Inside the front cover was an advertisement from Cordilleran calling for interested parties to check out the *C.C. Times's* sister periodicals to learn about the goings on in other microcosms spread across the region.

"No, I don't need a fly rod and I already have snow shoes!" Michelle grumbled when she clicked on the folder for Volume No. 5, which included the August 1982 issues of the *C.C. Times*. "Stupid pop-ups!"

A young woman wearing a knit hippie hat seated at the table in front of them turned and whispered, "It's a timing thing. They launch you to sponsor sites based on average click-response time." To prove her point, the young woman tilted the chewed end of her pencil in the direction of a tall, slender man with strawberry blonde hair seated two tables over. The man was stabbing his finger in frustration at the keyboard. She told Michelle to wait for the pop-up, and then click the 'X' box to make it go away. Michelle thanked her, and the young woman stuck the pencil back between her teeth and turned back around.

"What was that date?" Michelle asked.

"The twenty-third," Melanie replied.

"You'd think that I'd have that committed to memory by now," Michelle mumbled while scrolling through that August Monday's edition. She wondered what she was doing that day so many years ago; how excited she was to begin her freshman year at Huron College. *Was I already there?*

"Anything?" Melanie asked.

"Not yet." Michelle scrolled some more. "Wait! Here it is. Take a look." Michelle moved aside so that Melanie could slide in closer. Together, they read about the mysterious disappearance of Dylan Streeter from the Panner's and Picker's Rendezvous event.

"That's awful," Melanie said. "Who was Dylan Streeter?"

"I don't know," Michelle said. "Jodi didn't say. Remember the other day when you read about that guy named Laney?"

"*Oh!*" Melanie said with alarm. "I do. If this Jodi person is implying that the disappearances are connected, what do you think it means?"

"I don't know," Michelle answered with equal concern.

They continued to read. Much like the piece about the recently missing William Laney, this article was comprised of a lot of filler talk because there was little to tell. The police didn't have many facts, at least nothing that they were willing to share. The only thing in common between the two cases, beyond that both men had disappeared from a mountain-man-type event—which in itself was intriguing—was that both had an expertise in archeology and had disappeared under mysterious circumstances wearing period clothing. Michelle chewed at her lip. She glanced to Melanie, who was looking back for answers. *What was it that Jodi wanted her to find?*

"I'm not sure that we can trust this Jodi person," Melanie commented, upon reading the article a second time.

In spite of Melanie's skepticism, Michelle refused to give up hope that Jodi was trying to help. She had an idea. Michelle typed the name Streeter into the help function on the computer screen, where she was taken to a follow-up article written some months later. Here again, she found nothing exceptional until she read the term *linsey-woolsey* used to describe a scrap of fabric found in the woods not far from where Dylan Streeter had gone missing.

He was wearing a linsey-woolsey garment at the time of his disappearance...

"Oh, my god!" Michelle squealed. She clicked back to the original article as fast as possible.

"What is it?" Melanie said with a shiver of excitement.

"*There!*" Michelle pointed to a face in the original crime-scene photo taken at the Rendezvous, after the police had been summoned. "See that guy?" She pointed to the younger of the two policemen in the photo. "He was one of the officers that day at the field station when I found that skeleton. He spoke to me!"

"Are you serious? What does that mean?"

"I'm not sure." Michelle was breathing rapidly when she realized that the clothing on the skeleton was linsey-woolsey, and that the young officer in the photo was one of the authorities who took the skeleton away without processing the scene. "There was no mention of it anywhere on the radio or in the newspapers. The body just disappeared. This has to be what Jodi wanted me to see!" She then read the photo caption and discovered this was not all. Although the young officer was not named, his superior was—sheriff Hollis Walker.

Michelle thought she was going to be sick.

Melanie swallowed hard before asking, her voice tremulous, "Isn't that the name of the guy who's in charge at the Conservancy?"

Michelle also swallowed. "Yes, something like that. My contact, Beth, calls him Bud. She has to clear things through him and another guy named Joe Hayden, who I think actually runs the day-to-day stuff." Michelle's mind raced. She struggled to wrap her head around the connection between what Jodi implied was a long-standing relationship between the Conservancy and the local authorities.

An uneasy pall settled over their workstation. The body language of the young woman in the hippie hat and that of the man with the strawberry blond hair suggested that they were listening in.

Lowering her voice, Melanie asked if Michelle recognized anyone else in the photo.

"No," Michelle said, still pointing to the computer screen "Just him—that officer kneeling in front of Bud Walker."

Tarryall Mountain Foundation
Copper Mountain, Colo.
1:25 P.M.

"Do you really think you found the body of that man?" Melanie asked.

They'd spoken little since leaving Cordilleran and picking up I-70 west out of Denver. The topic of conversation, when they did speak, was the relevance of the warnings embedded in Jodi's cryptic emails, which were all too clear now: they were stepping into the murder trails of Dylan Streeter and William Laney.

"I don't know. Maybe…probably." Michelle had now dismissed the notion of a mysterious third-party hacker group, now that she saw the officer's face in that photo from six years before her discovery of the skeleton. "Whatever happened then must still be going on. I'm sure of it. What the Conservancy told Connor was a smokescreen. I also get the feeling that Jodi doesn't know whom she can trust. What do you think?"

Melanie had to admit that she agreed.

They drove on in silence, mulling over the situation that loomed ahead.

The communities of Lawson and Idaho Springs were distant memories when Melanie's phone rang. "It's Kerry," Melanie said, her mood brightening. "Hi Kerry! What's up? Where are we? Somewhere west of Denver, why? What's going on? Uh-oh, What's wrong?"

Michelle's heart sank.

"Are you serious? What are you going to do? I see. Uh-huh. Uh-huh. Right." A sigh. "I understand. Don't worry, we will. I'll tell Michelle. Yes, we will. And Kerry, please be careful. Love you, bye." Melanie rang off. Her slouch said it all.

"Is she alright?"

"No," Melanie said firmly. "I mean, she is, but Kerry can't come. Not right away at least. Something's come up with work. That special needs patient of hers I was telling you about? He's escaped."

"*Escaped?* When?" Michelle gasped.

"Between Saturday night and yesterday morning. Kerry wanted to let us know in case we hear something on the news."

"On the news? Does she have any idea where he is?"

"Not yet. That's the problem. Something else has also happened. She wouldn't talk about it. I think that's why she mentioned the news."

Michelle waited for Melanie to elaborate.

"Kerry was at a conference in Florida, about to board a plane to come here, when she was notified. She's on her way back to Washington state now to help with the search."

Michelle sensed the strain in her friend's voice. "Mel, from everything you've told me about your sister, I'm sure everything will work out for the best."

"Thanks," Melanie said. "Appreciated. I'm sure of it, too, but I still worry. Kerry is one of the few who can manage him. My concern is that I don't know if anyone *can* control him when his violent personality takes over, especially outside of a controlled environment."

"I see," Michelle said. "Hopefully the authorities will have found him by the time she gets home."

Melanie's demeanor brightened. "Yeah, hopefully. Kerry did promise to come, once the situation is under control."

"Now, that's good news!"

They were enjoying a return to normalcy when Michelle's cell phone sounded off in her cup holder like an angry rattlesnake. The sound made them jump. Michelle had forgotten to switch it off vibrate mode after leaving Cordilleran. "It's Mark, our camera guy," she said, seeing his name pop up on the view screen. The call lasted less than a minute, when Michelle trilled her lips and tossed the phone back into the cup holder.

"Let me guess, he can't make it either."

Michelle frowned. "Not until tomorrow morning." She checked the GPS for their arrival time. "Tell you what. What do you say we stop for lunch first? I've had enough stress for now. It'll be lunchtime by the time we get there, anyway. I say we eat, and *then* go to the Conservancy. We can meet them for a while, feel out the waters, and set a schedule. I'll tell them that we don't want to do any exploring until Mark gets here. After that, we can head back to Breckenridge and check into our hotel."

Melanie liked the idea. It was a safe and simple plan.

"With any luck," Michelle said, "Mark won't get here until later in the morning. Maybe Kerry will be on her way by then."

———

Copper Mountain was nothing like Michelle expected. Being the fuddy-duddy homebody she was, Michelle never once made the five-mile, as the crow flies, jaunt over the spine of the Tenmile Range to visit Breckenridge's sister ski-bum town back in her college days. Nick always said that she had the home range of a deer, and that wasn't much. Denver and Colorado Springs might have been several hours to the east, but they were in the direction of home and shopping. But Copper Mountain? It was a half-hour's ride in the wrong direction, on the wrong side of the mountain, and, thus, a place completely outside her comfort zone.

"This is gorgeous!" Melanie said, taking in the scenery. "You really were never here before?"

"No," Michelle replied, embarrassed that she'd missed so many past opportunities. Breckenridge was a metropolis compared to the quaint mountain-village feel of Copper Mountain. The setting was different as well, far more open and majestic; the bright, grass-covered ski slopes offered eye-popping contrast to the surrounding dark of the evergreen forest cover and the gray, craggy peaks beyond. The resort community occupied a low-lying opening at the base of the mountains that provided a spatial relationship between mountain and plain that her field-camp area simply did not have.

A flow of off-season tourist traffic buzzed around the village community. Michelle decided to leave their car in the common-area lot off of Ten Mile Circle so that they would be forced to walk off lunch. The Eagle BBQ made for a fine choice that required a walk. It didn't take long to canvass the walkable west half of town, which was just as well because it would be the right time to head to the Conservancy by the time they made it back to the car.

"This can't be right," Michelle remarked when she queued in the address for the Tarryall Mountain Foundation. "The GPS says that it's right here. Look."

So, back out of the SUV they climbed, and to their surprise, discovered that they'd already walked past the place—twice. The Conservancy occupied a street-level end unit fronting Ten Mile Circle off of the lot where they were parked.

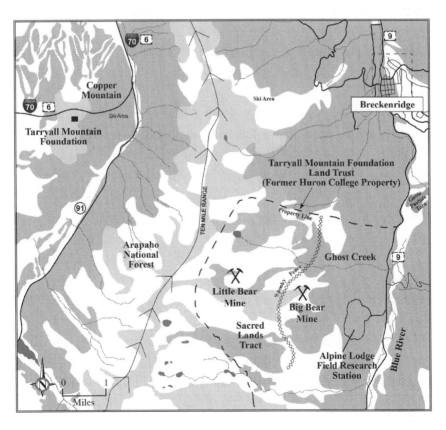

"You honestly didn't know the place was right here?" Melanie asked with no small measure of relief in her voice.

"No!" Michelle answered, sharing in Melanie's feeling of relief. "I thought it was going to be some lodgy place out in the sticks, didn't you? I wish I'd checked. This changes everything."

"Seriously!" Melanie agreed. The Conservancy's unexpected location in a busy and high visibility place erased the undercurrent of unspoken anxiety they shared about disappearing without a trace, like Dylan Streeter and William Laney, in some godforsaken tract of forest outside of town.

The melodic ring of a doorway chime announced their entrance into the Conservancy's street-front office. Inside, a huddle of adventure seekers decked out in all the trendy outerwear pored over a topographical map with an older gentleman whom, by his attire, Michelle figured was a retiree working for the Conservancy. To their right, a second Conservancy spokesperson, younger, perhaps in his late fifties, obliged a family's interest in some area point of interest. The staff member attending to the trendy sorts looked up from the map to say that someone would be with them shortly. Michelle thanked him with a wave then whispered into Melanie's ear, "So far so good."

Melanie returned the whisper, asking Michelle if she recognized either Conservancy representative.

Michelle said that she wasn't sure.

An immense wooden plaque welcoming all visitors to the Tarryall Mountain Foundation hung above the central corridor behind what doubled as an information desk and checkout counter. The common area walls were painted in soothing earth tones. Framed pictures enticed patrons to explore everything that the wilds of Colorado had to offer. A collection of beautiful, hand-hewn wooden tables to their right provided space to meet with Conservancy staff. Michelle noticed that the highly lacquered tables complimented an equally gorgeous map cabinet stationed in a near corner: a commissioned set. Michelle meant to nudge Melanie, only to find that Melanie had drifted off to browse the pamphlets in a nearby kiosk.

Laughter from an office behind and to the right of the information desk caught Michelle's attention. She took a few steps in that direction, squinting to read the collection of nameplates vertically arranged next to the doorway. There was a Derrick Schmidt, Carol Jones, Judith Barrie, and a Vikki Atkinson, but no Jodi something or other.

Michelle took another step closer and peered inside. She saw a young woman of perhaps twenty with a foot propped on her desk throw a pen at a young man of similar age seated several desks over. The young woman did a double take when she realized that she was being watched. *Don't sweat it,* Michelle mouthed. The young woman acknowledged Michelle's discretion then grimaced at her partner, letting him know that they'd been busted. A folded paper sign drawn with multiple colors of ink and resting on the corner of her desk announced that this was *Kaycee's Place.* Michelle noticed that Kaycee's partner in play pretended not to be embarrassed. His desk, too, had a kitschy sign identifying him as *Derrick "Storm" Schmidt,* and below that, a sheet of printer paper taped to the edge of his desk read: *D-Man's Weather for Today.* Michelle laughed at the forecast: "Hot and sunny with periods of rain, a snow shower possible."

Ah! Interns. To be young again.

"Hello? Can I help you?"

Michelle looked around to find a middle-aged woman with shocking white hair coming her way from the hall corridor behind the information desk. "Yes. Hi! I'm Michelle Snow," Michelle said, using her penname.

"Of course! We've been expecting you. I'm Beth Stockwell," the woman said with a welcoming smile. "I feel as if I know you already. No trouble finding us, I hope?"

"None at all." Michelle glanced over her shoulder for Melanie, who was doing a duck shuffle in their direction from the kiosk with a fist full of brochures clutched in her hand. "And this is my friend, Melanie Sutton."

Melanie stuffed the brochures into a pocket and repeated the introduction.

"Please, call me Beth." She then took Melanie by the shoulders and said, "You're even more beautiful than I imagined. I could only guess what you might look like from what I read in Michelle's book. And do please accept my condolences."

The unorthodox greeting was overwhelming. Melanie was touched that Beth Stockwell expressed her feelings about the loss of her brother. Whatever the Conservancy had to hide, whatever it was into, Michelle and Melanie were encouraged by the thought that Beth Stockwell was someone whom they could trust.

Beth asked if they needed anything. She then gestured toward the back room that continued to occupy a part of Michelle's attention. "We call it the *Play Pen*," she said with a titter.

As if on cue, D-Man Schmidt emerged from the Play Pen. He glanced toward their guests and said, "I beg your pardon, Ms. Stockwell. Have you seen Carol or Vikki? We need to do that thing for Mr. Monroe this afternoon"

Beth looked to the clock on the wall and scowled. "I asked them to escort those hikers to Mayflower Gulch. They're not back yet? Call them. Tell them to get a move on and get back here to help you with the preparations."

"Yes, Ms. Stockwell," D-Man said, and went back inside. They watched him retrieve a two-way radio from the charging station along the back wall of the Play Pen. Beth maintained her focus on D-Man until she was satisfied that her message was appropriately sent.

"That was Derrick, one of our new summer hires." Pinching her eyes close together, Beth said, "I keep telling him—all of them—to keep track of the time. Kids these days don't pay attention to anything!"

Michelle laughed. In his defense, she said, "I remember being just like him." Then pointing to the sign on Storm's desk, added, "I like his weather prognostication. It reminds me of my field-camp days when the only thing predictable about the mountain weather was its unpredictability."

"Isn't that the truth!" Beth concurred with a laugh.

"Beth? Are these our guests?"

It was the older gentleman who'd been attending to the trendy sorts. Michelle instinctively looked around. She discovered to her dismay that she and Melanie were the only remaining outsiders in the building.

"Yes, Teddy," Beth said, her voice tight. "This is Michelle Snow and her friend Melanie Sutton—you know, that boy's sister. Michelle, Melanie, please meet Teddy Monroe." Beth took an immediate step back.

Submissive, was Michelle's read.

Monroe's greeting was obligatory rather than genuine. Tall, thin, and craggy-faced, Teddy Monroe was a tough read. His steely eyes were vacant and impenetrable. Monroe, Michelle knew from reading the Conservancy's list of officers on their web site, was Tarryall's acting president. His name was listed beneath that of Bud Walker—the former town sheriff—who carried emeritus status with the Conservancy. "It's a pleasure to meet you, Mr. Monroe," Michelle said, hoping that returning his uninspiring words with pleasantry would break the ice. "I'd like to thank you and Tarryall for helping me with my project."

"Not a problem," Monroe said, unmoved by Michelle's outreach. "Don't hesitate to let me know how I may be of assistance." A glimmer came to his aged eyes when he looked at Beth and asked, "Does Joe know that they're here?"

"I don't think so. Let me check."

They watched Beth hurry down a central corridor to the deeper recesses of the office. Monroe turned away without speaking to place a call on his cell. He then answered an incoming call on the office landline.

"That guy gives me the creeps," Melanie whispered.

"He's not very friendly," Michelle agreed. "Did you see how Beth cowers when he's around? And she's a Conservancy officer."

"I did!" Melanie said, struggling not to show her anger. "I get the idea that this is a good ole boys club."

"Michelle!" a heavy voice called from the direction of the information desk.

Startled by the unexpected hail, they watched a powerfully built man emerge from the same corridor. The fullness of his proportions was not apparent until he cleared the desk area. Behind him came the same Conservancy employee they saw earlier with Monroe, and behind him, trailing at a measured distance, was Beth Stockwell. "I'm Joe Hayden," the big man said. "Glad you could come. Safe travels?"

That voice! I remember that voice.

"Yes," Michelle said trying to conceal her intimidation. It was the same voice she often heard in the background while speaking with Beth. No wonder the poor woman cowered, having to work with such unpleasant and physically imposing men. There was something else about Hayden's voice that she couldn't place.

"Didn't startle you, did I," Hayden challenged, his manner bragging; eyes all but undressing Michelle and Melanie without shame.

Teddy Monroe, they might have misread, based on a first impression biased by Jodi's warnings that something malevolent lurked beneath the surface of the Conservancy's public face. Joe Hayden, however, came as advertised—a bully. What the man lacked in height was more than compensated for by mass, an incredible thickness of muscle shrouded by a layer of age fat, a cocky swagger, and an unsettling glare. Michelle gauged him to be not much older than she was, perhaps sixty, but with the physical prowess of a man twenty years younger. He had a massive head that he kept shaved to accent the facial scars that marred an otherwise handsome face. Simply put, Joe Hayden *wanted* to intimidate people.

"Of course not," Michelle lied. "It's been a long couple of days, with the drive and all. We're both a bit rammy."

"Right. And you must be Melanie Sutton," Hayden said, shifting his glare.

It was a demand, not a question. Melanie forced a tight smile.

Hayden again sized them up. He then introduced Bill Clay, a tall, gaunt man with soft features, and asked Beth to retrieve a folder from the information desk. "What have you told her?" he asked her.

"Nothing yet, Joe," Beth said evenly. "I figured you wanted to tell her."

"Tell me what?" Michelle asked, concerned that her plans were again on the verge of falling apart.

The door chime sounded, disrupting the conversation…and in walked the tall man with the strawberry blonde hair.

Another surprise.

Michelle thought she would explode.

Relief came when the tall man glided into the room and, surprised by the girls' presence, ignored the Conservancy staff to address Michelle with a refined air. "Hello, ma'am," he said, looking from Michelle to Melanie. "I believe I was seated several desks over from you and your friend this morning at Cordilleran."

"Can I help you?" Hayden demanded. He was clearly ruffled by the stranger's disregard for professional etiquette.

The tall man ignored Hayden's posturing. "My apologies," he said. "I'm Dave Kerrigan. I have an appointment with Bud Walker. He's expecting me, though I'm embarrassed to say that we did not set an exact time. I hope now isn't inconvenient."

Hayden was at a loss. "I'm not aware of this," he said, and looked in the direction of the back offices. "Bud's attending to something at the moment. Why don't you wait here while I speak with him. Bill Clay, this is…what did you say your name was again?"

"Dave Kerrigan," the man with the strawberry blonde hair repeated. "Like I was saying to the lady, I was in Denver this morning, at Cordilleran Media Resources, looking up an article that covered the properties I wanted to speak to Mr. Walker about. I'm thinking of sweetening the pot." Then giving a nod in Michelle and Melanie's direction, Kerrigan hoped that their search was also successful.

"Quite. Thank you. We found everything we were looking for, and then some," Michelle felt compelled to say.

Hayden acted like he was puzzled.

Michelle found humor in Joe Hayden's discomfort at not being in control of the situation. She surmised that he had to be wondering just what it was she and Melanie were researching at the news-media outlet. Michelle wanted to laugh at the thought of Hayden poring over back copies of the *C.C. Times* into the wee hours of the morning until he reached the article with the picture of his boss reporting Dylan Streeter's disappearance.

Bill Clay escorted the attaché-wielding Kerrigan to one of the commissioned tables.

Hayden wanted to say something to Michelle when he was interrupted by a call. The ring came not from the Play Pen docking station phone clipped to his belt, but from his personal cell, which he retrieved from an opposite pocket. Whoever it was, one look at the display screen gave Joe Hayden pause for concern. "This is Joe. Yes, sir. Affirmative. A few minutes ago. I don't know, sir."

Despite Joe Hayden's alpha personality, whoever it was on the other end of the line was a bigger dog. *Bud Walker perhaps?* The girls noticed that Beth was also nervous. It wasn't a reach for Michelle and Melanie to assume that the call was about them.

"That's not going to happen, I can assure you," Hayden promised the anonymous caller. "Yes, sir." Hayden turned away from his visitors. He then placed his hand over the mouthpiece. "This is going to take a while." He asked Beth to show Michelle and Melanie around. "Give me half an hour," he added, and stormed off down the corridor.

Beth asked if they would like to take a walk. Michelle said that she would, and Beth escorted them on a tour of the immediate area that Michelle and Melanie had explored after lunch. Liberated from the testosterone infused atmosphere of the Conservancy's office, Beth Stockwell was a completely different person, brimming with

Rick Ley

confidence and far more outgoing than she had been during any of their previous telephone conversations. Melanie was right: the Tarryall Mountain Foundation was a good ole boys club. Michelle felt sorry for Beth. She probably didn't get many opportunities to interact professionally with others of her gender.

They walked and talked, stopping every so often to admire the light green tiger striping of the summertime ski slopes. Mostly they talked about the *Foundation*, as Beth preferred to call her place of employment. Michelle thought that the random chatter was Beth's polite way of venting her relief at being able to speak freely. But when she continued her rambling, Michelle became concerned, as did Melanie, because at no point did Beth Stockwell give the impression that she was Jodi.

Tarryall, they did learn, was a non-profit organization that held lands in trust, or purchased property outright, for the purpose of protection from future development. Beth estimated Tarryall's current holdings to exceed thirty thousand acres.

"It's become something of a status symbol for people to entrust us with their property," Beth cooed with pride. "We're approached all the time by wealthy clients who want to impress their friends."

"That's…interesting," Michelle said, fighting the urge to call such people ridiculous.

Was there actually a level of one upsmanship beyond the yacht or McMansion?

"In some instances, the Foundation will flip a property for more desirable lands, so long as the client has expressed his consent in advance." Beth further revealed that Foundation senior employees like her each receive a base salary with an accelerator clause entitling them to a percentage of gross sales exceeding that year's territory goal. Since the Foundation—the Conservancy, Tarryall, the list of names and nicknames kept getting longer—did more buying than selling, *sales* consisted primarily of monetary donations solicited from businesses, philanthropists, and the smattering of visitors who signed the guest registry. Each employee was responsible for a different region of the country that rotated yearly so that no one employee continued to reap the benefits from the lucrative east and west coasts. "We all get our turn at the prize," she said, excited, making it a point to mention that her territory for this year was the California-Washington corridor, including Alaska and Hawaii. "All remaining funds, once salary, operating expenses, and sales perks are accounted for, are allocated toward the purchase of additional property, or for special projects that enhance the monetary and ecological value of existing properties we currently manage."

This was a fascinating bit of discovery that Michelle was sure to include in her book, but what she really wanted to know was the Conservancy's plans for the Sacred Lands tract. Beth assured her that the Foundation was going to keep the property, owing to its popularity. The Sacred Lands tract was an asset by virtue of its history, even if the mines were making the property increasingly difficult to manage. Beth expressed with pained amusement the ironic blunder in logic that followed the Foundation's decision to make the mines off limits to the public, except for special invitation. Intended to decrease the organization's headaches, the action had the opposite effect, increasing public interest and spawning so much whack-job tripe that Beth joked the Sacred Lands had become their very own Area 51.

"Oh, brother!" Michelle said, batting her eyes in disbelief. Maybe she hadn't misjudged the locals after all.

"My, yes!" Beth tittered, correctly reading the astonishment on both girls' faces. "There were so many rumors flying about that we even printed a pamphlet to dispel the nonsense. I'll make sure to give both of you a copy when we get back to the office."

"Did it work?" Melanie asked.

Beth turned beet red. "Not in the least! In fact, it further complicated matters. On the good side, we've seen an increase in the number and size of charitable contributions since the pamphlet was published."

They stopped at a bench with a nice view of the action happening around them. Beth continued to talk, mostly with Melanie. For reasons she couldn't explain to her satisfaction, Michelle was discomforted at the notion that the Conservancy would use the pamphlet as a marketing tool. A tragedy had occurred there—her tragedy, and Melanie's, too. Granted the matter hit close to home, and Beth's explanation was reasonable, and maybe it was just in Beth's delivery, but still...

Distracted, Michelle didn't notice the folder Beth was holding for her to see. "What's this?" Michelle asked. Inside, she found a copy of the authorized entry agreement for the mines. It had been marked-up yet again with red pen, this time only where the Little Bear mine was concerned. "I don't understand. Nothing's changed," which was probably true to anyone outside of the legal realm. From what Michelle could tell, the wordsmithing hadn't altered the document's content or meaning in the least. "Is there a problem?"

Beth expressed her frustration. "This came from legal this morning. Don't ask me why alterations were made, other than because they had the opportunity to do so. I spoke at length with your agent and our lawyers over the weekend, and they told me that everything had been settled."

It took every bit of will for Michelle to hold her temper.

"Don't fret, my dear!" Beth said calmly. "I don't see this as anything more than an inconvenience. Bud Walker and Teddy Monroe are working out the details. You'll like Bud. In the meantime, there's no reason why you can't still see the remainder of the property. So long as you stick to the terms of the rest of the agreement, everything should be fine. We can set you up to do that first thing in the morning."

Michelle waited for her nerves to settle. She thanked Beth for her honesty, more so for being her advocate. One way or another, this balsa-wood glider of a project was going to make it through the wind tunnel of red tape. But not without Michelle first throwing in her own complication. She explained her photographer's dilemma, saying that she didn't want to begin her groundwork until he arrived, which could be anytime tomorrow. Until then, she said that she and Melanie would shift their base to Breckenridge to see if any of the shopkeepers from back in the day who were still in business were willing to talk.

<hr />

Evening Star Hotel
Breckenridge, Colo.
7:34 P.M.

"My turn," Melanie said, grabbing her things and making a beeline for the bathroom. "Whew! Steamy in here," she said, fanning the air to clear a path through the curtain of fog.

"I should have warned you," Michelle giggled. "I couldn't find a switch for the fan."

"Darn it!" Melanie replied, popping her head back into the main room. "Mind if I borrow your shampoo?"

"Not at all. They didn't give us any?"

"Ah…Not that I can see. What kind of place is this?"

The Evening Star may be a hotel on paper, but it was a motel by any other name. Connor Lewis had taken care of the arrangements; and, yes, Michelle knew that publishing budgets were tight these days, but *"Come on, Connor!"* she bitched loud enough for Melanie to interrupt spreading out her toiletries on the bathroom countertop. She would have paid for a better place, for Melanie's sake if nothing else, had she been forewarned. "We can get another place," Michelle called out, making no effort to hide her irritation.

"You don't have to shout!" Melanie kidded. "It's fine. Besides, I'm too tired to pick up and move."

Michelle plopped down on her bed. She propped a pillow behind her and relaxed against the headboard. To the place's credit, the Evening Star did have remarkably comfortable beds. Splayed out with her computer parked between her legs and a remote in her hand, Michelle realized that she was too tired to compute or watch TV, and closed her eyes. The steady soft hiss of the shower was soothing. Michelle soon drifted off into that pleasurable twilight domain between sleep and consciousness. She found herself floating about, weightless as a feather, bumping against fluffy clouds, comforted in the fact that the day had gone well. She might not have gotten any closer to unraveling the Jodi mystery, but she did find the Conservancy staff mostly accepting of her presence—and, more importantly, she didn't get herself or Melanie hurt.

A knocking sound pried her from her siesta. Michelle blinked her eyes open and stretched. Melanie was drying her hair. She must have fumbled the dryer against the mirror or bathroom countertop. Michelle had no sooner closed her eyes than she heard it again. The knocking was coming from the front door. Michelle slid the laptop aside and pulled herself up with a groan. She shuffled her way across the carpet, expecting to find housekeeping coming to ask if the room met their expectations. She would of course say yes, and ask for a courtesy bottle of shampoo for Melanie. Without thinking to check the peephole first, Michelle opened the door and, to her dismay, there stood Dave Kerrigan.

Michelle ducked back inside.

"Don't be alarmed, Ms. Kozlowski. I mean you no harm," the man said, holding up a hand in deference.

"Who are you?" Michelle demanded, peering out from behind the door she was using as a shield.

"If you please," the man said, and reached inside his suit jacket for his credentials. "I'm Special Agent Ron Sanderson with the FBI. May I come in?"

For the briefest moment, Michelle was gripped by the same immobility she experienced in her nightmare. She scrutinized the man's credentials. They appeared to be in order. Michelle backed up to allow the agent inside the moment she could do so without fear of falling down. "Am I in trouble?" Michelle asked.

Special Agent Sanderson answered her question with a comment. "You don't seem surprised." He canvassed the room, observing the layout, looking for the roommate.

"Sir, I'm not sure what to think." This much was true. Having experienced so much extraordinary turmoil in her life, the sudden if not timely presence of government intervention was somehow fitting.

"Please, call me Ron," The agent said. "In regards to your question, from the Bureau, *no*. From others, this remains to be seen. It's our responsibility to ensure that nothing happens to you or your friend."

"Our responsibility?" Michelle cut a glance in the direction of the window.

"You needn't bother," Sanderson told her. "You won't see anyone."

The whirring hum of Melanie's hair dryer abruptly stopped, casting the room into silence. "Were you talking to me?" Melanie called from the bathroom.

"Mel, are you decent? Can you come out here?"

Melanie did, and in a repeat of Michelle's recoil, made a dash to safety.

"It's okay," Michelle said. "He's from the FBI."

"The FBI?" Melanie replied, her voice a thin squeak. She eased out from behind the bathroom door. "Is this about the Conservancy? What happened?"

Sanderson repeated his introduction, saying, "If you mean the Tarryall Mountain Foundation, that answer is yes. Nothing, however, has happened; at least nothing yet. Like I just told Ms. Kozlowski, that's what we're here to prevent."

Michelle confirmed that everything the agent said was true.

"What *is* going on, Special Agent—I mean, Ron?" Michelle asked. She then asked that he call her and Melanie by their first names, and wondered how he knew her last. All of her communications with the Conservancy, including the booking of the hotel room, were made under her maiden and penname, Snow.

"In due time. A few more introductions are in order first. If you don't mind?" Sanderson motioned for Michelle to open the interior door to her left. "Your choice of accommodations was most fortuitous. I should add that I did take the liberty to have your room moved so that we would have three adjoining rooms. My room is there." Sanderson pointed to the interior door to her right.

Michelle opened the left door. She hesitated before the second and still closed door that opened to the adjoining room.

"Go right ahead," Sanderson encouraged. "They're waiting for your knock."

Michelle grabbed the knob and knocked lightly. The door opened almost immediately, pulling her forward. She found herself looking into the face of a vaguely familiar woman with blond hair and a bobbed haircut.

"It's a pleasure to finally meet you, Ms. Kozlowski. I'm Catherine Solomon. And this," Solomon said, stepping aside for Michelle to see, "is my associate, Janelle Stone."

Catherine Solomon was petite and attractive with an athletic build. Michelle gaged her to be around thirty. Janelle Stone was about the same age, and tall like she was, with long, flowing, loosely curled hair, but with brown hair rather than Michelle's fawn color. Melanie commented that besides the similarity in names, Michelle and Janelle could be mother and daughter. Michelle welcomed Catherine and Janelle inside, their presence having an immediate and reassuring effect that Michelle and Melanie appreciated. "This is my friend, Melanie Sutton," Michelle said, "though I'm guessing you already know that."

"Yes," the Solomon woman said, walking in Melanie's direction. "Please, call me Cat."

"And I'm just Janelle," Ms. Stone said with a polite wave from the doorway.

Michelle and Melanie sat on facing edges of their respective beds. Special Agent Sanderson took a seat across from them on the credenza near the window, where he could peer behind the curtain and keep tabs on the parking lot and front door. Cat and Janelle, meanwhile, maneuvered a couple of chairs to the foot of each bed.

"I met Catherine several years ago under circumstances very similar to yours, Michelle," Sanderson said with a soft chuckle.

Michelle looked at Cat.

Where do I know her? She's someone...

"In the process," Sanderson continued, "we discovered that the company Catherine and Janelle work for uses sophisticated surveillance techniques that the Bureau finds in its best interest to use when we're stretched thin. We've since developed a mutually beneficial relationship that's helped the Bureau's investigation into Tarryall." Sanderson warded off competing questions from the girls, saying that he would fill them in with all they needed to know after he made one last introduction. Sanderson used his phone as a walkie-talkie. "This is Sanderson. Are we clear?"

"Affirmative," they heard an oddly familiar masculine voice reply.

"Very good. You can come in now."

"Roger that."

Footfalls soon approached, followed by a single knock, and, when the door opened wide, in walked Kris with a 'K.'

"Ms. Kozlowski, Ms. Sutton, I'd like you to meet Special Agent Ryan Wells."

The girls' mouths fell open.

Special Agent Wells gave them a salute of recognition. Rather than stepping forward to meet them, he maintained his post at the front door, where he could peek out from behind the heavy drape to monitor the street traffic where Sanderson could not. Wells did, however, apologize for his deception and said that he and his partner Special Agent Amy Morgan very much enjoyed the opportunity to get to know them better over dinner. Amy, he said, was parked down the street watching the vehicle traffic coming in and out of the motel.

The protection detail notwithstanding, Michelle couldn't help from becoming angry. Melanie had taken a liking to Kris with a 'K,' even if she thought she would never see him again. Right or wrong, Melanie was clearly crestfallen, and like Michelle, didn't appreciate being used. "So," Michelle said hotly, "Kristian Fletcher was just a cover...and I don't recall who you said you were," she continued, speaking to Sanderson.

"That is correct, Michelle," Sanderson answered on Agent Wells's behalf, calling her Michelle for the first time. "Dave Kerrigan is the name I am using. We need to maintain our covers in the event that Tarryall checks our backstops—which they did mine, though I'm reasonably certain it was only for real estate acquisition purposes. Might I add that I'm impressed that *you* checked on Agent Wells's backstop. You both have been as careful as we hoped you would be."

"*Treasure Island* is one of my favorite books," Wells said, jumping into the conversation. "Fletcher Christian might be too much of a coincidence in the right circles, so I flipped the name around and doctored the spelling. I got nervous when you knew what a palynologist was. I thought impersonating a pollen specialist would be safe. I never had someone press my cover that quickly before." Perceptive, Wells next addressed Melanie's all too poorly concealed disappointment. "You can still call me anytime," he said with that rock star smile of his.

His words teased a dusky blush.

"Wait a minute!" Michelle blurted. "How did you...How long..." Michelle's mind was spinning so rapidly that she couldn't formulate a complete sentence.

"Let me explain," Sanderson said in a soothing voice. He reached into his suit-coat pocket and pulled out a sheet of paper. He unfolded it and handed it to Michelle. "This is a search warrant allowing the FBI to monitor your communications with Tarryall. You fell onto our radar last fall when you first contacted the organization about your book project."

Michelle's face tightened. "Since last year?"

"You have nothing to fear, Michelle; nor do you, Melanie," Cat interjected, sensing the need for feminine intervention. She explained that the surveillance permitted the Bureau only to record Michelle's business related discussions and electronic transmissions with Tarryall made from her cell phone and computer. Cat completed their part by saying that she, too, was once under investigation, and regretted the necessary intrusion.

Sanderson thanked Cat and expressed his own sincere hopes that Michelle and Melanie didn't find the Bureau's presence too unsettling.

Cat took in the exchange between the FBI agent and the women that followed. A smile parted her lips. "You know, Michelle, like Ron said, I was literally standing in your shoes four years ago. The world was crashing in around me, and Ron and his team were my lifeline. You can trust him and Ryan. Our job—Janelle's and mine—one of them at least, was to scrub through your phone and electronic transmissions looking for names, and from there figure out the connection between those names: Tarryall, and the greater syndicate organization that Tarryall belongs to. It has been our job since the two of you were vetted to keep tabs on your schedule and itinerary so that the Bureau could arrange for your protection. Rest assured that we did not invade your privacy in any other way."

"That's correct," Sanderson concurred. "In fact, I would like both of you to sit down with Catherine and Janelle and review the transcripts of your correspondences with Tarryall. You can see for yourselves. We also have a number of questions you might be able to clarify."

"It will help you think of things you otherwise might have forgotten," Wells inserted.

"What things? A crime organization? Tell me you're not serious." Michelle was incapable of keeping her voice from rising.

How on Earth can this be happening to me again?

Sanderson looked to Wells, who said that the coast was still clear, before continuing. "Let me begin by saying that the Tarryall Mountain Foundation is a legitimate and reputable business." And after a weighty pause added, "It is also a front."

Michelle tensed. Melanie stared back at the FBI agent with an icy glare.

"Thought so," Sanderson said sagely. "I see that you're not all that surprised. We have evidence that Tarryall—the Conservancy, as you call it—is one of an untold number of cells working both together and independently as part of a multi-national art and antiquities smuggling ring."

"A smuggling ring? In the middle of Colorado?" Michelle wasn't certain whether she should laugh or be sick.

"Don't be fooled into any false sense of security," Sanderson warned. "These people are ruthless and not afraid to kill to protect their interests. Just ask Catherine. She can tell you first-hand what these people are like."

Michelle was struck with the sudden recognition that Cat Solomon was the blonde woman whose face was splashed across the media outlets, along with that of her husband and their two friends, a few years back. They were survivors of some pirate-museum treasure-heist debacle, or something in Haiti, or was it the Bahamas?

"That was you?" Michelle asked.

Cat smiled. Janelle pointed at Cat with proud confirmation.

Had she looked into the mirror on the wall, Michelle would have observed her porcelain skin was as ashen as Melanie's. "You think they're the same people? I mean, part of the same ring?"

"Tarryall? Yes," Sanderson said solemnly. "A different cell, of course, but we're certain that at least two of the individuals you met today report to a common entity higher up in the organization."

Michelle's heart fluttered.

Sanderson abandoned his casual repose and leaned forward. "You do not have to do this. I would totally understand if you decided to cancel your plans. We can prepare an exit strategy and ensure that you both arrive home safely. The Bureau, of course, would be most appreciative if you elected to continue with your book research. You have my personal promise that every resource will be made available to ensure your continued safety—as well as that of your husband and his friend, Mr. Orrey—until there's no longer a credible threat."

Now her throat tightened. Michelle hadn't considered how her actions in Colorado might place Nick or Chris in harm's way. "Nick doesn't have anything to do with this. Why would he be at risk?"

Sanderson was direct. "Tarryall has been following your husband and his friend since Saturday." And in response to the gasp that followed, continued, "And we've been tailing him. In fact, we've been monitoring your movements since you and your husband arrived in Charleston."

Michelle connected the dots. "That was you following Nick and Chris around last week?"

Sanderson smiled. "The Bureau, yes. We've since made contact with counsel on both sides of the litigation to apprise them of the situation. We want what happens here to have as little influence on the outcome as possible." He then mentioned as delicately as possible that Nick and her agent Connor Lewis were read in last night.

"Nick knew since last night?" Michelle blurted.

"Please, don't get upset. We needed you and Melanie to act as natural as possible when you met with Tarryall today. That's why you were kept in the dark." Pressing, he asked, "Could you have gone in blind, knowing what you do now, and not arouse suspicion?"

Michelle's frustration melted away. Sanderson had made his point.

"You and your husband can resume your normal dialog, we only request that you refrain from talking about specific details that could get either of you into trouble. Act as if nothing out of the ordinary is going on. Cat and Janelle can help you with that. Lastly, your husband will be awaiting your call when we're done here."

Michelle said that she had no intention of turning back, and agreed to do what she could to help the FBI gather more information on the Conservancy.

"Absolutely," Melanie said, adding her support.

Feeling guilty, Michelle then asked if Nick was upset with her.

Sanderson's features softened and he said, "I believe that his first words to Special Agent Granby were, *'Not again!'*"

A murmur of laughter rippled through the room.

"He's fine. In fact," Sanderson confided. "My colleague was inclined to think that he was rather expecting something like this was going to happen. Your husband also agreed to cooperate to the extent of your choosing."

A hand grasped Michelle's arm. It was Cat. Michelle didn't realize that she had moved to the foot of her bed. "Your husband's in good hands," Cat said. "The FBI assigned a two-man detail headed by James—James Granby—who, along with local law enforcement, are watching over him around the clock. I don't know what I would have done without James, or Ron for that matter, when I was going through my ordeal."

Michelle was recovering by the moment. Still, she had questions, lots of them. "I don't understand what I can do. Why not just go in there with a search warrant, or something?"

Sanderson anticipated this question. "Because we don't have anything concrete. To be honest, this is the first opportunity we've had to have operatives—in this case the two of you and Agent Wells—working from the inside. If we can gain a better understanding of how Tarryall works, we can use this information to make the inroads necessary to one day bring down the greater organization."

Operatives...

Michelle got all tingly. Participation in a covert op? As exciting—and ridiculous—as that sounded, it was not a decision to make lightly. There would likely be no turning back. She asked Melanie for her opinion.

"Why not?" Melanie said, pouncing at the chance, her enthusiasm unleashing a bout of excitement. "You're sure we'll be safe, right?" she asked the agents.

"Absolutely," Sanderson promised.

"I'll be by your side the entire time," Wells affirmed, with another rock-star smile.

"And Janelle and I will be right here, helping the Bureau, and providing you with whatever you need, " Cat promised.

"Yes, anything," Janelle added for good measure.

"What do you say, Michelle?" Melanie asked, her eyes at once determined and hopeful. "I'll never get the chance to do something like this again."

Caught up in the moment, Michelle was all too happy to agree, albeit with the nagging reservation that she might have just signed them up for a deal to combat the devil. On the bright side, they would be venturing into the unknown armed to the teeth with support.

"Very well," Sanderson concluded. "I thank you—the FBI thanks you—both of you." He tapped on the credenza to catch Wells's attention.

"Still nothing outside," Wells said.

"Good. You've yet to arouse undue suspicion," Sanderson said cheerfully. "Now tell me, have you figured out who Jodi is? Is it Ms. Stockwell?"

Michelle blinked. "Oh—right..." she said, recalling that the FBI was monitoring her electronic footprint. She curled a lock of hair around her finger. "No. I don't think so."

"She gave you no indication?"

"No."

Sanderson took some notes. He asked Melanie for her thoughts. Melanie agreed with Michelle that Beth had ample opportunity to say something when they were alone in town. She and Michelle were also in agreement that none of the other Conservancy personnel they met were likely candidates. For what it was worth, Melanie said that they found Teddy Monroe and Bill Clay standoffish, and that Joe Hayden was a bully.

"I see," Sanderson said, making more notes. "That was my assessment as well. Joe Hayden is a person of interest we want to learn more about, especially his specific involvement and who he reports to within the greater organization."

Sanderson's words were discomforting. Michelle wrestled with a recurring knot in her stomach. She had scarcely said yes and was already getting cold feet. "Is whatever the Conservancy—Tarryall, I mean—is into really that important to bring in the FBI?"

Wells stopped his street peeping long enough to say, "More than you can possibly imagine."

"What do you mean?" Michelle asked.

A playful glimmer splashed across Sanderson's face. He piqued Michelle and Melanie's curiosity when he posed a seemingly offbeat question: "Have either of you heard of Cíbola?" The look he received was like that of two skeptical owls watching a mouse climb a tree.

"*N-o*," Michelle drawled.

Melanie trolled her memory. "*Wait!*" she said. " Like in the National Treasure movie?"

"Yes!" Sanderson applauded. "Very good."

Melanie described the part in the movie where Nicolas Cage holds a piece of wood inscribed with an Indian hieroglyphic clue to Cíbola up to a traffic camera, before tossing the clue off a bridge so that sidekick Riley could later hack into the street-cam system and download a picture.

"*R-i-g-h-t!*" Michelle drawled again, only now with sudden recollection. "I remember! He threw the thing into the river so that the bad guys couldn't have it."

"That's right!" Melanie followed, to the amusement of everyone in the room. "The hieroglyphics were a clue to—"

"Cíbola," Sanderson repeated, rounding out the scene. "Might I add that you chose your conquistador well, Ms. Snow, or should I say that *he chose you!* And isn't it also true, Ms. Sutton, that you are related to Coronado?"

Sanderson's compliment teased a bow from his operatives-in-training.

"I am!" Melanie said, proud of her Spanish lineage and the inherited skin tone that defined the origin of her Mediterranean name.

Michelle waited with baited breath, as did Melanie, wondering just how the lanky agent was going to weave the Hollywood Cíbola treasure, Coronado—and by extension the Ghost Creek legend—the Tarryall Mountain Foundation, and the eerily similar situations concerning the disappearance of two missing men, into a tapestry of circumstance that made sense.

There was work to do first. Wells broke off his street-side surveillance, said something to Sanderson, and hurried past Cat and Janelle to grab, of all things, an ice bucket. "Don't start without me," he said with a devilish grin before slipping out of the motel room under the guise of Mark Boone, photographer, just arrived from a previous assignment, and much in need of the ice machine.

The real Mark Boone, Sanderson explained, would not be coming because Mark Boone didn't exist. Remarkably, he was a figment of Connor Lewis's imagination, concocted following the FBI's initial call to Michelle's publishing company some weeks before. It was Lewis who, to Michelle's surprise, exhibited genuine concern for her safety. Michelle had usually found Lewis to be cavalier with trivial details like the safety of his clients and the rights of others when there was money to be made in the world of print. "Just go ahead, it will all work out," he was famous for saying. Maybe it was his way of increasing future sales by trivializing danger while adding an element of intrigue for his charges…whatever.

Michelle was also humored to hear that Lewis threatened to obstruct the FBI investigation if the Bureau didn't ensure that she and Melanie were provided with a continuous escort. Sanderson deemed the request reasonable and assigned Ryan Wells to assume his protector role in the guise of a third-party cameraman. Lewis thought that the photographer angle added an extra layer of credibility to Michelle's book project, and with that, Mark Boone's identity was born. "Your literary agent is a good man," Sanderson made it a point to say. "I assured him that we would keep the two of you safe."

With Wells off patrolling the grounds, Sanderson excused himself to check messages and dashed off to the room he shared with his partner. This gave Michelle the time she was looking for to call Nick, who delighted her by answering on the second ring. Nick was in exceptional spirits. There was none of the "I told you so's" that she expected to hear, and they talked nearly non-stop. When Nick said that he was thankful to hear that she and Melanie wouldn't be "going it alone" with only a photographer, Michelle laughed and told him that she had just said the same thing to Melanie, about how comforting it was to have Big Brother hiding in plain sight to save the day. She calmed what remained of Nick's concerns when she said that Tarryall was treating them as well as could be expected. The only hiccup came when Nick described the close call he had that afternoon with a Conservancy henchman named Ian Prescott, which, he explained, was defused by the timely intervention of his own guardian agent G-Man, Steve Bonino.

The conversation resumed its merry rambling when Nick explained how his sleuthing had turned the PSTRE case on its ear. Wide-eyed and listening, Michelle was expecting to hear more, but the next words she heard were those of Agent Granby, to whom Nick had handed the phone. In a repeat of what Cat and Sanderson had said to her and Melanie, Granby promised to keep her husband safe in her absence. He downplayed the Prescott incident to her satisfaction and attentively answered all of her questions, assuring her that Nick was never in any real danger. Granby then thanked her for her assistance and handed the phone back to Nick. It was a call Michelle wished would never end. And upon hearing with her own ears Nick's promise to support her no matter how far she decided to take matters, Michelle let out a relieved breath. There would be no stopping her now.

Michelle enjoyed what remained of the respite. Melanie had moved to a second chair beside Janelle, where she was immersed in a lively conversation with the Bureau support team about how she was handling the sensitive nature of the book project in terms of the loss of her brother. It was a touching gesture. *Ghost Creek*, Cat informed Michelle, was required reading as part of their preparation for what the FBI was calling Operation Timberline.

An operation…with a real government sanctioned name… required reading?!?

Michelle was speechless. Agent Wells was correct: whatever it was she had stumbled onto was much larger than she could have possibly imagined.

A dull pounding sound at the front door halted the conversation. Sanderson, who had recently returned to the room, looked away from his notepad. He glanced behind the curtain. "It's Ryan. Janelle, would you let him in?"

Janelle opened the door and in strode Ryan Wells with not one but a brace of ice buckets, one tucked under each arm, both holding a collection of brown-necked bottles.

"All clear," Wells said to Sanderson. He handed the ice bucket containing the larger number of bottles to Janelle. Turning to face the girls, Kris with a 'K' explained that Agent Morgan had observed a suspicious vehicle enter the parking lot. "Not to worry," he said. "The Evening Star is also the place to go for a covert hook-up, if you catch my drift."

"Very well," Sanderson said, placing his notepad down beside him. Speaking to Wells, he said, "I just spoke with Perry. He and Cullen are in position."

Wells nodded.

Michelle was confused and looked to Cat for clarification.

"They're operatives from the FBI resident agency office in Glenwood Springs, which covers Summit and surrounding counties. Special agents Cullen and Perry are coordinating with the local authorities in the event that we need their support."

Sanderson added for reassurance that local law enforcement had not picked up any chatter from the Conservancy since their arrival, either. "It appears that Tarryall remains none the wiser."

Wells supported Sanderson's assessment. "What?" he said in mock surprise to the inquisitive eyes fixed on the second ice bucket, still crooked in his arm. "It's root beer. We're still on the clock. Besides, who says you can't learn a few tricks from watching cop shows?" Wells placed the ice bucket down on a nearby table and retrieved his service piece from the ice.

The female contingent did a double take. Even Sanderson was amused. Janelle looked into the bucket she was still holding to see if it also contained a weapon.

"I decided to check the lock on my room," Wells said. "It's a little trick that once served its purpose on an undercover narcotics case."

"What happened?" Melanie asked, impressed by her favorite agent's act of clandestine cleverness.

"I walked into the room, dropped one bucket as a distraction, and drew my weapon from the other the moment I saw that the suspect had taken the money offered by my partner. He never saw that coming and surrendered without issue. Soda anyone?"

Amidst a round of giggles, Janelle passed the bucket she was holding. Wells took two root beers from his bucket and handed one to Melanie.

Michelle found the exchange heartwarming. Melanie accepted the beverage as if she had just been given a prom corsage.

"If I remember correctly," Sanderson said wryly, keeping the mood light by needling Wells on his unconventional methods, "there was some paperwork that needed to be filed afterward... something about abandoning your service piece?"

"Worked, didn't it?" Wells replied nonchalantly.

"Touché!" Sanderson uncapped his bottle. He waited for his audience to take a few sips from their beverages before calling the conversation back to order. "Both of you might be interested to know," he began, addressing Michelle and Melanie, "that it was a little known Spanish explorer by the name Pánfilo de Narváez, and not Coronado, who's responsible for our being here today. It was the survivors of Narváez's ill-fated 1527 voyage who passed along a story about a place of vast riches that gave rise to the legend of Cíbola—the mythical Seven Cities of Gold."

The girls glanced wide-eyed at one another, and then to Cat and Janelle.

Janelle gave them a wink. Cat said, "You're going to like this."

Sanderson took a swig from his root beer. "Cíbola, you see, was the purpose of Coronado's journey into the American Southwest. More importantly, his search for Cíbola gave rise not only to the Ghost Creek legend that you so eloquently bring to life in your book, but to an even more amazing legend, possibly rooted in fact, that your inadvertent meddling into Conservancy affairs stands to bring to light and expose Tarryall for who they truly are."

Michelle scooched her way to the edge of her bed.

Melanie did likewise, copping her favorite Michelle response. "This sounds like the makings of a Scooby Doo ending!"

"We certainly hope so!" Sanderson replied.

Michelle was overcome by a sudden wave of panic. She had either missed, forgotten about, or—heaven forbid—deemed Cíbola inconsequential during her research of Coronado's travels for *Ghost Creek*. As for the explorer Sanderson just mentioned, she was unfamiliar with him altogether. "I never heard of Narváez."

"Nor did I until 2012 when certain events put Tarryall back on our radar," Sanderson said, hoping to address her confusion. "I was called in by Agent Granby to track Tarryall's movements because of the nature of some suspect *merchandise* being moved on the open market." Sanderson paused for few seconds of introspection. "A fortuitous change in career path to criminal justice enabled me to combine an academic passion for archaeology and art history with the Bureau's needs as part of Operation Timberline. I believe that I overheard you and Catherine talking about it earlier?"

"None of the specifics," Cat said.

"Very well."

Eager to hear more about the operation, Michelle pressed Sanderson for an explanation.

"In due time," he promised. "First, I need to fill you and Melanie in on some history. It's the story behind the merchandise—artifacts,

Rick Ley

if you must know, and I'll leave it at that for the time being—that establishes their value, which I am afraid appears to be great enough to kill for. I need both of you to understand precisely what we're up against. I don't mean to scare you, but you need to know just how precarious your situation could have been had we not known what we do now about Tarryall. Those emails? Make no mistake about it, they're serious."

Cat's dour expression magnified Sanderson's concern.

"Michelle and I were thinking that they might be a call for help," Melanie said, hoping to find the Bureau in agreement.

Sanderson weighed Melanie's words carefully. "Could be...or a warning."

Melanie drew a breath.

"We thought about that, too," Michelle said. "It just sounds worse hearing you say it. Mel and I still want to stick it out, right?" she said, looking to Melanie. "We need answers."

Melanie nodded.

"Again, good to hear!" Sanderson said, applauding their commitment. "Now then, let me tell you a little story."

And with that, Ron Sanderson embarked on a tale of fact and fancy so profound that it made Michelle and Melanie's involvement in the Bureau's Tarryall investigation seem almost trivial by comparison.

—

"They wandered for eight years before they were found?" Michelle said, amazed that anyone could survive in the wild for that long, anywhere, let alone in a foreign land.

Sanderson nodded. "Even more remarkable is that only four would survive to tell the tale of their ordeal."

"How many did you say they started with?" Melanie asked, still shaking her head. Like Michelle, she found the enormity of Narváez's men's achievement astounding.

"Around six hundred."

"It's incredible that any survived at all," Michelle gasped. "And this all happened even though their plan was to settle Florida?"

"That's correct. Narváez's plan was to establish colonial settlements in Florida."

"And that was like twenty years before my ancestor explored the Southwest?" Melanie asked.

"That's also correct, Ms. Sutton. Narváez set sail from Spain in June 1527, arriving in what we know today as the Dominican Republic later that year. After re-provisioning the fleet in his homeland Cuba, he then sailed on to Florida the following April," Sanderson said, filling in more gaps. "If all had gone as planned when he arrived in what's now St. Petersburg, he probably would have founded a settlement and expanded outward from there."

"Which didn't happen because you said the local Indians sent him on a wild goose chase," Melanie said with a little laugh.

Michelle sat by quietly listening, making mental notes for her book.

Sanderson echoed Melanie's amusement. "In a manner of speaking. It was his following of bum leads in the hopes of fame and fortune that would be Narváez's downfall, as it would be for your forebear, as well as for some of the characters in the Ghost Creek legend." He was careful not to include Garret with the unfortunate Ghost Creek lot, and seeing that neither of his operatives-in-training caught his drift regarding Coronado, Sanderson quickly moved on to new ground. "Yes, it was local Indians who sent Narváez and the majority of his men on an overland search for food and gold reported to be in Apalachee tribal lands, far to the north near the Florida panhandle."

"What about the others?" Michelle asked. "What did they do?"

Sanderson sipped at his root beer. "Good question. Narváez sent a detachment north by sea along the Gulf Coast to meet him at the Apalachee lands. Narváez, though, ran into increasingly hostile natives along his route, and when he reached the Apalachee in June 1528, he found…surprise, surprise that the Apalachee were a destitute lot who didn't appreciate his presence. They fought for several weeks, at which point Narváez decided to cut his losses. Why he would accept the advice of another native at that point is mind boggling. Maybe he was desperate, who knows? Anyway, he and his men turned south back towards the coast, where they pushed their way through snake-ridden swamps and chest-deep water in search of a second promised land."

"Yuck!" Melanie managed with a shiver. "I hate snakes. I hope they made it."

Cat shared Melanie's sentiments.

"They did, and arrived at what is known today as Apalachee Bay south of Tallahassee, sickened and weak and, unfortunately none the richer. There, Narváez and his men convalesced. They built five ships and set sail westward through the Gulf that September."

"What about the ships Narváez sent to follow him up the coast?" Michelle asked.

"Ha!" Sanderson laughed. "That's right. I almost forgot. Lucky for them, they never found Narváez near the Apalachee lands. They searched for him on land and sea for over a year before giving up hope and, therefore, avoided the fate that befell their captain and the majority of their crewmates. As for Narváez and his men, they followed the Gulf Coast, eventually landing in Galveston, Texas with a crew of only eighty out of the nearly two hundred-fifty that started west from Florida. But not Narváez, he never made it. He died when his ship—in reality not much more than a cut out log—was lost at sea."

"That's awful." Michelle said.

"Indeed. It's amazing to think how few explorers lived to tell about their adventures, let alone accomplish something of value to make them famous. This makes Coronado's legacy that much more remarkable."

This got their attention.

Sanderson said that he would be getting to Coronado shortly, and asked that Michelle and Melanie hold their questions. Taking another swig from his bottle, he said, "Álvar Núñez Cabeza de Vaca assumed control of the expedition after Narváez's passing. It was Cabeza de Vaca who played a pivotal role in Coronado's future." Draining the bottle, Sanderson relayed that Cabeza de Vaca and three others were all that would remain by 1532, four years after they landed in Texas; that it was from this low point that they continued on foot in search of fame and glory, first west through Texas, and then into New Mexico and Arizona, before eventually arriving in Mexico.

"Those poor men," Melanie lamented. "I can't imagine."

Sanderson looked in Wells's direction.

"Still good," Wells confirmed.

Sanderson cleared his throat, and with a dose of unexpected drama said, "Here's where things get interesting. Fast forward four more years to 1536, and imagine their surprise when a group of Spaniards on a slave trading expedition in northern Mexico happen upon three of their countrymen and the black Moor slave Estevanico wandering aimlessly in search of somewhere. This was the first that anyone had heard from the lost Narváez expedition in nearly a decade."

"Wow!" Michelle said

"Wow is right. If that wasn't enough, they still had to walk seven hundred miles to reach the creature comforts of the capital of New Spain in Mexico City."

"Jeez!" Melanie muttered.

"Tell me about it," Cat said, praising the men's will to live. "You're hard-pressed to find people willing to *drive* ten miles to the grocery store today, let alone walk seven hundred miles across a scorching desert after finally being found."

"Needless to say, the leader of New Spain—the Viceroy Antonio de Mendoza—was fascinated to hear a first-hand account of the terrible hardship of Narváez's failed expedition...though I rather think he was more interested in the stories about the 'cities of unlimited riches' Cabeza de Vaca said he heard about from some natives they encountered on their journey."

"*Uh-oh!*" Michelle interrupted, to Sanderson's amusement.

"You recognize the trend!" Sanderson remarked. "After falling for two false leads and being lost and given up for dead, you would think that Cabeza de Vaca would have kept his mouth shut!"

"What happened?" Melanie asked.

"The Viceroy succumbed to temptation and sent a Franciscan friar named Marcos de Niza and the slave Estevanico to confirm Cabeza de Vaca's story. Fray Marcos, as he's sometimes called, completed his mission in 1539, and in spite of the loss of Estevanico to some hostiles, returned with glowing news. He claimed to have seen a golden city located high up on a hill that the natives called Cíbola."

"They did find it!" Melanie cheered.

"In a manner of speaking, yes," Sanderson said cautiously. "You will be pleased to know that it is here where your ancestor enters the picture. The Viceroy must have had some reservations about the friar's report, because that fall, he sent yet another man by the name of Diaz to verify Fray Marcos's assertions about Cíbola. Diaz made it as far as the Chichilticalli Pueblo ruins in southern Arizona before weather forced his return. On the way back, he stopped to inform the Governor of the Kingdom of Nueva Galicia that he could not substantiate the friar's claim—that man, of course, was Francisco Vásquez de Coronado."

Michelle had to admit that Ranger Rick had nothing over the FBI agent's oratory prowess. All the same, the wait to find how all of this involved the Conservancy was excruciating.

Sanderson recognized her frustration and promised that the FBI's interest in Tarryall and Coronado's *true* legacy would become clear shortly. "The Viceroy was undaunted by Diaz's less than glowing report. The temptation must have been too much to resist. He invested a considerable sum of his own money and drafted Coronado to help him assemble what constituted an army of twenty-five hundred Spanish soldiers, Indian allies, and various followers, along with enough provisions to get the expedition under way in pursuit of Cíbola. Coronado left from Compostela in the territorial province of New Galicia, in February 1540, with Fray Marcos serving as guide. They marched across northern Mexico and into southern Arizona through some of the most inhospitable terrain imaginable. Coronado reached Cíbola in early July of that year, only to be bitterly disappointed. There was no great city of gold located high on a hill, only a Zuni Indian pueblo carved into the rock face."

The disappointment that registered on the girls' faces—Melanie's in particular—was unmistakable.

"Coronado was outraged; they all were. The friar had lied. Worse, Coronado had invested a vast sum of his own wealth in the expedition, and for what? Nothing. He would send Fray Marcos back to New Spain in shame.

"Why would the friar lie?" Michelle asked.

Sanderson smiled. "It appears that the good friar was duped by wishful thinking and a trick of the light. Friar Marcos apparently never set foot in Cíbola. Seen at a distance, in the right light, and with a vivid imagination, some scholars think that Fray Marcos mistook the golden hue of the sun's reflection on the rock face as evidence of a city made of gold."

"That's absurd," Melanie said, taking the insult to her relative's reputation personally. "What kind of idiot would think that? No wonder Coronado was angry."

"Alas, it was a time less learned when imagination, no matter how fantastic or unrealistic, carried as much weight as fact, particularly when spoken by someone with clout, like a clergyman. Coronado, though, had more pressing matters to attend to. His men were tired and many were on the verge of starvation. He demanded entrance into the village. When the normally peaceful Zuni refused, tempers flared and a fight ensued that resulted in Coronado being wounded. The Zuni, of course, were no match for the Spaniards and were soon overpowered. The 'Conquest of Cíbola,' as some call it, did not take long to come to an unfortunate conclusion for both parties. Those Zuni not killed retreated deeper into the hills, and Cíbola, Coronado would discover, proved to be nothing but a collection of seven Zuni villages centered around an area of the high ground called Thunder Mountain—I can dispense with the unpleasant details if it bothers you," Sanderson said, recognizing Melanie's discomfort over the continued disillusionment.

"No, it's fine. " Melanie said. "Being able to say that I was related to a great man in history was one of the few bright spots of my childhood. Look at me," Melanie said pointing to her face, "We have to be related, right? All I'd have to say is that Coronado was my distant uncle, and for a few minutes I was the girl all the kids wanted to be with. I suppose that I always chose to ignore the dreadful things he must have done. What happened to those poor Zuni was disgraceful. What did they have for weapons, arrows?"

Sanderson explained that Coronado, although under strict orders not to attack the indigenous populations he met on his journey, engaged the Zuni only after his men were first fired upon. "Remember, they were hungry," he reminded her.

Melanie appreciated Sanderson's encouragement, even if he was only trying to make her feel better. "I can take it," she said when Sanderson forewarned her that history doesn't get any kinder to Coronado, or the tribes he encountered.

Sanderson continued. "Being so far from home and with nothing to show for his effort, Coronado made the best out of a bad situation and pressed on. His secondary objective was, after all, a mission of discovery, and the northern reaches of New Spain remained uncharted. For instance, he was the first European to see the Grand Canyon and Colorado River."

"See, Mel! Uncle Frank wasn't all bad," Michelle said, making Melanie laugh.

Sanderson also laughed. "I doubt anyone has called him Frank before," he said with a vigorous tap of his pen against his notepad. "No matter what you may think of him now, Ms. Sutton—Melanie—Coronado was a courageous man with the responsibility for thousands under his command in a distant and hostile land."

"He did what he had to do to survive, I guess" Melanie was resigned to say.

"I couldn't have put it any better. Don't forget that," Sanderson said. He glanced at his watch, checked his phone for messages. Finding nothing pressing, he said, "And now, ladies, I believe it's time to explain how Coronado's past collides with Tarryall's present."

Michelle looked to Melanie with a glint of excitement.

"You'll want to pay close attention to this," Cat said. "This *is* why we are here."

"Catherine couldn't be any more correct," Sanderson remarked to Melanie. "Dubious as it might seem, you can take pride in knowing that your ancestor's reach reverberates to this day. After leaving Cíbola, Coronado made his winter encampment along the Rio Grande near present day Albuquerque. At some point he heard stories of yet another place of immense wealth in gold and silver, called Quivira, from a Pawnee Indian captive the Spanish called the *Turk*."

"He must have had dark skin like me!" Melanie quipped.

"The case exactly, I understand. Racial profiling was alive and well, even in the fifteen hundreds!" Sanderson took another root beer from the nearest ice bucket while the ripple of laughter settled. Opening it, he savored the initial bite of carbonation and said, "Coronado took the Turk at his word, and in June 1541 set forth with a contingent of his men, led by the captive, eastward into the Great Plains in search of Quivira. They eventually reached the Arkansas River in southwest Kansas, near what is now Dodge City. They turned north from there, reaching Quivira country that July or August. Coronado scoured the countryside for nearly a month to no avail, finding little more than random groupings of Wichita or Pawnees living in thatched huts, tending to their crops. Like all of the tribes he encountered to that point, the Quivirans were an impoverished lot that lived off the land. The only item of value that was found was a single copper pendant. His mission a failure—and please forgive me for saying this—a frustrated Coronado had the Turk killed. He then began the long march home."

"And the connection is exactly?" Michelle asked.

Sanderson leaned forward until he was as close to Michelle and Melanie as possible and said, "In 1980, two amateur archaeologists unearthed some artifacts in central Kansas that they claimed belonged to the lost kingdom of Quivira. Of particular interest were several partial bracelets, a few amulets, *and* a copper pendant that closely matched the description of the one found by Coronado."

"*Oh!*" Michelle said, the connection becoming suddenly less murky. Melanie, too, made the connection.

"Told you!" Cat said, knowingly.

Sanderson paused to let his audience think. With regard to the commotion that such discoveries bring, he said, "As you might expect, excitement over the find rocked the antiquities world. Then, strange as it might seem, nothing more was heard about the discovery until 1982, when Dylan Streeter disappeared from the Panner's and Picker's Rendezvous event in Climax. Why the sudden secrecy, we don't know for certain."

"Maybe they were secretly marketing the items?" Michelle offered.

"Could be," Sanderson agreed. "Or, the archaeologists were under a lot of pressure to move the goods and decided to let the attention die down. Whatever the reason, the Bureau was called in over some peculiar elements about the case. Our intelligence revealed that Streeter had a connection to the artifacts—we surmise it had something to do with their authenticity, based on his area of expertise. The Bureau was careful to conceal from the media that both the amateur archaeologists and the artifacts went missing at the same time as Dylan Streeter."

The shock that still others may have been killed was palpable.

"Why cover it up?" Melanie asked.

"Because of the hysteria it would create. Even then, the Bureau saw this as something bigger than it seemed: we just didn't know how big. We had no idea who Tarryall was at the time, and Operation Timberline would not officially exist for another twenty years."

"The Streeter case went cold until 2012, when the pieces reappeared on the market in Europe. In 2013, the pieces were then rumored to be back in the States, where they remained underground until the most recent event occurred."

"Mr. Laney's disappearance," Michelle said.

"That's correct. We know without question that William Laney was involved, but to what degree, beyond being a victim, remains to be seen. Because no sign of him has yet surfaced, we fear that he suffered the same fate as the archaeologists and Dylan Streeter. And this brings us around to the body you found at the field station, Michelle—I am rather certain that you found the remains of Dylan Streeter, though I think you already suspect as much."

Melanie had become so rigid that Michelle thought she could feel waves of tension radiating from Melanie's body through the floor to her feet at the base of the opposite bed.

"Your reaction to that photo in the C.C. Times article was all I needed to know to confirm my suspicion." Sanderson reached inside his suit jacket and pulled out a manila envelope. He unfastened the clasp and handed it to Michelle.

Melanie jumped over to Michelle's bed and leaned in close.

"You no doubt are still wondering what I meant by Coronado's true legacy?" Sanderson teased, dangling his earlier comment.

Michelle and Melanie nodded vigorously.

"Well, Ms. Sutton, your ancestor may not be remembered for finding fame and fortune, but the missing Quivira artifacts discovered several decades ago are legendary by association. As for their value, I can't count that high. Let's just say that if they were any less prized, the Tarryall Mountain Foundation might never have fallen onto our radar and the memories of Dylan Streeter, William Laney, and the two missing amateur archaeologists would have been lost to history. It may have taken Coronado almost five hundred years, but his lasting legacy—and I dare say yours as well—is about to unfold. Please, open the envelope and take a look inside.

Her fingers trembling, Michelle pulled two sheets of photo stock from the envelope, turned them over...and gasped at a haunting face from her past and present peering back at her.

Register Mesne Conveyances
Meeting Street, Charleston, S.C.
10:37 A.M.

"Be yourself and act like nothing's out of order," Special Agent James Granby reminded Nick. Granby glanced at his watch. "Wait here for me to leave. Ten minutes should do it."

"No problem," Nick answered as coolly as his nerves would allow.

"And feel free to use that number I gave you."

"I will. Either you or your partner will be shadowing me the whole time, right?" Nick asked for reassurance.

"Yes," Granby chuckled. "Remain calm and all will be fine. We're here to make sure that nothing happens to you, just like Special Agents Sanderson and Wells are watching out for your wife and her friend out West. There's no reason to believe that anything should happen, so long as she remains on script, and you don't do anything foolish yourself."

There was that word again, *script*. Granby mentioned the term several times last evening. As anal-retentive as the government was to work with, he wouldn't put it past the Bureau to actually have a *101 Uses for a Civilian Operative* guidebook available for agent training. He mused at the thought of Granby thumbing through the chapter titled: *How to Convince Your Civilian Operative that There's Nothing to Fear When Tailed by an Assassin So Long as He Sticks to the Plan.*

Granby bent over to pick up one of the empty D-Squared boxes he asked to use as a prop. "Each of you can return to your normal lives as soon as we're comfortable that your wife and her friend have returned safely from Colorado." He started toward the door.

Turning at the frame he said, "I would like to thank you and Mr. Orrey again on behalf of the Department for helping us take some very dangerous people off the streets." He continued, only to stop again on the porch. "Remember to call me or Special Agent Bonino the moment you feel threatened, or if something just seems abnormal. We'll be right there to take over." And with that said, Granby continued to the curb.

Nick waited a good fifteen minutes before taking his leave. "Here we go again," he said to the walls around him. He knew from the start that Michelle's rekindled meddling into the Ghost Creek legend was a bad idea. History implied that the place held too many secrets better left unchecked. And he was right. For reasons beyond anything imaginable, his wife's doings now found them under FBI surveillance, being used as pawns in a game not to just bust up an illicit crime ring of international proportions, but for their *OWN PROTECTION*, no less! What could possibly go wrong?

The one consolation, Granby assured him, was that his own safety wasn't in question until last Saturday, following Michelle and Melanie's departure for Colorado, when Granby and Bonino observed a lone white male tailing him back from the marina. The question he'd been meaning to ask, but didn't really want the answer to, was how the thug knew how to find him in the first place. Whatever. It didn't matter. That was Granby's problem. There was nothing he could do but go about his business as usual, keep a keen eye out for trouble, and hit the floor when the bullets started to fly.

If only she would have told me about the emails…

He stepped outside and *didn't* get shot. That was encouraging. Michelle mustn't have pissed them off yet, Nick joked under his breath. He feigned the need to look up the one-way street for traffic before walking around to the driver's side of his vehicle, where he quickly slipped inside and pulled away from the curb. Nick passed several men in parked cars on the way to the Bull Street intersection. Waiting for the cross traffic to pass, Nick looked into his rear-view mirror, wondering if one might be his stalker.

Nick was relieved to find the drive through town equally uneventful. He was feeling about as normal as could be expected by the time he was rolling up I-26 toward PSTRE. He resisted the temptation to pull off the highway to top off his coffee and grab a breakfast sandwich per usual. The last thing he needed was for an ill-advised diversion to turn into a killer's opportunity.

Chris was waiting for him in the parking lot when Nick arrived. He was leaning against the hood of his car and facing the parking lot access with his arms folded across his chest.

Nick pulled alongside and grabbed a clipboard from the passenger seat.

"How'd you sleep?" Chris asked.

"Not so good. You?"

"About the same."

"Yeah. That was a bit much to take all in one sitting. We talked more this morning. That helped."

"Good," Chris replied. "Notice anyone following you?"

"Thank goodness, no."

"That's good. What did Michelle have to say?"

Nick frowned and stuck his hands in his pockets.

"Uh-huh. Didn't tell her, did you?"

"Christ. That Granby guy put me in a pickle. He told me not to."

"And you listened?"

"What if I did tell her and she did something goofy? If the whole thing blows up, it'll be my fault."

Chris started to laugh. "You keep telling yourself that."

"I know," Nick sighed. "I'm a dead man either way. As are you for not telling her for me—we're in this together, brother. Of course, we can always hope that that jackass pops us off first."

"Ah!" Chris cackled. "That's what I like about you, Nick. Always thinking! Now what do you say we go look at that culvert again?"

They walked in the direction of the PSTRE-Athens property line to verify Nick's doubly-dead-box discovery about the true nature of what had been assumed to be an oddly-placed stormwater culvert that discharged onto PSTRE property.

"Is Secret Agent Man and his partner going to be camped out in the parking lot when we come back?"

"Dunno. I didn't ask. Why?"

"Just wondering what to expect," Chris asked.

"Wait!" Nick corrected between breaths. "I take that back. Granby said that he would be sticking with us while his partner—Steve Bonino, if I remember the name correctly—keeps tabs on the bad guy."

"Works for me," Chris said, and they continued on.

Nick paused to scrutinize one of the piezometer-well PVC stickups.

"What are you thinking?" Chris asked.

"Nothing. I had this really weird dream…it's nothing. Come on, let's go," Nick said, offering no further explanation.

They stopped at the presumed stormwater-drainage culvert that was cut low into the dirt just on the PSTRE side of the property line. The purpose of the feature didn't make visual sense because it appeared to provide discharge from one piece of flat ground to another: what was the point of that? Largely covered over by grass and mostly in-filled with detritus, there was no indication that water had flowed into or out of the pipe for quite some time. At best, the structure posed nothing more than a landscaping hazard. Nick took a step back to survey the area. "This has to be the tar pipe," he said. "I don't recall any other feature like this one on the property, do you?"

"No. Is that a copy of the letter?" Chris asked. "Can I see it?"

Nick handed him the clipboard and pointed to the first bullet.

"Incredible," Chris murmured. "Talk about a smoking gun. Carlyle's going to have a shitfit." Chris lowered the clipboard. "I'd say this has to be it," he said, gesturing to the culvert.

"Now what are you thinking?" Chris asked, interrupting Nick's introspection.

"I still can't believe she didn't tell me about those emails," Nick fumed.

Chris ignored him and again scrutinized the letter, looking up from time to time for another plausible location for the tar pipe.

"Worse yet, now I have to stand around with a thumb up my ass all day until the FBI pays her a visit this evening. I could kill her, only I'd be waiting in line! How in the hell does this keep happening, Chris?" Nick groused himself into a lather. "What are you doing?" he snapped when Chris began crawling around on the ground.

"What do you think?" Chris replied, laughing at Nick's lament. "I'm looking for a tar pipe. Yuck!" Chris said when he reached his hand inside the small clearing he made in the overgrowth. He continued to egg Nick on. "You're the one who decided to stay married to her after the first two disasters." Chris shook a glop of dark gray muck from his hand. "I should have put on a second set of gloves so I don't get any of this crap on me. Here, take a look." Chis pulled back the mane of grass covering the culvert opening.

"*Huh!*" Nick said upon seeing a surprisingly small diameter pipe. With the way that the soil had been humped up around it, he was expecting something larger. This pipe was certainly too small to be used for stormwater conveyance. "Is that cast iron?"

"Not sure. Let me dig a little more."

"I just wish she would have told me," Nick rambled, still lost in his distraction. "Does it smell?" he asked when Chris brought his hand to his nose and sniffed at his muck-covered fingers.

"Ick!" Chris recoiled at the wretched odor. "Definitely oily. Not real strong, just rank." Rubbing his fingertips together to discern more about the material, he asked, "What do you think would have happened if she did tell you about the emails?"

"We would have had a fight and she would've gone anyway."

"So true!" Chris said sagely. He rocked back on his haunches, and with Confucius-like wisdom said, "The way I see it, she owes you big time. Whether she went with or without your blessing, she did go, and now the Feds have been dispatched to protect us."

"*You're right!*" Nick said, "She does owe me." Getting back to the matter at hand, he asked Chris for the verdict after Chris ran his fingers back and forth across the grass to wipe the oily spooge from the pipe off his glove.

"Smells like tar sludge to me," Chris said, excited as always when trouble lurked. "I also think that the pipe is made of terracotta and not cast iron." Chris looked around, pursed his lips. "Do you see a rock or anything that I can use as a hammer? I'd like to break off a piece and check."

Nick found a rock of sufficient heft in the grass not far away. He handed it to Chris, who promptly smacked it against the pipe's flange. The end crumbled into several pieces. "That's not good," Nick said when Chris held up a piece of the busted pipe for him to inspect. Staring at the piece in cross-section, Nick could clearly see the red hue of the century-old fired clay beneath the rind of tar and grime. This was not good at all. Made of such a fragile material, the odds were better than even that the terracotta was compromised at any number of places along its length during subsequent earthworks activities. This in turn meant that it would have leaked like a sieve wherever broken. From there, it was only a matter of the creosote following the right geologic conditions to PSTRE's production well.

"What's not good?"

Gerry Dawson, the sourpuss PSTRE superintendent, was standing behind them. "We'd appreciate a little heads up next time," Chris said smartly. Dawson craned his neck to look at the disturbance Chris had made in the grass. "Can you tell us what this was for?" Chris asked.

Dawson made a grumping sound and lumbered off.

"No help. I don't trust him," Chris said.

Nick shrugged.

"You know, Chris, we haven't put any borings around here yet. I don't see any signs of gross contamination. I'd feel a whole lot better if we could write off the tar pipe as a non-source. I'm not sure what that will get us, but it would be something."

"Agreed," Chris said. "It would be information either way. I know that it's still on RCE's to-do list. I think they're planning on coming back Thursday. I've been playing phone tag with Sam to see if he can't move that up." Chris eyed the tar-pipe outfall on a straight-line course back across Athens's property. Puzzled, he asked Nick to again read the meat of the letter. "They *did* use creosote to treat logs over there," Chris said, pointing to a logical area on the northwest portion of the Athens property.

"Correct."

"Why then did Carlson say that they hadn't?"

"Maybe he doesn't know that they did."

"You don't believe that, do you? I didn't think so," Chris said, reading the doubt on Nick's face. "My man, I'm telling you something is definitely rotten in the State of Denmark!"

"How long have you been saving that one for?" Nick quipped.

"For about as long as it took me to read Hamlet in college-lit class, or the Count of Monte Cristo for that matter."

"That long. Never finished either one, did you?"

"Shit, no!" Chris laughed. "That's what Cliff's Notes are for." Flicking a hand in the direction of Athens's back forty, he then said, "I've been racking my brain trying to figure out their game plan. Carlson made it clear that they knew about the log treating operation on the North Property identified in the letter, which we agree is one and the same as Parcel C."

"Yes," Nick agreed. "I plan on confirming that when we're done here."

"Why then the song and dance? Why not hit us with that chestnut the moment after we threw down our drilling findings? It's not like we wouldn't find out whatever it is during discovery."

Chris made a good point. They contemplated Athens's play.

"What you have in your hand suggests that the gentleman's agreement favors PSTRE. Even if Athens has a copy of the same, I can't see how Carlson can claim that Athens never used creosote on their property when the partial document we have says that they did. *Unless!*" Chris said, interrupting his train of thought, "their end game is to embarrass PSTRE."

"How so? That seems like a reach to me."

"Could be. I don't know. We're really flapping in the wind right now."

What ifs aside, there was nothing more that could be gained at the site today and they needed answers. Chris asked Nick for the correspondence he found in the Doubly Deads. He would pass it on to Smitty and describe the corroborating tar pipe that lay in disguise as a run-of-the-mill drainage culvert. Nick meanwhile promised to complete a thorough deed search, then reconvene with Chris back at M&C's office, where they would hash matters over with Smitty and Brant.

"You going to be alright?" Chris asked. "I can follow you over if you like."

"Shit. I'd almost forgot about that. No thanks. I'll be fine. Meet you back at the shop."

<hr />

Wasn't it a silver car I saw pass Ashley House this morning? Or was it gray??? Wait! Wasn't Granby's car gray?

Nick was relieved to find curbside parking in front of the O.T. Wallace County Office Building. For three-quarters of an hour, from the time he pulled out of the PSTRE parking lot to his brief stop to refuel to now, he was preoccupied with searching his mirrors for what Granby described as a white male about six feet tall with short, dark hair and driving a silver-colored sedan. How convenient. That description could have described about three of every ten com-muters he saw, not to mention the handful of cars with drivers still in them parked in his immediate vicinity. His grim reaper unsub could have been any one of dozens of people at any given moment.

He found solace inside the county office building. There, Nick chatted up a passing security guard who pointed him in the direc-tion of the Register Mesne Conveyances office, the pompously sophisticated sounding name for the place where mundane things like deed searches were performed. "RMC is upstairs, Room 210," the guard said, and moved on. Nick was scoping out the lobby for anyone suspicious when a professionally dressed woman asked if he would like to follow her. "I'm going there myself," she said. Nick thanked her and followed her to the second floor.

Nick's paranoia subsided inside the deed-recorder's office. There was no better place for danger phobes like himself to hide than in a sterile office filled with musty ledgers. If the stereotype in his mind held true, any felon entering RMC's inner sanctum would stand out like a sore thumb.

He got right to work. Nick took a seat in front of a computer terminal and entered the property-owner name, which called up what he expected to be the latest PSTRE deed. Instead he found the document recording the 1977 name change to Palmetto State Transformer and Relay. "That's right, there would have been an official recording of that," he said softly, and printed a copy for his records. He then flipped to the last page, which referenced the deed citation for the previous 1927 business-name change to Palmetto State Electrical Supply. Here, he hit an electronic dead end and summoned the assistance of a kindly attendant named Adeline, who escorted him to the stacks of deed books where all of the deeds older than 1997 were located. *"Old school!"* Nick said, happy to explain how much he hated scrolling through microfiche.

"It makes me nauseous, too," Adeline agreed.

Nick moved his things to a desk near the stacks. On his note pad he scribbled the following headers in neat columns across the top line: *Date, Book, Page, Grantor,* and *Grantee,* beneath which he transposed the information he'd acquired thus far before flipping the appropriate deed book open to the page containing a hand-written copy of the 1927 name-change record. Digging further, he hunted down the transaction that portioned off a part of the PSTRE property to Athens, and finally the original PSTRE deed when Palmetto State Electrical Supply purchased the property from the Middleton estate in 1889. Review of the property description in the 1889 deed revealed that the Middleton family still retained all lands for a considerable distance to the west, north, and east.

The digging became murkier the deeper Nick dove back in time. Middleton's landholdings, including the piece carved out to PSTRE, had changed hands many times all the way back to the early 1800s, the property splitting and reforming again and again, all for the family-value discount of one dollar per transaction. It was a confusing mess that had obviously confounded all six of PSTRE's previous consultants, none of whom bothered to decipher the comings and goings of farm-property sales between kin. It was this lack of attention to detail that confounded Nick as well: Parcel C—aka the North Property—remained a mystery.

Properties...

Of course! Now having personally reviewed the deeds, Nick recognized that what was clearly missing was the fact that PSTRE must have made a second, later land acquisition from the Middleton estate that none of the previous consultants had picked up on. It was this missing clarification in the Phase I reports that had led him and the M&C team to wrongly assume that Parcel C was a separately designated portion of PSTRE's existing Parcel A property.

Nick returned to one of the microfiche machines. He suspected that the answer lay in the Athens property description, and he was right. With Adeline's help, he found the current Athens Petrolatum deed and again worked his way back through time. PSTRE was cited as owning the properties both *north* and south of Athens Petrolatum. "Sonofabitch!" Nick muttered. This meant that PSTRE acquired what now is known as Parcel C from the Middleton estate in a separate transaction sometime after the 1889 purchase of Parcel A and before the northern 27 acres of Parcel A were sold to Athens in 1891.

He knew what he needed to do next and flagged down Adeline one more time. He asked to see a copy of the area plat map, which showed the existing property boundaries and identified ownership. She said this would be no problem and went to the center island where the flat maps were stored. Curious, she asked what his purpose was for coming in today. Nick provided the same time-proven reason he always did: he was working for a confidential client that was refinancing an area property, and that the process included an area-wide environmental risk assessment. "We wouldn't want our client or his lending institution stuck with cleaning up someone else's mess."

"That's nice," Adeline said, hefting a heavy stack of blue-print-sized plat maps from a metal file drawer. "Your work must be very rewarding."

"Just doing my part," Nick said with Maytag-repairman sincer-ity. Evasive yet to the point, the explanation preempts many of the thorny questions that can arise with identifying a client or specific property by name in conjunction with danger words like *purchase* or *sale*. He watched her flip through the stack, then return the plats to the same file drawer, before opening another.

"You said the area near I-26 and Montague?"

"Yes. Is that a problem?"

"Not at all. Portions of that area have been rezoned. I should have thought of that. We store those plats over here," Adeline said, moving to a separate file cabinet.

A disturbing feeling came over him. In the matter of less than half an hour he had solved the Parcel C dilemma that had eluded six previous consultants. It was too easy. Nick couldn't shake the notion that they were being hoodwinked. Stan Merrill knew more than he was letting on. What little he knew of the man, Nick didn't like. He wouldn't put it past Merrill to bully, coerce, or otherwise collude with an unethical consultant to stifle knowledge that might affect securing a low interest refinance loan from his bank. And if he was capable of this, what else might he be hiding from his legal team?

Adeline spread two different maps across the center island and asked, "Is this what you're looking for?"

"It's exactly what I'm looking for," Nick answered, pointing to one of the plats. He jotted down the parcel number beneath the name *City of Charleston*, which was listed as the current owner of the property adjoining Athens's north boundary. Nick thanked her and asked if Adeline would make two copies of the plat.

"That will be five dollars per copy. Is that okay?" she asked.

Nick said that was fine and returned to one of the workstations to scroll through more microfiche. One keystroke and a minimum of scrolling was all it took. The City of Charleston acquired Parcel C from PSTRE in 1928, two months to the day from the date on the tar-pipe correspondence Nick resurrected from the D-Squared waste bin. Again, it was way too easy.

Finished for now, Nick took a walk around. The RMC office had become quite busy. A steady stream of patrons came and went; still others remained seated with eyes glued to monitors or lugged heavy deed books to and from the stacks. Nick sidestepped a professionally clad woman on her way to the stacks—a real estate agent, he reckoned by her impeccable attire. He was in her way. In fact, he was in a number of people's way. Spying a series of framed maps on a far wall, Nick decided to wait there for Adeline to return with copies of the plat.

They were four maps arranged left to right from oldest to newest, and dated 1704, 1885, 1886, and 1905. The sequence represented a two-hundred-year snapshot of the early history of the city from the days of old Charles Town to Charleston at the turn of the twentieth century. The purpose of the two middle copies was obvious. The former, from 1885, represented a rebuilt post-Civil-War Charleston and the next, dated September 1886, depicted the destruction of all that rebirth in the wake of the great earthquake of August 31 of that year. Nick was intrigued by how turn-of-the-century Charleston didn't look all that different from today.

It was the oldest framed work, from 1704, that intrigued him most. It was a cartographer's line-art rendition of the city that looked unflatteringly like a crude science-fair representation of a human intestine, complete with an appendix-like attachment on the end called White Point that jutted out into the harbor. The reason for the work's crudeness was the artistic license taken with the deeply incised west coastline of the peninsula on the Ashley River-side, and the slightly less dissected Cooper River-side coastline to the east. The most prominent feature on the map was the great Granville Bastion that dominated the southernmost chunk of peninsula facing the Cooper River, an area that included the central business district where M&C's office stands today. The bastion, a notation said, provided early civil defenses against the French, Spanish, and Native Americans.

Nick found the map fascinating because it showed how much of the peninsula had once been covered with wetlands and a surprising number of small streams that snaked their way toward the rivers and harbor.

"Fascinating, isn't it?" Adeline said.

"Oh, hi," Nick said with surprise. He was concentrating so intently that he didn't hear her approach. "It is. I never knew there was so much water. It looks so different today."

"It sure does. That was before they filled in most of the creeks and drained or covered over much of the wetlands."

"That's interesting," Nick said. "Makes sense, I guess." He snapped a picture with his phone. There was something about the map and Adeline's remark that tugged at the back of his mind. He noticed that she was holding more than he expected. "You have something for me," he asked, following Adeline to a vacant corner of the center island.

"I do," she said, laying out the two copies of the map Nick had requested. "I don't know whether you need to see all of the properties owned by the City, so I made you two copies of this map as well. I realize that I didn't ask you first, so there's no charge."

Nick appreciated Adeline's generosity. He must have looked confused because Adeline was quick to explain.

"Look here," she said, simultaneously pointing to Parcel C located at the top of the plat Nick had requested.

"Okay," Nick said.

Adeline then laid down the copies of the second plat and fanned her hand across the lower half of the sheet. "The City also owns most of these."

"Really?" Nick said, not yet sure what to make of this information. "I'd better take a copy of this plat as well. Thanks."

Adeline smiled. She then said something Nick did not expect. She pointed again to Parcel C. "See this parcel ID? Now look at these here, here, and here. See how they have two extensions that follow the root ID?"

Nick nodded.

"This means that any parcel with a designation like this one was originally associated with this mother property." Adeline pointed back to Parcel C.

Nick massaged his beard. He thought about the once immense Middleton Estate and the fact that he didn't pay attention to the acreage for Parcel C. He was rather certain that the parcel size wasn't mentioned in any of the Phase I documents, either. "You're saying that this mother property was once much larger before being subdivided by the owner prior to being sold to the City?"

"Exactly. The first two-digit extension means that all these lots were derived from this one." Adeline said, pointing to Parcel C. "The single-digit second extension at the end means that the lot was sold as part of a bulk sale."

"Fascinating." Nick tapped a finger at a smattering of lots all ending with a '-1' and similar extensions. *PSTRE sold Parcel C to the city in a bunch of pieces.* "Why would they do that?" he asked.

Adeline offered a few suggestions, the leading one being that it was probably simpler for the city to work its own system and acquire the entire acreage through a series of smaller plots purchased at lower dollar values that did not require upstairs approval. "You might also want to go to the City Special Projects Office. The City is planning to redevelop portions of the central peninsula. They can tell you where if you think this will help with your investigation."

Another patron asked Adeline for assistance. Nick thanked her for her help and said he would flag her down again later if he had more questions. He scooped up his notebook and the copies of the plat maps she made for him, and returned to his workstation to make some final notes. Nick was summarizing thoughts when two large hands appeared on the tabletop at the periphery of his vision. Nick looked up to find a stranger leaning over him, and recoiled with a start. "Who are you?" he demanded.

"I'm Special Agent Steve Bonino," the stranger said, flashing his credentials.

"What happened? Is Michelle alright?"

"She's fine." Bonino leaned still closer and whispered. "A man wearing blue jeans and a t-shirt will be entering the room at any moment. He has a tattoo on his left forearm. He's the one who's been following you. I'm here to make sure nothing happens."

Nick stole a glance in the direction the doorway. "Who is he?"

"All you need to know for now is that his name is Ian Prescott."

"What do I do?"

"Nothing. Act like he's anyone else. If he talks to you, talk back. If he makes you uncomfortable, say that you need to get your work done and start packing your things. If he persists, pretend that you received a call and I will move in."

Nick stiffened when he saw the shadowy form of Ian Prescott slip into the room.

"Remain calm," Bonino said, in a low, firm voice, before playing his part. "Over there? Thanks," Bonino said more loudly than necessary to draw Prescott's attention.

"Yes," Nick replied. "No, over there, about half way down," he answered, reading Bonino's body language. He motioned toward a section of the stacks with a good line of sight to his workstation. "Let me know if you need any more help," he added for good measure. Bonino nodded his approval and headed for the stacks.

Ian Prescott was not what Nick expected. Were it not for the tattoo, he could have been mistaken for anyone else in the room.

Casually dressed in a decent pair of blue jeans and a polo shirt, he had a young face that could be trusted. So much for stereotypes.

Nick resisted the temptation to stare at Prescott as the Tarryall thug wandered about the room, sizing up the layout and means of escape. Here and there, Prescott looked in his direction. Nick wondered why he would risk later identification by revealing himself here and now. Beyond the wallet bulge in his back pocket, there was no evidence that he carried a weapon.

Nick was distracted by a commotion off to his left. A patron had lost hold of several meaty deed books, which hit the floor with a thud. When he looked to where Prescott was last standing, Nick was dismayed to find Prescott gone. He looked about as nonchalantly as he could, and found him partially obscured by a recess in the stacks two rows over from Bonino: Prescott was staring back at him with dead, soulless eyes. That's when Nick realized that Ian Prescott wasn't carrying a weapon because he didn't need one—he was the weapon. Nick suppressed a panic response. He needed to remain focused. One wrong reaction and he could foil the sting and put Michelle and Melanie's lives in danger. It was not a good time for the foot traffic to dwindle.

Finding himself trapped between the conflicting states of fight or flight, Nick was at a loss for what to do. He was finished and could have packed his things and left like Bonino suggested, but thought better of it. That would be too suspicious at this point. Instead, he pretended to check his notes against the information on the microfiche reader for another minute or so. With any luck, he could then pack his things and make his exit with any of the other patrons who looked as if they were wrapping things up.

No such luck. Like it or not, he was about to find out what he was made of one more time. For a second time, Prescott slipped from view. It would be several heart-skipping moments before he heard footsteps approach from his right, at the edge of his peripheral vision. A cutting glance confirmed his worst fears; Ian Prescott was walking with purpose in his direction. Prescott then did something unexpected. He stopped to take out his phone and place a call. Nick seized the moment to corral his things. Unfortunately he missed the opportunity to take his leave, as Prescott had continued his approach and was now too close for Nick to leave without risking a face-to-face encounter.

Stay calm!

"Excuse me. My bad," Steve Bonino's voice rang out. Nick swiveled about to find Special Agent Bonino inexplicably standing between him and Prescott. The agent's timely presence forced Prescott to change course and continue on.

"No problem," Prescott said coolly to the taller Bonino, who acted sincerely apologetic, his own cell phone still held close to his face. Prescott continued on out the door in the direction of the restrooms.

"How close are you to finishing?" Bonino asked.

"I'm done," Nick said. "What do you want me to do?"

"Go wherever you were going to next. I'll wait here to see what he does. I'll keep Prescott preoccupied if I have to. Local police are waiting outside in an unmarked car to resume the protection detail."

Nick made a hasty retreat. Behind him he could hear Special Agent Bonino already speaking with Granby. "James? Steve. I sent you a photo. Have Sanderson's people look into the number I captured from Prescott's phone."

CHAPTER 8

TUESDAY

Evening Star Hotel
Breckenridge, Colo.
10:43 A.M.

M ichelle was remarkably calm. Repetition does that; the rehashing of agendas and contingencies until the requirements of the operation are second nature. It helped that Cat shared her own and in many ways similar experiences of several years before.

"You'll do just fine," Cat assured her.

Michelle appreciated the vote of confidence. Of course she would. She was a survivor, with the support of the federal government and a best friend to help bring the Conservancy down. "You did too know something," Michelle grumbled at the photo of the sheriff and his deputy from the C.C. Times article: a young Joe Hayden and his boss Hollis *"Bud"* Walker, the Conservancy's retired leader and, if titles still meant something, continued guiding voice, working behind the scenes on the illegitimate side of the business, pulling strings. The sight of the corrupt cops disgusted her. She had placed her trust in them in her time of need, and they betrayed her. Hayden, in particular, had questioned her with apparent compassion on that dreadful day following her grisly find in the Ghost Creek valley. It was all a sham to pump her for information about the skeleton she found and what she might say that could come back on the Conservancy. No matter how angry they made her, or how confident she was in her ability to dupe them now, Michelle couldn't help but shudder at Hayden's malicious eyes. They all but jumped out from the photos in her hands.

A hand pushed the photos aside. It was Cat. "You need to maintain focus. I don't know if this helps, but I will never forgive Brett for what he did to us. I learned to cope with it and you will, too."

Brett Carr was Cat's Joe Hayden, a former college friend living a secret life—a pirate's life—who manipulated her husband and college chums into joining him on a pleasure seeking treasure hunt in the Bahamas that went horribly wrong. Carr, Cat explained, put his friends in harm's way in a race to find the pirate Bartholomew Roberts's lost treasure. He took advantage of her husband's knowledge of pirates to solve a riddle, scrawled in Roberts's hand, on a map Carr found in a crate of goods he plundered during the 2010 Pirate Museum heist. The map revealed the location of the treasure—only Carr's partner in crime, a Haitian named Marchand, found them and the map first. Believing Carr had double-crossed him during the heist, and that Brett absconded with some of the treasure, Marchand sought revenge and moved his captives into the Haitian mountains, where he tortured them into revealing the location of Roberts's treasure. *The boys*, as Cat referred to husband Pete and friends Damon and Rey, needed all the help she could muster to help bring them home.

Point taken. There would be time enough later for Michelle to reconcile her emotions.

"Let me see that," Wells said, asking Melanie for her daypack. "What do you have going on here?" he commented, holding the heavy pack at arm's length by a frayed strap, twirling it about, scrutinizing the exceptional wear and tear on an otherwise new rucksack. For the past half hour, he had silently watched Melanie struggle to manage the nylon frizzies plucked from the bag's exterior, while he attended to his own much larger pack filled with various cameras and secret spy stuff.

With a frown, Melanie explained how it got that way from plowing through the underbrush at the Garden of the Gods.

Wells smiled.

"What's so funny?"

"You just called me Mark without thinking."

"Finally!" Melanie said with relief, to a congratulatory cheer from Cat and Janelle. Odd as it might seem, the hardest thing she and Michelle had to prepare for was not the difficulty of acting normal in the face of danger, but remembering to call Ryan Wells by his Mark Boone alias. First Kris, then Ryan, and now Mark? It was all so confusing and unnatural.

"This will help," photographer Boone said to Melanie. He took a lighter from a zipper pocket of his own pack and began burning away the loose strands, cauterizing the frays on Melanie's daypack straps. "Good as new," he said when finished. He then handed the pack back to Melanie for her inspection.

"Thank you!"

"Don't mention it. Tell me, do you have one of these?" Wells tossed Melanie his lighter. "Always keep a lighter with you in the event that you're stranded and need to start a fire."

Melanie nodded and tucked the lighter into a zipper pouch.

"How about a flashlight?"

Melanie said that she had one of those, and scooped up the extra AA batteries the FBI agent tossed her way.

"Good to always have spares," he advised. "You never want to rely on the flashlight app on your phone; it drains the battery you might otherwise need so you can use the GPS app or make a call. Now, how about a whistle or an air horn?"

Melanie proudly held up the whistle she said she kept to scare away bears.

"Or *people*…or to alert someone if you need help. Excellent."

"Emergency poncho?"

Michelle found the exchange illuminating. She would have to admit that she would be woefully underprepared in the face of adversity. She also found the sequence amusing in a geeky flirtation sort of way.

"Why are you looking at me that way?" Melanie asked Michelle with a playful scowl.

Michelle's eyes twinkled when she said, "Oh, no reason."

The front door to the agent's room opened, then closed with a thud. Seconds later, Sanderson leaned through the interconnecting doorway dressed in Dave-Kerrigan-persona business casual. "Everyone's in position and local law enforcement is on standby. How are we doing in here?" he asked his partner.

"All good. Michelle and Melanie are ready," Wells replied.

"We're ready!" the girls rejoined.

"I know you are," Sanderson encouraged his troops. "And remember," he said to Michelle, "you're in charge. You know what you can and cannot do. Don't hesitate to exercise one of the contingencies your photographer, here, explained to you if either of you feel threatened. *Mark* will make the necessary adjustments on the fly. All you and Melanie will need to do is to follow his lead, right?"

"Right!" Michelle and Melanie repeated.

Sanderson checked his watch. "It's seventeen 'til, now. I'll let the others know when you've gone."

"Hold on!" Cat said. "We're not quite ready."

"Yes! We can't forget those," Wells said, regarding the communication devices Janelle was holding in her hand.

"What's this?" Michelle asked, accepting an attractive crystal-pendant necklace.

"There's a GPS locator in the pendant," Janelle said.

"It's beautiful!" Michelle asked Melanie to help her put it on. "I feel so James Bond!"

"As you should…and so will you!" Janelle then said to Melanie, handing her an equally attractive woman's watch.

"We'll be able to track your movements from here on our laptop," Cat explained.

Special Agent camera guy Boone shook his wrist to show off his own tracking device.

Sanderson gave them a salute for good luck and ducked back inside his room to inform his counterpart James Granby, two time zones to the east, that the operation was about to get under way.

⸺

Alpine Lodge Field Research Station
Breckenridge, Colo.
1:35 P.M.

They piled into Michelle's SUV. Melanie took the passenger seat while Wells eased himself into the back, a camera suspended from his neck. The rear was filled with their packs, over-sized camera equipment, and layers of outerwear scattered in such a way as to give the impression that they were air-drying. As she eased the SUV into the Highway 9 traffic, Michelle found herself even calmer now than she was inside the hotel room.

The Conservancy was put off-kilter by their unexpected arrival. It was part of Sanderson's plan to keep Tarryall off balance. It put Michelle in command of the situation, allowing Wells to get lost in the distraction to place surveillance equipment in strategic places around the office.

"We—ah—didn't expect you so early," Beth managed, stepping out from behind the counter to greet her guests. The way she looked over her shoulder was a dead giveaway that her good-ole-boy superiors would not be pleased.

"I'm so sorry," Michelle lied. "I was so excited to get started, that I kinda forgot to call. I hope that's okay. This is Mark, my photographer—Mark?"

Wells looked up from the custom-made table he was admiring. "Oops! Coming."

They watched photographer Boone sweep a hand across the table as he hurried towards them, his first task already complete.

In addition to the radio receiver he'd tucked inside the table's box apron, Wells affixed an imperceptibly small button camera in the river-rock-textured matting of a framed photo that faced the room's interior.

Michelle made the introduction. "Beth Stockwell, this is Mark Boone, our photographer. Mark got in late last night."

"A pleasure, Ms. Stockwell. Might I add that the woodwork on those two tables is exquisite."

"Thank you! We enjoy them. Along with that map cabinet over there, they were made by a local craftsman."

"I was admiring that, too. Local wood, I presume?" What he failed to mention was that he planned to install a remote listening device behind the map cabinet. The cabinet's location was an ideal spot for nefarious conversations to be held outside of earshot.

"What are you doing here?" a masculine voice rumbled from the direction of the office hallway.

It was Joe Hayden, and he was clearly irritated.

"Joe? Michelle said that her party arrived last evening and that she couldn't wait to get started. I told her you weren't expecting her this early."

Michelle looked away to avoid ruining the operation by expressing her contempt for that pig of a deceitful man. She was livid that Beth Stockwell was actually apologizing to Hayden for their unexpected arrival. It was a fortunate exchange nonetheless because it told Wells all he needed to know: that Joe Hayden was the man in charge. Wells relieved the situation when he thrust out his hand. "Hi, I'm Mark Boone. If you'd like, we can come back later." He looked around, ducked his head to look up at the sky outside. "I can take some area shots, a few of the establishment…Hold on!" he said, unexpectedly looking from Hayden to Michelle. "We have to get one you and Mr. Hayden and Ms. Stockwell beneath that Tarryall sign up there."

They turned in unison to look at the sign.

The subterfuge worked. A rattled Hayden cleared his throat. "No, that's fine. I need to clear a few things up first. You said it was Mark, right?"

Of course he knew his name was Mark. Cat said that Tarryall had checked the Mark Boone identity alias and faux blog web site several times, as recently as yesterday.

"That's right. Mark Boone. Let me give you my card." His wallet purposefully barren, Wells fumbled about until he opened a side pocket on his pack that contained a small stack of business cards tied by a rubber band. He gave one to Hayden, but not until first handing one to Beth.

Hayden accepted the card as suspiciously as he shook Wells's hand. If Hayden was put off by the snub, he didn't show it. He asked Beth to show their new guest around and trudged off down the hallway.

Beth offered her canned speech about Tarryall's mission, adding a few new details for Michelle's and Melanie's benefit, and took them on a tour of the office. She made it a point to stop at the table set and map cabinet that had grabbed cameraman Mark's attention earlier, to explain the craftsman's work in greater detail. When Beth wasn't looking, Wells made it a point to show the girls where he had hidden the surveillance bugs.

Next up was the Play Pen. It was much larger than Michelle anticipated. Beth explained to newbie Boone that it was here that the junior staff worked, and that the rear area to their right was a combination workshop and place where maps could be spread out. "Here's where all the behind-the-scenes business takes place," Beth said proudly. Stationed smartly on a wall-length countertop behind the junior staff desks was a bank of charger cradles missing their phones, and next to that a sundry assortment of field equipment and supplies.

"Where is everyone?" Michelle asked.

"In the field. Everyone that is, except for Joe and me. Some of the kids should be trickling in soon. I don't expect the men until later."

Michelle was disappointed. She wanted Wells to place names with faces. *Wait!* Where is he?

Wells was leaning against the wall next to the doorway leading to the interior hallway with his camera at the ready. "Pretend I'm not here," photographer Boone said, and clicked a few photos. "Everything I shoot belongs to the publishing company. I might also mention that nothing Michelle chooses will be published without Tarryall's approval."

"We appreciate that," Beth answered. "But that will be Joe's call."

Again with Joe...

"Of course!"

The dialog was flowing so smoothly that Beth didn't think twice about the awkward way in which Boone took the next photo, a whimsical shot of the lady trio, while holding his camera at a screwy angle. "Who says it always has to be about work?" the faux photographer said. What they didn't realize was that Wells had just used his balance arm to place a bug on top of the doorframe. Beth liked the photo and asked if she could have a copy. Photographer Boone pulled out a pen and note pad and asked for her email address.

Beth escorted them back to the common room. She asked that they wait there while she attended to a patron who had walked in off the street. Wells whispered into Michelle's ear, asking if she and Melanie were shown the senior staff offices yesterday. Michelle said no and asked if that was a problem. Wells shook his head. He then pulled out his phone to show her the text he received from Cat and Janelle at the Evening Star: "LAC," which was short for that the surveillance was coming in "*Loud And Clear.*"

Michelle could just pinch herself. Everything was happening like clockwork. She and Melanie were pulling off their parts splendidly, allowing Special Agent Wells to plant spyware as if he was decorating an office. The sudden appeal of being an FBI operative dimmed, however, at the sound of Joe Hayden's huffing. He walked past without so much as acknowledging their presence to say a few words to Beth, who had just shown the patron back outside. Wells drifted off to one side, pretending to clean his camera lens. Melanie joined him. Michelle overheard Wells remark to Melanie to remain aware of her surroundings. Hayden, he pointed out, was a smoker with reduced lung capacity.

"I suppose you want to see the mines?" Hayden asked Michelle from across the expanse.

"Actually, Mr. Hayden, I'd rather we walk the grounds today to get our bearings, if you don't mind. It's been so long. I don't want to miss anything. Maybe tomorrow for the mine tour?"

Was that a glimmer of relief?

"Sure, sure," Hayden answered, his voice losing its edginess. "Let me get my keys. You all can come with me."

Score another one for Operation Timberline. Sanderson was adamant about only one thing: that, for their safety, they not go into the Little Bear mine. It was that mine, as opposed to the Big Bear mine that Huron College used for educational purposes, that was a sticking point for Tarryall. Sanderson surmised that Tarryall was hiding something, stolen goods perhaps, in the depths of Little Bear, and he didn't want to risk putting the team in jeopardy. Michelle just did her part perfectly by pushing the thorny obstacle of mine entry off until another day. Wells gave her a wink of approval.

———

"This is like something out of Storybook Forest! I'm *s-o-o* jealous!"

Melanie's comment even pried a chuckle out of Hayden.

"I can't believe that I'm actually here, Mel!" Michelle said, staring with fond remembrance at the cedar huts protruding from gaps in the foliage as far as the eye could see. They were worn now, and overgrown in a way that was reminiscent of John Hammond's abandoned Jurassic Park compound. Michelle, though, could look past the years of neglect and envision the place as it was in its glory.

"Where did you stay?" Melanie asked.

Michelle grabbed Melanie's hand, tugging her forward. "Follow me!"

Hayden plodded after them at his own slower, pace. Wells brought up the rear, assuming his photographer duties long enough for Hayden to pass.

Melanie was right; this place was like Storybook Forest, the way they had to meander through the aspen and conifer forest on winding, gravel lanes. All that was missing were the giant mushrooms and wandering gnomes. Here and there, the gravel expanded outward to accommodate groupings of student bunk housing—two here, three congregated there. Michelle stopped to laugh at one of the *non-sanctioned*, non-graveled footpaths made by students to cut off an annoying bend in the path leading to the mess and lecture hall. "Soil compaction was all the rage back then," Michelle quipped. "We used to get yelled at all the time for being lazy—that we were going to kill all the trees if we kept stepping on the roots and packing down the soil."

"Really?"

"Uh-huh. Plants and trees can't get enough oxygen, and the increased runoff removes water that would normally soak into the soil. I went back to Huron last year after I don't remember how long and saw that the school finally admitted defeat, and paved over all the little goat paths we made across campus over the years."

Michelle's eyes teared with fond memories as she stood outside the bunkhouse she had shared with Tracy for those several mostly glorious summers. The structure was showing its age now, like the others, and yet it greeted her all the same, as if it were only yesterday and she was returning from a day in the field.

"Stop it! You're going to make me cry, too." Melanie gave Michelle a little shove. "It's a really big bunk house," she said, wiping a cheek against her shoulder.

"We got lucky. There weren't many girls that first summer session. The profs gave us the biggest places so we would feel more comfortable. That we stayed on for the entire summer season sealed the deal. It gave Tracy and me seniority for the next summer session. When it became clear to the field-station directorate that we would keep coming back so long as your brother decided he was going to stay at school, they even allowed us to keep some of our things inside over winter, so we didn't have to take them back home in August."

"Aww! That was nice."

They turned at the sound of Joe Hayden's huffing.

He smirked when he saw that they'd shed a few tears. He then reached for the retractable key ring on his belt and fumbled through the collection of keys until he found the right one. "Excuse me," he said and stepped past to loosen the padlock.

One look inside was all it took for the remainder of the memories of those heady days to come flooding back. Michelle rushed inside and flopped onto the left bunk—her former bed—now just a layer of plywood sheeting with the mattress gone. "I've dreamed about doing this again for a long, long time."

Melanie sat down on Tracy's bunk. They heard the little click of a camera shutter capture the moment for posterity.

"Thank you, Mark. I definitely want to include one of those."

"I took several. You'll have some good ones to choose from," photographer Boone promised.

Michelle then sprang to her feet and hurried to her former study-carrel nook. She took one look at the wooden top and exclaimed, "*Oohh!* Mel, come look!"

Wells was amused that Hayden had to hurry to get out of Melanie's way.

Melanie gasped at the initials *MS 'n GS '85* carved into the woodwork, along with other student graffiti that accumulated through the years prior to Michelle's tenure. "That's you and Garret!" Melanie exclaimed, "It's still here after all these years." She took out her cell phone and snapped a picture.

"I got that, too," photographer Boone again promised.

Michelle had trouble pulling herself away from the rekindled bond with her former home away from home. She now led them to Nick and Garret's former quarters. Here, it was Melanie's turn to reminisce about the brother she barely knew. She sat at Garret's desk for several minutes, imagining what all his positive thoughts might have been: about Michelle, the studying he relished so much, what his life was going to be like after college. Then looking around, she commented with a derisive smile how war-torn this bunkhouse was compared to the one that Michelle shared with Tracy.

"It was a real disaster," Michelle said. "I can almost still smell the boy stink," she added, wrinkling her nose.

They shared a laugh, including Hayden for a second time.

"*Eew!*" Melanie joked. "I can imagine. Where should we go next?"

Michelle didn't have to think twice. "To the field station!"

They crunched their way along the gravel path, Michelle recounting one memory after another as much for Melanie's sake as hers. Joe Hayden followed at a distance, keeping pace with photographer Boone, who again lagged at the rear. Hayden expressed his displeasure by remarking that Boone was taking an annoying number of photos.

All of the joy Michelle felt inside the bunkhouses turned to sorrow when they reached the field station. It was once much more than a place to study and grab a bite to eat; it was the hub of student life. Michelle could almost hear the structure, neglected as it was, cry from its soul for a return to the glory days when its walls buzzed with life. Michelle couldn't hold back the tears. "It wasn't supposed to be like this," she said. Melanie rubbed her shoulder and said that she understood.

Michelle's sadness turned to a slow burn when they stepped inside. The place was a shambles. The once orderly tables were pushed into a heap; everything else determined not to have value lay scattered about. It was a slap in the face, a disregard for the great tragedy that had occurred here.

Melanie sensed Michelle's bitterness.

Just stick with the plan and get out of here, Michelle told herself, and urged them along.

Michelle's mood brightened briefly when they reached the library, a collection of shelves and wooden built-ins that formerly contained sundry reference texts and study aids, in addition to copies of each thesis or dissertation completed by students who studied the local geology and ecology for their graduate work. Her mood changed when she saw a small collection of dust-covered blue and green-bound graduate research documents strewn across the floor. The college wouldn't have purposely left something so valuable as a thesis or dissertation behind, nor would an advocacy organization with any sense of ethics or responsibility. Michelle saw this and just knew that Joe Hayden and the Tarryall Mountain Foundation were despicable to their core.

Michelle decided to leave before she said something she regretted. Needing a distraction, she asked Hayden to take them to Satan's Lair. She always found the pile of rocks something of a novelty in spite of its reputation as a symbol of foreboding, at the heart of the Ghost Creek legend. "I used to go this way every morning for my research," Michelle explained to the others who followed her along the trace of a gravel path that had become more overgrown than the rest. Putting distance between herself and the field station did the trick, and before long she was feeling much better. "I'd like to show you where my favorite mountain-bluebird subjects used to nest."

"They were named after *Flintstones* characters, right?" Melanie asked.

"Good memory! I named them Fred and Wilma. *Look!*" Michelle pointed. "There's one over there."

"They're beautiful!" Melanie said, stopping short, hoping to catch the serendipitous encounter on film. "Mind if I take a picture?"

"Of course! That's why we're here," Michelle said. See how they don't have any orange on the breast like our eastern bluebirds?"

A ring tone caused the birds to take flight. It was Hayden's personal cell, and not the two-way pool phone clipped to his opposite hip. From his reaction, it was clear he wasn't expecting a call.

Having reached for her phone, as well, Michelle was surprised to find that she had four bars of coverage. She tried listening in on Hayden's call. Wells did the same while sharing camera tips with Melanie. Something was up. Hayden kept grunting in frustration and paced about. Michelle made out Beth's distant voice saying the name Kerrigan. Sanderson was still doing his part to keep Tarryall off balance.

"Impressive cell coverage you got here," photographer Boone said when Hayden terminated his call.

"Huh?" Hayden replied, still agitated. "Yeah. We had a booster tower installed when we started the mine tours." He pointed up the mountain.

Hayden's comment sparked a devious urge to tease out more information. "I was wondering, Mr. Hayden," Michelle asked, "how did Tarryall come about purchasing the property from the college?"

"We bought it right after the accident. They were looking to sell. Sorry for your loss—both of your losses. Ready?"

"Sure," Michelle said to the curious response. She ignored Hayden's curt and unsympathetic gesture of concern, and as they continued walking, pressed, "Were you working for Tarryall then— you know, as part of the transition?"

"In a manner of speaking."

Gotcha! Michelle said to herself, proud of her manipulation skills. She pretended to stumble as an excuse to catch Wells's attention. The telltale narrowing of his eyes was all she needed to know that he also caught Hayden's slip.

"You're not kidding," Melanie said. "This thing is really creepy. No wonder it scared the bejeezus out of people. I have to send a picture to my sister. She'll be thrilled. You said we got bars, right?" Melanie snapped a few photos, and started thumbing away on her phone.

Michelle and Hayden had taken turns playing follow the leader through the woods all the way to the Ghost Creek valley. Michelle led the way from there, downhill along the south bank *almost* to where the creek enters the Blue River. The legend described the collection of granite boulders that gave the appearance of a serpent as being perched next to the Blue River, when it fact they were located at the base of the floodplain on the opposite side of the highway from the river. Engrossed in the legend for as long as she was, Michelle gave Melanie a stupid look when she apologized for forgetting to tell her this little but seemingly important detail. Not to worry, Melanie said she was impressed all the same by the feature's fearsomeness that, for centuries, symbolized evil to Indian, prospector, and student alike.

"Sent!" Melanie said with the satisfaction of knowing how pleased Kerry would be to see the object of so many people's fears. "My sister also gives lectures about various psychological topics. The power of suggestion and its role in fight or flight response is a fan favorite. Kerry says she's constantly looking for new examples to share with her audience. This spooky stack of rocks is perfect!"

Michelle asked how so.

Melanie pointed to the stone structure. Opening her arms wide, she said, "If I never heard of the legend before and you asked me what I saw, I'd have to say nothing. No, wait…how about a squirrel eating a nut? That I'm familiar with the legend, in this setting and on a gloomy day, and yeah, I can see how people would see the monster it's supposed to be. I'm picturing one right now."

"I see what you mean," photographer Boone said, amused at his own recoil from a dark stump in the forest to their left. "For a moment there, I thought that was a bear."

"See?" Melanie said between breaths. "Whew! I'm still getting used to this thin air." She pulled in a lung full and continued. "We start talking about scary things, and now you're seeing monsters," she said to Boone. "Kerry says it's ingrained in our evolutionary drive for survival, which keeps fabrications like the bogeyman and superstitions alive. All it takes is for someone to stir the pot in a place like this, where legend has worked its way into the fabric of the community, to perpetuate a myth and incite fear."

"Ha!" Michelle challenged, "And, you're like me and like to hold on to childhood fantasies like UFOs—or Garret's Bigfoot. You know, you hope that one day you'll see one of those, though deep down you know that'll never happen."

"Well put!" Melanie giggled. "Now let's get out of here."

It was just as well. There was nothing more to see, and Hayden was again getting antsy. Sticking to the script, Michelle avoided the temptation to ask where it was that she had found the *The Body*, the disinterred remains of what they presumed was Dylan Streeter. Instead, she asked to see the Big Bear mine. Hayden was again receptive. In lieu of trudging straight back up the long slope they'd just come down, Michelle asked whether he minded if they walked the circuitous route the school used to take. "It's longer," she said to Melanie and photographer Boone, "but it's a dirt road and a heck of a lot easier than that." She pointed up the treacherous mountainside to make her point. Hayden shrugged and off they went, following his huffing lead.

It took longer to reach the Big Bear mine than Michelle remembered. No wonder the college repurposed a school bus to shuttle the students to and from the field station. Kids being kids, it would have taken forever to herd them to and from the mine on foot.

Standing before the wood clad frame of the mine entrance, Michelle was overcome by that long forgotten smell of rock and timber. Her mind drifted to the days of yore, when grizzled miners worked metal ore from the Earth, to the mine's rebirth as an educational tool. The sad-fond feeling that came with looking into this gateway to the past must not have been lost on Hayden, who inexplicably let down his veil of indifference to ask questions about what Michelle remembered most about the mine. Was he genuinely interested? Who knew? What mattered was that he gave no indication of being aware that it was he who was under surveillance. Hayden even offered to show them the refurbishments Tarryall had made to the entrance-level area of the mine. "It's quite a bit different than you remember," he said.

Michelle couldn't resist the urge to look inside, if only for a few minutes to reconnect with her past. "Hey, Mark? Could you come here?"

Wells was across the parking lot with Melanie, taking photos of the mine portal. "I got several good shots of just the entrance, and several with you and Mr. Hayden in the foreground." He wandered over. "What's up?"

"I'd like to take a look inside," Michelle asked. "Not the whole mine, just the part Joe said Tarryall fixed up for the tourists."

"Sure!" Boone said. "You're the boss. After you."

Hayden instructed them to wait while he turned on a generator housed in the prefab shed beside a pair of porta potties at the edge of the parking area.

Wells took advantage of the time to compliment Michelle on how well she and Melanie were doing. He also let her know that he planted two surveillance cameras just inside the tree line to capture anyone coming to the parking area or entering the mine. When Hayden returned, they followed him inside.

"Wow!" Michelle said. "And no, you're right, it didn't look like this when I was here. I'm impressed."

"We've had a good response," Hayden boasted, and invited her to look around.

Tarryall had created a mini-museum filled with mining artifacts that Hayden said came mostly from the deeper recesses of both mines, and below the level—in Big Bear at least—where the students were allowed to go. Many of the metal pieces had been refreshed with clear coat so that they popped to the eye. Even Huron's pride and joy, the single rail car and spur, got a spit-shine polish: the tracks were ground down to a fresh surface, and the ore cart gleamed like shiny enamel. Unfortunately gone was some of the old timber smell, now sealed off by the finishing chemicals used to bring the grain of the timber supports back to life. Hayden responded to her comment about the same, saying that the remainder of the mine still looked and smelled like it always did. A nice touch was the photos that showed the harsh reality of what life as a hard rock miner was really like. When Melanie commented on the mix of old and new lantern lights, Michelle pointed to a particular one and asked that she take a picture. It was one of the Huron College-era *middle-aged* lights, she said, that Garret likely purchased as part of his junior professorship responsibilities.

"You might want to tell your guy not to go wandering off on his own," Hayden commented.

Michelle looked in the direction that Hayden had nodded. She saw movement in the distance, down one of the timber-supported corridors leading deeper into the mine. She yelled for her photographer to get back.

"I thought we had authorization," Boone hollered in return, his voice echoing off the many stony surfaces.

"We do," Michelle said crisply. "But you need to wait for the rest of us. Mr. Hayden said it's dangerous to go wandering off in the dark."

Boone double tapped his flash.

"Mark!"

"*Kidding!*" Boone said, and rejoined the group.

Hayden asked if she wanted to tour the mine, since they were there. Michelle declined. As much as she wanted to, she didn't want to risk losing any of the gains she had made with Hayden's trust. Not just yet. "I still want to see everything else first," she reiterated, to Hayden's satisfaction.

Michelle's heart raced with every uphill step toward the forbidden Sacred Lands. No matter how much she prepared herself for this moment, she still couldn't shake the dread; all of the terrible memories of that day when so many died and her life was changed forever.

They followed the trace of the former mine road Garret had used to take unsuspecting geology students to the Little Bear mine to conduct their field-camp studies. Michelle stopped at the remnant of the former fence the college had half-heartedly erected to mark the boundary separating the active field-station grounds from the Sacred Lands beyond. She explained that it was installed to appease a vocal group of local heretics who had difficulty separating superstition from reality. Constructed of reclaimed barbed wire, all twisted and rusted, it wasn't much of a deterrent. "I used to call it the *spooky fence*," Michelle said with a little laugh. "The professors said anyone caught coming from the Sacred Lands would immediately be sent home at their expense, and that drinking privileges for the rest of us would be revoked. It was a persuasive policy."

They all laughed.

"I'd say so!" Boone said, taking a picture of the abandoned fence, now mostly obscured by weeds. He looked up and down the road they were walking. "You gotta tell me how he did it, fool everyone the way he did?"

Michelle gave her head a disbelieving shake. "I've asked myself that question a million times…keeping two groups of kids in the dark for an entire summer session several times over is beyond comprehension. Ultimately, it was dumb luck. Garret hedged his bets that his students, being kids and all, would be lazy and unobservant. It also helped that we heeded the professor's wishes and steered clear of the Sacred Lands. In reality, though, I think it was this," she said, reaching into her back pocket to pull out her phone. "We didn't have cell phones. Communication back then wasn't instantaneous. If there was any suspicion, any interest in checking it out had passed by the time the kids from the day shift at Big Bear ran into those getting ready for their night work at Little Bear."

"There was one who did catch on," Melanie said softly.

Michelle gave a heavy sigh. "You mean Dave. Dave Hoffman." She struggled past the memory of her friend to explain how Hoffman, a contemporary of hers and an anthropology student at Huron, had caught on to Garret's deception while following out an assignment by one of his professors, and sought proof of Garret's trickery to use student labor for his own ends behind the school's back.

"My brother killed him."

They pressed on into the Sacred Lands.

"Hmm," photographer Boone hummed when the silence that followed lasted a little too long. "And you didn't go there—to Little Bear—until that day?" he asked.

"No," Michelle replied.

"You couldn't have seen much of Garret at that point."

"I didn't. Our relationship was pretty much over by then, and I had started seeing Nick." She lamented how their lives might have turned out differently had she never mentioned the trace of what turned out to be mining-era wagon-wheel ruts leading into the Sacred Lands one day while sharing a picnic lunch with Garret. It was that innocent comment that stoked Garret's curiosity and that led to his finding the lost Little Bear mine.

"From everything you've told me," Melanie said, "my brother would have found the mine on his own."

They continued on mostly in silence, save for the sounds of their feet kicking up weathered granite pebbles. Before long, they made one final turn in the road that terminated at a small turn-around. Unlike the Big Bear mine portal, Little Bear's had not been refurbished. Hayden explained that only limited private tours were given of this mine.

"I didn't think it would be this hard," Michelle said, looking into the ominous maw of the Little Bear mine. It challenged her, daring her to step inside. She took a step back instead. One sight of the place was all it took for the years to melt away.

Melanie shivered at the puffs of cold air that belched from the blackness: it was as if the mine was breathing on them. "I can't believe you went rushing in there."

"What choice did we have? Garret was beyond hope and Tracy charged on up there after him. We each had our reasons for feeling responsible. Nick and I had betrayed her, and Dave Hoffman blamed himself for setting Garret off in the first place." Michelle ran her fingers through her hair. "It was awful, Mel, just awful."

Michelle asked Hayden what happened once the tumult over the rescue and ensuing investigation had settled.

Hayden's response was maddeningly indifferent. "What do you mean what happened?" he asked. "Nothing happened."

A sci-fi ring tone cut the pregnant pause that followed. "Sorry! That's me," photographer Boone said. "I thought it was on vibrate." He looked at the screen and frowned. "I need to take this." Michelle waved him off and they heard, "This is Mark," trailing off toward the distant edge of the turn-around.

"Nothing at all?" Michelle asked in disbelief at Hayden's apparent apathy about the event that resulted in such a dreadful loss of life and that effectively shuttered the field station and nearly claimed her and Nick in the process. "Something had to have happened." She didn't care how dangerous Joe Hayden might be; he had crossed a line and she was pissed. Michelle demanded an answer.

"You've got to be kidding! I just got here last night," they heard Boone say in the background.

"Not really," Hayden said with the same disinterest, as if what had happened was a garden-variety domestic dispute. "Sure, there was some local media interest for a while, until the forest fire that August, but not much after that."

"Look, I've got three days slated for this assignment. I can leave Thursday."

Michelle fought to maintain her focus over Boone's distant ranting. "Fine," she persisted. "So when did the school first contact Tarryall about selling the property, or was it the other way around?"

"I don't remember. You need to ask Bud Walker. You can ask him if he's in when we get back."

As frustrating as he was, Joe Hayden was a singing bird of useful information. Between his police affiliation and admitted association with Tarryall at or about the time of the tragedy, he most certainly was in a position to know something, and yet he had nothing to offer. Why Tarryall had failed to craft a story—any story—to appease even a modest journalistic inquiry like the one

Michelle made during her 1990s research for *Ghost Creek,* or her current book project, was nothing short of baffling. Confident or just plain dumb, in Michelle's eyes, claiming ignorance screamed that there *was* something to hide.

"Amy, that's who! She's the travel coordinator, right? How's that my problem? Come on, this is bullshit! What does Lewis have to say? Of course he's not taking calls. So what am I supposed to tell his client?"

The photographer's latest outburst again caught all their attention. They watched as a flummoxed Mark Boone stomped his way in their direction.

"What's going on?" Michelle asked. Whatever the call was about was off script.

With deepest sincerity, Boone said that he had bad news. "I've been double booked."

"What does that mean?" Michelle snapped in honest confusion.

Boone huffed. "That was my firm. Scheduling booked me for another assignment, apparently without knowing I was already supposed to be here." He thrust his hands on his hips and stared blankly past her to the mine portal beyond, tapping a toe in mock agitation. "Look," he said, his eyes coming back into focus. "I'm sorry. I usually get a heads-up. This time I got nothing."

Michelle's eyes narrowed. "How could this happen? When do you have to leave?"

"Tomorrow."

"Tomorrow!"

Boone nodded glumly.

"What about my agent? What does Connor say?"

Photographer Boone feigned a dejected smile. "They haven't been able to reach him. I'm told that my people will explain everything, but the fact of the matter is, I can't stay."

Wells was crafting an exit strategy, but for what purpose? Michelle hoped it was nothing serious. "I don't know what to say," she said to Hayden.

Hayden remained noncommittal.

"Look, Mr. Hayden, I take full responsibility for this," Boone said. "I know that you and your organization went to a lot of trouble to accommodate us. If I missed something on my end, I'm truly sorry. This is wrong." He broke off the apology to again stare at the mine, now tapping a contemplative finger to his chin. "Work with me," Boone asked. "I assume that Tarryall has pictures of the insides of both mines?"

"We do," Hayden said with a spark of interest. "Back at the office."

"And Michelle, do you really want to go in there?"

Michelle took one look into Little Bear's maw and said, "Not really. I did until we got here."

Melanie did her part by giving Michelle a thankful hug.

"Whataya say that we forget about going into the mines altogether and take a look at what photos Tarryall can offer? Between those and everything else I've taken so far, I'm sure that you will have more than enough to work with."

The relief on Hayden's face was unmistakable. "That works for us," he said, his tone bordering on grateful and friendly. "We have plenty that you can use," he said to Michelle.

"Great!" Boone said with a smile. "Michelle, would that work for you?"

Michelle pretended to mull over the option. It actually wasn't a new option. Chris had proposed she do the very same that first night they arrived in Charleston. "That's fine. You will amend your fee?"

"Not a problem," Boone agreed.

They milled about the mine grounds a little while longer. Michelle asked Hayden a few general questions. She even gathered her will to stand inside the mine's head frame alongside Melanie long enough to say that they had done so. Having seen enough of the field-station grounds and Sacred Lands, she asked that Hayden take them back to Copper Mountain to pore through Tarryall's photos.

"Michelle? Can you hold up a sec?" Boone asked. "I thought of something."

Michelle was following Melanie inside when she stopped part way through the doorway. "We'll be right there," Michelle called ahead to Hayden at the front of the line. "Mark wants to talk to me about something."

Hayden looked past her to the chagrined lump of a photographer standing on the sidewalk. He grunted an acknowledgement and continued inside.

"Do you know Frankie Wilson?" the photographer asked loud enough for Hayden to hear. "Has Connor mentioned him?"

"I don't think so," Michelle answered uncertainly. "Should I?"

"Just wondering. He's in my line of work. He owes me a favor," Boone said, reaching for his phone.

Hayden paid them no mind, having turned his attention to straightening up one of the handcrafted worktables that had seen activity after they'd left for the field-station grounds.

"What are you doing?" Michelle asked in a bit of a panic. She thought the charade was about over.

"Here," Wells said, and handed Michelle a folded piece of paper. "I need you to call this number when I give you the signal."

Michelle looked at the number. It was not one that she recognized. "What is it?"

"It's the number that Ian Prescott, the man following your husband, called on Monday."

Michelle recalled with a nervous chill listening to Sanderson describe the moment following Nick's close encounter with Ian Prescott, when Nick's Bureau shadow, Steve Bonino, took a picture of the view screen on Prescott's phone. She hadn't stopped wondering what the call was about. Was Prescott calling to give his Conservancy employer the disappointing news that he was interrupted from completing his mission to eliminate his target? "Then what am I supposed to do?" she asked.

"We simply want to know who takes the call and what their reaction is. If someone answers, act surprised and say that you received a text to call this number. If they ask to see your phone, show them. If it goes to voice mail, leave a message sounding confused and ask for whoever's phone it is to call you back. Got it?"

Michelle nodded and she and Melanie followed the FBI agent back inside.

———

"You're all back early. How was the tour?" Beth Stockwell asked, emerging from a side room to their left. Photographer Boone rushed over to relieve Beth of her struggles to manage a box of promotional pamphlets that was much too heavy for her to carry. Hayden appeared content to allow their guest to come to her aid while he walked a clutch of empty plastic bottles and soda cans to the recycling bin.

"Something's come up with Mark's schedule," Michelle said. "I'm afraid that we have to cut our visit short."

"But you just got here," Beth managed, still huffing from the exertion and brushing off the dust that transferred from the heavy box to her clothing.

Hayden interrupted to say that Michelle was going to use Conservancy photos of the mine interiors, instead of doing the underground tours. "That is still your intent?"

"Yeah," Michelle said, showing as much disappointment as she could muster.

Hayden didn't waste more time talking and lumbered off to the archives located in the rear office area.

"You're not going to see the mines?"

"Maybe another time," Michelle said to Beth with even more dejection.

A UPS driver walked in carrying several packages. Beth scurried over to sign for the delivery.

"Is it me, or does Beth seem relieved?" Michelle whispered to Melanie.

Melanie thought so, as did Agent Wells. Wells motioned for them to move to a spot with a good view of the Play Pen and rear office corridor. The same young woman whom Michelle and Melanie had seen yesterday was seated at *Kaycee's Place*. She was making small talk with another young woman of similar college age, who was making annotations in India ink on several topographical maps spread across the map desk.

Michelle and Melanie were leaning forward to get a better view of the woman at the map desk when her two-way radio made a chirping sound. They watched her struggle to decide whether to finish recording the notation she was making or respond to the hail. It was humorous when the phone chirped a second time before the poor child could make up her mind; but when it then chirped again, the humor was cut short when an authoritative voice demanded that she stop what she was doing and pick up.

Frustrated, the young woman literally dropped everything to retrieve her two-way, and in doing so inadvertently bumped aside the book holding down one corner of the collection of maps she was working on. There wasn't time to keep the maps from rolling back and knocking over the open bottle of India ink used to refill her drafting pens. The bottle toppled over, and, with a curse, she used her free hand to whisk the dribbling bottle off the table and onto the floor.

Melanie rushed over to pick up the bottle before the remaining ink had the chance to spill out onto the floor.

Not expecting a stranger to come rushing to her aid, the young woman jumped. With a start, she introduced herself as Vikki and thanked Melanie for the help. Waving the two-way in her hand, she said, "I need to take this," and responded to the impatient caller. "Yes, Mr. Walker," the young woman blurted, while cutting a nervous glance in the direction of the corridor doorway. "It's Vikki. I'm sorry, Mr. Walker. I'm almost done…I still need like five minutes."

"I'll be there in five," the surly voice threatened.

They didn't know that Walker was in the building. His imminent departure meant that the call Michelle hoped to avoid needed to happen now. She didn't wait for Wells's signal to slyly unfold the paper clutched in her hand.

Wells noticed, and did his part by distracting Beth with an explanation as to why he was the one responsible for their cutting the visit short.

A peek at her phone proved that, sure enough, Cat or Janelle or some FBI tech support nerd holed up somewhere had sent her a text that read: *"Call Me."* At the top of the screen, and beneath the time, was the same local 970-area-code phone number that was written on the paper.

Michelle placed the call. To her surprise, it rang through not to Joe Hayden's personal cell, a cell belonging to one of his cronies, or to a landline in one of the offices down the directorate office corridor, but to one of the remaining two-way field phones resting in their charger cradles along the back wall of the Play Pen.

The young woman at *Kaycee's Place* craned her neck as far back as she could from her seated position to see which phone was disrupting their afternoon. "I got it," she groaned to coworker Vikki with a most exaggerated effort to rise from her chair.

Michelle was encouraged. Selfish or not, she had had enough of playing the role of secret operative for the time being. She hadn't gotten herself or Melanie—or Nick or Chris for that matter—hurt thus far, and so wished to back out from her duties gracefully before she did something to screw things up. Thinking about it, logic dictated that thug Prescott's Monday call had to be of a general nature. Tarryall surely wouldn't have been so irresponsible as to risk ordering a hit on anything less than a secure personal line. *But still…*

"Please don't tell me we acted that way when we were her age," Melanie joked. The Kaycee woman could have spent far less energy by simply standing up and turning around.

"Stop that!" Michelle teased. She secretly appreciated Melanie's kind effort to calm her nerves.

Remaining in character, the Kaycee woman made a lackadaisical approach toward the ringing phone. When she saw the all too familiar 513 area code number for Michelle's Cincinnati number on the phone's view screen, however, there was no mistaking the shock on her face, and she snapped her head about in a panic.

"Jodi!" Michelle said without thinking. The last person she expected to be Jodi was some college intern. She scanned the list of nameplates hung all in a row outside the door, stopping at the one that read *Judith Barrie*.

Her cover blown, and with a complexion white as parchment, Kaycee—Jodi, whoever she was—rushed to her desk, holding the two-way radio at arm's length as if it might be radioactive. She opened one of the larger side drawers with her free hand and frantically rooted around inside. Her panic deepened when the reality set in that she was holding the object of her search.

Michelle stared into Jodi's ashen face and mouthed, *"We need to talk."*

"What's going on here?"

They flinched at Joe Hayden's sudden appearance. He was standing in the doorway, a photo album in hand, watching the scene play out—the end of it at least. *Did he actually hear me say that?* Michelle wondered, hoping not, cringing that she could have been that stupid.

"Oh, hi!" Melanie said sheepishly, standing from her kneeling position at Vikki's feet. "You're probably wondering what I'm doing. I was helping…I'm sorry, I forget your name," she said to Vikki. "This fell on the floor," Melanie continued, holding the bottle of ink between her fingers.

The spur-of-the-moment ad lib was so timely and so plausible that it caught Hayden completely off guard. His features softened.

"I thought I heard a phone ring," he said

"It was a sales call," Kaycee lied.

Michelle watched Kaycee casually clip the problematic phone to her waistband while further distracting Hayden by swatting a lock of hair away from her face.

Clever girl.

"What did you tell them?" Hayden demanded.

"I told them we don't accept solicitations, and they hung up."

The subtle tug at the corner of Hayden's lip suggested that the lie had worked. Michelle noted that he did, however, take stock of the number and location of the remaining pool phones.

Does that mean anything?

"There you are!" Beth said, speaking past them all to Bud Walker, who emerged at last from his office. "You need to meet our guests before they leave. Joe did tell you that they were here?"

"I'm aware." Walker answered with a nod of recognition. "Is there a problem?" he asked, taking his place beside Hayden at the corridor entrance to the Play Pen. They made for an intimidating presence.

Wells cursed. He had let Walker slip past his guard, and was out of position to effectively monitor the situation in the Play Pen. He was particularly concerned with what Michelle's reaction would be at seeing the former sheriff standing again beside his former trooper subordinate. There also was no telling what Kaycee Barrie might say or do. Not one to leave the operation in the hands of fate, Wells reverted to his football playing days and called an audible. He pried himself away from Beth and fired off a note to Sanderson to initiate the *555*-countermeasure contingency.

The Evening Star was listening. Wells had hardly caused his own small disruption by filling the space between Michelle and Melanie to introduce himself to Walker when the landline phone started to ring.

"Tarryall Mountain Foundation, this is Beth, how may I help you?" Listening. "Yes, he's here." More listening. "I will do that. Can I put you on hold?" Beth looked at Hayden, and said, "It's Dave Kerrigan. He wants to speak with you. He says it's urgent."

"I better take this," Hayden said to Walker. "We were supposed to meet. He has more information on the property." Walker urged Hayden along and Beth patched Agent Sanderson's Kerrigan alias through to Hayden's office.

Bud Walker turned his attention to his guests. Like counterparts Joe Hayden, Teddy Monroe, and Bill Clay, Walker was only as cordial as he had to be. He introduced himself by his given name, Hollis, and like Hayden, made a slip by saying that he was proud to be a part of Tarryall since its inception. Old and withered, Walker was a shell of the intimidating man Michelle that remembered. Still, he demanded respect. It was those pale, piercing eyes and erect posture that suggested a proper breeding somehow gone horribly wrong.

Walker thanked his guests for coming, and wished Michelle well on her book project. He even expressed his regrets that they had to leave prematurely. Walker then cut the conversation short to help his lagging intern Vikki pull the remaining details together for the field-recon project she was working on.

All told, it was a productive day. They had made solid inroads, between the personal acquaintances, the planting of surveillance bugs, and the gathering of insight into the day-to-day operation of Tarryall's legitimate business front. And while it was true that they hoped to catch a bigger fish, there still was hope that they caught the right small one. Wells passed on the Barrie name, and a plan was in the works to intercept her on her way home from work. They would not have to wait long because it was by the grace of Joe Hayden's helping hand that Judith "Jodi"—"*Kaycee*"—Barrie was snagged in Operation Timberline's waiting net.

"Doing anything important, Kaycee?" Hayden asked, upon his reappearance from the depths of the corridor, without making a sound beyond his incessant huffing.

Surprised at hearing her name called, Kaycee said, "Not really. Should I be?"

Hayden rolled his eyes, a reflexive response to a history of daft answers.

"Remember the tall gentleman with the family property he wants to sell? His name is Dave Kerrigan. I need you to meet him now. He had to cancel our appointment for this afternoon, and has some documents we need to see." When Kaycee asked why he couldn't simply mail them, Hayden erupted. "They're time-sensitive, that's why!" he snapped. His anger having got the best of him, Hayden thrust a torn sheet of notebook paper in Kaycee's face with Kerrigan's number written on it. "Meet him at the Safeway parking lot in Frisco—*Now!*"

"This might be her," Janelle said.

Sanderson glanced up from the status report on his Colorado task force's findings that he was drafting. "I think you're right," he said, and snapped his laptop shut, placing it on the floor behind Janelle's seat.

"Have you heard from Agent Granby?" Janelle asked.

"Yes. There's been no movement by Prescott. Nothing at all out of the ordinary."

"Michelle will be relieved."

Sanderson hummed. He flashed his lights. The driver in the approaching car lifted a finger of recognition, and pulled alongside the Bureau's rental. "Ms. Kaycee Barrie?"

"I'm Kaycee," the young woman said, with a happy-go-lucky smile. "Mr. Kerrigan?"

"Not exactly," Sanderson said with a matching smile and held up his credentials. "I'm Special Agent Ron Sanderson with the FBI; and this," he continued, leaning back, "is my colleague Janelle Stone. Please remain calm," he said in response to Kaycee's instant discomfort. "We're here to help…and no, you weren't followed."

"Are you sure?" The young woman asked in a slow, searching, desperate voice.

"I'm certain, Ms. Barrie. Now, I understand that you also go by *Jodi*?"

"How—"

Sanderson cut her off. "I presume you know where the Breckenridge Brewery is on Main Street, at the south end of town?"

"Uh-huh," Kaycee answered with a compliant nod.

"Let's meet there, in Breckenridge, and talk. You lead. We'll follow."

The brewpub traffic was brisk, just as Sanderson hoped it would be; sufficiently busy so they could blend in with the crowd; noisy enough but not too loud to allow for unhindered conversation. He requested a table along a far wall with access to the kitchen, in case an alternate means of escape was needed—and to monitor the kitchen traffic in the event that a Tarryall mercenary decided to use the rear entrance. With his back facing the wall, Sanderson also had a commanding view of the front door.

He recited a simple story for Kaycee to remember: his plane was delayed and he asked if she would join him for an early dinner while he explained some of the details about the family property he planned to relinquish to Tarryall for posterity management. Janelle Stone was his daughter, who accompanied him on the trip west. Janelle's female presence, in addition to serving as a line of communication with Cat back at the Evening Star, was designed—as it had been for Michelle and Melanie before—to make the clandestine meeting less intimidating.

Kaycee watched a server pass by. She then canvassed the brewpub for anyone acting suspicious. Comfortable that no one was paying undue attention, Kaycee leaned across the table to ask in a low, pleading voice, "Will you help my mom, too?"

This was unexpected. Sanderson looked to Janelle, who shrugged. "Do you have reason to believe that both of you are in danger?"

Nervous shifting was followed by another cautious look around the brewpub.

"It's okay, Kaycee," Janelle said. "You can trust us."

She started shaking. "Mom…She's scared."

"Okay." Sanderson took out his government-issue notepad. He commended Kaycee for her bravery and asked, "What is your mother's name?"

"Beth Stockwell."

Sanderson blinked.

Janelle started madly thumbing a text to Cat.

"Who's threatening her?" Sanderson asked.

"My uncle…Joe Hayden."

"Your uncle?" Sanderson said in disbelief. Janelle stopped her texting midsentence. This complicated matters. Sanderson slipped his phone from his pocket to call James Granby. He talked openly in front of Kaycee, observing her reaction. Granby agreed to authorize an additional protection detail. In closing, he reminded Sanderson that he had his work cut out for him. Frightened or not, expecting one family member to stay the course and roll on another was always a crapshoot. They hung up.

Sanderson was intrigued that the young woman didn't seem the least troubled by the call he just made. "Ms. Barrie—Kaycee—do you know why we're here?"

"You're after them."

"You mean Tarryall?"

Kaycee nodded.

Sanderson made more notes. "You sent the messages to Michelle."

Another nod.

Sanderson made note of this as well. Janelle resumed her texting.

Convenient timing. Wells arrived with Michelle and Melanie. They were seated at a table near the door.

"Kaycee, would you kindly acknowledge that person over there?" Sanderson was pleased to find Kaycee not at all confused by Michelle's presence.

Kaycee raised her hand. Michelle waved back and joined them.

Like Sanderson, Michelle didn't know what to make of Kaycee. She didn't fit the profile of the perpetrator Michelle had in mind behind the Jodi communiqués. She took the remaining seat beside

Kaycee, who was listening to Sanderson's explanation of photographer Boone's true identity. Kaycee's reaction was one of continuing relief.

"You might be interested to know that Kaycee, here, informed us that Beth Stockwell is her mother, and that Joe Hayden is her uncle."

Michelle did a double take. She didn't have the foggiest notion how to respond, so she said nothing.

Sanderson resumed his questioning about Kaycee's family history.

"My father abandoned us when I was a little girl. I don't remember much about him. His last name was Barrie."

"I see," Sanderson said. "Your mother—Beth—did she raise you alone?"

"For the most part. Mr. Hayden, he's not my real uncle. He helped some. Mom never called him my dad," and then with sudden and unexpected sharpness snapped, "*because he's not!* Mom had to call him something, so he became my uncle."

"I see," Sanderson repeated. "You call him *Mr.* Hayden. I take it this is not out of respect?"

Kaycee shook her head. "No. It's what he told me to call him."

"And calling him your *uncle,* was that his idea, too?"

Kaycee nodded.

One look at Janelle's expression was enough for Sanderson to recognize how infectious the contempt was for Joe Hayden. He asked if Janelle was relaying all of this on to Cat. Janelle said that she was, and Sanderson continued, directing his next question to the Barrie girl. "You asked if we could protect you and your mother. I presume that you're referring to Joe Hayden? Has he hurt either one of you?"

"Not exactly," Kaycee said with her face drawn tight. "It's not that. Mom's afraid of him because he's a bully. He threatens people." Kaycee gave Michelle an anxious look and said, "Things got worse after you contacted Tarryall and told them you were writing another book."

"Why?" Michelle asked. Her fear of Joe Hayden turned to anger and then resentment for everything he did and did not do for Beth and Kaycee.

"I dunno. At first it just made them upset. Your name would come up and I'd hear him say how your first book almost ruined everything."

"Ruined what exactly?" Sanderson asked. All Kaycee Barrie would have to do was say something about an illicit operation, and the Bureau's long-held suspicions would be proven true.

"I don't know."

Sanderson pushed his disappointment aside. "You said *they*. Who are they?"

"My uncle and Mr. Walker. Mostly them, but the others, too, like Mr. Monroe and Mr. Clay, though not as much." Speaking to Michelle, Kaycee said, "Mom was really stressed out when you said that you wanted to find out more about that body. It got real quiet for a time. There was a lot of hush-hush stuff going on between the elders after that. They got really edgy and took it out on my mom. There were lots of threats, telling her not to say anything to you."

"Can you give any specifics?" Sanderson asked.

Kaycee shook her head slowly. "Not really. They were more like implied threats, about things only they knew about."

"I'm so sorry," Michelle said. "I never intended for anything like that to happen."

"How would you know?" Kaycee asked. Her breathing became labored. "It got even worse after what happened to that Laney person. I heard them say things like the same thing might happen to you if you kept sticking your nose in where it didn't belong."

Michelle swallowed.

Janelle stopped her texting.

"You mean Hayden," Sanderson asked.

Kaycee nodded. "And Mr. Walker. Mr. Monroe, not so much, but he went along with whatever they said."

Sanderson leaned forward and said in a barely audible whisper, "Do you know what happened to William Laney?"

"I don't know for sure, but I'm pretty sure that they killed him." Averting her gaze, Kaycee said, "My mom really likes you—she's afraid, you know…"

Michelle took another hard swallow.

"Why didn't she turn to the police?" Sanderson asked.

"She always told me that they couldn't be trusted. I didn't know why until I made the connection that my uncle and Mr. Walker used to work for them, and that they probably still had connections on the inside."

"That's understandable," Sanderson said. It would take a long vetting process to clear all of the current Breckenridge and Copper Mountain officers of any ties to Tarryall. Hearing this, however, reminded Sanderson to warn the other Bureau agents to keep their eyes and ears open to those officers they had vetted.

"And that's when you first contacted Michelle—following the Laney disappearance?"

Kaycee looked nervously around the brewpub before saying with considerable unease, "Not exactly. We all heard about Mr. Laney's disappearance the night it happened. It was big news." She blushed when she explained that the next day, Play Pen cohorts Storm Schmidt and Vikki Atkinson saw Bill Clay and Joe Hayden carrying something heavy through the woods in the direction of the communications-tower shed, which was to the west and upslope from the Little Bear mine.

"I gather that they weren't supposed to be there," Sanderson chuckled, finding humor in what Kaycee's blush implied.

"No!" Kaycee said with a coy smile. "Storm and Vikki are seeing one another. They sorta made a detour from what they were supposed to be doing. They were in the Sacred Lands—you know—fooling around when they were interrupted. They kinda didn't want to stick around. They told me what they saw when they got back, and I waited until after work to check it out." Kaycee then said that between what she saw, all of the strife swirling over Michelle's looming arrival, the Laney abduction, and her mother's escalating stress level, she was convinced that the dark secrets that kept her mother tied to Tarryall included murder. Bill Clay and uncle Joe Hayden, she was certain, had killed Laney, and were in the Sacred Lands to dispose of the body. Kaycee reached into her shoulder bag to pull out a folded piece of paper, which she handed to Sanderson.

On the paper was a string of GPS coordinates. "You already gave us these," Sanderson said.

The way Kaycee solemnly shook her head sent shivers up their spines. One look at the coordinates was enough for Michelle to know that these ones were different from those in Kaycee's Jodi post. "These are newer? You think this is where they buried William Laney?"

That's when it clicked. Until now, Sanderson had more pressing concerns, and had relegated the Jodi coordinates to the back burner. "My god!" he said, pondering out loud, wondering with distinct embarrassment why he hadn't considered their purpose, until now. "Those other coordinates…that's where you think they buried Dylan Streeter?"

Kaycee looked at the agent with tired, sad eyes and said, "I think so."

<hr />

City Special Projects Office
Meeting Street, Charleston, S.C.
9:07 A.M.

Nick awoke from a fitful sleep. It was little consolation that he had seen no more of Ian Prescott yesterday, or that Chris and Granby took turns visiting with him until the nightly detail of unmarked squad cars took their place. The simple fact that he had seen his would-be assassin in the flesh rattled him. He did have the opportunity to speak with Michelle after Granby's Colorado counterpart had made his introduction. Michelle expressed how sorry she was for getting him and Chris involved in her mess. That helped. He brightened her mood when he said that Chris actually liked the attention. They pledged to be safe and hung up. As much as speaking with Michelle calmed him, Nick understood all too well that he would not feel anything like normal until this latest fiasco was behind them.

Then there was the dream, the third in as many nights, that awakened him with a shudder. Like the others, it occurred in the wee hours and was more vivid than the last. What they were about, unfortunately, remained maddeningly elusive, the details vanishing like smoke within seconds of awakening.

He drifted off again, only to be roused by a muffled thump that caused him to again rise from his bed with a jolt. He stuck an arm out to turn on a light, only to knock the nightstand light on the floor. Thankful not to find someone looming in the shadows, Nick rushed to the window and threw open the sheer. *"Whew!"* he muttered, relieved to see a lone female jogger taking advantage of the dawn twilight to get in a run before work. Across the street, a familiar neighbor was in the process of beginning the daily grind… *just a car door.* Nick looked at the clock he managed not to knock on the floor. It was a quarter of six. He crawled back into bed, focusing on all the fun he had on Sam Piersall's boat over the weekend, until his nerves settled, and he fell back to sleep.

Granby put in place a new protocol to follow. Nick would receive a call from him at eight in the morning, earlier if necessary. The purpose was to apprise Nick as to whether it was safe to leave Ashley House and whether there were any changes to the morning schedule from the night before. So that there was no misunderstanding, Granby assured him that receiving a call was a good thing. The agent called precisely at eight to inform him that there had been no movement by Prescott and, more importantly, that Operation Timberline's surveillance team had not picked up any suspicious chatter or unusual actions from Tarryall or any of the other identified cells within the arts and antiquities smuggling ring.

It was a beautiful morning. Nick fought the urge to say *screw it* and walk into town. He said good morning to Mrs. Mockingbird, who squawked angrily at his intrusion into her domain and, deciding to play it safe, retreated to the safety of his car. Two more days and it will all be over, he reminded himself...*Just two more days.*

The drive to the City Special Projects Office was uneventful. Nick circled the block, his mind simultaneously looking for a spot to park and thinking about the bizarre entwinement of Coronado's failed search for gold, the possible discovery of an actual Quivira treasure, the Ghost Creek legend, and Michelle's improbable link to a perhaps now non-missing body—make that bodies—whose discovery could topple a multi-million-dollar international smuggling ring. Such a thought was nothing short of absurd. What wasn't absurd was the realization that he might have misjudged his old friend Garret all these years. Nick found a parking spot close to the building. "I'm sorry Garret. I hope you found peace," he said softly and exited the car.

Nick leaned across the information desk and announced his presence. He heard rustling somewhere in the back, then nothing and hailed again. A faint voice said he would be right there. Nick bided his time observing the stark interior. Why, he wondered, were government offices everywhere so sterile? Painted in utilitarian white with no decorations to speak of or background music to break up the monotony, it was no wonder that some employees went postal. Nick knew that he wouldn't last a day working in a place like this.

"Can I help you?" A younger man named Patrick asked. He asked if Nick had waited long and placed an arm full of rolled prints onto the countertop.

Nick assured him he had not. He asked Patrick if he could speak with someone about the city's plans for their holdings near the I-26/I-526 interchange.

"That would be Karen Lanier," Patrick said. "You need to speak with her. She's the engineer in charge of that area. Karen's in back. Please follow me."

Finding himself in a bouncy frame of mind, probably because he could pick and choose his own hours and place of work, Nick couldn't help from rolling *Karen Lanier the engineer* around in his head while following Patrick into the deeper recesses of the City Special Projects Office. What the place lacked in charm, it more than made up for in effective use of space. Drafting tables, CADD and computer workstations, a small art department, and an immense print room were smartly located around the periphery of two long center islands that dwarfed the one at RMC where he performed his deed search. Nick's good humor was stymied when Patrick pointed to Ms. Lanier.

Yowzer. There was nothing whimsical about Karen Lanier. In fact, she was the epitome of the government drone: frumpy with a melancholy workface that testified to the effort it took just to get up each day. Nick felt sorry for her. Time and place were conspiring to erase all semblance of her femininity. To her credit, she was polite enough, if one considered a strained grimace as a sign of welcome.

"Karen? This gentleman wants to talk to you about our properties near the split," Patrick broadcast from a good ten feet away. He waited to be dismissed.

Nick got the feeling that it was proper form to wait until being summoned, so he remained where Patrick left him.

Another woman breezed past without so much as acknowledging Nick's presence. "Good morning, Karen," she said. "How are you feeling today? Good, I hope?" The interloping coworker disappeared into another room.

"I'm managing, thank you," Lanier replied.

"Hang in there. You're in the home stretch now." The coworker said, as she disappeared.

Pregnant! Nick flushed with embarrassment. That explained a lot. He'd caught poor Karen on a rough day when all she probably wanted was for *it* to be *out.* "Ah, Ms. Lanier?"

"Yes, please come over. I didn't mean to keep you standing there," she said. "I'm usually not so out of sorts. What is it that I can help you with? And please, call me Karen."

Nick introduced himself. He used the same line he did with Adeline, adding that his client was also an investor looking to purchase additional commercial or light-industrial-zoned properties with rail and interstate access in the Charleston area. "I was at the RMC office yesterday working on a project for my client. An Adeline over there recommended that I see you."

"Adeline!" Lanier said fondly, her expression chasing the melancholy away to expose a hidden beauty. "She's such a sweetheart. She must have told you about the properties we're planning to put back into circulation."

"She did."

"Did you also try any of the real estate websites?" Karen asked, motioning for Nick to follow her to one of the center islands.

"Not yet. Recommendations?" Karen recommended he try the real estate classifieds in *The Post & Courier* for a start. Nick helped Karen spread a roll of maps she pulled from an upright filing box.

"Nope," Karen said. "We need North Charleston. That's my jurisdiction. These cover the area south of Calhoun. Would you mind helping me? My arms aren't as long as they used to be." She smiled, rubbing at the growing belly that affected her reach.

"No problem," Nick said with a supportive laugh. "When are you due?" He asked, rolling up the remaining maps. He paused when he spied an unframed copy of the same buried-stream map he saw yesterday at the RMC office pinned to a cubicle wall.

"The bane of the structural engineer!" Karen commented, glancing at the map.

"How so?" Nick asked.

"All those blasted filled-in creeks and wetlands make foundation design a real headache."

"I take it that's the voice of experience?"

"More than you can possibly know," Karen said with a pained expression. "You can't imagine the water-management problems I have to contend with to install subgrade utilities in a tidally influenced area with a high groundwater table." She rolled her eyes. "The soils don't play nice."

Her comment intrigued him. Nick contemplated the map some more. If he was right, one of the long in-filled stream courses he was observing meandered across Athens's and PSTRE's properties—*both* PSTRE properties. On second look, so did another. The screwy drilling findings were suddenly becoming clear. He was thinking small when he needed to be thinking much larger.

"Man's incessant desire to control nature," Karen commented. "We are an arrogant species. When will we ever learn?"

"You could look at it as job security!" Nick said lightly.

Karen Lanier gave him a playful slap. "That's too funny. I'll have to remember that one."

They continued to scrutinize the map, contemplating the intricacies of the subterranean soil profile like art connoisseurs, only struggling to tackle a shared problem for different reasons.

"Look," Karen said, waving a hand from the buried-stream map to yet more pictures of the 1886 earthquake devastation clinging to the half-wall of a worker cubicle, "They filled in the streams and wetlands so that the city could be built on top, and then comes the earthquake. The channels and wetlands may have been filled, but they still act as a conduit for water. The shaking built up the pore pressure in the water-saturated sediments, causing sand boils to shoot water into the air. Liquefaction of the sediments caused many of the buildings to sink and tumble. Mexico City was built on a filled lakebed and suffers from the same issues, only on a grander scale. There, the earthquake waves bounce back and forth across the former lake basin and cause far more damage than should be." With a smirk she said, "A woman never would have built one city, let alone two, on such unstable ground."

"I can't disagree," Nick said. Karen's last comment might have been a tad overreaching, but she did provide him with the additional information he needed to refine his working model about contaminant flow beneath the Athens and PSTRE properties. Creosote had leaked downward from the unlined pits and from breaches in the tar pipe, encountered the poorly consolidated channel deposits from the long buried streams, and took off from there. This was not at all good for PSTRE.

"Seven weeks," Karen said, still staring at the buried-stream map.

"Excuse me?" Nick asked. "I didn't catch that?"

"Seven weeks. You'd asked when I'm due. Thanks for asking."

Karen laid out a copy of the same blueprint-sized plat map that Nick perused the day before with Adeline. The principal difference was that Karen's copy highlighted with gray shading the hodge-podge assemblage of City of Charleston-owned properties in the vicinity of the I-26/I-526 interchange. Karen's map also included a GIS rendering of the area transportation infrastructure, along with certain other features and landmarks. The collection of properties sold to the City by PSTRE stood out by virtue of its combined size. It was by far the largest chunk of remaining undeveloped real estate owned by the City in the area.

"Do you know what your client's needs are?" Karen asked.

Nick took cues from the plat to craft a response that conveniently homed in on the former PSTRE holdings. He waved a finger around an area that included Parcel C. "I'm sure he'd be interested in an area around here, considering its proximity to the interstate. Do you know if the secondary roads in the area can handle a significant volume of tractor-trailer traffic?"

She asked Nick to hand her the stapled set of half-size sheets beside him. "It's my bible. A detailed summary of the City's holdings." She then asked for the City ID code for one of the parcels within the area of his finger swirl. "Any one will do for starters," she said. She also asked for a business card. "I can forward to you the detailed specifications for any properties that interest you. The specs identify zoning, whether the City is planning to purchase, lease, or retain the property, acreage, utility status, development requirements—information like that."

Nick handed her his card. He chose a property near but not too close to Parcel C.

"Here we go," Karen said, placing the detailed summary on the center island so that she and Nick both could see. "We should be in the right area." She scanned the page and then the several that followed. "I don't have this area committed to memory. I've been tied up until recently with facility improvements at the rail yard. I'm sure you must have seen it if you drove around the area."

Nick said that he had.

Karen tapped a finger against several sequential entries. "I see that we have several projects planned for this area that your client should be made aware of."

"Projects?"

"Properties slated for imminent transaction or redevelopment. We call them projects. You're in luck. See here? This entire area is designated for light industrial use. This said, if your client's interest is commercial retail, special accommodations are sometimes granted."

"Good to know." Nick asked how the City determines future property use.

"The Planning Commission meets on a regular basis to discuss town and public goals and interests. This particular area was selected for light industrial development because it doesn't fit in with the City's recreational initiatives. It's my understanding that the City wants to get some of these properties into circulation to raise the capital needed to help counter the anticipated financial burden of redeveloping other more tourist friendly places closer to the water."

"That makes sense." Nick asked about the City's time frame for breaking ground.

"As soon as humanly possible," Karen said with a pained smile.

"There is a lot of pressure to get this area into service. And that," she said with a sigh, "can't happen until the baseline environmental surveys have been completed for *all* of the City's properties, including those not planned for immediate action."

"I'm not sure if that makes sense, but okay."

"It's awkward. We conduct the baseline survey to establish property value and incorporate future use limitations into the redevelopment process. It's a requirement we have to remind the planning commission about from time to time. Not that the environmental work is necessarily a burden, mind you. We can work around most issues during the design phase of work—unless, of course, the issue proves more extensive than initially believed. Then it turns into a cluster; that's why we insist that the baseline surveys are completed first."

Nick could relate. He groaned. "As if it's your fault for finding the contamination you were asked to look for." He asked if Karen's people had found any environmental issues that he should make his client aware of.

"Come to think of it, there are. Follow me," she said, giving Nick a wave to follow her to a nearby drafting table where she proceeded to peel off several over-sized CADD-drawn sheets. She handed the discards to Nick to drape over a chair. "Boy, this has been awhile," Karen said when she found the appropriate one.

It was a plat titled, *Summary of Areas of Concern*. Nick frowned. On it, he counted four and possibly two additional former PSTRE-owned properties subdivided from the initially larger Parcel C, including the property currently adjoining Athens's north boundary, where the City identified an environmental issue that required attention. There were far more than Nick thought there should be for such an underdeveloped area. He wondered what PSTRE was into all those years ago, and why none of the AOCs were noted in any of the Phase I reports.

Stan Merrill...

"Not what you expected?" Karen asked in response to Nick's scowl.

"Frankly no," Nick said, not bothering to conceal his irritation. "I'm only aware of these two sites," he said, pointing to the current PSTRE and Athens properties. "The others didn't show up in any of the state or federal databases when I ran the report. When did the City perform its assessment work?"

"That was quite a while ago," Karen said to Nick's dismay. "I've been here going on five years, and this was the first project that I was assigned. Work was stopped when the money was pulled for budget reallocation. My guess is that's why notification of a release wasn't called in to the state for these properties, and that's why you didn't find them in the database reports. Rest assured the state will be notified shortly now that this is a priority again."

"Of course," Nick said. "Would you mind walking me through what was found?"

"Sure!" Karen said, happy to oblige. "This will help me get reacquainted with these properties and let me see what I'm up against. If I remember correctly, each site was in a varying state of investigation or remediation. These two, here and here, I do know were simple tank removal jobs. As you can see, neither was a leaker. All we'll need to do is pull together the final report."

"Got it," Nick said, reading the fine print typed within the property limits for both properties.

"I can make you a copy of this sheet," Karen said, saving Nick the time to copy down a bunch of notes.

He thanked her.

"Not a problem. Once the reports are completed, I'll sign off as the lead engineer and send my approval upstairs. That's how it's supposed to work, anyway. Now, this one here was a former farm dump—I remember that now."

Nick made a mental note of the metal items, glass, and household debris that were discovered. The property was located not far from Parcel C.

"As it says here, most of the junk has been removed. The rest will be removed and we still need to collect samples. Who knows what we'll find: maybe something, maybe nothing." Karen next pointed to the property adjoining Parcel C to the east. "This one was a head scratcher, as I recall. We identified a magnetic anomaly and did some digging but didn't find any junk. There were, however, significant elevated concentrations for…" Karen leaned in close to read the print, "lead, copper, zinc, and chromium. No idea what's going on there, though it doesn't appear to have anything to do with what the former owner did then or does now."

"You mean this company, Palmetto" Nick pointed to PSTRE.

"Palmetto State Transformer and Relay," Karen said, reciting the complete name. "Correct. We're quite familiar with the company and its current and former business practices, considering it sold so much real estate to the City."

Nick was getting a bad feeling. "The magnetic anomaly? Did you use geophysics or just a metal detector?"

"Geophysics—a full suite. It's standard practice for all baseline surveys. It's how we identified all of the lagoons on this property." She pointed to Parcel C.

"Lagoons?" Nick said, his heart sinking. "Do you know what they were used for?"

"Palmetto and the other company you mentioned, Athens Petrolatum, used to treat telephone poles with creosote in unlined pits. Here, let me show you." Karen asked Nick for the parcel ID number. She then flipped to the project-summary detail for Parcel C. "You can see them quite clearly in the GPR output."

And there they were, laid bare before him, PSTRE's very own Pearl Harbor. Lined up in procession like the USS Maryland, Tennessee, Arizona, and Nevada in a Battleship Row were the four lagoons that corresponded with the four *pits* referenced in the 1928 internal legal correspondence; and beneath those, tucked just inside the Athens property line, was the USS Pennsylvania dry dock equivalent, Pit 5. Small print associated with Pit 5 indicated that it was "*Filled <1893.*" The information was damning to the point of laughter. No wonder that smug ass Cresson was dumbfounded at the meeting. Nick shook his head. He turned to Karen and said, "The documentation I have talked about ponds. I figured they were old farm ponds related to the original Middleton estate. This looks like a real mess. What's the City going to do with the property?"

"This remains to be seen. It's going to be a long time, if ever, before this property gets back into circulation. I shouldn't say that," she corrected. "It will eventually be developed. We first need to perform the characterization work to determine the magnitude of the problem. Then there will be the cost-recovery phase, planning, and so forth."

"Cost recovery?"

"The City's not going to pay for the cleanup if it has anything to say about it," Karen said without calling out PSTRE by name. "Now, if your client is willing to assume the environmental risk," she added wishfully, "I'm certain that a suitable arrangement could be worked out, for which I would be eternally grateful. I have enough to contend with for the time being," she added rubbing at her belly. "I would see to it that your client is extended every courtesy."

Nick asked if the City had contacted the former owner.

Karen said that she doubted it, though it was only a matter of time now that area redevelopment was back on the City's radar. Karen regretted that she had to cut their conversation short. "I almost forgot about my ten o'clock," she said. "Come on, follow me, and I will make you that print of the AOC plat."

Nick followed her into the print room to a large-format printer crammed in an awkward arrangement between the closet where the paper stock was kept and a small computer workstation. "Can I help?" Nick asked.

"No, I got it. Thanks," Karen answered with a grunt. "We're used to it. It's only temporary. We needed to make room for a few new toys and have to make do in the meantime."

"Sure I can't lift that for you, then?" Nick asked again when she struggled to load a new roll of large-format paper into the printer. Karen again declined. "It's an insurance thing," Karen said, before shoving the paper into place with a huff. She stood up, placed her hands in the small of her back and arched. "Actually, you can help," she said. "I need to align the roll and it's so dark in there that I can't see a darn thing. Would you mind turning on the light and getting me my glasses? I left them on that desk over there by the window."

"Sure thing," Nick said, glad to help. He flipped on the switch and went in search of her glasses. Karen Lanier may have been an engineer, but she was anything but fastidious when it came to housekeeping.

"I think they're on the shelf."

"Thanks," Nick said. He scanned the cluttered shelf above an equally cluttered desk. "Found 'em." The glasses were hiding in plain sight in front of a framed portrait of what he guessed was her daughter's little league softball team. The photo toppled when he reached for her glasses. Nick righted the photo and did Karen the favor of wiping off the layer of dust that had accumulated on the frame. He couldn't resist trying to pick her daughter out of the lineup. "Your daughter, she the third from the left? She's cute."

"Yes, thank you. It's last year's team. They made it to the City-league finals," Karen boasted. "I got it," she followed. "The print will be ready in a few minutes."

Nick was re-setting the photo when he noticed an all-too-familiar face standing in the back row. *"No way!"*

"Did you say something?"

Nick ignored her. He couldn't believe it, just like he couldn't believe the lettering visible on the sleeves of some of the players—the letters *A.P.* stitched in artistic script within a red, white, and blue patch...*Sonofabitch!*

MacDonald & Carlyle Law Firm, LLP
Broad Street, Charleston, S.C.
12:17 P.M.

Nick was parked at a red light not far from M&C's office, reflecting on his shocking discovery, when he was alerted to an incoming text. It was Michelle. He checked on the condition of the traffic light, and then his mirrors for the stalker who may or may not be there. The traffic inched forward in anticipation of the coming green. Michelle's text pleased him. All was well, and she and Melanie were looking forward to their tour of the field-station grounds later that day. "Wish you were here!" she said in closing. Nick tossed his phone into the passenger seat when the traffic moved forward on the green. He liked that Michelle was sending him regular progress reports; it allowed him to trace her whereabouts in his mind.

Having spent more time conversing with Karen Lanier than planned, Nick had lost track of the time. It was past noon. No wonder his stomach was growling. He picked up his phone and called Granby. "Change of plans," Nick told him. He was going to stop for lunch before heading into the office. Granby appreciated the call, and told Nick that his counterpart was keeping his eye on Ian Prescott, who indeed was tailing him at a distance. Granby also said that he'd spoken with Special Agent Sanderson in Colorado that morning, and all was good. Encouraged by the good news, Nick pulled into a diner for some comfort food.

Having his fill, Nick got back in the car and drove the remaining distance to the office. He found a spot along Broad not far from M&C's office. As chance would have it, he bumped into several M&C employees also returning from lunch, and tagged along. He soaked in the banter between the junior attorneys about the throes of several of M&C's other cases. Nick also appreciated their interest in the special arrangement he and Chris shared with Bill Carlyle. One asked for his business card and said that he might give him a call about another case. They parted ways at the staircase inside. Nick trudged up the stairs, whereby he followed Chris's telltale cackling to a conference room down the hall and to his left.

"There he is!" Chris called as Nick was making his way down the hall.

Chris was seated along the near side of the conference-room table, his head half twisted around and canted at an angle. Brant was seated next to him at the head of the table. Smitty was there, too, standing in a far corner with his back turned, his cell pressed to one ear and a finger plugged in the other. A sense of tension in the air put Nick on his guard.

"Guys?" Nick said to Brant and Chris with a cautious drawl. "What's going on?" Smitty remained in his corner with his back turned.

Chris looked at Brant and said, "Care to do the honors?"

Brant crossed his stubby fingers. "We're waiting to see who fires whom first," Brant said, almost pleased to announce the possible dissociation of PSTRE and M&C.

"*What?* Is this because of what I found out yesterday?"

"Told you!" Chris said, pivoting around to take in Nick's reaction.

"You are kidding, right?" Nick insisted.

"No," Brant responded with uncharacteristic mischievousness.

"Why are the two of you looking at me that way?" Slowly, Nick realized that he was the butt of some kind of joke.

"I bet Brant that you would react like this was all your fault, which you did. The expression on your face was priceless."

Nick took the joke in stride. He called Chris a wiseass and took the seat opposite him, on the far side of the table. Smitty remained deep in conversation with his back still turned. "Who is he talking to?" Nick asked.

"Bill," Brant said. "Bill and Ainsley marched over to Stan Merrill's office this morning. You and your wife did your jobs too well. Merrill apparently didn't understand that we'd be going through *all* of his records with a fine-toothed comb to avoid this very fiasco. Chris says that you were right; as it turns out, Stan does have an arrangement with a slime-ball geologist to provide him with bogus Phase I documents to manipulate the bank."

"He admitted that?" Nick said in disbelief. "And he didn't think that we'd figure things out?"

Nick's questions didn't require an answer. Brant expressed his frustration. "As you know, Bill and Ainsley also have a country-club relationship with Stan Merrill. This changes everything. They're furious over the breach of trust, and Merrill—well, he's pissed about everything else."

"I never intended—"

Brant told Nick to save it. "We have to protect the firm first. What you found in that box and the reality of PSTRE's title history have saved us further embarrassment. The long and the short of it is, Stan Merrill lied. Quite frankly, I don't care which way it goes. I will tell you, however, that if we do continue to represent PSTRE, Stan Merrill will be put on a very short leash." Brant relaxed his fingers, "Need I ask how you made out at the City Special Projects Office"

Nick rolled his eyes.

"Like I thought," Brant scowled. "Save it for Smitty." Brant looked in his direction. Finding Smitty still ensnared in discussion with Carlyle, he said, "Now's as good a time as ever," and slid a folder in front of Nick.

"What's this?" Nick asked, flipping open the folder. Inside was a client-summary sheet.

"Our new client—Evan Barrow. He's a friend of Smitty's. We have a proposition for you," Brant said, shelving his irritation over the PSTRE mess. "How would you like to work with us on a little climate-change litigation?"

That was about the last thing Nick expected to hear. So much for being the PSTRE-case sacrificial lamb. Climate change? Now that's a step up from a Hatfield and McCoys feud between tar slinging log rollers.

Brant explained that Barrow was a self-made entrepreneur and inventor with a niche in the alternative energy market, where he designed fuel-efficient engines. Barrow became embroiled in a lawsuit over the offer of free electricity to his apartment-complex tenants during the beta testing of an advanced air-driven engine concept of his that used a tablet-sized solar panel and standard mechanical parts for an ignition source.

"A type of pneumatic pump?" Nick asked.

"More or less, only Barrow claims that his concept can convert compressed air energy to mechanical work powerful enough to move cars. The difference with Barrow's invention, we are told, is in the ignition source; his concept eliminates the need for a fossil-fuel energy source. You can imagine the implications for commerce and the energy market."

"No kidding!" Nick said, marveling at the concept. "That'd be a game changer. Talk about opening the door to a slew of new markets. So what's the problem? You said that he offered free electricity to his tenants. Who wouldn't want that?"

"Someone with an axe to grind against progressive ideology."

"Oh, brother."

"And the Earth is flat and the Moon is made of cheese."

As much as Nick was intrigued by what Brant was telling him, he wasn't in the mood for one of Chris's digressions. Chris had no sooner said, "It's real Hillbilly Elegy shit," when Brant described the political climate in the area of the southern Missouri community where the case would be tried. They were all interrupted by a sigh coming from Smitty's corner.

"I see that Brant is filling you in on Evan's situation," Smitty said, making his way back to the table.

"We just scratched the surface," Brant answered.

"We can use your help," Smitty said to Nick. "This comes at an inconvenient time for Evan. He's in negotiations with two firms, one is a Big Oil firm in Texas looking to marry itself to an alternative energy future, and the other's a Swiss firm eager to do the same."

"Wouldn't that be something," Nick said, thinking out loud, "the auto industry some day merging with the energy market."

"Huh!" Chris laughed, agreeing that market pressures and in-step advances in technology will eventually make that happen; much like the advances in smart phone technology merged with technology that enabled people to do everything from remotely manipulate household climate control to communicate with the satellites in the sky to find their location on the Earth. "The people get what they want, and business makes a killing on all the emerging markets."

"And in the process, we do the right thing and set the precedent that leaves future generations with a better place to live."

"Both of you may be more right than you know," Smitty said. "Evan tells me that's not beyond the realm of possibility. The Big Oil people he's speaking with actually already have their engineers working on the concept. We'll see." Smitty glanced to his watch. "I didn't realize I was on the phone that long. Back to the point, what we have is an attack against ingenuity and technological advancement that would set a very bad precedent, should we lose. If Evan continues to get too much flak, he says he has no problem taking his business overseas. That would be most unfortunate. He can use our help, and it's a big opportunity for the firm. We hope to include you on our team."

"Love to," Nick said, glad to be involved in what would/could be a groundbreaking case.

"That's what I hoped you would say. Remind me later to have your contract amended. But first," Smitty continued with a sage smile, "we have to get PSTRE's butt out of the fire."

"There's been a compromise?" Brant asked.

A paralegal stopped by with a packet of documents for Smitty's review. Smitty accepted the package and asked him to close the door upon leaving. He then collapsed into a chair and tossed his glasses onto the table. Collecting his thoughts, Smitty took a deep breath. He then indulged the team on the fallout from M&C's morning marathon session with Stan Merrill. "We have reached a compromise. And there's been a change in lead counsel. Bill's removed himself."

This development took the others by surprise, more than if they had lost PSTRE as a client altogether.

"Bill was against keeping PSTRE as a client. Ainsley, however, wants to keep up appearances, so Bill suggested that Ainsley take lead chair."

"Are you fine with that?" Brant asked.

"It's not my choice, but it is their company. We both know that Bill is better suited to deal with the case. Bill, however, feels personally betrayed, and can't guarantee that he'd continue to look out for PSTRE's best interests. I get that. The chain of command will otherwise remain the same." Smitty then attempted to rally the flagging morale with a resounding, "Let's move on, shall we?" He asked Nick to enlighten them with whatever new facts he discovered in town. "Some good news, I hope?"

Nick gave his head a regretful shake. An unanticipated consequence of the Evan Barrow interlude was that it gave him time to bring together the disparate pieces of bad news and develop a plan of action that just might enable PSTRE to navigate around the legal nightmare to come. "No good news, I'm afraid," he said. "But I think I have a plan."

"A plan?" Smitty said. "Fair enough. I'll consider anything even remotely positive at this point."

Nick asked that they bear with a thinking-on-the-fly delivery. He led off with, "First, PSTRE should drop the lawsuit against Athens for contaminating the production well."

This caught their attention.

"Why?" Brant asked.

"Let me show you." Nick spread the plat maps he obtained from Karen Lanier on the table. On top of these he placed a copy of one of the drilling summary maps he doctored up over lunch to show the approximate locations for the buried streams and former creosote pits.

"What's this?" Smitty asked with alarm. He traced a finger across the caption typed within the polygon shape representing Parcel C.

Nick relayed the City's plan for area redevelopment. "The findings from the City's preliminary environmental assessment.

And these," he said, pointing to various other polygons, "are the findings for the other former PSTRE properties that the City of Charleston owns."

Smitty frowned.

Chris crowded in next to Smitty and Brant so that he could also read the text.

"What's this, then?" Smitty asked, pulling the copy of the drilling-summary map annotated by Nick's doodles in front of him.

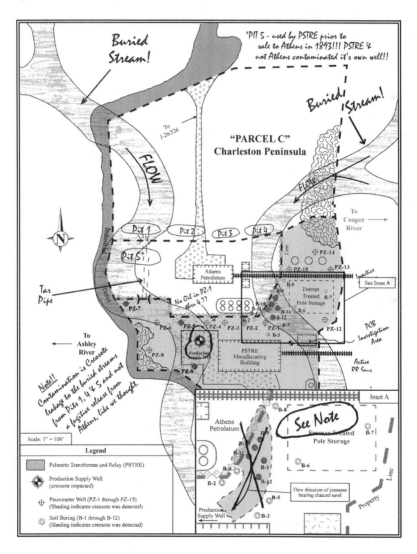

Nick took out his phone and selected the picture of the buried-stream map. He traced the snaking course of one of the streams on the map. "This is one of the streams that the City had in-filled back in the late seventeen or early eighteen hundreds. And here is where I think it crosses through both the Athens and PSTRE properties. It's a best guess, and I did take some liberty to make the map fit our data, but I think you get the idea. It's a pretty good fit. I gathered from talking to Karen Lanier, the engineer in charge, that buried streams and wetlands are a sticking point around here." Nick again pointed to the picture on his phone. "There were copies of this map in both the deed recorder's office and at the City Special Projects Office."

The information was telling: PSTRE had contaminated its own property, not to mention Athens's and who knows how many other properties south and down gradient from Parcel C.

Smitty smacked his head with a groan. Brant chuckled, saying that he was familiar with the buried-stream map but had never given it a second thought. Chris remained uncharacteristically quiet.

Nick added insult to injury when he showed them the photo he took of the City's internal findings for the ground-penetrating-radar investigation that corroborated the partial 1928 legal document he found in the Doubly Deads. "Remember those little curved things marked 'ponds' on the fire-insurance maps?" he said, poking a finger at the Battleship Row of former creosote pits, and then to the approximate location for Pit 5 that the City determined from an interview with a retired Athens employee.

Smitty looked as if he might vomit. "When did they do this work?"

"At least five years ago according to Ms. Lanier, when the City first planned to redevelop the area before the funding was pulled."

"But they're moving forward now?" Brant asked. "I'm not aware of this. Time frame?"

"As soon as possible, I'm told." Nick then offered a window of hope. "Ms. Lanier said properties like Parcel C will take time to develop, considering the amount of environmental work needed to be done. Guys—" Nick said, so that there was no misunderstanding, "I didn't mention names and she didn't give me the impression that Athens's intent on pulling the City into its suit against PSTRE is common knowledge. Ms. Lanier and the City are, however, familiar with PSTRE's history and will expect PSTRE to bear some if not all of the investigation and remedial costs associated with Parcel C. She indicated that PSTRE could be hearing from the City at any time."

Nick's words hung in the air. Smitty, Brant, and Chris took turns looking from the plat maps to the map photo on Nick's phone to his buried-stream mock-up.

"For this reason," Nick continued, "I recommend that Ainsley advise PSTRE to approach the City about purchasing Parcel C back from the City and, if possible, look into deepening their production well."

Smitty contemplated what Nick had to say. Although on board with the plan in theory, he still had serious reservations. "They're already hemorrhaging money. I doubt seriously that Merrill will entertain the notion without some incentive."

Nick smiled. "About that, Ms. Lanier told me that she would be 'eternally grateful' if my anonymous client would take Parcel C off her hands. She doesn't need the headaches, nor does the City want to get involved with contesting PSTRE for reimbursement. She said certain accommodations could be made—like say, getting around the water-use moratorium. I'm also thinking that if PSTRE acts quickly and offers to purchase and self-remediate Parcel C, this would undermine Athens's lawsuit and make them—and not PSTRE—look like the bad guy. Surely Merrill has to see the benefit of having the City in his corner, rather than having it as an enemy. Besides, the City plans for a light industrial use for the area. I think it would make for great PR for the City if it can show how it's helping a local, long time business step up into the international market. Like I said, Ms. Lanier told me that she would see that all possible concessions would be arranged if Parcel C...*went away*."

Brant looked at Smitty with an excited glint in his eye. "This could work!"

"Hold that thought," Smitty said, matching Brant's enthusiasm. "Yes…yes, we can work with this." He snatched his phone from his pocket, called Ainsley, and asked that he get ahold of Bill and meet them in the conference room. "They'll be here shortly," Smitty said. He then asked if Nick thought about how PSTRE might offer push-back against Athens.

Building on the momentum he'd established, Nick brought his plan home with the final piece of discovery he was sure would leave M&C dumbfounded. *"Ah, yes!"* he said, again reaching for his phone and proceeding to scroll through photos. "Didn't the timing of Athens's disclosure at Friday's meeting seem odd? Here we go into the same meeting with the intent of surprising Athens with our findings, only to have them turn everything back around on us. What's the chance of that happening? And what gave them reason to go poking around in the first place? I get it if it was in response to Stan Merrill's insistence that they had contaminated PSTRE's production well, but as far as I understand it, Athens didn't do any of its own investigation work, right?"

"What are you driving at?" Smitty asked.

Brant, as did Chris, hunched in closer to the table.

"I'm saying, what if they had a little help?" Nick selected a photo and enlarged it. He handed the phone to Smitty and waited for what it showed to sink in.

"Help me. What am I looking at?" Smitty asked, staring eagerly at the photo.

"It's Ms. Lanier's daughter's softball-team photo," Nick said. "I saw it on her desk. Check out the coach."

"No shit!" Smitty said in response to the man dressed in coach's attire standing behind the team. He handed the phone to Brant, who held it in front of him to share with Chris.

"Fuck me!" Chris said. "That's Hal Cole!"

Brant resumed his chuckling, finding humor in how everything was falling into place.

Smitty saw MacDonald and Carlyle lumbering down the hall and frantically waved for them to hurry.

"This should be more than enough evidence for PSTRE to amend its lawsuit against Athens to collusion or industrial espionage, right?" Nick hoped. "Ms. Lanier said that Cole used to serve on the City Projects Office board of directors. And there's more," he added, waiting for Smitty to take the phone back from Brant. "Look at the shoulder patch."

Smitty took one look and started to laugh at that all-too-familiar sponsorship patch stitched onto each girl's shirtsleeve, in the center of which were the distinctive letters A. P. for *Athens Petrolatum*. It was a watershed moment: PSTRE, despite all of Stan Merrill's faults, had been set up from the start.

CHAPTER 9

WEDNESDAY

Evening Star Hotel
Breckenridge, Colo.
7:26 A.M.

Kaycee's disclosure put a new perspective on the Tarryall investigation. What started out as an intelligence-gathering mission had become a full-blown protection detail with life and death consequences, and the clandestine search for the remains of two men: Dylan Streeter and William Laney. The focus of the investigation changed so abruptly that Sanderson took time between calls to his Bureau counterparts the previous evening to speak privately with Michelle and Melanie about his mounting concern for their safety. "Our people can take it from here," he said, thinking the girls would be thankful for the reprieve. On the contrary, Michelle, having regained her vigor thanks to having the Jodi riddle resolved, protested at the thought of being cut out of the operation with the end now in sight. When Melanie seconded Michelle's feelings, Sanderson relented, but not without first giving them a warning: "I don't want either of you to take any unnecessary risks!"

The inscrutable variable continued to be the Tarryall Mountain Foundation. How much did they know? Kaycee Barrie had been careful. She preserved her anonymity by using her personal computer and *HikerChic* screen name to covertly contact Michelle through area coffee-shop servers. She even used her childhood nickname—Jodi—reserved for a few of her closest friends. It was a clever ruse that even slipped past Cat Solomon's affinity for name etymology. But she wasn't perfect. Kaycee made her first misstep when, in a panic after overhearing the Tarryall elders say that Michelle and her friend might meet "Bill Laney's fate," she used a pool phone she found in a vacant desk drawer to send her truncated "*STOP AVOIDING ME!! THEY WIL—*" email message. Clearly, the phone was found again among her possessions and placed back into service to be called later by Ian Prescott. Who relocated that phone and answered Prescott's call remained unknown, though Sanderson suspected it was Joe Hayden. Kaycee's second mistake was a derivative of the first: her reaction to Michelle's calling the same wayward phone. There was no mistaking Joe Hayden's suspicion. Kaycee's first mistake threatened her safety; her second put them all at risk.

To clarify Michelle's confusion about why Ian Prescott would have been so careless as to contact Tarryall on a pool phone, Sanderson explained that the move wasn't as reckless as she might think. Cat and Janelle, he said, had back traced Prescott's call to a pre-paid cell phone, and found that the call originated from a Charleston-area cell tower. Review of Tarryall's call-log history for the day and time in question revealed that Prescott's call—presumably again to Hayden for status purposes—was initiated by a nameless sender, and received by an anonymous recipient using one of a dozen service lines assigned to Tarryall, all generically identified in the phone company records as *Tarryall MTN FDN*. The call, therefore, would have provided the Bureau with nothing more than circumstantial information had Nick and Special Agent Bonino not caught Prescott in the act of contacting Tarryall.

On a brighter note, Kaycee's revelation about the locations of possibly two gravesites gave Michelle an unexpected bump in status within the investigation hierarchy because of her skills at aerial photography interpretation. Long into the night, after Sanderson sent Kaycee back to Tarryall with phony real estate documents in hand, they pored over the photography Michelle had purchased from the vendor she and Nick used for their environmental work.

Michelle pointed out the 1989 and 1993 false-color infrared photo anomalies that coincided with GPS coordinates for what should be Dylan Streeter's current resting spot.

For Cat and Melanie's benefit, Sanderson repeated what Kaycee told them at the Breckenridge Brewery about how the hoopla surrounding William Laney's disappearance had brought back a long forgotten memory from her youth about a phone call she overheard between Bud Walker and a man with a singsong voice. Kaycee, Sanderson said, remembered hearing the man with the singsong voice say the name Streeter loud enough that she heard it through the receiver from several feet away, and an oddly submissive Walker promising that *"it"* had been taken care of over ten years before the call. Curious, and with nothing more to go on than a vague memory to look somewhere upslope from Little Bear, Kaycee went on an against-all-odds search and found an artificial arrangement of small boulder-sized rocks that suggested a shallow grave.

Another revelation was Kaycee's age. At twenty-six, she was older than they suspected. This was telling because it demonstrated how the years living a life of oppression and isolation at Joe Hayden's hands had stunted Kaycee's development. Instead of a maturing young adult, the poor child remained stuck on a developmental par with her teen-aged Play Pen peers. Simple math, using Kaycee's 1992 birth year and the year 2000, the approximate year she remembered Walker's call with the man with the singsong voice, suggested that *it*—Dylan Streeter's re-interment—occurred in 1988 or 1989. This timing, if true, lined up conveniently with Michelle's 1988 discovery of *The Body* and the revealing blue-green blips on the 1989 and 1993 aerial coverage. How Streeter's body might have been initially disinterred and then ended up in the Ghost Creek tributary for Michelle to find remained anyone's guess. Plugging both sets of coordinates for Dylan Streeter's and William Laney's presumed final resting places into Google Earth placed both gravesites within fifty or so feet of one another, and conveniently within walking distance of the Little Bear mine.

Rick Ley

Hot on the trail of discovery, Michelle rummaged through her daypack and retrieved Garret's journal that outlined his own inquiry into the location for the Ute prophet Badger Heart's grave. She reminded Sanderson of that part of the Ghost Creek legend where the prospector John Parker stumbled upon an old grave, and Garret subsequently discovered a suspicious pile of rocks in the same general area. "What if," Michelle asked, "Garret didn't find Badger Heart's grave like he thought? What if in reality he found the dumpsite of a third Tarryall execution?"

This wasn't an outlandish thought. It was while they were discussing Tarryall's use of the Sacred Lands tract for a potter's field that Sanderson threatened to pull the plug on the girls' continuing involvement. Final word on the matter came from Cat, who reminded Sanderson that Michelle and Melanie deserved the right to exorcise their own demons, much like she, husband Pete, and friends Rey and Damon had done. Besides, she reminded him that they could use Michelle's familiarity with the Sacred Lands to their advantage.

The preparations resumed at six-thirty a.m. sharp with Cat's gentle rapping at the interior door. Janelle arrived shortly after with a bag of breakfast sandwiches and a carrier tray brimming with cups of coffee and all the fixings. Nestled on top of beds and in comfortable chairs, Michelle, Melanie, Cat, and Janelle ate while they rehashed the plan discussed the night before. It was a simple plan, a literal walk through the woods, as Sanderson put it. He would drop Michelle, Melanie, and Special Agent Wells off along the highway south of the field-station turn off. Michelle would lead them from there, through the woods and up the mountain to the gravesites, using a hand-held GPS device.

"I think we should go this way," Michelle said to Cat and Janelle. She traced a course on the topographic map that reached the gravesites from a round-about, uphill position. Using the same logic she did the day before when they walked the field-station grounds, Michelle described how the topographic lines along the route she was recommending were less bunched together, meaning the slope was less steep and easier to climb.

"Makes sense to me," Cat said. "And less likely to give any of you a heart attack! You look confused," she said, turning to Melanie.

"I am, but not about this."

"What then?"

"How this all came about…how we got here," Melanie said. "I don't understand how someone in Europe could positively identify the Quivira artifacts after they'd gone missing for however long that was. Didn't Ron say they were seen by only a few people and never authenticated?"

"I can help with that," Wells announced, emerging from the room he shared with Sanderson, but not without first addressing a question from Cat about status. "We're on schedule," Wells confirmed, to Cat's satisfaction. "Amy's in position south of town with Agent Hernandez, and the Denver team is on their way. They should be in place before long down in Alma. Local law enforcement has been monitoring Tarryall's office since five this morning, and report no movement."

"And back east?" Cat asked.

"All good." Wells glanced at Michelle's mock-up. "Found a route for us to follow, I see. That certainly looks a lot easier than the way I probably would have gone."

"Should be a piece of cake, " Janelle said cheerily.

Wells routed the conversation back to Melanie's original question. "How did we get here, you ask? I should start by saying that reality makes for a much better story than the one Ron gave you the other night. He was on vacation, sitting on a beach with his family, when he received a call from a museum-curator friend in Madrid, whose expertise happened to be New World conquistadorian antiquities. The curator friend told Ron that a legitimate buyer in Aberdeen, Scotland took what he believed to be early Native American artifacts to a local appraiser for valuation. The Scots appraiser was suspicious of several bracelet pieces that looked similar to the lone photograph of the lost Quivira artifacts that he remembered circulating for awhile in the early eighties."

"The appraiser remembered that?" Michelle said.

"Ron says that the art world is a dichotomy of sorts: conservative about provenance and close-knit on the one hand; shady and free-wheeling on the other. Considering the dollar stakes involved, memories are long on both sides, and the art-community guardians are diligently self-policing. Anything of Quivira's magnitude—from Coronado's search for it to the intriguing nature of the treasure's discovery to its suspicious disappearance—therefore, would hardly be forgotten, even if the goods didn't resurface for several decades. The Aberdeen appraiser did his job by contacting a colleague in London, who compared photos of the suspect merchandise with the original photo and agreed that the supposed lost Quivira artifacts had resurfaced. The London connection then conferred with his Spanish counterpart, who contacted Ron because of his involvement in Operation Timberline."

"Who would have imagined that a chance observation like that would lead to Tarryall's world closing in the way it has?" Michelle said wistfully.

Wells chuckled. "It didn't happen quite that simply. All we had was a buyer with no dossier or criminal record to speak of, so we instructed our art-world contacts to keep their suspicions to themselves until we had more information—like the name of the seller or potential future buyers—who, we hoped, would enable us to connect the dots and make inroads. Simply put, the Quivira artifacts were too valuable not to catch Timberline's attention, if they had indeed lost track of them."

"You're saying that the Quivira relics were kept in play in a game of cat and mouse? Wasn't that risky?" Michelle asked.

"Absolutely. It wasn't a decision the Bureau or other agencies involved took lightly. But it was worth the risk. We at least knew where the treasure was, part of it at least, so we waited. We caught the break we were hoping for the following year when more Quivira items showed up in the States. This happened not long after the San Antonio art heist. As you know, Cat did her part to connect Brett Carr with that robbery and with the pirate-museum heist and the Strickland Gang crime ring."

"And they all had ties to the Timberline Organization, correct?"

"Yes, very good," Wells said to Michelle, who was pleased that she was able to keep all of the names and affiliations straight in her head. "It's Ron's opinion that some of the lower end items from the San Antonio heist showed up on the market as quickly as they did to serve as a smoke screen for the movement of the remaining Quivira artifacts."

"Is that normal?" Melanie asked.

"It's not unheard of," Wells said. "The San Antonio items were peddled on the open market without backchannels, as if whoever was moving the goods wanted to draw attention. We think this produced the intended distraction that tied up local and federal resources; and with one exception besides Brett Carr, the perpetrators did an excellent job making certain our leads dried up before arrests could be made. The one suspect we did manage to nab was a gold mine of information. He took a plea deal that revealed many useful names, including our friends at Tarryall."

"Are you serious?" Michelle said.

"Imagine our luck!" Wells smiled. "Who would have ever thought that, for all intents and purposes, a recent crime like that one would lead right back to some of the same individuals who fell onto the FBI's radar before either of you were even in college?" Then bringing Melanie's *how did we get here* question home, Wells was pleased to say, "Then you come along and contact Tarryall about your book, and here we are."

"Now you know how easy it is to be sucked into a government investigation of organized crime!" Cat said, jumping in on the conversation, making light of her own Timberline misfortune.

Wells supported Cat's assessment. "I can't say I disagree. Innocent people sometimes do get caught in the way. The informant also shed light on how far Tarryall's tendrils had spread into the community. Trust me when I say that the FBI is keeping tabs on a number of others, and not just here in Breckenridge. You are but one example of Tarryall's reach."

"Welcome to the club, I guess," Michelle said, sighing at the thought of there being others like her, whose actions were being monitored that very moment by Tarryall and the government alike.

"You could say that." Wells said giving Michelle a comforting smile. "That's why we were reluctant to use local law enforcement until we had vetted everyone who was to be read in on the operation."

"We should be fine, then?" Michelle asked, aware that Joe Hayden was only recently retired from the force.

"I'm certain of it," Wells said to her satisfaction.

"Do you know who Tarryall reports to?" Melanie asked.

Cat tapped at her notepad. On it she had drawn a triangle filled with circles arranged in a series of rows. Above the rows of circles she drew a line that formed a smaller triangle at the top.

Melanie giggled. "It looks like a Christmas tree."

"That's not far from the truth. From what we know, Timberline is a glorified pyramid scheme. Each circle—or ornament—" Cat said, with a giggle of her own, "is an individual cell within the organization that reports to certain other organizations higher up the tree."

"Why are these ones filled in?" Michelle asked.

"We believe them to be inactive for various reasons, like no activity within the past few years, or they've been arrested or killed for cause. And these half-filled circles here, they're cells that have been infiltrated to one degree or another and are still in operation."

"Killed for cause?"

"Y-e-s," Cat said, massaging the word as she said it. "In some instances, we believe the organization suspected that one of its cells was under investigation, and had the members eliminated before they could be arrested or brought in for questioning."

The girls listened uneasily. Rather than dwell on the frightful things they couldn't control, Michelle decided to move on. "These open circles," she said, pointing to several that included Tarryall at the very bottom of the pyramid, "I take it they're active and haven't been compromised?"

"That's right," Cat said. "Or they're ones we don't yet know enough about to make an educated guess as to their status."

"For what it's worth," Wells clarified, "you can take pride in knowing Tarryall is the oldest still operating cell that we're aware of. That they've been around for this long speaks volumes about their security measures and importance within the organization. As Ron may have mentioned, we believe they use the mines as a distribution hub for stolen property. Can you think of a better place to hide contraband than in an abandoned mine?"

Put that way, Michelle wasn't sure whether Tarryall should command respect, or only more fear.

Wells interrupted that troubling thought with a philosophical observation about the milestone that the Bureau's Tarryall investigation might one day be seen as. Speaking to Melanie he said, "When Ron said that your ancestor's legacy remained to be determined, what he meant was that Coronado's legacy might be rewritten, here and now, by the two of you."

This they didn't expect. "Rewrite history?" Melanie asked. "Us? How would we do that?"

Special Agent Wells folded his arms and said, "Coronado, like so many conquistadores before him, set off in search of fame and fortune that came at the expense of others. What if, half a millennium later, he's also remembered as the man whose search for mythical cities of gold ultimately resulted in the downfall of what may be the greatest arts and antiquities smuggling ring of our day?"

Cat cleared her throat. "Might I add that, if this happens, you and Michelle will have brought closure to countless grieving individuals and their families."

"I never thought about that," Michelle said, humbled by the thought.

"Neither did I," Melanie concluded with a triumphant smile.

Michelle began counting all the little circles on the Timberline pyramid. "How many are there?" she asked.

"There's many more than I drew here," Cat said. "There are thirty-seven, if I remember correctly."

"The organization isn't two-dimensional either," Wells added. "It's actually three-dimensional, like a real pyramid, where cells also interact across family lines when circumstances warrant. Presumably, some form of tribute is paid to those cells within the same family, as well as to others higher up the tree, like in a traditional pyramid scheme. At the top, above this little line, is *management*. We're not certain who they are. We only know that they operate in the shadows above the tree line—or *Timberline,* hence the name. It's management who we ultimately want to take down."

"Ron did say that, too." Michelle then thought of something rather perplexing. "It sounds like the FBI knows more about what it *doesn't* know, than it actually does."

"Again, I can't say I disagree," Wells said with a dismissive wave. "Keep in mind, though, that the prospects of wealth and an even greater fear of reprisal for missteps are powerful motivators to be careful, and to keep quiet."

Michelle understood exactly what Wells meant: just ask James Streeter and William Laney.

"But like I said before, every now and then we do catch a break, like with you, Cat, and Kaycee Barrie, who move our investigation forward."

"About that," Melanie asked Cat, referring to Damon Elliott, who received the brunt of Marchand's retribution during the Brett Carr debacle, "Your friend, is he okay?"

"Damon!" Cat sniffed, with no effort to conceal her lack of sympathy about his Caribbean kidnapping. "If Damon wasn't who he was, he would have been institutionalized!"

"Oh!" Melanie shuddered.

"Don't fret about it," Cat said, just as lightly. "Not even a zombie burial in the Haitian mountains could kill Damon Elliott! I think he wears it as a badge of honor." Then soberly, she added, "To his credit, Damon isn't as careless as he used to be. I'm just glad it wasn't me, or I'd still be a basket case."

Sanderson made his entry. "We're set," he said, ending the discussion. "Everyone's in place and we have authorization to proceed." To Michelle he said that Nick was fine, and then to his partner asked if they were ready.

"Ready," Wells said. "One last comcheck and we're ready to roll."

"Very good. Let's meet outside in ten." Sanderson left a few last minute instructions with Cat, then promised Michelle and Melanie that their involvement in Operation Timberline would soon be over.

The Sacred Lands
Breckenridge, Colo.
8:31 A.M.

Michelle struggled to keep her anxiety in check as Sanderson maneuvered the sedan through the morning traffic toward Breckenridge. Melanie was less successful at containing the adrenaline rush, which manifested itself in a bout of shivers that Michelle could feel vibrate through the seat.

"It's perfectly normal to be nervous," Sanderson said, speaking into the rear view mirror. "Remain focused and try to relax. Remember—"

"We're just going for a walk in the woods," Michelle repeated what Cat, Ryan, and now Ron beat into her's and Melanie's heads all morning.

"That's right," Sanderson said again for reassurance.

What they were about to do was so simple and so low risk that Michelle had to remind herself not to lose her composure. She grabbed Melanie's hand and gave it a squeeze. Melanie reciprocated in a sign of solidarity that she, too, was ready to meet whatever challenges lay ahead.

The traffic lightened and they passed quickly through town. Sensing something wrong, Michelle glanced in Melanie's direction to find her friend staring ashen-faced at her phone "Mel?"

Sanderson looked into the rear-view mirror. Wells turned around.

Melanie continued staring into her phone until the next text message appeared on the screen. "It's Kerry! She's in Alaska."

"Alaska?" Michelle reinforced Melanie's alarm.

"Her patient, the one I told you about who escaped? He made his way to a fishing camp. They're weather bound and he's in a fugue state. She says he's holding them hostage."

"He has your sister?" Michelle said so sharply that Sanderson pulled the car to the berm.

"No, she's fine. Sorry. She's at some kind of base camp. One of the campers was able to escape and report what happened. Kerry says her patient snapped when they became fogged in. And there's something else…the campers…they're being hunted by a wounded bear."

"Jesus! She's going to be safe, right?"

Melanie nodded. "Kerry says she'll be fine. They can't do anything until the weather clears. She wanted me to know in case we hear something on the news."

"Excuse me," Sanderson said softly. "Are you good?"

Melanie assured them all that she was fine.

Sanderson turned off the engine. "Ms. Sutton, while I feel for your sister and the others, we must remain focused. Please extend my best wishes and let her know that your next contact will be when our work here is done. Is that understood?"

"Of course."

"Good. Let's get you and Michelle back safely first, and then I'll see if there is anything I can do to help. Fair enough?"

"Thank you!" Relieved, Melanie fired off one last text. She wished

Kerry and her patient well and promised she would get back in touch soon. In closing, she said that she and Michelle were about to take 'a walk in the woods,' and tucked her phone back into her pocket.

Sanderson restarted the engine and pulled back onto the highway. He pulled over again not long thereafter, about a hundred yards south of the field-station turn off. No traffic was coming in either direction. He gave the girls a final pep talk and some parting instructions while they grabbed their daypacks. "Stay calm, be alert, and try to enjoy yourselves. If anyone from Tarryall shows up, say that your photographer's flight was postponed and you wanted a few more scenery photos for cover art. Ryan has a flight itinerary, should someone ask. Go to the coordinate locations, look around, and get out. If you do find something significant, we'll call in the cavalry once you're back at the hotel." To his partner Sanderson then said, "Ryan, call me when you're close to the road. I'll swing by and pick all of you up. If I'm not there, keep walking south down the highway until I get there." Wells nodded, and Sanderson drove off.

To the small string of cars that passed after Sanderson pulled away, Wells and the women looked like any other trio of day hikers who had left the comfy confines of their hotel suite for a day afoot. Michelle removed her GPS from its hip case and turned it on. Melanie looked over Michelle's shoulder as Michelle scrolled through her file of waypoints until she reached the one marked "BH" for Badger Heart. Michelle pleaded with Wells to allow her a cursory look for the possible gravesite described in one of Garret's journals, since it happened to be on the way to the other locations. Wells agreed and off they walked into the aspen fringe at the base of the mountain, and out of view.

It was tough going until Michelle got her bearings. "This way!" she said, seeing familiar territory ahead. "Be careful," she added, forging ahead, using subtle nuances in the topography to their advantage. Wells remained a few yards behind, keeping an eye out for danger, observing the same landscape for evidence of other potential graves.

Onward, upward, and with increasing ease, Michelle guided them on a north by northwest course in the direction of the fabled Ute prophet's grave. Picking up the pace, they crossed the dilapidated remains of Michelle's *spooky fence*, and entered the Sacred Lands. The knoll that trapper-turned-prospector John Parker dubbed Little Bear Mountain was not far ahead, and to their right.

"I think I found something!" Melanie called out. She was in the lee of Little Bear's shadow when she spied a geometric arrangement of mostly hand-sized boulders.

"It *could* be a grave," Michelle said, with less conviction. It certainly was a pile of rocks, and the arrangement was arguably squarish. "I guess there's only one way to find out," Michelle said, and dropped to her knees and began pulling rocks aside.

Wells showed up in time for Michelle to pull a triangular piece of something from the shallow pit she and Melanie were creating.

Michelle held the fragment up to a shaft of light and squinted. "It could be a piece of pottery."

Wells asked to see it. "Could be," he said. "You should hold onto that." He watched her wrap it in a tissue and slip it into her pack. Wells meanwhile looked intently at the pit. Not seeing anything suggestive, he advised that they move along.

Michelle was disappointed. The search for Badger Heart's grave would have to wait for another day...*like after we bring Tarryall down.*

It took some doing to negotiate an expanse of deadfall that a recent tornado had left behind. This forced them to adjust their course across a precarious stretch of ground that ultimately led them above Little Bear Mountain into an area beyond which Michelle was familiar. Wells halted their progress so they could catch their breath. He called Sanderson with the good news that thus far, the Sacred Lands was not proving to be the cemetery for the damned they feared it might be. When finished, he stepped in behind Michelle, who held her GPS pointed in the direction of their remaining targets. "Looks like they're just over there," Wells said. "You can wait here if you like."

Granted, the thought of again coming face to face with *The Body*—or any other body for that matter—was becoming less appealing with each step, Michelle nevertheless remained resolute in her conviction to bring this mystery to a close. So did Melanie who, having taken Cat's words to heart, said she couldn't rest comfortably knowing that there might be the remains of two men out there in need of coming home.

"As you wish," Wells said, and pressed on.

The stench of decay stopped them short of their mark.

The wind then shifted and the smell disappeared. Wells had just held up his own GPS when the wind picked it up once more, making the electronic gadgetry unnecessary. With trepidation, they followed the wretched scent to a cluster of aspen trees, where Wells told Michelle and Melanie to remain where they were while he investigated. Wells was solemn-faced when he returned. "This way," he said with a wave.

Hearts pounding, the girls willed themselves forward, creeping slowly behind Ryan Wells toward a pile of recently heaped rocks.

"Maybe it's just a deer," Michelle said nervously.

"Yeah, maybe," Melanie supported that hope.

Ten feet more and they were staring down at what unquestionably was a grave.

"It's horrible!" Michelle said, pulling her shirt over her nose.

Melanie did likewise, burying her nose in the crook of an arm.

"Stay back," Wells advised with a pushing motion.

The girls obeyed, stepping back.

Wells circled the low, sloping pile of rocks, taking pictures, looking for signs of who—or what—was buried beneath. He stepped over a few stray boulders, then knelt.

"Do you see anything?" Michelle asked.

Wells craned his neck, trying to catch a glimpse of what was hiding within the dark recesses between the stones. "No," he said with a frown, and got back to his feet. Reaching into a pocket, he retrieved a pair of surgical gloves. Wells snapped them on, then repeated the process, snapping a second pair over the first. "Better safe than sorry," he said and resumed flipping rocks aside. Each pull brought with it a fresh pulse of stench.

"I think I'm going to be sick," Melanie said and turned away.

Michelle stepped in the opposite direction out of a sympathetic impulse. The breeze mercifully carried much of the putrid odor between them. Michelle looked on with mounting horror, finding herself transported through a wrinkle in time to an alternate dimension between myth and reality. There was no getting around the realization that she was living a scene right from the Ghost Creek legend when the scheming Dan Thompson discovered the decaying remains of Garret's soul mate, the miner John Parker, not far from this very spot. It was Thompson who had set into motion the grand plan to exploit Parker's claim that culminated in the development of the mines that unleashed the latest round of Coronado's curse… if one was inclined to believe in such nonsense.

Wells continued casting rocks aside. Nothing. He then circled to the near side where the rocks were piled higher. Wells struggled to shove a particularly large boulder aside that dislodged several smaller ones along with it. This cleared the way to an angular slab of rock that took every bit of his strength to move. The wretchedness that wafted up from beneath was unbearable. Taking short breaths through his mouth, Wells continued, stopping a few stones later at the sound of Melanie's scream.

<hr>

Evening Star Hotel
Breckenridge, Colo.
8:56 A.M.

All was quiet at command central when Sanderson returned to report that the operation was underway. Cat pivoted the computer she and Janelle were using so Sanderson could see that the tracking devices were working. He leaned in close to watch three colored blips inch their way across the mountainside. "Excellent!" he said, taking a seat in one corner near the air conditioner. Cat said that James Granby had called, asking him to call the Denver Field Office as soon as possible.

With Janelle faithfully monitoring the view screen, Cat took the opportunity to check in with Missy Sparling, her protégé at ICF, about the deep dive into Tarryall's corporate finances and the personal accounts of Joe Hayden, Beth Stockwell, and Kaycee Barrie that she had requested. Cat wanted to know what if any familial history showed up between the two women and Joe Hayden.

A cell phone rang. "That's mine," Cat said, spying her reawakened iPhone on the credenza next to her purse. "Good morning, James," she said. "Ron? He's sitting across from me. He's speaking with the Denver office, like you requested. Why? Is everything alright?" Cat snapped her fingers in Sanderson's direction.

"I think I know what this is about," Sanderson mouthed in return, motioning for her to keep talking with Granby.

Cat then made a sharp gesture for Janelle to quit fiddling with the plug-in device used to record the live screen display, and continue paying attention to the monitor.

Janelle tapped excitedly at the three pulsating dots, now converged at the coordinate location of William Laney's purported grave. "Tell me they found something," Janelle said, "Is it him?"

Cat shook her head; raised a finger. "Uh-huh. Uh-huh. Oh, my! Are you sure? Excuse me while I put you on speaker…James, do you hear me?"

Sanderson hung up on his Denver colleague.

"I hear you," James Granby's baritone voice crackled from the phone's tiny speaker.

"James, its Ron," Sanderson said. "Is it true? What can you tell me?"

"Not much," Granby grumbled. "I was informed by Agent Donaldson that Kaycee Barrie didn't show up for work this morning. Her mother called the police, who called Donaldson, who called me when you couldn't be reached."

It was Sanderson's turn to grumble. He had received a call—this call—from the Denver team while dropping off Special Agent Wells and his charges, but let the call go to voice mail.

"Ron, they pulled Ms. Barrie's car from a ravine at Dillon Reservoir."

Heaviness hung over the room like fog.

"Do you know where that is?" Granby asked.

"I do," Sanderson said, scratching at his scalp in agitation. "Condition?"

"Donaldson says it doesn't look good."

"Specifics?"

"There's not much to report yet," Granby said. "Initial reconnaissance suggests she didn't negotiate a turn and went off the road. Her car was found partially submerged; she might have been underwater for some time. You better coordinate with Donaldson to make sure that only vetted personnel are in command of the scene, and see to it that an agent is standing guard at the hospital."

"Copy that."

"*RON!*" Janelle interrupted. "You better look at this…I think something's going on."

They all watched as Michelle and Melanie's two red dots veered away from the Laney target location, going in different directions. Wells's green dot, meanwhile, remained disturbingly stationary.

"What the hell?"

They were still on the line with Granby when the call came. Sanderson thrust a hand into his pocket and pulled out his phone. He took one look at the view screen and croaked, "*It's Michelle!*"

<hr/>

The Sacred Lands
Breckenridge, Colo.
9:07 A.M.

"What is it? What do you see?" Michelle asked, stepping nervously back and forth in response to Melanie's scream.

"*There!*" Melanie wavered a finger.

"I see it," Wells gasped in his struggles to slide the slab aside some more. Unable to reach his camera, he asked Melanie to document the scene for him.

Teetering on the edge of throwing up from the stench, Michelle lost it altogether at the sight of the period clothing pant leggings and exposed patch of skin. The leg, if it could be called that, had been contorted, flattened by the combination of decay and the crushing weight of the rock. "*William Laney,*" she said sadly, her voice trailing to an imperceptible whisper.

"We accomplished what we came here to find. Let's go," Wells said, pulling himself away from the rock pile.

"You're going to call Ron, right?" Michelle asked.

The resounding *whump* of bullet striking flesh prevented a reply. Time stood still in the instant it took for Michelle and Melanie to fully realize what was happening. The FBI agent's body first arched upward, and then was propelled backward in a spray of blood when the second slug struck home. It happened so quickly that the report of the gunfire fracturing the air was lost in the wake of the hollow thudding sounds of lead striking flesh and—

…the sound of a snapping stick.

"*RUN!*" Michelle shouted at the sight of Joe Hayden and Bill Clay converging on their location, guns in hand, from higher on the mountainside. A third muzzle flash from Clay's weapon and the sound of the bullet ripping through foliage was all it took for the girls to double their effort across the precarious ground. It was a near miss. Michelle looked over her shoulder in time to see Hayden, the former cop with weapons training, steady his aim: he wasn't likely to miss like his subordinate. Michelle was practically towing Melanie through the woods when she made a jerking turn, causing them both to stumble, and then tumble into a screen of evergreens.

An aspen thicket forced them to separate on the far side. This saved at least one life when Hayden's belated shot tore into the dividing cluster of trees, missing Melanie by mere inches. Had

Hayden shot a second earlier, he might have struck them both. For better or worse, the thicket also forced Hayden and Clay to part ways. Clay followed Melanie, whose flight took her uphill. "You're mine!" Hayden barked, and set off on a downhill pursuit of Michelle.

Michelle once again found herself in a fight for her life, and her previous experience helped to focus her mind. Frightened but not desperate, she had the foresight to use the larger trees to her advantage, weaving her way around the largest trunks, denying Hayden a clear shot. She also used her hands and arms to grab ahold of and slingshot her way through the low-hanging branches, propelling her body downhill in a herky-jerky manner, making her that much harder to hit. Finding a patch of ground that favored running over hurtling, Michelle risked making a call for help. Fumbling with a slippery phone across uneven terrain proved nearly impossible. It took every bit of concentration she could muster to thumb one-handed through her contacts and stab at the tiny blue number beneath Sanderson's picture to execute the call. To her relief, the agent answered on the second ring. *"Michelle! What's happening?"* She heard the urgency in Sanderson's voice. *"HELP US!"* She screamed before her ankle buckled. Stumbling but not falling, Michelle worked through the pain and then shouted, *"HAYDEN AND…AFTER US…THEY SHOT RYAN!"*

"We can see you on the monitor," were the next words Michelle could make out between heavy breaths, the swishing of branches, and the crunch of rocks and sticks beneath her feet. "Catherine is calling for help. Are you hurt?"

"NO!" Michelle sobbed, almost falling again.

"Can you see them now?"

Michelle managed a glance over her shoulder. *"Yes!"* she said more calmly now. "Hayden…he's after me…you have to help Melanie. I don't know where she is."

"We can see her just fine," she heard Sanderson say, his voice strong, measured, reassuring. "She's running just like you. We're coming to get you, Michelle. Maintain your course and head for the highway, and do not—and I mean *do not*—go into the mines. Go to the road and we will find you. Got it?"

"Ye—"

"You're breaking up. Agent Wells?"

"You have to help him…Found Laney!"

"We'll help Agent Wells…That's good, Michelle. You're do—"

"*SHIT! SHIT! SHIT!*" Michelle cursed in a panic when she preempted the call in her effort to readjust her grip on the phone. It was just as well. She did what she needed to do and made contact; talking was only slowing her down, and ahead lay a tangle of fallen timber—and a decision to make.

Good! She could barely make out the sound of Hayden's footfalls, as he lagged farther and farther behind. Energized, Michelle decided to barge through the tangle instead of running around it and lose what gains she had made. It took no more than a few steps into the deadfall to realize that she had made a terrible mistake. There was so much more in the way of fallen tops to negotiate than there appeared to be at a distance that she became ensnarled. Michelle's progress slowed to a crawl and, regrettably, Hayden quickly reclaimed his losses. A bullet peeled the bark from a nearby branch. It didn't help that her bootlaces had pulled loose, and that her feet were sliding around inside her footwear.

She heard a cracking sound. Hayden! He was closing in. She then heard his feet skid to a halt just in time for her to leap between arching limbs and avoid being struck by a bark-chipping shot that gored a ragged hole into a large fir tree ahead. She might have dodged the bullet, but not the branches that raked parallel gashes into her face from her forehead to the bridge of her nose. Hitting the ground, Michelle rolled to her feet and kept on running, wiping the blood away as she went.

She risked another look over her shoulder. Having taken note of her struggles, Michelle noticed that Hayden chose to circle around the fallen timber, which required his retreating up hill to negotiate some of the densest treetops. Older, slower, and suffering from cigarette-addled lungs, Hayden disappeared again from view. Free of the tangle and entering familiar territory, Michelle quickened her pace, stumbling recklessly downhill in the direction of the highway. When she heard voices drift her way from below, she lurched to a stop. Grabbing onto a sapling for support, Michelle willed her heart to stop pounding long enough so that she could listen.

There it was again! Talking…a masculine voice and….Michelle couldn't make out whether there were two individuals, or only one talking to another on cell phone or two-way radio. She panicked. What if it was Tarryall? It had to be. Ryan's partner, Amy Morgan, was the closest law enforcement officer to the field station. Or was she? *Did Ron say she was working with another partner?* Michelle was conflicted about what to do: keep heading in the direction of the voice and hope that it wasn't Tarryall, or keep stringing out her descent along the mountainside. The seconds mounted. Her heart nearly stopped when the first distant sounds of Joe Hayden's footfalls reached her ears. He was still out of view, but getting closer. Michelle decided to skirt around whoever may be waiting below. If she could just make it to the highway near the field-station drive, she could either hide there in the woods with a good view of the road, or perhaps risk crossing the highway and hunker down on the far side until Sanderson or a law enforcement vehicle arrived.

Michelle emerged from the forest onto the former ore-haul road leading to the Little Bear mine. She hadn't thought about this road, even though they had walked it only yesterday. It was a tempting and surely faster route down the mountain, but wouldn't that be the course Tarryall would expect she would take and post a guard along the way? Compounding matters, she again heard the masculine voice. It sounded much closer now, reaching her ears from every direction, depending on how the wind blew. Her panic mounting, Michelle ignored Sanderson's advice and headed for Little Bear. At least there she could hide and call for help again.

Michelle shuddered once more at the looming blackness of Little Bear's mouth. She thought about how very little had changed over the thirty years since she was rescued from this very place. Part of her was surprised Tarryall wasn't already waiting here for her, considering the mine was both familiar ground and a logical hiding place. Or had they thought of that, too? She heard something…like a heavy shuffle pushing through fallen leaves. *"He can't be!"* Michelle gasped when the shuffle turned into distinct footfalls. She had been entirely too predictable. More disturbing was the rate at which Hayden had made up lost ground. He was so close Michelle swore she could make out the sound of his huffing. There was no time to dally. Joe Hayden would emerge from the woods at any moment. Not willing to give him the satisfaction of an easy kill, Michelle steeled her frazzled courage and slipped into the mine.

Inside, she was struck by sensory overload: the darkness, that stale smell of old mine timbers, and the oppressive chill that rocketed her past to the present. Michelle risked turning on the flashlight function on her phone. That helped. A good feeling emerged from all the bad ones when the light cast its rays across the antechamber, triggering her memory of the fact that the Little Bear mine was set up very similarly to the mine she was more familiar with down at Big Bear. Encouraged that she might know where she was going, Michelle scampered through the antechamber and down the inclined pitch of the main gangway to the gallery of passageways ahead. She took advantage of the backlighting to take a left turn at the first junction. If she remembered correctly, this passageway offered a tradeoff of few options for hiding in exchange for the nearest and easiest means of descent to the next lowest level of the mine. She was fortunate not to have hesitated any longer because the searching rays of a much stronger flashlight announced Joe Hayden's arrival.

The nerve-numbing sounds of lead striking tree and ground forced Melanie to climb ever higher up the mountain, toward the gray barren grounds above the tree line. She hadn't experienced true fear before, the hopeless feeling that all was lost. If forced into the open ground of the alpine tundra, Melanie knew it would be only a matter of time before she was cut down.

Melanie hadn't planned on running uphill. She only did so to avoid colliding with Michelle on the far side of the evergreen screen. This was neither here nor there when the pursuit started because she was still in reasonably good shape from all the tramping she'd done as part of her wolf-recovery project. She was getting used to the oxygen-deprived air, and as a matter of course quickly distanced herself from the unassuming man she barely paid attention to on Monday. Regrettably, when she lost sight of Michelle, she lost both her navigator and means of support. Fortunately, she had committed the topographic map and Google Earth imagery pretty much to memory, and in doing so decided to continue working her way uphill diagonally in the direction of town, hopefully tiring her pursuer in the process. She planned on making her downhill turn along the far sides of the Little Bear and Big Bear knolls, using the promontories as cover. If she could do this before Clay made his own turn, Melanie was sure she would be home free.

Bill Clay had other ideas. His first volleys were non-focused, striking helter-skelter off to Melanie's left. Making the necessary correction, Clay then focused his shots to a point below her, forcing Melanie into climbing ever higher and farther from safety. The wolf to Melanie's moose, Bill Clay knew that it was his prey that would tire first.

She saw a flash of brown ahead, and then an equally out-of-place glint of gray shining through the trees. Melanie headed in that direction, desperate for anything that resembled cover. The tower shed. *Of course!* How could she have forgotten? Hayden mentioned it the other day; so did Kaycee yesterday to Michelle and Special Agent Sanderson. Unfortunately, it didn't hold much promise. A single-room shack made of plywood nailed to thin studs tacked to a square wood frame that floated on the flattest available ten-by-ten-foot piece of mountainside, the tower shed offered pathetically little in the way of protection. What looked like an outhouse stood next to the north wall, facing the highway below; and beside that were several jerry cans of fuel and what she guessed was a chemical-storage locker. It was not much, but it would have to do. She only needed to survive long enough for help to arrive.

Melanie reached for the door and tried to barge inside. Instead of opening, she collided face first into the door. Looking up, Melanie saw that the door was dummy locked. She hastily pulled the lock from the hasp, turned the handle and pushed, and still the door would not open. Pounding on it in frustration, she was surprised when the door recoiled outward. Melanie didn't give it a second thought and ducked inside. She wasn't thinking when she then used her body to slam the door closed, only to fall back outside. She caught herself, and struggled her way back inside. "Stupid!" she cursed. The door was a problem. *Wait!* No it wasn't. *That's odd…* Melanie spied a heavy gauge hook and eyelet mounted near the top that secured the door to the jamb, which she fastened tight. That's when it occurred to her that Tarryall must have built the tower shed to serve a secondary purpose, as a safe house in the event of emergency. Why else mount the door so that it opened outward, in bear-proof fashion, making it difficult to break inside? Melanie was struck by the irony that it was she and not some Tarryall goon who was using the tower shed as a panic room.

She took stock of her defenses. There were windows on three sides, each small and set high on the wall. It would be a challenge, but not impossible for her to reach one and squeeze her way through, if she had to. More importantly, it would be virtually impossible for Clay to break in from outside. A work counter cluttered with electronic equipment and repair items consistent with communications maintenance spanned the back wall. The shed was barren otherwise, except for a heavy wooden office desk made from what looked like construction scraps…and two sleeping bags.

"*Bastards!*" That's how Hayden and Clay eluded the patrols. They must have slipped out during work hours yesterday, before

Sanderson's joint task force was in position, and stayed the night in the tower shed for this very reason: in the event Michelle and her party doubled back for some unauthorized snooping around.

Melanie searched for her phone in vain. She cursed. It must have fallen from her pocket during her escape. She took out her anger by sweeping an arm across the cluttered work counter, scattering tools and supplies that clattered loudly onto the floor.

A hail of bullets tore through the door and adjacent walls, casting pencil thin shafts of light into the shadowy interior. Melanie dived for cover behind the desk, which she had the sense to flip over and use as a shield. Expecting the outburst, she maintained her cool. She betrayed her location, however, when she bumped into the back wall beneath the work counter. A moment's silence was followed by the sound of footsteps, and then more shooting. Melanie tracked Clay's movements by the sound of his footsteps and the emerging bullet pattern. She moved so that there were at least two solid objects between her and her assailant. Being shot at was one thing; truly frightening, however, was the realization that Bill Clay was unleashing his fury, all without saying a word.

If the tower shed was supposed to double as a safe house, then it was failing miserably. At least Melanie had the heavy desk to hide behind…for now. The firing ended when Clay stopped to reload. Melanie heard rustling, then the mechanical snap of another magazine being rammed into place, and the shooting resumed. She had to do something fast. Bullet holes were converging to form larger holes and lines, and, unfortunately, the desk she was using for a secondary cover was starting to decompose, the particleboard and glue construction spalling apart in increasingly larger pieces with each impact—at this rate it wouldn't hold up for much longer. And then there were the ricocheting slugs and pieces thereof that bounced with abandon about the tiny space.

Obviously, Melanie had another problem: she didn't have a weapon, something—anything—to check Clay's assault. Nothing jumped out at her when she first entered the shed, and Clay hadn't given her time to look since. Melanie moved about as best she could in her search, sneaking out from behind the desk when Clay was shooting elsewhere, ducking back behind the bullet-riddled backstop when her scurrying gave away her location. Her situation was dire. She could see Clay with ease now between the widening breaches in the wall, meaning that soon he would be able to see her as well. Melanie grabbed a pair of tin snips, and then a utility knife, and after that an even smaller pair of scissors, discarding each because they were useless.

The rain of slugs continued to pound the tower shed to pieces. There was no time left for Sanderson's people to make a grand appearance upon the scene. She had to do something now or there would be no one left for the authorities to save. Any more firing and Clay could simply push his way through the walls and finish her off.

Melanie spied a screwdriver dangling over the edge of the work counter. She grabbed it and retreated swiftly back to the safety of the overturned desk. She took advantage of a convenient lull in the weapons fire to evaluate her chances of a window escape. Melanie frowned. Sure, she could knock it out and probably struggle her way up and through, but then what? It was a noisy proposition that would take time that she did not have. Besides, Clay would probably hear the glass break and be on her before she even hit the ground. No, that wouldn't do. Desperate, eyes flitting about, Melanie noticed the one avenue she hadn't thought of that could offer a realistic, if cumbersome means of escape: the convenient lack of a floor. The floating frame was flush to the ground in most places, but here and there, and conveniently near the closest corner of the work counter, the frame was propped off the ground by a large rock. Melanie shed her daypack. Lighter, thinner, and feeling decisively less protected, she slinked her way on her stomach to the groundhog hole of sorts, and tried to squeeze her way through.

It was working. She first slipped an arm, and then a shoulder through to the other side. Having taken up caving as an extra-curricular activity in her college days, she was glad to have those spelunking skills come back to her now. Placing a foot against the near corner of the desk for leverage, she pushed with all her might, pivoting to squeeze her head and upper torso between the frame base and ground. It was an incredibly tight fit, but the loss of a little skin was a small price to pay for freedom. A little more wriggling freed her hips, and she made her escape in a fraction of the time it would have taken to go by window, all without making so much as a distracting noise.

The firing stopped. Melanie froze. Did Clay hear the desk move when she pushed off it with her foot? Was he waiting for her to make her next sound? Not to fear, at least for the time being, she heard a grumble—the first audible sound she heard Clay make—then a rash of metal-on-metal sounds and the pounding of a fist against the stock.

Clay's gun was jammed!

Melanie resisted the urge to run. Clay would soon enough discover that she'd escaped—or fix the problem and resume firing with calculated shots. Through the bullet-ravaged openings Melanie could see Clay through the far wall stalking his way around the perimeter, trying to peer inside. Melanie was at an impasse about what to do; then she had an idea. It was risky, yes, and something she would never have considered doing if desperate times didn't call for desperate measures.

She skirted around the backside of the tower shed, and then the north, town-facing wall, keeping low, keeping at least two walls between her and her would-be assassin. She then peered with trepidation around the front, easterly wall for signs of an accomplice. She breathed a sigh of relief. There was none. This meant that help wasn't coming, either, at least not soon enough. Melanie tried to remain optimistic. She hoped that Cat and Janelle were tracking her movements on the computer screen and sensed that something had gone wrong, and that Sanderson's cavalry was closing in fast. And then there was all of the shooting—in mid-morning, in the middle of the week, so far away from anywhere that anyone would take his

AR-15 to shoot—someone had to have heard it, right? Certainly, someone had to have called the cops…or so she hoped.

Collecting her nerve, Melanie waited for the right moment to sprint across the front of the tower shed when Clay concentrated a brief burst of gunfire on the corner from which she had just escaped. "*Made it,*" she whispered with relief, having assumed correctly that Clay's senses would be too focused on the task at hand to notice her sudden flash of movement past the many bullet-hole windows, or to hear the patter of running feet. And now she waited some more.

The wait was excruciating. Melanie again had to resist the urge to take flight and stick with her on-the-fly plan, which was becoming seemingly more reckless by the moment. Whether she wanted it to or not, the time for action came sooner than later when Clay emptied what proved to be his last clip. Peering through a peephole, Melanie was shocked by the hatred in Clay's eyes. She never witnessed such malice. Yet as frightening as he appeared, Melanie couldn't get over how pathetic the man was to have abandoned all sense of sanity over a ridiculous quest for wealth that didn't belong to him or his people. And for this she couldn't resist a triumphant sneer when it occurred to her that it was she who held the upper hand. Bill Clay, distracted as he was in an overconfident quest to make certain she didn't live to tell her tale, was playing right into her hands.

He kicked at, and then pounded furiously at the door. Melanie managed another nervous laugh. Hayden's lap dog had forgotten Tarryall's built-in failsafe against break-ins. Realizing his error, Clay then started yanking at the door with all his might. It took but a handful of rage-jacked tugs to pop the internal hook and eyelet from the door and frame, and Clay barged inside to find the tower shed…empty. That's when Melanie burst from cover, slammed the door shut, flipped the exterior safety latch, and shoved the screwdriver home in place of the discarded lock.

Clay went berserk. Amidst a flurry of expletives, he charged the door, ramming into it with a crashing thud that made the bullet-weakened structure shudder. Melanie jumped back, frightened at first, then proud for having trapped her predator. Her joy vanished just as quickly when Clay started yanking savagely on what remained of the door. Although wedged in tight, the screwdriver shaft was too long for the short area between the hasp and overhanging sheet metal of the roof. Melanie saw that with each powerful tug the screwdriver was acting as a lever to pry the hasp screws free. She was going to make a run for it per her plan when her hand brushed against her leg…and the lighter she'd forgotten she'd removed from her daypack to cauterize the vegetation-plucked frizzies before leaving the Evening Star.

Melanie pulled the lighter from her pocket, stared at it for a moment, and with a wicked thought contrary to everything she believed, flicked it on. The sound of the spark wheel striking flint was all it took for the deranged animal trapped inside to turn into a pleading fool. Through myriad holes of Clay's making, Melanie looked without compassion at the desperation in Bill Clay's eyes. She still could have run, but didn't. She had to end this now, even if it meant committing an unspeakable act, just in case Bill Clay managed to escape and tried to finish her off. Turning her back on the man who had tried to kill her, Melanie hurried to the outbuilding. There, she kicked at the jerry cans until she found one with enough fuel to get the job done.

"*WHAT ARE YOU DOING*?" Clay shouted, his voice an enraged tremble, before resuming his yanking, then pounding at the walls in a desperate attempt to beat his way through the bullet-ravaged plywood.

Melanie picked up the jerry can, unsnapped the cap on the spout, and sniffed. Just as she thought: *gasoline*.

"No! Don't! What do you want?" Clay pleaded as he watched her return through the bullet-hole openings.

Melanie couldn't help but glare with contempt for the man, for Joe Hayden, and for Tarryall and what the organization had done to ruin so many lives. Even so, it was difficult for her to splash fuel on the door. This was until Clay's demeanor returned to its former fury and Melanie was forced to accept that Clay had no intention on stopping until one of them was dead. Reaching into her pocket, Melanie pulled out a tissue. Then, using the lighter Ryan Wells said she should always carry with her, she ignited the tissue and tossed the flaming ball of paper in the direction of the building.

The tower shed burst into flames in one great *WHOOSH!* Melanie listened with grim satisfaction to Clay's pitiful screams and his frantic beating on the walls. In the end, the fire was too aggressive, the wood framing too dry, and the breeze just right to fan the flames to a roll that climbed high into the air. Melanie watched until she was sure that Clay could not escape, before walking away.

The Sacred Lands had claimed another victim.

Sanderson sped down Highway 9 as fast as the conditions allowed. He was less than a mile north of the field station when he saw the first faint wisps of smoke rising from the treetops in the vicinity of the mines. By the time he emerged from around a slight jog in the road, the wisp had transformed into a thick column of smoke. *What the hell?* It could have been a spurious forest fire, but Sanderson knew otherwise. He didn't believe in coincidences. This had something to do with Tarryall. "Call Agent Morgan," he spoke to the hands-free driver-assist system that dialed Special Agent Morgan's number. "Amy? It's Ron. I see smoke above your location. Where are you?"

"I'm at the field station now. I saw the smoke as well. Special Agent Hernandez went to a clearing for a better view. The smoke's coming from high on the mountain."

"Any sign of Ms. Kozlowski or Ms. Sutton?"

"Negative. Nothing here."

"Roger that. Hold your position until I get there, in case one of them makes it down the mountain. Have Agent Hernandez head to the coordinates for the Laney grave that Ms. Solomon forwarded to each of you." Sanderson then paused before adding, "And Amy, there's been no movement from Ryan's location."

"Copy that," the female voice responded.

Sanderson hung up. That was a difficult call to make. The tension in Amy Morgan's voice cut through her professional response. She and Ryan Wells were close. Sanderson didn't want her rushing into a situation that might cause her to make a rash decision.

The morning was an utter disaster. Sanderson had grossly underestimated Tarryall. Not only was one of his agents down, Kaycee Barrie was near death, and her mother and the remaining Tarryall directorate didn't report in to work—and now his two civilian operatives had been compromised. His next call was to Cat Solomon. "Catherine? Status."

"Ron, we just lost Michelle's signal," Cat said, dashing Sanderson's hope for good news. "We think she might have gone inside Little Bear."

"*Shit!*" Another problem.

"I hate telling you this," Cat reported to her beleaguered boss. "Something's also going on with Melanie. Her position hadn't changed for almost ten minutes now in the woods way up near the tree line—*WAIT! Hold on...*" This was followed with ringing excitement, "She's on the move...coming your way now...and *fast*... straight down the mountain."

"Very good," Sanderson said, trying to remain optimistic, his mind running through the various scenarios as to how Melanie's moving dot on the computer screen could be interpreted.

"Ron," Cat said, disrupting his introspection, "Janelle just heard on the police scanner that fire fighters and police are on their way to the field station. Is there something we should know about?"

Sanderson explained that he saw smoke high up on the mountain. When asked about Ryan Wells's electronic signature, Cat was hesitant to inform him that it hadn't moved.

Sanderson peeled to a gravel-grinding halt in the field-station parking lot. There, he met Amy Morgan in front of the main building. The smoke was unavoidable. A dark cloud covered a large swath of sky, turning the clear day to hazy twilight. Sirens were heard in the distance, becoming louder by the second. Sanderson asked Amy how she was holding up and placed a hand on her shoulder. "We don't know anything yet, Amy," he said. "Ryan's strong." This lifted her spirits. Sanderson then requested she hold her position until the fire department and local law enforcement arrived, after which she was to follow him to the Little Bear mine where Cat said they lost Michelle's signal.

The sound of something large crashing through the understory reached their ears before Sanderson had the chance to leave. They drew their weapons.

"*There!*" Special Agent Morgan said, pointing into the trees.

"I don't see anything," Sanderson said.

Melanie appeared from the wall of green, waving her arms and screaming, "*DON'T SHOOT!*"

The agents raced to intercept.

"I didn't mean to do this!" Melanie sobbed.

Sanderson enveloped her in a bear hug, his gun still drawn and pointing into the trees. "Clay?"

"*NO!*" Melanie managed, collapsing into his arms.

Sanderson lowered her to the ground, checked her for injuries. "You all right? What happened?"

The cacophony of sirens and noise pulling up the winding drive announced the imminent arrival of emergency services. "I got this," Morgan said, jogging off after them.

"I left him in that cabin…you know…that shed," Melanie said between sobs. "I didn't want to do it. Am I in trouble?" she asked, pointing despondently at the billowing clouds of smoke she'd created. The fire had taken off to the point that glowing embers were being carried on the wind.

Sanderson wasn't sure what to say. He asked her again if she was hurt, and what had happened. Melanie struggled to explain how she and Michelle saw Ryan Wells gunned down by Joe Hayden and Bill Clay, who had appeared from nowhere. From there, she described how she became separated from Michelle, and how her hopeless run up the mountainside culminated in the inferno that burned Bill Clay alive inside the tower shed. Bawling helplessly over the fact that she had killed someone and started a forest fire, and the fact that Michelle was nowhere to be seen, Melanie pleaded, "You have to help her!"

"We will," Sanderson assured her, cradling Melanie in his arms. "You did what you needed to do to survive," he said, and left it at that. He released her when he heard Amy Morgan's voice over the sirens. Sanderson waited with Melanie until Morgan hurried over with a paramedic, before taking off at a sprint toward Little Bear.

Michelle hid in a recess in the rock wall leading to the next lowest level of the mine. It was dark, chilly, and save for the intermittent tap of dripping water, she heard nothing. She used her hands to rub opposite arms to ward off the cold. There was nothing Michelle could do but wait for Hayden to make the next sound. Although the mine entrance was not far away, the little light entering the chasm had all but vanished the moment she slunk down the corridor. This, along with the thin skim of gravel and occasional chunks of rock covering the mine floor, complicated moving further in either direction without giving away her position. And then there was the void ahead. It was similar to the one she recalled from the dream that she surmised her subconscious had reconstructed from the several times she had visited the Big Bear mine back in school, looking for Garret or Nick. She recalled these openings being areas where the ore was extracted, something like that. Michelle thought these unguarded areas were unsafe back then, when the mine was lighted. Now, without any light whatsoever, they were downright treacherous.

"If you ever wanted to redeem yourself, now would be the time," Michelle mumbled to Garret's spirit. Talking to herself gave her something to do while she waited to break up the insufferable silence. Hayden was out there, somewhere. Michelle so wanted to hear his voice, just to know where he was. Ideally, she would hear him call from somewhere deeper in the mine; if she heard that she would risk life and limb to bolt for the light of day, and race down the mountain to safety.

Was that a flicker? Michelle's heart skipped a beat. She held her breath, willing herself to peer out from the recess. The direction from which she'd come was lighter now, her eyes having adjusted to the darkness. She could just make out the faint outlines of the rock wall she was hugging, the infinity pool intersection of the mine floor and cliff-face headwall into the void to her left. She cocked her head, hoping this would improve her hearing. Still there was no sound.

There it was again! A faint flicker, far ahead down the corridor near her would-be route of escape. Joe Hayden had indeed followed her into the mine. He wasn't below her like she hoped, but at least she had a fix on his location. Michelle reevaluated her position, and decided to hold tight. The recess still afforded the best means of protection until Special Agent Sanderson and his many resources swarmed into the mine.

She saw the flicker again, this followed by a diffuse beam of light that became sharper and brighter with each rhythmic drip of water overhead. Then came the sound of shuffling feet, and after that the haunting form of Hayden's silhouette dancing in the gamboling light.

Michelle ducked back into the recess, ahead of Hayden's searching beam. She froze, all except for her heart, which sent surge after surge of coursing blood that roared in her ears. The flashlight beam snaked ever forward, sniffing out its target, the footfalls louder with every step. Joe Hayden would be on her at any moment.

Michelle reacted without thinking. She could have waited for Hayden to pass and then doubled back to the mine entrance like she initially planned to do, but no; instead, she rallied what was left of her fear addled psyche and charged from her hiding place with a banshee scream. The bull rush tactic caught Hayden completely off guard, forcing a reciprocating scream of surprise. His feet skidded on the gravel, and, for one precarious moment, he nearly toppled over the headwall.

Almost...

Michelle gave away over one hundred pounds to Hayden, and lost her advantage the moment his feet regained traction. Hayden growled, grabbed Michelle by the shoulders, and threw her against the mine wall. Her head struck the granite with a smack that filled her eyes with pinpoints of light. Dazed, Michelle staggered, trying to get away; but Hayden grabbed ahold of her again before she could take a few steps. He leaned into her, pinning her to the wall. Hayden may have been stronger physically, but Michelle's will was more than a match for his brawn. She struggled against his might, holding him off as best she could until she regained her faculties. Upon doing so, Michelle used the close quarters to her advantage, preventing Hayden from using his superior strength to its full extent. Between labored grunts and shallow screams, Michelle inched her way along the raking granite, little by little bettering her situation, buying time. The harder she struggled, the more determined Hayden was to use his bulk to his advantage.

"You couldn't leave well enough alone!" he snarled. "You had to come back!"

But it was a labored snarl. For all his strength, Hayden quickly tired, his growls turning to wheezing huffs. This invigorated Michelle, who stepped up her struggling. It was hard work that sapped her strength as well. Not helping were the shards of quartz protruding from the rock face that tore into her flesh, sending tendrils of blood down her back.

Hayden's threats soon gave way to deep gasps for air. Sensing the tide had turned, Michelle took advantage of her better conditioning to apply leverage against the rock wall and push Hayden away. She added short punches, angering Hayden, whose attempt to pin her to the wall only pushed his quarry that much farther from his grasp.

Michelle had all but escaped when she kicked into a stub of rock protruding from the mine floor. She fell and had just risen to a crouch when Hayden crashed down on top of her, draping his ape-like arms around her middle, and squeezing tight. The pressure forced out a cough, but Michelle was able to draw in a second breath before Hayden could reposition his grip, and this time she was ready for his next squeeze and held her lungs tight. When Hayden tried wrestling her away from the protective barrier of the wall, Michelle matched his advances by setting her hands and feet as wide as possible in a four-point, defensive stance.

"We should have killed you months ago!" Hayden growled, and with a jerk nearly flipped Michelle over.

Not to be outmaneuvered, Michelle remembered girlfriend Tracy's brother's wrestling matches that they had attended back in Darrtown. She avoided being rendered defenseless by grabbing ahold of the back of Hayden's thighs and turtling. The idea was to draw herself tight into a defensive shell while keeping Hayden as close as possible, and let him waste his strength trying to turn her over. It worked. Hayden soon lost endurance, and his grip loosened enough for Michelle to draw in a few deep, rejuvenating breaths. Refueled with oxygen, Michelle now had the strength to break free from her captor's grasp and rise to her feet in an awkward pirouette motion. She just as soon stubbed her toe against another mine-floor protrusion, only this time her footing held, allowing her to push back—*hard*.

It all happened so fast. With the ball of her left foot planted firmly on the nub of rock and her right foot flat against the mine wall, Michelle thrust herself forward, low and hard into Hayden's midsection. Her actions were overwhelming, causing the surprised Hayden to stagger backward and drop the flashlight he had somehow managed to hold onto. In spite of her pains to wrench herself free, she still couldn't shake Hayden's hold on her shirt collar. He windmilled his free arm wildly about, trying to regain his footing, but before either had the chance to scream out in alarm, Joe Hayden pulled Michelle along with him over the headwall and into the void.

It took every bit of effort to keep the desperately screaming

Hayden beneath her, as they fell. The flashlight, which was kicked over the side ahead of their fall, cast shafts of light in all directions like a disco ball. The last thing Michelle saw before it smashed to pieces was the mine floor hurtling up at her at blinding speed.

She crashed on top of Hayden, whose chest collapsed in a violent wheeze. Michelle's chin struck the side of Hayden's head, stunning her, stopping her world until her shoulder plowed into the rocky floor an instant later, this sending shock waves of pain through her body. She rolled off of Hayden, clutching at her shoulder, to the broken collarbone that tore through her shirt. She then reached for her chin, which felt numb and ragged, and finally to the neck that Garret broke that dreadful July day three decades before.

How far had they fallen? It wasn't very far, but far enough. Michelle struggled to her knees, only to fall back moaning. She wanted to crawl, but couldn't put any weight on her right arm, so she picked it up with her left, cradling it like a sling. That felt better. When she realized that her feet were still dangling off into space, she inched herself away from the edge as carefully as she dared in the darkness. What did that mean? With her legs back on firm ground, she reached out with her good arm, finding the edge of yet another headwall, and swore. It was then that she realized with heart-rending panic, that they were on a bench cut into the rock, which meant that she was trapped between levels with no way to climb to safety.

She heard a moan, and then movement. Adrenaline sprang Michelle to her feet, the effort spawning waves of disorienting pain that made it difficult to maintain her equilibrium. She was dizzied when a foot swung out into nothingness. Recovering, she kicked into Hayden, who groaned again, then moved some more. Michelle reached desperately to her back pocket for her phone. She fumbled with it with her good arm. She then fumbled some more with the slippery device until she found and turned on the flashlight app. What Michelle saw when she pointed the blinding light into Hayden's face was not a raging monster, but a desperate and literally broken man. She would have been justified to exact revenge on the man and organization that fueled Garret's delusions and affected so many lives over the years, but she didn't. In fact, Michelle found herself feeling nothing at all. Joe Hayden had taken care of all the retribution necessary by destroying his own life in his attempt to end hers.

Raising a hand to fend off the light, Hayden backed away, tottering, wobbling to avoid the blinding glare streaming from Michelle's impromptu weapon. He made an awkward stop, gasping for breath, the effort stimulating a wet rattle deep inside his staved-in chest. Michelle thought Hayden might recover when he swiped at the air. She then thought he was going to lunge at her when she realized that his hips were moving in the opposite direction. It was over, and she did feel something. Michelle looked with pity at the bully who no longer had the will or the capacity to hurt anyone.

Staring vacantly into her eyes, Joe Hayden garbled what sounded like a plea, slipped over the side, and was gone.

<hr />

Ashley House
Ashley Avenue, Charleston, S.C.
6:47 A.M.

The rupture started as the failure of a single mineral grain, miles beneath the Earth's surface. First one grain broke, then another, in a cascading response to the continental stresses placed on the poorly healed suture in the basement rock buried far below. The failure released a shock wave that reached the ground surface seconds later, causing catastrophic devastation.

Traveling upward at nearly five miles per second, the compression wave front reached the surficial deposits, where primary wave energy was converted to undulating surface waves that wreaked havoc on all things not structurally sound. Water saturated sediments lost all semblance of cohesion, forming a soupy mess of quicksand, mud boils, and blowouts that erupted like pustules. Where the groundwater found a pathway to the sky above, it was propelled into the air like so many geysers. Everywhere the land was conflicted into spasm. The ground surface rolled like waves on the ocean, throwing all things loose into the air and toppling buildings. Cries of mayhem and despair cut through the train-like roar.

Nick was jolted awake by the vividness of the dream. He patted at his body for confirmation that he wasn't covered in mud. The last thing he remembered before awakening was sinking, along with Chris, into the depths of a patch of liquefied earth that appeared without warning beneath their feet. *Just a dream*, he told himself. All the same, Nick raced to the window like he had yesterday morning after his last nightmare, just to be sure. Everything was still standing where it was supposed to be, and all was thankfully silent, save for the sound of the distant morning traffic…and Mrs. Mockingbird's incessant chattering.

Dream or not, Nick realized that the nightmare might not be over, because it could explain the one detail not related to the PSTRE case that had confounded the project's technical staff, the inexplicable variability observed in site water levels: *EARTH-QUAKE!*

What he was thinking wasn't crazy. He had looked up enough information about the regional geology in preparation for the PSTRE case to know that the United States Geological Survey considers Charleston to be a high hazard seismic area. The problem was that he had nothing more than speculation to support his theory. But there was something, something that the dream rekindled about an article he once read—something that had rattled evasively around in his head ever since he'd learned of the chaotic water levels at the PSTRE site…something about earthquakes and spasmodic water levels. If he could only remember… *"Ahh!"* Nick gasped loud enough to set Mrs. Mockingbird off onto another one of her jags. He worried that the notion gnawing away at him was just an overreaction to inconclusive information. But what if he was correct?

It was a quarter of seven. With sleep out of the question and Granby's morning call still a ways off, Nick decided to mull his thoughts over in the shower. That did the trick. Water therapy overturned the rock that the dream had loosened, and out from under popped the article he tried in vain to remember. Nick quickly dressed and raced to his computer. While the essence of the article supported what he was thinking, Nick was undecided about what to do. *Call Sam, that's what!* Nick found Sam Piersall to be level-headed, the perfect choice to use as a sounding board to test his theory. Sam's voice was distant, distracted. Nick gathered that he was in a car. "Sam? It's Nick, where are you?"

"Hey, Nick! What's up?" Sam replied, back to his collected self. "On my way to a job. Did I miss something? Am I supposed to be with you?"

"No, nothing like that. Sorry. Have time to talk?" They did, and Nick was relieved to find Sam receptive to his earthquake idea. Sam in fact said that he, Jay, and RCE's hydrogeologists had kicked around the very same idea the other day. It just so happened, Sam told him, that there had been a recent uptick in seismic activity in the area.

"You haven't spoken to Chris about this yet, have you?" Sam asked.

"Heavens no! I wanted to run it past you first. You know Chris, he'd just as likely laugh his ass off as run the idea up M&C's flag pole just to see what excitement he could create. I need some evidence before I go to him with a crazy idea like an earthquake did it."

"I hear you!" Sam agreed. "He's an excitable one. About those deep wells used for earthquake prediction that you mentioned," Sam said in response to Nick's summary of the article he was reading on his monitor, "I think I can help you with that."

"*Yeah?*"

"Pretty sure. That's something we've also kicked around. We haven't had the time to look into it. I'm heading up the coast now. We're performing pump tests on a new water-supply well field in Dorchester County. We've been monitoring background water levels there for the past week. Two of the wells are quite deep; one's about two thousand feet, and the other bottoms out at around twenty-two hundred. I don't think they're as deep as the ones they use over in Japan and China, but who knows? Should be deep enough to see something, I would think."

"That's great, Sam!" Nick said. He couldn't believe his good fortune. "Not that I want you to see anything, mind you, but if you do...." Nick let Sam complete the thought.

"Roger that," Sam agreed whole-heartedly. "That'd be quite the bomb to drop on the M&C boys. And if you're right, and we live to tell the tale, it'll make for a heluva good paper! Hey, look," Sam then said, bringing their conversation to a close, "my exit's coming up. Let me go and I'll check out the data when I get there, and call you back."

"Thanks Sam."

"Bye."

They hung up.

Nick went downstairs to put on a pot of coffee. He was in the kitchen when Granby made his morning call. Nick breathed a sigh of relief when Granby said there was nothing new to report, and that Michelle's Colorado hurrah would be kicking off later that morning. "We don't expect any problems." Granby went on to say that Special Agent Bonino was on his way to relieve the local law enforcement detail that staked out Ian Prescott's motel room overnight. Nick thanked Granby for the update and said that he planned on remaining at Ashley House for the morning, unless M&C summoned him elsewhere.

Coffee cup in hand, Nick trudged back upstairs where he planned to enjoy the morning air out on the porch before it got too hot. On cue, Mrs. Mockingbird greeted him with a raucous squabble the moment he open the slider door. "Good morning to you, too," Nick volleyed in return, and settled into his favorite chair. He called and left a message with Chris, explaining his plans. With any luck, Chris would call back to report that they would remain in a holding pattern until M&C figured out what to do next about PSTRE.

Nick propped his feet on an end table and reached for his laptop. He tapped a few keystrokes and discovered that there was a considerable body of literature pertaining to earthquake impacts on groundwater, far more than he thought there would be. The subject had attracted a growing audience since the first and last time he gave the matter any thought years before. The use of wells for the purpose of monitoring changes in groundwater level and quality in the hopes of predicting earthquakes remained largely confined to Japan and China. "It's their bag. Earthquake prediction is more of an art than a science," Nick recalled Sam saying. Reading on, Nick learned that this predictive tool hadn't passed sufficient scientific scrutiny to be embraced by counterparts in the West. Cultural differences aside, Nick surmised that with fully one-quarter of the world's entire population living along the seismically spastic western Pacific coast Ring of Fire, the Chinese and Japanese, with so much more to lose, would be open to anything that might help predict a quake. The take away was this: that a radical change in water level in deep wells was considered an earthquake precursor. Water levels, the literature reported, often exhibit a gradual decline in the months to years before an earthquake. This is followed by an accelerated drop in level in the final weeks to months preceding the event, only to be followed by a rapid rebound in the days or hours before structural failure occurs and the Earth starts to shake. Nick couldn't recall if PSTRE's water levels followed all, or even most of these metrics, but the literature description and his real-time observation of the limited data available were similar enough to at least consider the aberrant water levels in PSTRE's wells as a precursor.

He didn't hear back from Chris until just before nine. Nick got his wish, and then some, when Chris said that PSTRE was put on hold indefinitely. This not only included the environmental work, but PSTRE's plans for expansion. This was serious, and naturally put Chris in good spirits. "Looks like we're going to have a little down time for some R&R, good buddy!" he cheered. Chris then thanked Nick for making him M&C's hero for bringing Nick to the team. "You're their new golden boy!"

"I don't know about that," Nick said modestly.

"No, seriously. You don't understand. You just turned everything—and I mean everything—on its head. The big guns, including Smitty, have been holed up behind closed doors with Athens's counsel pretty much since we left yesterday afternoon. Old man Merrill went ballistic. They had to take him to the hospital. And get this! Both company boards were called in. Hal Cole's ass is flapping in the wind right now. From what Brant was able to tell me—and you didn't hear it from me—PSTRE wants Cole charged with conspiracy and industrial espionage, like you mentioned. And that doesn't include what the City wants to do with him. Nobody knows how the City found out so fast. You didn't say anything, did you?"

"Like I would do that," was Nick's emphatic response to the turmoil he apparently created, just by doing his job.

"Good!" Chris replied. "They're circling the wagons now—all of them—trying to distance themselves from Cole and sort things out with the City. You don't want any parts of that."

"No kidding!"

"Don't worry about a thing," Chris said with certainty. "You're about as bulletproof as they come right now. By the way, why did you hang back at the house this morning?"

Nick's response was evasive. "There's something I needed to check out before coming in. It's probably nothing. We can meet later over a beer for a good laugh."

Nick was glad Chris didn't press for more details. Not yet. With indefinite time to kill, Nick slipped into something more comfortable and returned to the upstairs porch, this time with a glass filled with his new favorite non-alcoholic beverage of the Southern variety, sweetened ice tea.

The heat had ratcheted upwards of ninety—and the humidity! Any higher and even the bugs would start to sweat. Nick turned on the overhead fans, which pulled some of the dry, air-conditioned air from inside. Slouched in the same comfortable chair, and with the air tempered, Nick watched contentedly as a string of cars motored up the street. Not yet ready to put the compliments aside, he ran through all that had transpired over the action-packed past couple of days and had to admit that Chris was right: he was M&C's new golden boy. He had to be. He had changed the course of a legal proceeding and halted a company's business plan. Nick gave himself a congratulatory pat on the back.

Nick bookmarked one last article about the effects of earthquakes on groundwater geochemistry to discuss with Sam and decided that he had had enough of reading dry technical articles. He resolved to move on to something more interesting, like earthquakes in general and the gory details about the aftermath of some of the bigger quakes.

The United States Geological Survey, he read, estimates that approximately 500,000 detectable earthquakes occur each year around the globe. Of these, nearly 80 percent occur along the Ring of Fire, aka the Circum-Pacific Seismic Belt, the tectonically active ribbon of the Earth's crust that snakes its way around the globe like the seam on a baseball, from New Zealand to the south, then north to New Guinea and east past the Philippines before swinging north again along the coasts of China and Japan, then crossing the Pacific Ocean at the Aleutian Islands. From there, the Ring of Fire extends in a long southerly arc from Southern Alaska, Western Canada, the U.S. West Coast, and Central America before terminating off the coast of southern Chile. Nick whistled. Sure, he was a geologist, and yes he had seen the feature depicted countless times in print before, but he never once considered until now just how extensive the Ring of Fire truly is.

Not surprisingly, he read that the overwhelming majority of earthquakes register 3 or less on the seismologist's current measuring stick, the moment-magnitude scale. Such *minor* quakes, as they were called on the formerly used Richter scale, are rarely felt;

and, thankfully, fewer than one percent are of the *light* to *strong* variety, between 4 and 7, that can cause heavy damage. As for the rest, only 20 or so each year are of the *major* to *great* types that Nick had to admit got him as excited as a meteorologist in a Category 5 hurricane, because these are the quakes that cause serious damage: the Earth-altering outliers that destroy communities. Nick took particular interest in the fact that since 2004, great quakes have occurred more frequently than the historical average, at a rate of 1.2 to 1.4 events per year. And the largest quake ever recorded, a 9.5 temblor off the coast of Chile in 1960, spawned a tsunami 100 feet high along the Chilean coast that reached Hawaii fifteen hours later, striking portions of the Hilo mainland with wave heights reaching 35 feet. He whistled again upon reading that the Chilean quake was so strong that it shifted Earth's rotational axis, speeding up the planet's rotation and slightly shortening the length of each day.

Fascinating but not relevant to his pressing local concern, Nick focused his search closer to home. "Now that sounds interesting," he said in defiance to Mrs. Mockingbird's incessant harangue from her magnolia-tree roost, when he discovered an article describing the far-reaching effects of the largest U.S. earthquakes. The text began with the *big one*, the great Alaska earthquake of March 27, 1964, and the second largest temblor ever recorded. With an estimated magnitude of 9.2, the *Good Friday Quake,* as it is called, destroyed much of Anchorage and produced a tsunami that reached an astounding 219 feet in height at Shoup Bay, near Valdez inlet in Prince William Sound. The jolt shook Seattle's Space Needle, and shock waves continued to travel around the world for weeks. And to Nick's utter amazement, he read that the quake was so strong that it produced seiche waves causing swimming pools and small water bodies to slosh about as far away as Louisiana...and *cause fluctuations in water wells as far away as South Africa.*

"This could explain everything!" Nick said with such eagerness he frightened Mrs. Mockingbird into silence. The wonky water levels could be nothing more than a response to an earthquake that occurred half way around the world. He wasn't aware of any large recent quakes, and it might be a long shot, but it was worth checking into. He would do that, but first he wanted to find out more about the hometown earthquake that the locals seemed so proud to remember.

Nick was surprised to find that the cause for the 1886 Charleston earthquake remained something of a mystery. He recalled his geophysics professor at Huron saying that a contending theory at that time was that the quake was the result of slippage along one of the transform faults that jut like trellis-work from the Mid-Atlantic Ridge in the Atlantic Ocean. At issue is Charleston's location, so far removed from a crustal plate boundary. The Mid-Atlantic Ridge, where the North American Plate is continuously generated from magma upwelling, lays some 2,400 miles to the east of Charleston. Simply put, intraplate quakes don't happen that often, and when they do, they often defy simple explanation. Not up for discussion is the fact that intraplate earthquakes like those that occur in the eastern United States can be catastrophic, and this is a function of the geology.

Compared to the West Coast, where the North American Plate and Pacific Plate meet at the infamous San Andreas fault zone, and where crustal stress is released daily in the form of mostly minor tremors, earthquakes occur much less frequently in the East. This is because the bedrock, being so far removed from a plate boundary and less affected by tectonic movement, is less fractured and correspondingly more stable. Not subject to regular releases of energy, the stress continues to build in eastern rocks until the Earth eventually ruptures, sometimes with an unfathomable shudder. And when this happens, the shock waves, being less encumbered by energy-dampening fractures, travel that much farther than those that occur in the West. With an estimated magnitude of 6.9 to 7.3, the Charleston quake is the fifth largest recorded seismic event to strike the Eastern U.S., after the four major to great events that occurred near the small town of New Madrid, Missouri between

December 16, 1811 and February 7, 1812. It was the awe-inspiring power of the February 1812 tremor, which had an estimated magnitude of between 7.4 and 8.0, that caused waterfalls to form on the Mississippi River, and for the river to briefly run backward. Across the border in Tennessee, a portion of the land sank, creating the 15,000-acre Reelfoot Lake.

Nick tapped his finger on the screen when he read that the current theory is that Charleston and New Madrid overlay two poorly-healed active sutures deep within the crust, remnant sores from when the North American plate twice failed to split apart during the breakup of the supercontinents Pangea and Rodinia, hundreds of millions of years in Earth's past. More to the point, the literature stated that geologists have identified several faults near Charleston believed to be responsible for the local seismic activity that spawned the 1886 quake, and that these features, including a recently discovered fault buried beneath Virginia and the Carolinas, are related to the Pangean rift.

Nick read with increasing interest when he reached the part that mattered most—the devastating effects of the 1886 quake. It struck at ten minutes to ten at night, on Tuesday, August 31, 1886. With an epicenter located seventeen miles to the north near the community of Summerville, the Earth shook with ferocious intensity for about a minute over an elliptical area measuring 20 to 30 miles from north to south around Charleston. Saturated soil liquefied across vast areas. Mud boils erupted from the ground, forming tiny volcanoes that spilled water in all directions; mud geysers spewed ropes of earthy porridge; and where the land split, water shot into the air two stories high. When the quake ended, the railroad infrastructure lay in ruins and virtually all of Charleston's buildings were either heavily damaged or destroyed. Major damage was reported up to sixty miles away, and structural damage was reported as far away as Alabama and West Virginia. The shock wave was felt across 2.5 million square miles, from Boston and Chicago even to Bermuda and Cuba. Opportunists in a time of crisis took advantage of the mayhem when 43 of 64 prisoners escaped from the city jail. The one saving grace was that Charleston was still in its formative years: the official record identifies only 60 unfortunate souls who lost their lives.

Nick was humbled by the enormity of the event. How history had failed to give Charleston its due, compared to the likes of New Madrid and the much-celebrated 1906 San Francisco quake, was beyond his comprehension. Looking out over the idyllic bliss of the sleepy summer morning, it was even more inconceivable that such a catastrophe might happen again, and yet here he was contemplating the very thing.

⁂

Nick was oblivious to the approaching sedan until it came to a screeching halt in front of Ashley House. Leaping to his feet, his computer crashing into the railing, Nick watched with trepidation as Agent Bonino emerged from the car in tactical mode, his eyes scanning Ashley House and the nearby yards and the intersection ahead for signs of trouble. "What happened? Is he coming?" Nick hollered down from the upstairs porch.

Seeing only Nick, Bonino holstered his service piece. "Are you alone?" he asked.

Nick nodded.

"Get your phone and identification. We have to leave, *now*."

Nick didn't ask questions. The seriousness of the agent's actions, and his intonation were all he needed to know that he'd better get his ass in gear. It had to have something to do with Ian Prescott, but what? Nick went to retrieve his laptop, stopping when he came to his senses. *"What are you doing?"* He scolded himself, and instead grabbed his cell phone and raced inside to retrieve his wallet and shoes.

Bonino was waiting for him outside. He put a hand up, motioning for Nick to stop. "Wait," Bonino instructed. A man was walking his dog down the sidewalk. Bonino waited for the man to pass before saying, "Follow me." The agent kept his hand out to feel that Nick was following him while constantly surveying their surroundings all the way to the waiting sedan, where he prompted Nick to take the back seat.

Sitting in the back of what amounted to a squad car made Nick nervous, even if he was the Bureau's client and guest of honor. "Where are we going?" Nick asked.

"The airport," Bonino said, and reached for his radio. "This is Bonino. I have Mr. Kozlowski. We are clear to go."

"Roger that."

"Bravo team is on the move," Bonino replied, and pulled away from the curb.

A police escort joined them at Bull Street.

"What's going on?" Nick demanded. What he saw in Bonino's reflection in the rear view mirror was not encouraging.

"There's been a situation in Colorado, on the former school grounds."

"*Michelle!*" Nick sputtered. "Is she all right? What about Melanie?" His worst fear might be coming true.

"I can't tell you. We're still working out the details. What I can say is that we have an agent down. I was not informed about your wife, or her friend."

Nick was devastated, He was also frustrated and angry; too much was happening all at once. He didn't know what to say that would not come across as insensitive, offering only that he was sorry.

Bonino nodded. He turned on his turn signal and followed the lead cars onto the interstate. Bonino returned the favor and apologized for the situation, promising Nick that he would be informed as to what happened when the facts became clear. He also requested that Nick not attempt to contact Michelle or Melanie, so as not to add to the distraction.

Nick appreciated Bonino's honesty. Still, it took everything he had not to demand answers he knew the agent could not—or would not—give. To his credit, Bonino did offer some words of encouragement that lifted Nick's spirits. Special Agent Sanderson, whom he knew Michelle held in highest regards, was responding at the scene to coordinate a rescue effort, along with all available local and federal law enforcement. "Thanks," Nick said. He noticed that the squad cars had turned off their sirens. "What happens when I get there?" he asked.

"You're not going to Colorado," Bonino informed him. This is *your* protection detail," Bonino reminded him.

What was he missing? Something more was going on. "That guy—Prescott—he's coming after me. I thought you and Agent Granby were watching him."

Bonino kept one eye on the road as he spoke into the rearview mirror. What he said was sobering. "He's not coming after you yet. But we expect Prescott to be mobilized at any time. Special Agent Granby is on his way to take Prescott into custody before this happens. What we don't know is whether others are involved. You're being moved to a safe location until we are certain that the threat has been neutralized."

That made sense. "Where are you taking me?" Nick asked.

"Little Rock. There, you will be met by an agent from the local office, who will take you to a hotel where you will be assigned a protection detail until, like I told you, we determine that the threat has passed. You can go on to Colorado from there. Agents there will keep you informed." Bonino took a business card from his suit jacket and handed it over his shoulder. "You can also contact me if you have questions or concerns."

They spoke little else on the way to the airport, located in North Charleston. Nick tried to be optimistic, that Michelle and Melanie were fine, and that Prescott was working alone. Nevertheless, all he could think of while watching the planes come and go on their approach was that he couldn't get to the airport fast enough.

Nick was whisked through airport security and taken to the security office where he was introduced to the head of concierge, a tall, ebony-skinned woman named Marguerite. Bonino explained

Nick's special case situation, and, together, Bonino, Marguerite, and a contingent of TSA personnel escorted Nick to the boarding gate for the Little Rock flight. Bonino explained to Nick that he would be on his own but not entirely alone until the plane touched down, that there would be an air marshal on board keeping a look-out for trouble. Nick thanked Bonino and the others for their support. He was particularly appreciative of Marguerite, who followed him down the jetway to make sure that he made it safely on board. Marguerite said something to the captain, told Nick "Good luck!" and returned to the terminal.

Nick was watching her go when a hand clasped his shoulder. It was the captain.

"Sir, if you please," the captain said, motioning to a smiling flight attendant. "Shannon, here, will show you to your seat. If there is anything that we can do for you, please don't hesitate to ask."

They didn't travel very far.

"I think you will find this seat to your liking," Shannon said, halting their procession in business class.

"Wow! The red carpet treatment."

"Make yourself comfortable wherever you like," Shannon said, gesturing to three open seats. She said she would be back shortly with a complimentary drink.

Nick settled into the rear right side seat. Across the aisle napped a suit-clad man whom Shannon said would be his lone first class companion. This was nice, real nice. It was the least the feds could do for botching Michelle's protection detail. He so wanted to call her, to hear her voice, hear that she was safe; but he understood why Special Agent Bonino said he needed to heed his advice. Nick would have to settle for hoping to hear, when he landed in Arkansas, that the crisis was over…*Now, where is that drink?*

First class was everything that Nick remembered it was from the last and only other time he had the privilege, back in his Oregon days working on the MinTech project with Chris. True to her word, Shannon returned to pour him a cup of wine while the final passengers were filing into coach. Nick tossed the drink back, asked for another and threw that one back too, and was instantly buzzed. He must have been wearing his anxiety on his sleeve because, before he could settle into his seat and close his eyes, Shannon reappeared with a pillow in her hand. "You're reading my mind," Nick said, accepting her assistance with placing the pillow behind his head. She had scarcely returned to the galley when he started to drift off to sleep.

The sudden lurch of the plane being pushed away from the gate jostled Nick from his wine-induced stupor. Just as well. He didn't want to miss the palm trees and all of the memories he and Michelle shared before her departure, before Athens's ambush, and certainly before the G-Men's not totally unexpected appearance that twisted what had been a Grisham-novel experience into a Quentin Tarentino film. He fought back the urge to doze again when the plane jerked to a halt short of the runway. The captain announced that the skies were crowded overhead, and that it would be a few more minutes before takeoff. Nick took advantage of the partially open curtain to peer back into coach. He wondered which of the nameless faces in the crowd was the air marshal.

They started to move, slowly at first, and then with increasing speed. Nick adjusted the pillow to make certain he had the best view of the ground below. Takeoff was his favorite part of the flight, where the exhilaration of feeling the engine's power rocket the plane off into the wild blue yonder meets anxiety's dread that the plane might not successfully reach air space. He was watching the backdrop speeding away off in the distance when something weird happened. The plane seemed to have lifted then lowered again without actually leaving the ground. Really strange was when the plane was lifted to its highest point; Nick swore that, for an instant, he was looking out over the distant tree line. Whatever it was had happened so fast that he would have dismissed it as an effect from the wine, were it not for the feeling that his stomach had been lifted into his chest. Then it happened again, seconds later, the same rise and zero gravity fall feeling. It wasn't just him. Others noticed it, too; murmurings drifted his way from coach. There were also the disconcerted faces of the flight-attendant staff seated in front of him. The captain must have sensed something was wrong as well because he punched down on the throttle.

"What was that?" stammered the suit-clad man who had been dozing in the seat across from him.

"I don't know," Nick said with mounting concern.

All hell broke loose after that when the perturbation happened a third time, this time causing the plane to yaw sideways. *Not Good.* Nick gauged the situation was dire when distress replaced the flight attendants' disconcerted looks and the captain struggled to course correct the plane. Behind him, the murmurings escalated to screams of panic.

"We're going to crash!" yelled the suit-clad man.

"We'll be fine!" Nick said as calmly and firmly as possible.

Nick still wasn't sure what happened when the plane was then rocked a fourth time at the precise moment it shot suddenly into the air. He jerked his head forward and saw to his relief the captain pulling back hard on the yoke. Take off. They were airborne! The clamor behind him, however, became more intense. There was so much yelling and screaming, competing with flight attendant Shannon's urging for the passengers to remain calm, that Nick couldn't make out what any of them were saying, until one woman's frenzied scream rose above the rest: *"WE'RE UNDER ATTACK!"*

The woman's words sent shock waves through the plane. The suit-clad man, now fully awake, cowered in his seat, trembling with fright. Nick might as well have been staring at a reflection of himself. All things considered, the hysterical woman just might be right. Nick could only wonder what Michelle had stumbled onto in Colorado to prompt the Conservancy to sacrifice the lives of an airplane filled with innocent passengers, all to eliminate one single loose end—*him.*

The plane started to bank. Nick stole a glance into coach. Aside from general chaos, nothing seemed out of order. There was no weapon-wielding assailant rushing in his direction. He breathed a sigh of relief when he then saw, at the rear of the plane, a man whom he guessed was the air marshal trying to restore order. He was turning back around when he realized that the ruckus had gone from a concern about what might be happening inside the plane to something happening on the ground below. Being on the opposite side of the plane, with only clouds and sky to see, he had to wait for the plane to level out.

Nick was horrified by what he saw. It wasn't the Conservancy. It was something much, much worse. In the twenty seconds it took from the first rolling wave until now, the City of Charleston, for as far as he could see, was being reduced to ruins. He saw one building collapse after another. Heightened screams from coach and the word *"AIRPORT!"* then made him look feverishly for the airport…that was reduced to rubble. All Nick could make out was an airplane on a cracked runway feeder lane that had burst into flames, and several others that were strewn about like toys. Fires had erupted everywhere from burst utilities. Adding insult to the destruction unfolding below was the guilt Nick was feeling for not having called Chris about the now not so absurd thought he had about the water-level data.

The captain flashed on the interior lighting. He instructed the passengers to remain calm and said that they were not under attack. Charleston, he regretted to say, was experiencing an earthquake… and that they were the last flight to leave the old port city.

Granby was on foot in pursuit of Ian Prescott when the earthquake struck. Incensed at hearing the attack that felled Special Agent Wells and the uncertain status of Michelle and her friend, Granby did the only thing he could do to stem the tide and implemented the contingency plan. There would be no more bloodshed on his watch, if he had something to say about it. The only change Granby made to the plan was to reassign Steve Bonino to escort Nick to the airport. As for Ian Prescott, Granby would handle him personally.

Prescott was holed up in plain sight, in a Historic District motel several blocks from the accommodations Granby shared with Bonino, and on the way to Ashley House. This made monitoring Prescott's whereabouts convenient and the transfer of duties simple. Bonino had reported no movement by Prescott, and reports from local law enforcement were also favorable: no untoward activity had been observed in the vicinity of Ashley House. Granby afforded himself the luxury of a smile amidst bleak times. It helped that Prescott had nowhere to run. Granby would be knocking on—or kicking down—the Tarryall minion's door in a matter of minutes. In the event Prescott did manage to slip away, police cruisers were stationed at every major intersection, and additional cruisers were parked at the I-17 interchange. Despite these safeguards, Granby took nothing for granted. Tarryall had already outsmarted them once today.

Granby was getting out of his car when he saw Prescott heading down the exterior staircase of the motel complex. Granby cursed for not relieving Bonino sooner. He had hoped to corner Prescott in his room. Prescott at least gave no appearance of being in a hurry. Granby radioed local law enforcement that the suspect was on the move.

Criminals may be of sub-average intelligence, but this didn't mean they were without skills. Prescott made Granby (how, the agent had no idea) and ran for his car. Granby cursed again and doubled back to his own vehicle with the intention of blocking Prescott into his spot. Prescott, however, was that much faster and was pulling out of the lot by the time the bulky FBI agent could turn the key.

Heavy traffic on Meeting Street impeded Prescott's exit long enough for Granby to make up some ground. With one hand out the window affixing a police light to the roof and with a foot on the gas, Granby darted into a gap in the traffic and was in hot pursuit. He had to commend Prescott on his driving skills, for it was all Granby could do to keep the fugitive in sight. Granby put the nearest intercept cars on notice that Prescott was coming their way.

Granby caught a second break when Prescott failed to negotiate a jaywalking pedestrian at Charlotte Street. Prescott did manage to avoid the pedestrian, but he was moving too fast and clipped the front end of an absent-minded motorist pulling away from the far curb. The impact careened Prescott's car into the center of the street, where it struck vehicles going in both directions, bringing all traffic to a stop. Granby swiftly exited his car to warn alarmed motorists and pedestrians alike to stay in their vehicles, or head for cover. Ahead he saw movement inside Prescott's battered vehicle. Granby watched as a bloodied Prescott fell out of the passenger-side window, picked himself up on wobbly legs, and started running away.

"PRESCOTT, STOP!"

Granby waved furiously at the growing number of idiot onlookers with phones held high. *"PRESCOTT!"* Granby yelled again when the man did not respond. Not that it mattered. Granby could plainly see that the injured Prescott was posing less of a risk to public safety with each step. Dazed from the crash and streaming blood, Prescott had slowed to a stagger, and he gave no impression that he was armed.

Keeping an eye on Prescott, Granby stopped when he reached the cluster of cars caught up in the impact. He saw several individuals still inside their vehicles, in the throes of recovering their senses. "Don't move, help is on the way," he told them. Moving on, Granby paused again when he saw Prescott standing near the far side of the street, staring down at his feet. Oddly, not far away a pedestrian was also looking down with the same bewildered expression. Granby noticed it, too, when strange vibrations suddenly surged upward through the soles of his shoes, his feet, legs, and finally his torso, making his burgeoning middle-age bulge quiver. All around him, road grit danced on the pavement.

Mayhem. First came a low moan that escalated to a deafening roar, and then the ground began to buck. Windows shattered, sending shards of glass onto the street. *"GET AWAY FROM THE BUILDINGS!"* Granby bellowed over the roar of the quake, waving his bearlike paws to the swelling mass of pedestrians that poured out onto the street from the offices and storefronts. Granby lost track of Prescott in the chaos. He found him again stumbling up the middle of Meeting Street. The one saving grace of the influx of human traffic on the street was that a weakened Prescott couldn't fight his way right or left through the crowd in his slowing effort to get away.

Granby pushed his way past a cluster of fear-riddled captains of industry, knocked to the ground and rendered helpless when the first surface wave rolled beneath their feet. The sensation was so bizarre, so unexpected and disorienting, that Granby also fell, but unlike many, he crawled, undeterred, back to his feet. Granby had managed several strides in Prescott's direction when the second surface wave came, pitching him forward; it was all he could do to keep his footing. Prescott was not so fortunate and fell again, this time remaining down, giving Granby the time needed to close the distance. And he would have done this were it not for the horrific sight of the entire left side of Meeting Street—buildings and all—being lifted into the air and then settling back down when the third surface wave rolled through.

And then Charleston started to crumble.

Pieces of brick, stone façade, concrete, even iron railings rained down on the street below, sending the already terrified people into a heightened state of panic. Some raced haphazardly about, causing even more confusion; elsewhere, others huddled in terrified groups for protection. The situation had deteriorated so rapidly that Ian Prescott was no longer Granby's primary concern: saving lives was his calling now. Shouting and signaling, Granby urged the masses to remain calm and make for the center of the street where they were less likely to be struck by building debris. Nearest him, his efforts worked. An older gentleman and his wife grabbed ahold of one of Granby's arms and hung on for dear life. Granby urged them to stand behind him as he urged others to join them. His radius of influence, of course, could only extend so far.

"GET AWAY FROM THERE!" Granby shouted over the mayhem to a disoriented Prescott, who had stumbled into the sun shadow of a crumbling building. Too late. Prescott was gone an instant later when he was driven into the macadam by a section of the building that had fallen from the sky.

Meeting Street failed with the fourth great swell. The fourth roller came with such force that it knocked Granby flat when the ground simply fell away. Buildings were crumbling in earnest now, and fires, both large and small, sprang up in odd places from all the burst gas lines and fallen electric cables. Granby scuttled crablike away from the fissure that parted the macadam, as jets of water and mud shot into the air. The fissure grew in height as well. The land to Granby's right rose with the surface wave while the portion he was on stayed relatively flat until the macadam could no longer take the stress and ruptured completely, forming an escarpment several feet high. The sudden emergence of the macadam fault-line cliff face did come with the advantage that it provided cover from falling debris, and from being trampled. Granby took advantage of this to pull himself into the lee of the low cliff face. Huddled with his face to the escarpment, Granby reached for his phone. *"Ahh!"* he bellowed with anger at his own stupidity. No service. Of course there wasn't, the city infrastructure was in shambles. "James, hang in there," he said, willing his flagging morale when the hanging wall of the escarpment started to rise higher, ever higher, in response to the stress.

A plaintive cry pierced the cacophony of screams, the tortured wrenching sounds of failing concrete, brick, and steel, and the roar of the Earth tearing itself apart. It was a sound of desperation, of someone calling out for help. Granby dared to poke his head above the precarious shelter. On the near side of the street and just out of reach of the fall line of building debris, stood a young mother and her daughter clinging to one another for dear life. Granby could see that the mother was frightened to the point of incapacitation. He had to save them.

Granby looked skyward to the cracks snaking up the street-facing side of the building behind the mother and child. Near the top, the decorative façade was starting to pull away. Granby burst from cover. He used his football lineman's skills to clear a hole, brushing aside several frightened pedestrians who ignored the mother's plight and, without saying a word, scooped mother and daughter in his long arms and toted them back to the safety of the macadam shelter.

The last thing that James Granby would remember of the Great Charleston Quake of 2018, before day turned into night and all went silent, was the building crashing down upon them.

CHAPTER 10

FRIDAY

Denver, Colorado FBI Office
East 36ᵗʰ Avenue, Denver, Colo.
10:26 A.M.

An administrative assistant knocked at the office door, poked her head inside. "Special Agent Sanderson? Your guests are here. Should I escort them in?"

"Please. Thank you, Susan," Sanderson said, looking up from the chaos in front of him. "Catherine and I are at a good breaking point, I think." He waited for Susan to leave to collect the email printouts and other documents he and Cat had been hashing over, documenting the Timberline syndicate's swift movements since the Bureau's dismantling of its Tarryall Mountain Foundation cell.

Cat got up to leave as well.

Sanderson requested she stay.

"Are you sure? I have plenty to do."

"Don't even think about it," Sanderson replied with a glimmer of the enthusiasm he'd temporarily lost since Wednesday's Sacred Lands disaster. "I'm rather certain Michelle and Melanie will be delighted to see you again."

"I hope so!"

"And I guess you're as excited as I am to finally meet Michelle's husband. And speak of the devil," Sanderson said, rising to his feet at the sight of movement out in the hall.

Cat adjusted several chairs around the circular conference table that she and the FBI agent were using, while Sanderson went to the door.

"The two of you are a sight for sore eyes!" he said to Michelle and Melanie. "You're looking good. Please, come in."

"Thank you, Ron," Michelle said, stepping inside. "I'm not sure that I look as good as you say, but I'll take that as a compliment." She motioned to her slinged arm. "The doctor says I'll need surgery once the swelling in my shoulder subsides. And I still hurt all over, especially my ribs, but the meds help. I hope they're not making me seem too spacey."

"Not at all. And how about you, Ms. Sutton? You're looking splendid."

The kind words brought a rosy blush to Melanie's cheeks. "Thank you," she said, following Michelle into the room. "It sure is good to see you again—both of you!" Melanie added, excited at seeing Cat waiting patiently near the window. She asked about Janelle.

"Janelle's good. Thanks for asking. I'll pass the word along that you both said hi." Cat broke proper form and skipped across the room to give Michelle and Melanie a hug. "Make yourselves comfortable," she said, gesturing to the small table.

"A chair would be nice. Thank you, Cat," Michelle said. She took the nearest seat, wincing as she did so. Melanie took the chair to her left. "It's all over, right?" Michelle asked.

"Generally speaking, yes. You should have nothing more to worry about."

"I hear a *but*…"

"There are a few details that still need to be resolved, which I will explain," Sanderson interrupted. "But no, we don't think Tarryall, or the larger organization, will be giving either of you any more trouble. This said, I advise that each of you remain in our care a little longer, until we're certain the danger has passed." He turned his attention to his one remaining guest. "You must be Nick," he said to the travel-weary stranger standing just inside the doorway. "I'm Special Agent Ron Sanderson. Please, call me Ron. I've heard so much about you," the agent said, sweeping his hand toward the conference table. "I've also heard nothing but glowing remarks about you from my colleague back east. It's a pleasure to finally meet you."

"Same here," Nick replied, and gave Sanderson's hand a vigorous shake.

"We're glad that you made it out of Charleston unscathed," Sanderson said while Nick took a seat beside Michelle. "A terrible thing, just terrible." Sanderson's expression darkened. I understand the USGS upgraded the earthquake to a 7.4."

"I missed that."

"That's understandable, you've had a lot on your plate. How about the aftershock this morning? It was a 6.1."

"I did hear about that." Nick had yet to hear from Chris. News of this morning's quake only heightened his anxiety about his friend.

"As you might expect, the infrastructure around Charleston is in ruins, including Interstate 95, which cut off the main artery to Georgia and Florida. I understand it's at a standstill down there." Allowing the tight lines of concern on his face to yield to a whimsical smile, he then asked, "Tell me, where was it that you ended up Wednesday night, Omaha?"

"Yeah!" Nick exclaimed. "It was a mess. The air traffic was so backed up we kept being bumped from city to city. We circled around up there for hours. It wasn't until after six that we finally landed. Then it took all day yesterday just to get to Denver. I could have taken an Uber and gotten here faster, without all the stress." Bringing the conversation back to Earth, Nick extended his condolences about the loss of Special Agent Wells, to which Sanderson thanked him and shared a few kind words of respect. Now he understood why Michelle took to Sanderson so quickly. Ron Sanderson was an empathetic man who was easy to like. "If you don't mind me asking, how are agents Granby and Bonino? Are they okay? I understand they're still in the hospital." Expecting the worst, he then hesitated to ask about Chris and the others at M&C.

"They're fine—they're all going to be fine," Sanderson was happy to report.

Nick breathed a sigh of relief.

"James is pretty banged up, but he's as cantankerous as ever and eager to get back on his feet." Sanderson explained how Granby and the mother and daughter were saved by the void space created by the ruptured macadam that miraculously didn't fail under all the excess weight placed upon it as buildings continued to fall. They were rescued that afternoon, while Nick was still in the air. "As for Steve," he continued, "Special Agent Bonino has been discharged and will be back to his post later this week. I suppose that you were told about Prescott?"

Nick nodded.

"I think it's safe to say that he's still lying under that section of building. We will, of course, confirm his death." Sanderson's next words bordered on reverent. "As for your friends, Mr. Orrey and the others are also safe because of you and a mutual friend named Sam."

"Me and Sam?" Nick said. He looked to Michelle and Melanie, who shared in his obvious confusion.

"I will explain. But first, we have a lot to talk about." Sanderson took the remaining seat between Cat and Nick. "Let me start by saying that this is not a formal interrogation. To the contrary, each of you was asked to come here for another reason. All the same, I am hoping that the more we talk, the more additional details will come to light that will help us in our investigation of the Timberline organization." Sanderson pointed to the wall. "So that we're clear, what is said here will be recorded. Catherine, would you mind taking notes?"

"It would be my pleasure," Cat said, reaching for her note pad.

Sanderson provided Nick with a summary of how they got where they were, much like he'd done with Michelle and Melanie on Monday evening, filling in many more details than Nick had learned from Special Agent Granby.

Nick listened patiently. He appreciated the unabridged version of the story. Still, he was confused, angry really, with what had happened. It was all, so…farfetched. "You and Agent Granby make it sound like Tarryall is part of the mob."

"I understand your frustration," Sanderson said calmly. This is a lot to take in. If James didn't make this clear to you already, Timberline, of which Tarryall *was* just a part, is far from your typical criminal organization. What separates Timberline from its competition is its size and the breadth of its connections. Timberline, in fact, is the largest and longest running illicit, multi-national syndicate that we are aware of, outside of the Mafia."

"Okay," Nick said, processing this.

"It might help to know, and perhaps you already do, that the world of arts and antiquities isn't reserved for the cultured and refined. There is a subset that lacks a moral center. These are people who operate outside of social norms, willing to obtain their drug of choice, in this case arts and antiquities, by any means necessary— and Timberline is their supplier."

"That means what, exactly?" Nick pressed.

"To put it bluntly, these are not sophisticated people," Sanderson said, referring to Timberline's rank and file, including Tarryall. "They're common thieves, opportunists who hover around the law. Timberline's distribution of independent cells, spread across several continents, requires that it use violence on occasion to maintain order: it's not like the cells report to a common office, where their actions can be monitored directly. Then there's its clientele to contend with—rich, powerful people with secrets to keep. Retaliation for risking exposure cuts both ways."

"I get that. What I don't understand is the blatant violence Tarryall used," Nick said, without mentioning murder or attempted murder (or the lifetime of future nightmares he, Michelle, and Melanie were sure to face). "It doesn't track with what you just said. Why risk everything like that?"

"Because we tipped their hand, I'm afraid, the moment the

two of you and Ryan found William Laney's remains," Sanderson answered, speaking to Michelle and Melanie. "That changed everything. I'm certain overreaction wasn't Tarryall's intention; what did happen was apparently a gut reaction to everything at stake." Sanderson then echoed Michelle's own words to Special Agent Wells on Tuesday about how Garret was able to keep his deception a secret only because students did not have cell phones in 1988, saying, "In this age of instant communication—and the fact that you, Michelle, are writing a book on the very subject—Tarryall couldn't risk you calling someone, or asking too many probing questions that might prompt the authorities to look further than they might have. You had to be stopped."

"I suppose so," Michelle said, shuddering at the thought of how close Tarryall had come to doing just that.

"The level of violence Tarryall used doesn't happen often," Sanderson assured them. "It can't if the organization wishes to remain viable, and Timberline has—correct that, *had been*—around for a very long time. But it does happen."

Nick thought of poor William Laney and his senseless murder.

Cat created a welcome distraction when she took the liberty of bringing Timberline's sordid relationship with the ethically corrupt buyers of stolen goods into perspective. She used the 1990 Isabella Stewart Gardner Museum heist for her example because of the similarities in business practice between the perpetrators of that crime and Timberline, and because of the coincident discovery made yesterday morning, deep in the recesses of Little Bear, which she would wait for Sanderson to reveal. Cat described how two art thieves, disguised as police officers responding to a disturbance call to the Boston museum, overpowered two museum security guards, and over the span 81 minutes made off with 13 artworks by the likes of Rembrandt, Vermeer, Degas, and Manet valued at over $500 million. "It's the richest, still unsolved, art heist in history."

"It was the Mafia? Nick said, realizing that he wasn't off base after all.

Cat looked to her boss.

"That's what our intelligence suggests," Sanderson concurred.

"What happened to the artwork?" Nick asked.

"Reliable sources say that the heist was pulled off by mob members from the Philadelphia and Boston areas, much like Tarryall might collaborate with one of its sister cells. The artwork was presumably passed up the chain of command, and from there distributed to private collections from Connecticut to Philadelphia."

"That's incredible," Michelle said. "And nothing's been heard since about its whereabouts?"

"Not quite," Sanderson said with a quiet laugh. "The artwork reappeared in Philadelphia in the early 2000s, where it was sold at auction on the black market. A Dutch investigator claims that from there it fell into the hands of the Irish Republican Army. Did it? Does the IRA still have it?" Sanderson shrugged. "Could be, though I'm inclined to believe our intelligence that the art remains in the U.S. Our counterparts overseas have not received reliable reports or heard chatter from Timberline's European cells to suggest otherwise."

The discussion drifted from there to the Internet and social media, and the seeming impossibility of keeping anything secret for very long, especially a heist as extraordinary as the one that occurred at the Gardiner museum. Sanderson anticipated this, as it was a frequent topic of discussion among his law enforcement cohorts. He reminded them of what he'd said earlier about retribution, adding that not even a $10 million reward for the return of the artwork in good condition had been enough to break the coconspirators' veil of silence.

Details of the heist, as fascinating as they were relevant, had a calming effect. Michelle and Melanie felt increasingly at ease as the particulars fell into place. As for Nick, he found humor in Sanderson's use of the antiquated term *syndicate* in spite of the realization that the situation in which they were enmeshed was far more complex than he imagined. He made them all laugh when he said that the term brought back memories of watching the old Jack Lord version of Hawaii Five-0 with his parents growing up. Then, recalling something that Sanderson said before the discussion turned to the possible reasons behind Tarryall's actions, he said, "Agent Granby didn't tell me he was the one who pieced together the Timberline network."

"We wouldn't be here today if the FBI wasn't called in because of the bizarre nature of Dylan Streeter's disappearance, and if James hadn't noticed a common name between that case and two others over a three-year period back in the early eighties. It was a real needle-in-a-haystack find. It was James's persistence in the early days of his career that linked those cases to still others across the country and overseas and to the same arts and antiquities syndicate. This, of course, led to the creation of Operation Timberline, which has since grown to become a multi-national task force."

"All because of a name?" Nick said wistfully. "Whose?"

Sanderson asked Cat to do the honors.

Cat looked expectantly around the table when she said *"Teddy Monroe."*

"Mr. Monroe?" Michelle gasped. This was a revelation. "Are you serious?"

"Remarkable, isn't it?"

"I don't know what to say."

"Believe me when I say that I was as flabbergasted as you look now when James first told me. Suffice it to say, all of the evidence we had linking Monroe to those crimes was circumstantial. In Streeter's case, Monroe was only a secondary person of interest, who had recent contact with Streeter. Hollis Walker and Joe Hayden were also named in the original report, as they should have been because they were the police responders at the scene." Sanderson chuckled. "As James likes to tell it, the moment that defined his career was made by an off-hand comment from another agent the following year who said, 'I'm working on a case about as strange as that mountain-man disappearance you handled.' James asked if the other agent minded if he read the report, for curiosity sake, when he recognized Monroe's name. He did more digging and found Monroe's name also associated with the unsolved theft of a collection of seventeenth-century tapestries from a collector in Washington state the year after that. Patience and keeping an eye out for Monroe's name linked him to still other crimes. Then Walker's name popped up again, as did Hayden's and a few others that have come and gone since." So there was no misunderstanding, Sanderson made it clear that the FBI believed Teddy Monroe to be the original ringleader of the Tarryall cell.

"What am I missing?" Nick asked.

Michelle explained how she and Melanie had met Teddy Monroe on Monday. "He's this little old man. He wasn't exactly friendly, but he sure didn't look like a criminal."

Melanie agreed. "We thought he was a retiree volunteering his time at Tarryall."

"They often *don't* look the part." Cat said sagely. "I can tell you first hand that none of us thought Brett Carr was capable of what he did."

Nick was even more intrigued.

Sanderson leaned in close and said, "Do you recall that sensationalized account about the American who was turned into a zombie, and the pirate-museum heist of a few years back?"

"That was you?"

"I'm afraid so." Cat admitted.

"You are in the midst of celebrities, Nick," Sanderson boasted. "Catherine and her husband and friends helped us shut down the Strickland crime ring, not to mention tearing a piece out of the collective that pulled off the pirate-museum heist. It was Catherine's insight about a mutual college friend—Brett Carr—that linked two syndicate cases that James and I were working at the time. If she hadn't stumbled across our path, we'd probably be no closer to bringing either case to closure. The same can be said for your wife and Ms. Sutton. Without Michelle and Melanie's help, Tarryall would be carrying on business as usual."

Nick asked to hear more.

"Well," Sanderson said, "we apprehended Monroe after a search was made of his home when we realized that the Tarryall directorate, of which Monroe is a member, did not report for work on Wednesday. He was preparing to run. Monroe surrendered quietly, though he's been less than cooperative since, as expected."

"That's still good, right?" Nick said.

"Absolutely," Sanderson said, taking great pride in Monroe's arrest. "We're optimistic he'll change his mind about talking once he weighs his options." Still speaking to Nick, Sanderson looked in the girls' direction, chuckled again and said, "It might not have worked out as planned, but Melanie here—as I'm sure you've been told—single-handedly eliminated Tarryall cell member William Clay, while Michelle successfully fought off Joe Hayden long enough for me to arrive with backup to secure the scene. Clay and Hayden were particularly bad men." Sanderson flattered the girls by saying, "Your heroics have gained the admiration of every woman in the Bureau."

"They're building your statues as we speak!" Cat added, reaching across the table to grasp Michelle's and Melanie's hands in a show of solidarity.

"I'm awed!" Nick said humbly.

"As you should be," Sanderson said. "What they did out there, alone and against such odds, was extraordinary."

"You're sure I'm not going to be in trouble for starting the fire?" Melanie asked.

Sanderson quashed her concern with a resounding *"No!"* He reminded her that she did what she needed to do to survive, and that the damage was limited. "To the contrary, when I explained the situation to the authorities and how you locked Clay in the shed and set it on fire, the fire chief said, and I quote: *'No, shit?'*"

Melanie relaxed.

"I should warn you, though, that once the details start leaking out, don't be surprised if you're confronted by those who see things differently. Just ask Catherine."

"Ugh!" Cat lamented. "It was an exhausting experience. We found out the hard way that there's a world of people out there who find satisfaction making themselves feel good at the expense of others. These people have no problem telling you how things could have been handled differently, and that you should be held accountable for your actions. You'll see. I'd be glad to help you avoid some of the issues we had to deal with."

"I would like that," Melanie said.

"What did they say?" Nick asked.

Cat sighed. "I don't even know where to begin."

Sanderson cleared his throat. "Let's move along. I want each of you to meet with our public relations people before you leave, so you know what can and cannot be said about this case. And Michelle, I'm aware of why you were here in the first place, so this pertains especially to you. I promise full disclosure of all details for your book, except for those that could compromise our mission of bringing Timberline to justice. But not now. Is that understood?"

"Not a problem," Michelle said.

"Good. Now, before we proceed, I do regret to inform you that we still have a problem, which is why I strongly urge that each of you remain in the Bureau's protective care for the time being." Sanderson pulled the thinnest folder from the stack of intra-office Bureau correspondence in front of him. He opened it, removed an eight-by-ten photo, and slid it in front of Michelle. "Joe Hayden. We didn't recover his body."

The shock was palpable.

"I heard him fall…I heard him hit the ground," Michelle stammered in desperation. "He couldn't have gotten up!"

"'Chelle," Nick said, in a calming voice, "give him a chance to explain."

"Thank you, Nick. And I believe you, Michelle," Sanderson continued. "It isn't reasonable to conclude that Hayden could have walked away from multiple falls from those heights under his own power. Our forensics people found blood where you said he last landed. You can see that here in the photo." Sanderson pointed at a brownish-red smudge. "They also found two sets of fresh footprints in the dust leading away from the blood smear. We believe Hayden had help from Hollis Walker, who is also missing." Sanderson waited for the words to sink in. "It appears that Walker was hiding deeper in the Little Bear mine, to protect the considerable cache of stolen items Tarryall was hiding there. Our best guess is that he responded to your altercation with Hayden. The footprints led to a horizontal airshaft that exited the mountain well away from the mine entrance. They likely slipped away in the confusion."

More silence.

"That's interesting," Nick said, breaking the quiet. "Both mines were constructed at about the same time, and as I understand it, had pretty similar layouts. I don't recall an adit—sorry, that's the technical term—or other portal opening at Big Bear, the mine we—*Wait!*" Nick said, raising his hands in time out, "Why didn't I hear about Hayden and Walker being still at large on the news? How much danger are we really in?"

Sanderson considered Nick's concerns. "The short answer is, we don't believe that you are."

"Why not?" Nick demanded. "What's changed?"

"Yeah, what?" Michelle insisted.

"Because Joe Hayden and Hollis Walker have much bigger problems. Correspondence from our field offices tracking the movements of known cells tied to Tarryall report that they've all gone dark. We believe that the syndicate is liquidating its liabilities."

Nick was stunned. Michelle and Melanie drew in startled breaths.

"The body of a member from one of Tarryall's sister cells turned up within hours of the press release about the fire and Clay's death. We've excluded Hayden and Walker from the media because they're well-known members of the community. We don't want to exacerbate the situation by having frightened citizens meet an untimely knock at their door with violence."

"People would think it's them seeking refuge."

"Exactly, Michelle. Private justice will only get additional innocent people hurt. In lieu of a broadcast announcement, we're performing door-to-door searches and a rolling patrol of area streets. We've also been monitoring area and regional hospitals, and medical and veterinary clinics."

"And?" Nick asked.

"Nothing. Nor has anyone been reported missing or unexplainably absent from work. This and the fact that the syndicate reacted so quickly to the initial press release suggests that Hayden and Walker are long gone, if not already dead. Trust me when I say they are marked men." Sanderson then relayed some extraordinary news that not only tied neatly to Cat's example, but further explained Tarryall's actions as the act of desperate men. "Besides exposing the greater organization, the syndicate has lost what could amount to millions of dollars in stolen goods. Their interest right now is in finding Hayden and Walker."

When Sanderson finished describing some of the many paintings, sculptures, and other priceless items he saw down in the mine, Michelle looked to Cat and said, "This sounds just like that museum heist."

"It does indeed," Sanderson agreed. "I think you now can see why an attempt on your lives at this point would only put the syndicate at further risk of exposure,"

Cat added her support of the Bureau's beliefs. "If my experience means anything, they're not going to be that foolish. My husband, our friends...me, we survived our ordeal, and no one has come after us."

Melanie couldn't keep her frustration in check any longer. "You were supposed to be watching them. What happened?"

"I can't answer that right now, Ms. Sutton." The unspoken translation being that heads were rolling on both sides of the law.

"The guy following me? You're certain Prescott's dead?" Nick asked.

Sanderson took the battering in stride. "Yes. As I said before, Special Agent Granby watched Ian Prescott being crushed by a piece of a falling building."

"Ooof!" Nick cringed. "You did say that."

Sanderson unexpectedly changed the mood and tempo of the meeting by slapping his hands on the table. "Enough about this," he said, "let's turn our attention to something less distressing, shall we?"

Cat seconded the change in direction. "I think we all could stand to talk about something a little more uplifting."

"Sounds good to me," Michelle agreed.

"I would like that, too" Melanie added.

Speaking to Nick, Sanderson said, "You may recall that thanks were in order to you and a colleague named Sam—Sam Piersall, if I recall correctly."

"Something like that," Nick said with a shrug.

"It so happened that Mr. Piersall noticed similar irregularities in the field data the two of you talked about on Wednesday morning. Failing to reach you, Sam called your friend Chris, who relayed your mutual concerns to the legal firm for whom you and Mr. Orrey are working. It wasn't more than a few minutes after that that the earthquake started. This put your colleagues at MacDonald & Carlyle on alert and made the evacuation less traumatic. There were very few minor injuries, as a consequence. Your bosses, Bill Carlyle and Ainsley MacDonald, extend their gratitude."

"That's so sweet!" Michelle said.

Nick lowered his head in modesty. "They're good people."

Sanderson brought the significance of Nick and Sam's actions home when he said, "I dread to think what might have happened if you and Mr. Piersall hadn't spoken and gotten hold of Mr. Orrey. They all might be dead now." Then lightening the mood again, he said, "And lest I forget, we've seen to it that Mr. Orrey was put up in an area hotel not damaged by the earthquake. He will be in contact with you once communications are restored."

"It sure will be nice to hear that cackle of his again!"

Michelle kissed Nick on the cheek. Cat congratulated him on a job well done.

Without thinking, Nick changed the subject back to Tarryall, asking how Hayden and the others knew that Michelle and Melanie had gone back to look for the gravesites.

Sadness returned to Sanderson's pale eyes when he summarized the sequence of events that triggered Tarryall's protect-at-all-cost response: everything from Michelle's call using the phone number Special Agent Bonino had eavesdropped from Ian Prescott's phone to Kaycee Barrie's telling response; and, most importantly, Joe Hayden's presumed observation of said response. Sanderson sighed, "Their stakeout of the Sacred Lands burial ground was, in retrospect, an obvious action I should have anticipated, and I'm sorry. What happened after that, of course, including the attempt on Ms. Barrie's life was, as I just explained, an act of desperation."

So much for the uplifting discussion.

"Kaycee!" Michelle said, her voice pleading, eyes full of dread. "She's the one I told you about, Nick. How is she?"

Nick put his arm around Michelle's shoulder.

Sanderson reiterated for Nick's benefit what Michelle had told him, about how the FBI was alerted to Kaycee Barrie's accident around the same time that local law enforcement informed the Bureau that the Tarryall directorate did not report for work. As for her health, Sanderson regretted to say that Kaycee was still in a coma. "She was underwater for some time."

"You're certain that her car was tampered with?"

"Yes. It wasn't an accident."

Michelle pulled a pack of tissues from her purse. She took one and handed the pack to Melanie.

Michelle said that all Kaycee wanted to do was help, to find a way out for her and her mom.

Sanderson hummed his agreement, smiled. "Whatever happens, Kaycee's efforts certainly will not be in vain. Tarryall's cell has been destroyed and those GPS coordinates she provided will give four families closure."

"*Four families?* I don't understand," Michelle said.

Sanderson's smile widened. "You found William Laney exactly where Ms. Barrie's coordinates said he should be, and the other set led us to Dylan Streeter's remains nearby. Using ground penetrating radar and cadaver dogs, we also found the remains of two adult males, who we expect are the young archaeologists who found the supposed Quivira artifacts."

"Now what am I missing?" Nick asked.

Sanderson described the archaeologists' 1980 find and subsequent noncoincidental disappearance—like that of Dylan Streeter and William Laney. He pointed out the irony that the archaeologists were buried in the Sacred Lands, the very place where the Ghost Creek legend was born as a consequence of Coronado's actions centuries earlier.

Nick wasn't so much impressed with how the parts of this never ending nightmare fit together, as he was by the Conservancy's depravity in using the Sacred Lands as their very own burial ground. The thought made him shudder. He spread his hands in a *somehow this all makes sense* gesture.

"What amazes me," Sanderson said, "is that Dylan Streeter's remains have been buried and found twice, and that so many of the key players in our little saga have remained the same over time: Monroe, Hayden, Walker, and of course the three of you."

Nick smiled.

The conversation drifted at this point. Cat congratulated Michelle on accomplishing what she had set out do and more, and Melanie peppered Sanderson with many more questions about the fire, the ongoing search for Hayden and Walker, and whether funeral arrangements had yet been made for Ryan Wells. Michelle was idly listening to Melanie talk about her fondness for the late agent when she thought about Kaycee Barrie lying in a hospital bed, fighting for her life. *Her poor mother...*

"Beth!"

"Pardon?"

"Beth Stockwell. I forgot all about her. She must be devastated by what happened to her daughter." Thinking about it, Michelle added, "Beth's not one of *them*, is she?"

"We don't think so," Sanderson said softly. "And she's fine. Ms. Stockwell does, however, remain a person of interest, and has been remanded into police protective custody until we can vet her testimony and determine next steps to ensure her safety."

Michelle expressed her relief and asked if it was possible to see Beth again before leaving Colorado.

"We can manage that," Cat was pleased to announce.

"You can? When?"

"How about right now?" Sanderson answered with a mischievous grin. "She asked to speak with you. It's the reason why each of you was invited here today. She's waiting for you down the hall."

———

Nick helped Michelle ease her way back to her feet.

"Getting going is the hardest part," Michelle gasped.

"Do you need help?" Sanderson asked.

"I'll manage, so long as I don't do anything dumb. Thanks!"

Sanderson appreciated Michelle's take-it-all-in-stride humor. "Very well. If you will follow me."

"Ron, do you mind if Janelle and I pop in later? I'd like to see how she's coming along with the information from Joe Hayden's computer, and I need to check in with Kim Parsons back at ICF. She has Missy working on that other information you provided."

"Sure. No problem, Catherine. I can take it from here."

They followed Cat out of the conference room, where they parted ways.

Sanderson led the others down the hall. He knocked on a door to their left, which was opened by a stern-faced agent who ushered Sanderson and his guests inside.

This was a real interrogation room, the interior sterile and without character. It reminded Michelle of one of the interrogation rooms on the crime dramas she and Nick liked to watch, the room barren except for a single long table with a chair on one side and several on the other—for the good guys—and a seeing-eye camera looking down from a corner near the ceiling. In the lone chair, on the wrong side of the table, sat Beth Stockwell. Beth greeted her guests with a trace of a smile that managed to break through all the stress that had accumulated over the turbulent past several days.

"Michelle, Melanie, it's good to see you again," Beth managed, her voice weak. "I'm so thankful that both of you are all right."

"Ms. Stockwell, please forgive me," Sanderson interrupted. "Before we begin, let me remind you that you are still a person of interest in our ongoing investigation of the Tarryall Mountain Foundation. Do you continue to waive your right to have an attorney present?"

"I do," Beth said softly. "I have nothing to hide. Like I told you before, I want to put this behind me…behind all of us."

"Fine. Now, Ms. Stockwell, you requested to see Michelle Kozlowski and Melanie Sutton, to speak with them and answer their questions. Is this still your intent?"

"It is."

"Very well, then. Ms. Stockwell, you have the floor."

Beth began by apologizing for her transgressions, no matter how unintended or coerced. She then looked at Nick and said, "You are exactly as I imagined."

Nick appreciated the compliment. He said that Michelle and Melanie had nothing but good things to say about her, and that the pleasure was all his to meet the one person his wife believed to be her ally from the beginning. He also expressed his condolences for her daughter's condition, praising Kaycee for her bravery.

Beth slumped contentedly into her chair.

The apprehension that Nick's remarks lifted was unmistakable. Michelle took Sanderson at his word and asked, "Beth, are you saying that you didn't actively participate in any of the illegal things the Conservancy—sorry, Tarryall—did?"

"Heavens no, my dear!" Beth sighed, to Michelle's relief. "I could never do any of those things. Never! Never! Never! I asked to see you because I owe all of you an explanation."

Sanderson suggested Beth begin with when she met Kaycee's father.

"That would be best," Beth agreed. "I met Benjamin Barrie when I was a sophomore in high school. Bennie and I were in the same grade. Dylan Streeter was Bennie's half-brother and was a good bit older. Dylan was out of college and working as an archeological curator for a museum in Denver." Beth sighed again. "They couldn't have been any more different. As much as Dylan had his life together, Bennie was struggling to find his. Bennie had this wild streak that often got him into trouble. That's what attracted me to him, that and the fact he was incredibly handsome. My parents couldn't stand him, but I didn't care. I was the lucky girl with the gorgeous bad boy the other girls all wanted." She then sighed a third time, this time heavily and with regret. "I was young and dumb. I should have listened to my parents."

"I dunno. I had the biggest crush on the class bad boy when I was in high school," Michelle offered, hoping to cheer Beth up.

"Unfortunately, my bad boy fell under Joe Hayden's spell."

"*No!*"

"Lucky me, huh? Joe was two years older and the school bully. He was as physically gifted as he was ruggedly handsome. He had this swagger about him that attracted certain kids like my Bennie."

"I know the type. Sorry to hear that," Nick said.

"That was Joe. I'm sure the only reason he let Bennie pal around with him was because Joe knew Bennie could be manipulated. I never trusted Joe, and—"

"Why was that, again?" Sanderson interrupted, checking his notes.

"Why I didn't trust him? Because Joe was always into something shady."

"Can you give us an example?"

"I don't know," Beth wavered, searching her mind. "All right. This will probably sound funny to you, but there was this time in school when Joe had all these watches. It was a fad at the time—you know—to have things you couldn't really afford to look all high society. If you wanted one, you went to Joe and he would get you one…cheap. Come to think of it, it was around that time that Bennie really started hanging around Joe, at least more than usual."

"Go on," Sanderson encouraged.

"I have no idea where he got them. He could get other jewelry, too: you know, things like necklaces and earrings—things that only a girl would wear. That bothered me."

"Why?"

Beth seemed confused by the question. "Because boys don't do that. It wasn't natural."

"Of course not. Please continue."

"The pieces he got, whether they were watches or necklaces, were nice—too nice for the prices he was asking."

"You thought they might be stolen?" Sanderson pressed.

"Yes and no," Beth said, with a conflicting expression to match. "It bothered me that they might be stolen, yes, but I don't recall hearing anything questionable about what he was doing. I also don't remember any of my friends who bought stuff from Joe ever saying anything about their parents having a problem with us suddenly wearing expensive things. I also found that odd."

"Do you recall any suspicious burglaries back then?" Sanderson asked.

"No."

"I see," Sanderson said, underlining the word, *"No."*

It was becoming clear to Michelle that the overriding purpose for Sanderson's agreeing to Beth's request to speak with them was corroboration with her initial testimony and filling in the gaps.

"So that we're clear, you're saying you thought Joe Hayden might have been into something illegal, even then?"

Beth frowned. "Yes. I realized even then that Joe was probably doing something illegal."

Michelle found the admission heartbreaking. "You've been dealing with this for nearly your whole life? Beth, I'm so sorry."

"Please don't feel sorry for me. I made a bad decision. I should have walked away; I couldn't."

"Why's that?" Michelle asked.

"You must remember what it was like to be a teen-aged girl. All that pressure to get a boyfriend, then to keep up appearances until a better one came along. For me, that person never came. Worse, as time wore on, Bennie became domineering. There was also an issue with Joe, who also liked me, so there I was, caught in the middle between the two of them. It was a small school in a small community. There was no way I could leave one without being expected to take up with the other."

"There had to be other boys."

"Dating others was out of the question, for their sake. I was afraid of what Joe, or Bennie for that matter, might do to them. Bennie at least was a buffer from Joe. I thought that maybe if I waited it out, things would change. They didn't."

"I can relate," Melanie said. "I was once in a difficult relationship like yours."

Beth dabbed at her eyes. "Things did change, at least for a while, when Joe went to college. Out from under Joe Hayden's spell, Bennie came back around. If only that had lasted."

"What happened?" Michelle asked.

"Joe started coming home during breaks. He also changed his major to criminology to become a cop. I thought this was a good thing, that it would straighten him out."

"It didn't," Sanderson said, phrasing his question as a statement.

"No. Joe only wanted to become a cop so that he could use the law for his own purposes, and because of that Bennie was drawn right back under Joe's spell. Before long, it was 'Joe's coming home and he want's me to do this,' or 'I can't because Joe's coming home and wants me to do that.'"

"You didn't mention this before." Sanderson said, turning a page in his notebook. "Can you provide an example of 'this' or 'that'?"

"Oh, I can't think of anything specifically. It was always little things." Beth even gave Hayden some unexpected praise. "I do have to say that Joe always was entrepreneurial. He was always looking for a way to make money—you know, like cutting lawns, plowing snow, doing the odd job for people. I was naïve to think—hope, really—that Joe was asking Bennie to help to be nice. I eventually realized that Joe was only doing these things to get information on people, testing Bennie to see how far he could be trusted."

"Please explain," Sanderson insisted.

"It's what he did...it's what Joe did in later years with the organization. He'd gain people's trust, soak in what they told him, and then use that information against them."

"Did Joe Hayden recruit your boyfriend?"

"In the bigger sense, no. Bennie made a good lieutenant, but he wasn't up to scratch when it came to secrecy. I learned that it took constant vigilance, a continuing paranoia, to do what Joe and the others did at Tarryall to keep the trust of those higher in the organization; and, of course, to keep up the deception. That wasn't Bennie. He was loyal, but he could only be trusted so far."

"He sounds like that Strickland guy who Cat's ex-friend worked with," Michelle said to Sanderson.

"I agree. And as Catherine says, Brett Carr was her Joe Hayden."

Sanderson shared a summary of the Strickland crime ring and Brett Carr's overlapping involvement with two Timberline syndicate cells.

Nick asked if Tarryall had involvement with either organization.

"Not to our knowledge," Sanderson said, "though it wouldn't surprise us if they did, considering the value of the mine as a hiding place. Catherine and her firm are looking for a connection as we speak." Sanderson went on to say that, contrary to the FBI's assumption that Tarryall's influence was confined to the fleecing of ski-season tourists and wealthy mountain-retreat transplants, a preliminary inventory of goods recovered from the Little Bear mine suggested that some of the antiquities found in its warren of tunnels were consistent with a cache of cultural items stolen from the archives at the Natural History Museum of Los Angeles. Storage of stolen works from the San Antonio Art Auction heist, in which Brett Carr had taken part, therefore, was not out of the question.

Although Beth agreed with everything Sanderson said, she still reminded him of her earlier testimony that she was never privy to the *transactions* of property—meaning stolen goods—that occurred during what became for her a forced association with Tarryall.

Michelle had thought as much. Nonetheless, hearing that Beth was coerced to comply with Tarryall's misdeeds made her blood boil.

"I didn't say that I disagree with you," Sanderson said, jotting down more notes. "But let me be clear again, Ms. Stockwell, we will take the evidence wherever it leads, and I truly hope that it does not lead back to you." Sanderson poured himself a cup of water from the carafe on the center of the table, then a second one for Beth. He asked that she fast-forward to the disappearance of Dylan Streeter.

—And what followed was a tale of heartache and despair, followed by acceptance, and that of a long, downward spiral of dashed hopes, dreams, and spirit that echoed that of poor Garret, whose legacy landed them in this particular FBI interrogation room three decades after his untimely death—

"That day you found Dylan's remains in the stream…what happened began in 1982, that April I think. Joe had graduated from the academy and was working for the police force under Bud Walker, who was sheriff at the time. Bennie and I were living together, just making ends meet. Those were tough times. Bennie had become unbearable again and had fallen completely under Joe's spell by that time."

"Explain," Sanderson asked.

"Joe used his position to continue his high school ways, manipulating Bennie, filling his head with nonsense. At that point, I'd pretty much given up hope of finding something better for my life.

There didn't seem to be any place to go where Joe and his newfound power couldn't find me."

Michelle remained stuck on Beth's previous statement about Streeter. "You knew who I was talking about that day when we were on the phone. That's why you got so quiet."

Beth nodded.

Michelle wasn't sure how to take this. Should she be upset for not being informed about what Beth had allowed her to walk into? Chalk it up to one more instance of Calamity Girl happenstance? Whatever. Lamenting was only wasting time when she was intensely curious to hear what happened next. On a hunch, Michelle said, "But you didn't give up hope of finding a way out."

And she was right. With a resurgent smile, Beth said that, in spite of all his faults, Bennie was a dreamer. "He was always dreaming up the next get-rich-quick opportunity, even if he never had the means or ambition to see whatever that was through. But he kept on trying and I loved him for that. I'd pray that his next idea would actually work and we could make enough money to move far away, beyond Joe's reach, where we knew no one and no one knew us."

"That never happened," Melanie said sadly.

"Quite the opposite," Beth said with regret. "He pushed his luck too far instead. Bennie came home one day really excited, which made me excited, too. I thought maybe *this time* was it. When I asked what had him so worked up, Bennie turned my question around and asked if I'd heard about 'those relics that belonged to that Spanish guy.' I still remember those words as if I heard them yesterday. That was the beginning of the end. I had no idea what he was talking about. There was no Internet back then, and I didn't read the papers."

"The Quivira relics," Sanderson said.

"Yes."

"Bennie said that Joe asked him to talk to Dylan about convincing the men who found the relics to sell them to an interested buyer that was, of course, arranged through Joe. How Dylan and the men knew one another and Joe found out, I don't know. Bennie was excited because he was expecting a big cut. Dylan, I recall, didn't know that anything was out of order other than that his half-brother was concocting his next scheme. Bennie could have said no, and I told him not to get involved, but Bennie being Bennie, he would hear none of it. I had a bad feeling from the start; he was sure this time we were going to be rich."

"Would you say that Bennie and Dylan were on good terms at the time despite the differences in their ages and station?" Sanderson asked.

"On a social basis, like at family gatherings, yes they got along; otherwise, not so much. That's what made Joe's request so awkward. Bennie and Dylan saw very little of one another after Dylan went off to college. Regardless, and with pressure from Joe, Bennie badgered Dylan every few days for weeks before giving up, or so I thought."

"What changed?"

"What else? Joe. He stopped by one day after work some months later. He yelled at Bennie for not getting through to Dylan. They argued, and that's when I first heard Bud Walker's name mentioned. That's when I knew that Bennie had gotten himself into something deep. It scared me."

"You were frightened of Hollis Walker?"

"Of course I was afraid of Bud," Beth said, as if the comment was a stupid one. "If you can't trust the chief of police, who can you trust? What was he doing getting mixed up in the off-duty affairs of a subordinate like Joe Hayden, anyway?"

Point taken. Sanderson flipped through his notes again. He underscored Walker's name, made a check mark in the margin of the page. Thus far, Beth Stockwell's testimony remained true to her initial statement. He asked for clarification on the worsening arguments between Bennie and Dylan in the months leading up to Streeter's disappearance.

"Bennie responded to Joe's badgering by increasing his pressure on Dylan, right on up to the rendezvous. Dylan finally had had enough and said he would go to the authorities if Bennie didn't back off. Dylan insisted that the relics be donated to a museum."

"The relics weren't for sale, then," Michelle said in summary.

"No. That's what got Dylan and those other men killed."

Sanderson explained to Michelle and the others that Beth was informed of the two other bodies found in the Sacred Lands, presumed to belong to the missing young archaeologists, and urged that Beth move on to the day of the Panner's and Picker's Rendezvous.

Beth drew in a deep breath. "We had a run of gorgeous weather leading up to the event. The news said attendance was expected to be high. I was relieved because Dylan was going to be a reenactor, and I thought a large crowd would keep Bennie from causing a scene. I was also relieved when Bennie said that he had to run an errand for Joe that day. Then I heard that the relics and the men who found them might also be at the rendezvous, and I started to worry all over again. All I wanted was for the event to be over, because I knew Bennie would find a way to show up and cause a scene. I was at work that day when he burst into the office crying—I had never seen him do that before. He said that Dylan had gone missing. I thought I was going to die," Beth said, clapping a hand to her chest. "I dragged Bennie into a back room where no one could hear and made him swear that he didn't have anything to do with it. He said he didn't, which meant it had to be Joe."

Nick groaned.

Michelle responded by pounding her fist on the table. "He was a police officer!" she said, reflecting on her situation of a few years later. "How did you find out he was behind Mr. Streeter's disappearance?"

Beth grimaced with disgust. "Because Joe and Bud stopped by the house that evening. Bud did most of the talking. In no uncertain terms, he said that we were to come to him or Joe first if we heard of any rumors about Dylan…that he would hate to see anyone else get hurt."

Michelle and Melanie each drew in a breath.

"They threatened you," Nick said, the whole saga becoming clearer.

"Ms. Stockwell, this morning you said that neither man admitted to actually killing Dylan Streeter."

Beth sniffed. Michelle handed her a tissue from the community pack. "They didn't have to. The intent of their stopping by at our home instead of at the precinct was clear enough. To be honest, I doubt that they did it. They always had someone else do their dirty work. That's how they stayed clean...by letting others take the fall."

"Incredible. What happened after that?" Michelle asked.

"Nothing. It was back to life as usual with the exception that every time something about Dylan surfaced on the news, Joe fished around to make sure we hadn't said anything." Beth raised her hands in frustration. "What could we say? Fortunately, interest in what happened quickly died away. There's no doubt in my mind that Bud used his influence as sheriff to make that happen, and after a while, it was as if Dylan never existed. For me and Bennie, though, we had to live with the tension of not knowing what or when something might happen to us, all because Bennie didn't do what Joe had asked, and we knew too much. All it would take is for them to think that Bennie or me said something, and...you know. We lived in constant fear."

"That's a horrible way to have to go through life," Melanie said. "What you must have gone through reminds me of the dark days growing up with my brother and our family issues."

Beth remarked how she found a kindred spirit in Melanie after reading *Ghost Creek*. "We learned to cope with it. On the bright side, what happened to Dylan frightened Bennie. It brought us closer together."

"That's good," Melanie said.

"It was. Joe continued to use Bennie from time to time, probably just to keep tabs on him I'm sure. Our life was as good as could be, given our situation, right up until that college of yours, Michelle, purchased the field-station property."

Michelle leaned forward, as did Melanie and Nick. Even Sanderson, who'd already heard what was about to come, couldn't help anxiously waiting for Beth to continue.

"It was bedlam. Bennie and me, we didn't know why at first. We thought it was funny."

"Why's that?" Michelle asked.

"Because Bennie said how agitated Joe became, and that he overheard Joe arguing with Bud, who was arguing with Teddy Monroe, about what to do. Teddy was the ringleader back then. He recruited Bud and Joe, and created Tarryall through his real estate connections. Teddy leaned on Bud to use his position with the force to protect Tarryall and the organization you call Timberline, and here it was Teddy who let the property slip through his fingers in the first place."

"How's that?"

Beth looked at Michelle and smiled. "Because he could have used his real estate company to purchase the property in the late seventies, before this mess started. It instead went to a buyer who did the unthinkable, and gave it to the college several years later. That's when I knew, and I think Bennie did too, that they were hiding something—like Dylan's body—up there. The property was undeveloped and privately owned. With the topography as rough as it was, there was practically no chance of anyone finding a body buried there. But a college? A bunch of students and professors traipsing about would risk everything. We thought it was funny because it was good to see the shoe on the other foot for a change."

"That's right!" Nick said, smiling. "It was some benefactor from Minneapolis who went to Huron who owned the property. The family donated it to the school."

"That's right." And with that, Nick had unwittingly confirmed what Beth told Sanderson earlier that morning. Beth returned Nick's smile and said, "Then when word got out that the school was interested in using one of the mines for class work, that brought all the *waking the dead* ninnies out of the woodwork."

"You've got to be kidding?"

"I wish I was!" Beth responded to Nick's amusement with a derisive laugh. "Bud took advantage of people's fears to spread rumors that the college planned to exhume the body of that Indian prophet from the legend and use the mines to conduct pagan ceremonies. It was that sort of nonsense that led to your school's administrators being assaulted."

"That really happened?" Michelle gasped. She relayed the story she first heard at a fraternity-house party the night she and Garret got back together, about how a bunch of fantasy-driven rednecks, as she called them, accosted the administrators at gunpoint during a walkthrough of the property.

"The idea was to rile up the locals enough to scare the school off." Beth sipped at her water. "To answer a question I know you wanted to ask when you came here, we all haven't lost our marbles my dear. There were maybe a dozen or so who caused trouble, but as you know, it only takes a few bad seeds to cast a shadow over the rest of us."

"That's good to hear," Michelle said, relieved. She would make it a point to clarify this fact in her book.

Beth's expression darkened. "That uproar faded away as well, until the day you found that skeleton. You confirmed our worst fears about what had happened to Dylan." Beth then offered a snippet of information that took even Sanderson by surprise when she revealed that it was Michelle's discovery that led to Tarryall's creation. "It was Bud who thought up the Tarryall angle to create a land conservation company to approach the school about selling the Sacred Lands tract."

Susan, the administrative assistant, knocked at the door and poked her head inside. "Ron, a word?"

Sanderson suggested they take a break and rose to his feet. Nick had gotten up as well to stretch, when he felt a buzz in his pocket.

He pulled out his phone, glanced at the view screen, and chirped, "It's Chris!"

"Wonderful!" Sanderson said, and asked Nick to follow him into the hall where he would be shown to a room where he could catch up with his friend in private.

Left to their own devices, Beth filled Michelle and Melanie in on more sad yet fascinating aspects about her life under Tarryall's thumb. Particularly interesting was the despicable manner in which Joe Hayden had insinuated himself into every facet of her life, which happened in step with the increasing success of the legitimate side of Tarryall's business.

"Finding Dylan's remains changed everything," Beth said, "for better and for worse." Although forced to join Tarryall so that Hayden, Walker, and Monroe could keep an eye on them under the same roof, she and Bennie were paid handsomely for their silence. It was, as she explained, a golden handcuffs existence inside a prison cell without bars.

Michelle couldn't help but feel profoundly sorry for Beth, her own life problems suddenly paling in comparison to the drawn-out oppression Beth Stockwell was forced to endure.

The distant sound of cheering and clapping hands brought some much-needed relief. Moments later, Sanderson returned to the interrogation room bright with energy. "Ms. Stockwell, I have good news! Your daughter has awakened from her coma."

Beth was overcome. Michelle and Melanie hugged, then stood to meet Beth part way across the table for a celebratory embrace. Sanderson was quick to temper the optimism, if only for an instant, when he warned that Kaycee still had a long road ahead, but barring a setback, her doctor said that she should be fine.

"Her tests?" Beth asked.

"So far all negative for long-term brain and organ damage."

Beth closed her eyes and cried.

"Where's Nick?" Michelle said, excited. "He's missing this!"

"He's still down the hall." Sanderson answered, quipping, "His conversation with Mr. Orrey is apparently going too well, because Susan had to tell him to keep it down!" Sanderson asked where they were in the conversation.

Beth said she was explaining how she and Bennie struggled to make the best of a difficult situation after Michelle's unfortunate discovery. Struck by a sudden thought, she then asked if it would be alright for Michelle and Melanie to see Kaycee again, once her daughter had healed enough to receive visitors.

"I think that can be arranged," Sanderson replied. He then shared more good news, saying that he had forwarded Beth's witness-relocation request for a place where Kaycee could see palm trees.

"*Aww!* That's so sweet!" Michelle said. "Kaycee must have been adorable when she was a little girl. How old is she, twenty-five?"

"Twenty-six," Beth corrected. "And she was!" Beth beamed. "She was quite the tomboy. She loved playing with snakes and lizards, and all sorts of creatures that the other little girls were afraid of." A glimmer of sadness tinged Beth's eyes when she said that Kaycee dreamed of becoming a veterinarian when she grew up.

"Why didn't she?" Michelle asked.

Beth pursed her lips and said, "Joe, who else? But thanks to the two of you—and the FBI, of course—I now can send her to college. I promise to give her everything she's missed. There's so much I need to tell her, to make amends for."

"I don't understand," Michelle said.

"Bennie and I…we had Kaycee for all the wrong reasons, and she's had to suffer for our selfishness ever since."

"Please don't say that," Michelle said, feeling the need to reach for the pack of tissues. "What do you mean by, *for the wrong reasons?*"

Beth regretfully said, "Kaycee was born as a consequence of the distraction caused by the money coming through Tarryall's doors. Once the dust had settled, after the college sold the property and what little attention caused by your finding of Dylan's remains had died down, life got much better. So long as the money came in, it was as if Joe and the others could care less we existed. I actually looked forward to going to work for once, and Bennie and I were getting along as well as ever because Joe finally stopped using him. I let my guard down and we had Kaycee. I hope that she can forgive me."

"I sense another change happened," Sanderson interrupted.

Beth clenched her hands into tiny fists. "It's the story of my life. This time it was Bennie. Our situation didn't encourage the type of life in which to raise a child. I also found out the hard way that raising a family wasn't in Bennie's plans. Once they worked the kinks out of the mine-tour operation, life went regrettably back to normal because that's when Tarryall really ramped up the illegal side of the business. The influx of tourists coming to see the mine included many wealthy visitors wanting to put their land in trust with Tarryall."

Michelle noted that Beth called out the organization by name instead of saying *"we."*

"You mean Tarryall used the mine to attract potential targets?"

"Yes," Beth said, to which Sanderson nodded and asked that she continue. "Bennie must have not screwed up too badly because Joe started using him again, which gave Bennie the excuse to shirk his responsibilities. The more he did, the more we fought, and the more he pestered Joe to trust him with another assignment. And before you ask," Beth said, turning to Sanderson, "I don't know. We had a strict don't ask don't tell policy. I didn't want to know what he was into. I didn't want to know anything that Joe could use against me."

"Understood." Sanderson flipped through his notes, placing a confirmatory check next to his summation of that part of Beth's earlier testimony.

"Life got real tough the following year when Bill Clay was hired. Bud was retired from the force by then, and Joe was on his way out to come full time to Tarryall. I knew Bill was going to be trouble from the start. He was ruthless, the snake in the grass they brought into the fold as Joe's lieutenant to oversee the off-books stuff that Joe didn't want to get his hands dirty doing. He and Bennie didn't get along from the start."

"Was that because Bennie now felt he was an outsider?" Sanderson asked.

"I'm certain it was."

"What did Bennie do?" Michelle urged.

Beth frowned. "Bennie put all his efforts into impressing Joe, at the expense of what remained of our relationship. Then one evening, Bennie again came bursting through the door in tears. I knew immediately that something was wrong—really wrong. He said that he screwed up something for Joe. I remember feeling sick, and this time I did ask what he did. Bennie said that he and a partner were supposed to make a donation of valuable mineral specimens *disappear* in transit from the home of a patron in Centennial to the School of Mines."

This caught Sanderson's attention. "You mean the Colorado School of Mines in Golden? When was this?"

Michelle and Melanie observed that this must have been new information because Sanderson was scribbling madly on his note pad.

Beth finished her water. Her lips tightened into a long, thin line. "Yes, the school in Golden. It was 1993, because Kaycee wasn't one yet. Bennie said something about the collection being worth tens of thousands of dollars, and that they were supposed to make it look like the minerals were stolen from an inventory room at the school. He and an inside man, who made regular deliveries to the school, were inside the receiving room, but before they did whatever they were supposed to, they knocked over a stack of other deliveries that drew the attention of some staff, which led to their aborting the mission. Bennie said that he came up with an excuse to return to the school, but by that time the boxes with the collection in them had been moved. He said Joe was furious."

"This is coming back to me now," Sanderson said. "Go on."

"Bennie was so distraught; we both were. He started drinking and passed out early. I paced around for hours, wondering—waiting—for what Joe would do. I eventually fell asleep. When I awoke,

Bennie was gone. This wasn't odd. But when I got to work and he wasn't there and no one knew where he was, I got worried. When he didn't come home that night, I knew that I'd never see him again."

"Oh, Beth!"

Melanie leaned against Michelle for support.

"Did Joe…*you know*…have him killed?"

Beth surprised everyone when she said no; Bennie, she thought, simply ran away from his troubles.

"Again, to be clear, Ms. Stockwell," Sanderson cut in, breaking the uncomfortable silence that followed, "would you please explain for the record why you think Mr. Barrie wasn't murdered by Joe Hayden, or anyone else at Tarryall?"

"Because of the way they reacted to Bennie's disappearance. Joe sent Bill in search of him. He also called his contacts for weeks looking for Bennie, and nothing showed up. I could tell by their frustration that Bennie managed to slip away."

Beth choked up and asked for another glass of water. Sanderson poured her one, told her to take her time and speak whenever she was ready.

Beth took a sip. Swallowing hard, she looked skyward and said, "God please forgive me for saying this, but part me wishes they had killed Bennie."

This, they didn't expect to hear either. Michelle couldn't help asking why Beth would ever wish for such a terrible thing to happen.

Beth gave her a wicked look; expanded on her answer to Sanderson's question, saying, "Because Joe made my life a living hell after that. He used Kaycee as leverage until he was convinced I didn't know where Bennie was. After that, he dictated how Kaycee was to be raised as if she was his own."

"*No!*"

"He never took advantage of me or Kaycee—you know, *that way*. I will give Joe credit for that. I made it clear that I wanted nothing to do with him, and that was also fine. It was all about the business with him—the keeping of secrets and the money coming in." Beth then dropped a bombshell that stunned even Sanderson when she said that she and Hayden had an agreement not to tell Kaycee that Dylan Streeter was her uncle.

You never told her? How's that even possible," Michelle said, utterly befuddled. "And why?"

"Don't judge me," Beth warned. "You couldn't possibly know what it was like. I told Joe in no uncertain terms that I didn't want my daughter living like I was. I insisted she had some semblance of a life. Joe agreed because the less Kaycee knew, the less likely she was to ask questions that could jeopardize the organization."

"I understand," Michelle said softly. "I didn't mean to sound like I was judging you. It's just so much to take in."

"Same here," Melanie rejoined.

Beth thanked them for understanding. "I'm sure it's a lot to take in," she agreed. "I made Joe promise never to bring up Dylan's name, and he told me to tell Kaycee that her father and I simply drifted apart. It wasn't as hard as you might think. Bennie was never close with his family, and we didn't see them very often as it was. Since Kaycee was born out of wedlock, many in Bennie's family took issue with that, so it was easy to make the separation. My side of the family was more of a challenge, though only slightly so. They never warmed to Bennie. Because of that and all that had gone on that I never told them about, we had also drifted apart. They were shocked, of course, when I told them Bennie left us, but they didn't go out of their way to try to reconcile us either, which was just as well. This kept them safe, and made it easier for me to keep up the charade. It was Joe's family—and Bud's and Teddy's, and a few other real friends that came and went over the years that were Kaycee's family. She never knew any different."

"That had to have been awkward," Michelle persisted.

"Believe me, it was. But, again, I have to give some of the credit to Joe—to all of them, really. They treated Kaycee as if she was one of their own."

"But only to protect themselves and the organization," Melanie countered.

"I'm not making excuses for them. What they did was inexcusable. Joe monitored Kaycee's friends. He used his connections to check out their parents' backgrounds, and took advantage of some of them when he could. He allowed Kaycee to have sleepovers at our house, but she was not allowed to stay over at theirs. I could deal with that. There were always excuses to justify a *no* here and a *no* there. Then she got older, and some of her friends started talking about going to college. It was so much easier to foster hope for any other kind of life when Kaycee was..."

Emotion got the better of her, and Beth began to cry. Michelle and Melanie were already half way there and joined in; together they commiserated over false lives and lost dreams.

Sanderson flagged Susan down and asked that she find a box of tissues.

"I can't believe he wouldn't let her go to college," Michelle said, recalling that Kaycee wanted to become a veterinarian. "That's horrible, just horrible," she followed with a sniff and a swipe of her hand across her nose. "Now I understand. I can relate." Michelle shared with Beth the financial consequences her mother faced after her father passed away. "I at least got that chance. Can I ask why Mr. Hayden wouldn't let her go to school?"

Beth replied, as Michelle expected, that Hayden wanted to nullify the curiosity, insight, and scrutiny that comes with exposure to worldly endeavors like higher education, adding, "His concession was to hire interns so that Kaycee could live vicariously through their experiences."

Michelle erupted. She let her nerves settle before saying, "You mean those kids I saw at Tarryall—Storm and Vikki—they were hired under false pretenses?"

"They all were, for the past eight years," Beth said adding insult to injury. "Every year Kaycee would be given a new set of friends. It was so hard to watch her excitement come spring turn to depression at the end of each summer when it was time for the kids to go back to school. But we'd make it through together, like we always did, one day at a time, living the controlled life of a mobster family. Then you came back into our lives with that book project. Part of me hated you for complicating our lives; the other hoped you would expose Joe and the others for who they were." She grabbed Michelle's hands and gave them a squeeze. "Then I got to know you over the phone and hoped you would just go away so that they didn't hurt you, too. You've endured enough from this godforsaken place already." Beth's face then brightened, and with a heartfelt voice she said softly, "You can't imagine how glad I am that you were so doggone determined to get that story. You saved our lives. Kaycee and I will always be in your debt."

Staring across the table at a woman reborn, Michelle said, "You can thank my editor for that! It was all him. I'm ashamed to say that he was the one who kept hounding me. Besides, if there's anyone we all should thank, it's your daughter. Earlier you said that you hoped Kaycee could forgive you. Well, I think she already has. When we spoke the other day, I didn't see a sheltered little girl. I saw a strong, defiant woman wise beyond her years. She knows more than you think. I wouldn't be surprised if she already knows—you know… about her step-uncle."

Beth had to admit that, all things considered, Michelle was probably right. "Here I was, thinking I was protecting her all these years, when it was probably Kaycee who was protecting me!"

"I can't imagine how difficult it was for her to risk sending me those emails," Michelle continued. "That took real courage. If she hadn't, I'm sure Mel and I would have come and gone and nothing would have changed. What she did changed everything. And personally for us, by helping to shut down Tarryall, she gave Mel and me closure about what happened to Garret."

"I can't agree more," Melanie said. "I feel so much better knowing those terrible men won't be hurting you, or Kaycee, or anyone else any longer."

"That's right, Ms. Stockwell," Sanderson said, jumping into the conversation. "If your daughter hadn't reached out to Ms. Kozlowski, we wouldn't have been in a position to help you or your daughter. What Kaycee did jeopardizes the *entire* Timberline organization. Believe me when I say that the word is out and agencies around the world working on the Timberline case are grateful for your daughter's selfless deeds."

"That's my girl!"

Michelle asked Beth if she'd given any thought to what she was going to do, now that it looked like she and Kaycee could start over.

Beth answered the question with the enthusiasm of a lotto winner. "The first thing I'm going to do is give her the biggest hug! Then I'm going to tell her everything, and if she'll still have me, take her on a far away vacation, like Tahiti—if Agent Sanderson will permit me," Beth said, stealing a hopeful glance in Sanderson's direction. "We always dreamed of going there."

"I might be able to arrange that, provided your story checks out."

"It will, you'll see!" Beth said, overjoyed. "Then I'd like to send her to college."

"She'll make a wonderful vet!" Michelle said tenderly. She then gave Sanderson a playful glance.

Sanderson took the hint. His face reddening, he said, "I'll do what I can to ensure that you and Kaycee are placed in a college town—with palm trees!"

———

They all turned when they heard a faint voice out in the hall say, "Sir? Sir? No, that way…that door there;" this followed by the discombobulated shuffling of feet.

"Oh, brother!" Michelle groaned. "It's Nick. Only he can get lost in a hallway!"

Susan showed Nick to the correct door. She promised to return with a fresh carafe of water.

"What'd I miss?" Nick asked, without mentioning his navigation issues.

"Like everything!" Michelle teased. "Did you hear the good news about Kaycee?"

"I did!" Nick said, congratulating Beth on the wonderful news. He continued the celebration by walking around to Beth's side of the table and giving her a hug. He looked at Sanderson and said, "And?"

"Still going in a positive direction," Sanderson said, satisfying Nick's unspoken question about the status of Beth's testimony. Sanderson reciprocated with a question about Chris's status and that of the others in Charleston.

"Very good. Better than I expected; just a few bumps and bruises. Like you said, Bill and Ainsley got everyone else out in time, and Sam Piersall and the guys at RMC were pretty much all in the field when the quake hit. Their office in Columbia took a bit of damage, but nothing too serious, according to Chris." Nick then turned to Michelle and said with a sly smile, "Chris wanted to know if you got into any trouble yet!"

"What did you tell him?" Michelle replied with a giggle.

"That this time there's sure to be a movie! He's glad to hear that you and Mel are okay. He was really shaken up. Oh, yeah, and he extends his condolences to you and your daughter, Ms. Stockwell—and to you Agent Sanderson, about your colleague."

Sanderson expressed his appreciation with a silent nod. Beth said, "Bless his heart. You must be so relieved that he's okay."

"I am, thank you. They're all good guys, and I don't know what I'd do without Chris." At their urging Nick launched into a summary of the earthquake damage and the dramatic turn of events in the PSTRE case. "Chris says the town's still a mess. Martial law is in effect until they've sifted through all the rubble and finished checking out the buildings. On the bright side, Chris says the damage would have been worse if construction codes weren't similar to those they use in California. Somebody was thinking. That's why the death toll was so low. The people had time to get out."

"What's he doing now?" Michelle asked.

"Chris? You know him," Nick chuckled, "he can't sit still. He's helping M&C get back on its feet. Bill Carlyle is a pretty sharp cookie. He insisted that M&C's files were backed up daily and that a duplicate copy was uploaded to a secure server at his personal beach-house property up the coast in North Carolina, which was spared. They're setting up shop there for the time being. Chris says they lost only Friday's data."

"Thank goodness! That was smart," Beth said, welcoming the opportunity to continue talking about issues other than her own.

"You can't imagine," Nick shuddered. "The legal stuff is one thing; field data are another, entirely. Chris left his computer in the building like everyone else, and I left mine at the place where Michelle and I were staying when Agent Bonino scared the bejesus out of me, and said I had to leave *now*. If we weren't required to upload our files each day as well, we'd have lost everything, except for some raw data and graphics files RMC has on their end. The case would have been back to square one."

Michelle was confused. "It's still on? Why would it still be on if everything's in ruins?"

"That's a good question. I was surprised, too. As Chris put it, 'the spider is already rebuilding its web.' I'm not sure whether he was referring to the lawyers, or the city in general. Anyway, the situation isn't good, but it isn't as bad as you might think, either. Chris says that PSTRE's plans are on hold indefinitely. He's not sure about the damage to their building, but the rail infrastructure used to transport those big-ass rail-car transformers they make won't be repaired for who knows how long. That's the bad news. I'm sure they're also worried about not cornering the overseas market like they had hoped."

"I feel bad for them. So what's the good news?"

"Do you remember Mike Dodd, Athens's president?"

"Uh-huh."

"Chris says that Carlyle got Ted Carlson, Athens's lead counsel, to admit that Dodd and that slime-ball Hal Cole were in cahoots to set up PSTRE."

"*Thought so!* Michelle said, excited to discover her hunch was right. "They did contaminate PSTRE's well!"

"Not exactly!" Nick said with a Cheshire-cat smile. "It turns out that PSTRE did contaminate its own well, not to mention the surrounding area. I'm pretty sure about that, and that's still bad. *But,* Bill and Ainsley convinced old man Merrill to approach the City about buying the former pit-farm property—you remember Parcel C?—and take care of the problem."

"That doesn't sound like good news to me."

"It'll be a financial burden for sure. The upshot is, M&C also told the City that Cole leaked confidential City information about the contamination on Parcel C to Athens while he was still employed by the City, and *before* Athens could put its plan in motion to report PSTRE for contaminating its property. They did all that, and then the quake occurred. Chris said the City was not at all happy to hear this and agreed to help PSTRE, so long as PSTRE keeps up its end of the bargain and performs the cleanup."

Michelle laughed. "Talk about karma!"

"More like poetic justice. Dodd and Cole had apparently conspired to bankrupt PSTRE to settle that old family-squabble bullshit. And get this, Ted Carlson fired his client."

"Get out!" Michelle said, even more pleased at this turn of events.

"Athens is in a world of trouble," Nick boasted, proud of the legal maelstrom he set in motion.

"That's industrial espionage at the very least," Sanderson commented.

"That and sundry other charges Chris said M&C were planning to tack on." Turning to Michelle, Nick added, "I'm not sure if we'll have any role in PSTRE's new suit against Cole and Athens, but Chris did say that Bill wants us to be his technical advisors for the assessment and cleanup at Parcel C. We'll be working with our technical counterparts at the City.

"Looks like you did your job!"

"Looks like we did *our* job!" Nick corrected his wife.

Michelle thought for a moment, a twinkle coming to her eye. "Does this mean we'll be working from Bill's beach house?"

Nick turned a deep shade of red. "Yes…and no. Remember that other opportunity I mentioned that Smitty talked to me about?"

"*Y-e-a-h*," Michelle said, in a skeptical tone.

With his best salesman pitch, Nick said, "You always wanted to see the Arch. How about we first spend a little time in St. Louis?"

Cat was plugging her way through the first batch of Tarryall financial data lifted from the safe in Joe Hayden's office when she overheard Sanderson speaking with a member of the Bureau's Denver office in the other room. The second round of Beth Stockwell's testimony must be over, she thought. Cat checked over her notes one last time. She then made photocopies of the most intriguing pages from the hard copy files she was provided, and had just finished highlighting some of the more provocative parts, when Sanderson strode into the room. "Good timing!" Cat said. "I completed a first run-through of Tarryall's financials." She pointed to the stack of highlighted printouts next to her computer. "How'd it go? Did Michelle get some of the answers she was looking for?"

"More than she bargained for, I suspect. It went well, all the way around."

"Beth's statement is still holding up?"

Sanderson smiled. "That's checking out as well. She gave more details, and Michelle's husband corroborated some of her story. I seriously hope this works out for her. She appears to come as advertised."

"An innocent victim of circumstances."

"That about sums it up." He glanced at the several pages Cat was holding in her hand. "There are a lot of challenges ahead for Ms. Stockwell and her daughter, but I'm confident the road ahead will only get better."

"I bet seeing Michelle and Melanie lifted her spirits."

"It was good for all of them," Sanderson said, "especially when they heard that Kaycee's condition was improving."

"Oh, right!" Cat cheered. "That's wonderful news. Janelle and I can't wait to congratulate Beth."

"Speaking of Janelle, where is your partner?"

"You didn't see her next door?" Cat said with a frown. "She was talking with somebody named Brian in tech support about our Xana-Logic software, so that the Denver office can also join in on virtual meetings to expedite the investigation."

This time it was Sanderson who looked confused. "I must have missed her," he said with a glance into the room across the hall. "That's good. James says he's still amazed by the technology." Looking at the papers Cat held in her hand, he asked, "Are those for me?"

"They are!" Cat said gleefully. "Here, take a look." Cat spread out the photocopies on the table.

"What am I looking at?"

"Financial transaction records between Tarryall and what Janelle and I think are two curiosity shops in New Orleans. Janelle's been going through those file folders over there." Cat pointed to a neatly stacked pile of manila folders next to Janelle's laptop. "And those other stacks correspond to other Tarryall clients. We haven't had a chance to look through them yet in any depth, but I did ask Janelle to forward the names of the shops on to Missy Sparling back at ICF. We'll find out whether they're legitimate or not."

"Ms. Sparling, your protégé. Very well. Keep me informed of what you find out. Now, what can you tell me about these curiosity shops?"

"I'm still working on that, but I'd say they're shady at best. They appear to be legitimate on the surface, if you look at only what I'm holding in my hand. Why, then, seek to procure items from an entity like Tarryall? We dug a little deeper and discovered that neither has a website or Facebook page—fishy, right? This leads us to believe that they're probably operating on the dark web. We'll check that out next."

"That does sound fishy. What are they looking for?"

"Southwest Native American ceremonial artifacts."

"You don't say?" Sanderson said, intrigued. "Keep on it. I think you and Janelle are on to something."

Something in the way that Sanderson responded piqued Cat's interest. "What aren't you telling me?"

"It so happens that this morning we found a cache of artifacts in a chamber deeper in the mine that just might be what those curiosity shops are looking for. I'll see to it that a description of what was found is forwarded to your attention for you to match to the purchase orders."

"That would be great," Cat said. "I can't wait to get the rest of those little bastards. Oh, and I did get a chance to review the electronic files you sent over—and Kim says the next round of warrants to search the rest of the Tarryall directorate's electronic devices should be in by the end of the day."

"I heard that, too. Anything else?"

"*Yes!*" Cat said with a sly purr. "Remember yesterday when you were hoping that Hayden's computer would reveal a smoking gun? Well, I think I found one."

"Do tell."

"I found reference to computer banking records with a 242 area code."

"The Bahamas…that's interesting, very interesting." Sanderson chewed on this, his expression wavering from excitement to one of annoyance and concern.

"Is something wrong?"

"Come with me," he said with a wave of an arm, and walked out the door.

Cat had to scurry to keep up with Sanderson, past the room where Beth spent the last four-plus hours pleading her case, to the office space Sanderson was provided for his personal use. He ushered Cat inside and shut the door.

Cat sat in a chair on the opposite side of the desk. Straightening the lines of her skirt, she said, "Something *is* wrong. I've seen that look before."

Sanderson wagged his head from side to side. "The fact is, we don't know yet. But in light of what you just told me, we need to proceed even more carefully from here on out."

"I don't understand."

Cat had never seen Sanderson any more serious when he asked who at ICF had access to the electronic files recovered from Joe Hayden's computer.

"Not many," Cat said, nervously performing a roll call in her head. "Our tech support…Janelle, Missy, and me and Kim, of course. Why?"

"It's come to my attention that there was considerable chatter last night between several cells that suddenly went dark. The intriguing thing is—and what disturbs me most—is that none of these cells, as far as we can tell, have any known ties to Tarryall."

Cat felt a sickening feeling rise in her stomach. "What are you saying?"

"Catherine, one cell has Bahamian ties. I don't think it's a coincidence that this happened so soon after we started trolling through that first batch of files from Hayden's computer."

"You think there's a mole?" Cat said with growing alarm.

Sanderson resisted conjecture. "It might be nothing, but yes. We can't leave anything to chance. To this end, I took the liberty of contacting your boss, and told Ms. Parsons that until further notice only she and your team are permitted to discuss Operation Timberline. Is that understood?"

"Of course."

"Good. The same rule also applies to us on the Bureau's end. Besides James and myself, only several other agents will be read in from now on until we have some answers."

Cat was now even more alarmed. "You think the leak could also be on the federal end?"

Sanderson spread his hands. "Like I said, we don't want to leave anything to chance. If the leaks persist, then we'll know it's within our inner circle. We'll handle that problem, when and if it comes."

He reached into his pocket and removed a ring of keys. Sorting through them, he chose a small silver one that he inserted into the lock of a desk side drawer. "There's something else you need to see." He removed a spiral-bound notebook from the drawer and slid it across the table.

"What's this?" Cat asked, picking it up. She frowned at the scuffed covers and spiral binding misshapen from use.

"Take a look inside," Sanderson urged.

It took but a few seconds for Cat to realize what she was looking at. On each page, line after line was filled with alphanumeric code, and above each line there was a transcription written in tiny, impeccably neat red ink. "It's a ledger book. Where did you get this?"

"From an alcove in the mine near the largest cache. It wasn't too difficult for our cryptanalysts to crack, most of it at least. As you can see, it documents stolen items and Tarryall client want lists. I haven't had the pleasure yet of plowing through it in detail, but one name did stick out that I'm rather certain will tie to that Bahamian area code in one way or another."

"Don't keep me in suspense!" Cat said, excited now.

Sanderson pointed to a green tab near the back of the notebook. "I think you will find a name that's rather familiar to you."

Cat flipped through the notebook with mounting suspense, stopping when she reached the appropriate tab. She quickly scanned through the entries, her eyes halting at a name and matching code that Sanderson had highlighted in yellow. Cat stared thunderstruck at the name that suddenly brought the Bahamian area code into perspective with her own Timberline syndicate ordeal. *Rillieux.*

SUGGESTED READING

I hope you enjoyed *Reckoning at Little Bear*. Below you will find recommendations for further reading, as well as websites and Internet-search terms to perform your own inquiry into some of the book's subject matter.

FRANCISCO VÁSQUEZ DE CORONADO

Preston, Douglas. *Cities of Gold: A Journey Across the American Southwest in Pursuit of Coronado*. New York, NY: Simon & Schuster, 1992.

Preston chronicles his 1989 attempt to retrace Coronado's horseback journey from the Mexican border to Santa Fe, New Mexico. *Cities of Gold* is a fascinating read that shares some of the same challenges Coronado's army faced, traversing often inhospitable terrain, 480 years ago en route to the Seven Cities of Gold (Cíbola). Preston is a journalist and author, perhaps best known for his thrillers, co-written with Lincoln Child, and for the non-fiction works *The Monster of Florence* and *The Lost City of the Monkey God*—the latter recounting Preston's 2012 participation in a scientific expedition into the Honduran jungle in search of the lost White City, the place where ancestors of indigenous tribes reportedly sought refuge from Coronado's conquistador predecessor, Hernán Cortés.

Winthrop, George Parker. *The Journey of Coronado 1540-1542*. Golden, CO: Fulcrum Publishing, 1990.

Much of what is known about Coronado's journey through the American Southwest was first published in this reprint of

Winthop's original book by the same name, released in 1904. A summary of the expedition is presented in the book's first part. The second half is a translation of Pedro de Castañedas's first-hand account, describing Coronado's search for Cíbola and Quivira.

Search Terms
- Coronado (Francisco Vásquez de Coronado)
- Narváez expedition
- Seven Cities of Gold (Zuni-Cíbola Complex)
- Quivira

EARTHQUAKES

Charleston, SC

Stewart, Kevin G. and Mary-Russell Roberson. *Exploring the Geology of the Carolinas: A Field Guide to Favorite Places from Chimney Rock to Charleston.* Chapel Hill, NC: The University of North Carolina Press, 2007.

This fact-filled guide describes points of geological interest at various tourist and day-hike destinations across the Carolinas. The guide concludes with a brief discussion of the Charleston earthquake of 1886.

U.S. Geological Survey. *Ninth Annual Report of the United States Geological Survey to the Secretary of the Interior 1887-'88.* Washington, D.C.: U.S. Government Printing Office, 1899.

I had the good fortune to happen upon this publication in a used-and rare-book store in the early 1990s, when I first tinkered with writing a novel about the Charleston earthquake. This source presents a thorough scientific inquiry and anecdotal accounts of the event, and can be downloaded free of charge from the USGS Publication Warehouse at: https://pubs.er.usgs.gov/browse/Report/usgs%20Numbered%20Series/Annual%20Report/

Williams, Susan Millar and Stephen G. Hoffius. *Upheaval in Charleston: Earthquake and Murder on the Eve of Jim Crow.* Athens, GA: The University of Georgia Press, 2011.

In this intriguing book, the story of the 1886 earthquake is told amidst a backdrop of social change. Central to the plot are Carlyle McKinley, a member of the editorial staff of the Charleston *News and Courier* newspaper (whose account of the quake is also presented in the USGS publication above), and Francis Warrington Dawson, editor of the *News and Courier,* whose progressive views regarding human rights found him embroiled in the social unrest of the time. The controversial Dawson was murdered three years after the earthquake in a remarkable set of circumstances, also addressed in the book.

Earthquakes—General

Feldman, Jay. *When the Mississippi Ran Backwards: Empire, Intrigue, Murder, and the New Madrid Earthquakes.* New York, NY: Free Press, 2005.

Presented in a vein similar to *Upheaval in Charleston*, Feldman describes the devastating New Madrid, Missouri earthquakes of 1811-12 amidst an environment steeped in westward expansion, and social and political conflict. The book begins with the Indian chief Tecumseh and his famous prophesy that some believe foretold the coming tremors. Tecumseh rallied the northern and southern tribes to the failed British cause in the War of 1812. Feldman interweaves the Indian's plight with the far-reaching effects of the quakes, such as how the earthquakes exposed the cold-blooded killing of a slave by two of Thomas Jefferson's nephews (the slave's partially burned and dismembered body was discovered in the hearth of a cabin chimney toppled by the quakes), and the maiden voyage of the steamboat *New Orleans*. The murder helped shape history. Nicholas Roosevelt's vertical paddle-wheel invention embarked from Pittsburgh in October 1811, and was bound for New Orleans when the first New Madrid quakes struck that December: it was this successful test run of a steamship that could travel both down *and* up river against strong currents that opened the door to westward expansion via river travel.

Fountain, Henry. *The Great Quake: How the Biggest Earthquake in North America Changed Our Understanding of the Planet*. New York, NY: Crown, 2017.

Fountain pens a fascinating account of the second largest recorded earthquake in history, which shook coastal Alaska for five minutes on Good Friday, March 27, 1964. The devastation wreaked on the cities of Anchorage and Valdez, and especially upon the Indian village of Chenega—which lost a third of its population when a tsunami was triggered by a submarine landslide moments after the quake—is discussed in vivid detail. A focus of Fountain's narrative is George Plafker, the U.S. Geological Survey geologist, whose follow-up investigation of the quake helped confirm the then controversial theory of plate tectonics.

Websites

www.usgs.gov/natural-hazards/earthquake-hazards/earthquakes

Interested in knowing where the latest earthquakes occurred? Then this is the place to go. The website offers a wealth of other useful and interesting information, including earthquake location by region, details on some of the more famous quakes, how to receive real-time earthquake-event notifications, feeds and web services, where to see maps and statistics, and how to access earthquake-related software and publications.

www.scemd.org/stay-informed/publications/earthquake-guide

This is the website for the South Carolina Emergency Management Division. The webpage includes a link to the South Carolina Earthquake Guide, which includes information on the 1886 earthquake, the South Carolina fault zone, information on threat level and hazard preparedness, and access to related and relevant websites

Search Terms
- 1886 Charleston Earthquake
- 1811–12 New Madrid Earthquakes
- 1964 Great Alaska Earthquake & Tsunami
- Modified Mercalli Intensity scale (a measure of the amount of shaking that occurs)
- Moment Magnitude scale/Richter scale (a measure of the "size" of an earthquake)

MINING HISTORY AND GEOLOGICAL EXCURSIONS

Fiester, Mark. *Blasted Beloved Breckenridge*. Boulder, CO: Pruett Publishing Company, 1973.

In this intriguing book, Fiester traces the history of Breckenridge from the 1859 discovery of gold in the Blue River valley, through the gold-boom years lasting to the turn of the 1900s, to the mid-century galas held in remembrance of the Summit County community's storied past. Much more than a book about the area's rich mining history and all of the legend and lore derived from it, Fiester's liberal use of photographs and time-stamped anecdotes brings to life the personalities and civic groups that influenced the community in a portrait of everyday life from Breckenridge's rough and tumble beginning through its formative years.

Voynick, Stephen M. *Colorado Gold: From the Pikes Peak Rush to the Present*. Missoula, MT: Mountain Press Publishing Company, 1992.

— *The Making of a Hardrock Miner*. Kearny, NE: Morris Publishing, 1978.

These sources provide a nice overview of the rich mining history that put places like Breckenridge (and by extension, my fictitious Big Bear and Little Bear mines) on the map. Voynick's works also provide a glimpse into what life was like for the miners who earned their pay extracting precious metals from the Earth. It is interesting to note that in 1994, two years after publication of *Colorado Gold*, the Cripple Creek and Victor Gold Mine, located approximately 90 miles southeast of Breckenridge, opened on the site of the former Cresson Mine—one of the most famous mines from the heyday of the Pikes Peak Gold Rush. Unlike its predecessor, which was an underground mine, the Cripple Creek and Victor Gold Mine is an immense open pit. Tours are available, the proceeds from which are donated to the nearby Victor Lowell Thomas Museum.

Young, Otis E. and Robert Lenon (technical contributor). *Western Mining*. Norman, OK: University of Oklahoma Press, 1977.

— *Black Powder and Hand Steel*. Norman, OK: University of Oklahoma Press, 1975. The copy referenced herein is a reprint edition, March 2016.

Young's works provide a comprehensive overview of the Old West mining trade. *Western Mining* is a good reference source for those seeking a historical perspective of the mining techniques used from the early days of the Spanish and the Indians, through the early wave of Cornish miners who brought their metal-mining skills with them from England, to the Americans who followed. In his companion book, *Black Powder and Hard Steel*,

Young focuses on the lives and the challenges faced by a largely Cornish and Irish work force in the search for gold and silver, using technological advancements such as dynamite, the skip, the Bickford fuse, and the mine elevator.

Web Sites
www.friendsofgardenofthegods.org
www.gobreck.com/experience-breckenridge/breckenridge-gold-mine-tours

Search Terms
- Breckenridge gold mine tours (see the website above for area mines and tours.)
- Garden of the Gods (more information can be found at the website above.)
- Pikes Peak Gold Rush (Pikes Peak is located near the Garden of the Gods, and includes an auto road to the summit. Tours are also available.)

DINOSAURS AND ASTEROIDS

Alvarez, Walter. *T. rex and the Crater of Doom*. New York, NY: Vintage Books, a division of Random House, Inc. (originally published in hard cover by Princeton University Press, Princeton, NJ in 1997), 1997. The paperback copy referenced herein is a first Vintage Books edition, August 1998.

In 1980, Walter Alvarez—along with his father Luis, and fellow collaborators Frank Asaro and Helen Michel—published the article *Extraterrestrial Cause for the Cretaceous-Tertiary Extinction* in the journal *Science*. This article set off a firestorm of debate—both for and against the theory that a comet or asteroid killed off all non-avian dinosaurs (yes, birds are our living dinosaur descendants) as part of a global mass extinction event 66 million years ago. This is the story behind Alvarez's research, the extinction debate, and the search for and ultimate 1996 discovery of the smoking gun—the Chicxulub Crater—buried beneath Mexico's Yucatán Peninsula.

Ironically—as it adds intrigue to Ranger Rick's discussion during Michelle and Melanie's visit to Dinosaur Ridge—further incontrovertible proof of the dinosaur's extraterrestrial demise was proposed in 2019 by researcher Robert DePalma, Curator of Paleontology at Palm Beach Museum of Natural History (Palm Beach, FL). DePalma claims to have found evidence of the Chicxulub impact, dated to the day that the dinosaurs died, buried in the rocks of North Dakota's Hell Creek Formation, famous for its dinosaur diversity and former home to *T. rex*.

Brusatte, Steve. *The Rise and Fall of the Dinosaurs: A New History of a Lost World*. New York, NY: William Morrow, 2018.

This is another must-have book for the dinosaur enthusiast. Brusatte, a paleontologist at the University of Edinburgh, presents an engaging and accessible account of our current understanding of dinosaur evolution, including the birds. Brusatte takes the reader to some of the many places he's ventured to across the world in the search for dinosaur remains, and introduces many of the friends and colleagues he's made along the way—including Walter Alvarez, with whom he visited Gubbio gorge in Italy, where Alvarez identified the iridium-rich clay layer that led to his asteroid-impact theory.

Near the end of the book, Brusatte mentions his participation in the extinction debate. Ironically—again because this ties to Ranger Rick's discussion—recent findings suggest that, with limited exception, the dinosaurs were robust in terms of both number of species and anatomical diversity at the time of the impact, and not in a state of decline in response to volcanic outpourings from the Deccan Traps in India.

WebSites

www.cneos.jpl.nasa.gov

This is the website for the Center for Near Earth Object Studies (CNEOS). CNEOS is a part of NASA's Planetary Defense Coordination Office, established in response to a concern for global safety in the wake of the spectacular impact of the Shoemaker-Levy 9 comet that slammed into Jupiter in July 1994. CNEOS tracks the predicted orbit of all identified Near-Earth Objects, or NEOs, such as asteroids and comets, greater than 30 to 50 meters in diameter, with the potential to pass within 30 million miles of Earth (our Sun is 93 million miles away). On this website, the user can find the date, estimated time, and size for all identified NEOs forward to the year 2200 A.D., along with a wealth of other interesting information.

www.dinoridge.org

This homepage for the Friends of Dinosaur Ridge offers a wealth of information about Dinosaur Ridge that is sure to please dinosaur enthusiasts of all ages. The organization was formed in 1989, for the purpose of preserving the fossils at Dinosaur Ridge and nearby Triceratops Trail (in Golden, Colorado), and educating the public about the area's natural history during the Jurassic and Cretaceous periods. I had the good fortune of visiting Dinosaur Ridge in 1985, during my Waynesburg College geology field camp (and Doc Carnein was my teacher—thanks again, Doc!). It was a memorable experience I couldn't resist reliving through Michelle and Melanie's characters. And true to Michelle's recollection of her field camp visit—before the site became a Natural National Landmark, and the visitor's center and Dinosaur Ridge Trail was constructed—we geologists-in-training stopped at the side of a very busy highway to see dinosaur footprints, frozen in time (except for those regrettably jackhammered away), stamped in near vertical bedrock.

Search Terms
- Chicxulub crater
- Center for Near Earth Object Studies (see website link above)
- Cretaceous-Paleogene Mass Extinction
- Deccan Traps
- Dinosaur Ridge (see website link above)
- Morrison and Dakota formations
- Robert DePalma Tanis Site
- Walter Alvarez (asteroid impact theory)

THE ENVIRONMENTAL MOVEMENT, CONSULTING AND HAZARDOUS WASTE SITES

As an environmental consultant, I thoroughly enjoyed the opportunity to write about Nick's participation in the PSTRE case, and hope that you enjoyed this part of the story as well. Creating a fictitious case study proved every bit as challenging and rewarding as successfully leading a client through similar environmental issues in the real world. This said, most of the experiences and situations shared by Nick and the others in *Reckoning at Little Bear* were based in reality, adapted from experiences from my own professional career.

As for suggested reading, here are several sources from my personal library that I think you might find interesting. These books cover a range of subject matter, from Rachel Carson's book *Silent Spring*, credited with starting the environmental movement, to several high profile legal cases and cleanup actions. I also included the USEPA website, where you can find information on federal Superfund sites in your area.

Carson, Rachel. *Silent Spring*. Boston, MA: Houghton Mifflin Company, 1962; forward copyright © 1987 by Paul Brooks.

This is the landmark book that brought to public attention the effects that the indiscriminant use of DDT and other pesticides can have on the environment, birds in particular. The outcry that followed prompted a ban on DDT, resulting in the dramatic rebound in many bird populations, including the bald eagle, peregrine falcon, brown pelican, and American robin—and in the process, spawned an environmental consciousness that continues to this day.

Fagin, Dan. *Toms River: A Story of Science and Salvation*. New York, NY: Bantam Books, 2013.

Fagin presents a riveting account of the decades-long mismanagement of chemical dyes and other waste products at the 1,350-acre former Ciba-Geigy Corporation site and the consequences it had on the community of Toms River, New Jersey. Contamination from over 70,000 drums stored on the property between 1952 and 1990 was identified as the cause for a rising number of childhood cancers in the area. The ensuing legal battle between the victims and big corporations resulted in a multi-million dollar settlement between Ciba-Geigy Special Chemicals, Union Carbide, United Water Toms River, and 69 families with children diagnosed with cancer.

Gibbs, Lois Marie. *Love Canal: The Story Continues*. Gabriola Island, BC: New Society Publishers, 1998.

In 1978, the Love Canal disaster brought the dangers of living next to hazardous waste close—too close—to home. Conceived in 1890 by William Love as a planned model community, the project was aborted after the partial building of a canal intended to convey shipping traffic and provide hydroelectric power to the Niagara Falls, New York neighborhood. The 70-acre area was used subsequently as a city municipal dump, and then as a chemical dumpsite by Hooker Chemical Company, which later sold the property to the city, in 1953, for $1.00. A neighborhood was built overtop of the backfilled canal with the understanding from Hooker that the ground was safe. Twenty-five years later, President Carter declared the emerging health crisis a national state of emergency. Over two hundred families ultimately were evacuated from the most contaminated area. The cleanup was completed in 2004 at an estimated cost between 275 and 400-million dollars. The 1980 federal Superfund program was created, in large part, as a result of the Love Canal disaster.

In this book, Lois Gibbs, a Love Canal resident and spokesperson for the community, whose tireless effort was integral to bringing the disaster to light, presents the state of affairs at Love Canal as it was in 1998, twenty years after recognition of the tragedy. Although dated, Gibbs's account remains relevant from a historical perspective, and because the problem is still ongoing: 18 new lawsuits have been filed between 2014 and August 2018 in response to the discovery of dioxin and other toxic chemicals in an area sewer line dug in 2011, seven years after the cleanup was deemed complete.

Harr, Jonathan. *A Civil Action*. New York, NY: Vintage Books, a division of Random House, Inc., first Vintage Books edition, 1996.

In this true-life, Woburn, Massachusetts legal showdown, plaintiff's attorney Jan Schlichtmann represents eight families who claim that defendants W.R. Grace & Co. (via company division Cryovac), Beatrice Foods, Inc. (via subsidiary John J. Riley Tannery), and UniFirst Corporation contaminated supply wells G and H that provide drinking water to the community. The plaintiffs assert that the industrial solvent trichloroethylene (TCE) in their drinking water was responsible for the leukemia contracted by children in seven of the eight families. Although the lawsuit was filed in May 1982, the two-phase trial did not begin until early 1986. Costs incurred over the long duration of the legal process and Schlictmann's extravagant spending put a strain on his firm's financial resources. Schlictmann was compelled to reinvest a $1 million settlement received from UniFirst to support the larger case against Beatrice Foods and W.R. Grace. As Schlictmann's financial woes mounted, Beatrice Foods was absolved of responsibility, and Schlictmann was forced to accept a low $8 million settlement from W.R. Grace. Schlictmann's problems continued following the trial, as the families, disgruntled over the attorney's fees and small settlement of $375,000 per family, force Schlictmann to forego much of his fee. Schlictmann ultimately filed for bankruptcy.

Note: George Pinder, the plaintiffs' hydrogeology expert, worked for my first employer, Roy F. Weston, Inc., at the time of the trial. The contaminated wells became the Wells G & H Superfund Site. In 1991, the U.S. EPA accepted a $69.5 million settlement from five responsible parties, including W.R. Grace, Beatrice, and UniFirst. *A Civil Action* was adapted into the 1998 movie by the same name, with actor John Travolta cast in the starring role as plaintiffs' attorney Jan Schlictmann.

WebSites
www.epa.gov/superfund/search-superfund-sites-where-you-live.gov

This is a handy website I've used many times in the course of my work, where you can find the status of Superfund sites located in your area.

Search Terms
- Love Canal
- Rachel Carson
- Toms River Ciba-Geigy Superfund Site
- Woburn Toxic-Waste Trial

DISSOCIATIVE IDENTITY DISORDER

Baer, Richard. *Switching Time: A Doctor's Harrowing Story of Treating a Woman with 17 Personalities.* New York, NY: Three Rivers Press, 2007; Discussion Guide copyright © 2008 by Three Rivers Press, an imprint of the Crown Publishing Group, a division of Random House, Inc.

Switching Time is a disturbing true story about Karen Overhill, a physically and psychologically abused woman, whose mind created 17 identities to cope with the atrocities she experienced as a child—identities that followed her into a tumultuous adulthood. Baer, Overhill's psychiatrist, presents a vivid account of the horrific details of Overhill's life, the recognition of her condition, and the years of therapy needed to help Ms. Overhill toward recovery.

Nathan, Debbie. *Sybil Exposed: The Extraordinary Story Behind the Famous Multiple Personality Case.* New York, NY: Free Press, a division of Simon & Schuster, 2011.

In 1973, Flora Rheta Schreiber published the non-fiction book *Sybil*, based on the life of Shirley Ardell Mason, a woman with 16 alternate identities. The story of Mason's childhood, in many ways, mirrors that of Karen Overhill. The book and subsequent movie, starring Sally Field as the troubled Mason, shocked audiences and brought Dissociative Identity Disorder (aka DID, and formerly Multiple Personality Disorder) to public attention. Dr. Cornelia B. Wilbur, Mason's psychiatrist, diagnosed Mason with Multiple Personality Disorder. Wilbur's diagnosis has been brought into question, and in this book Nathan presents compelling evidence that Wilbur and Schreiber were frauds who preyed on the emotionally fragile Mason for their own ends.

I included *Sybil Exposed* because at the root of the matter, Mason appears to have been a victim willing to face her demons in any manner she could, even if that meant choosing to be complicit in Wilbur's and Schreiber's deception. Moreover, the Sybil phenomenon surely had something to do with my decision to plague poor Garret with the same malady to account for his actions in *Ghost Creek*. I can only hope that Michelle successfully played her part as fictional doctor herein, and vindicated Garret to your satisfaction.

Search Terms

- Dissociative Identity Disorder (formerly Multiple Personality Disorder)
- Sybil (Shirley Ardell Mason)
- Cornelia B. Wilbur
- Flora Rheta Schreiber

Made in the USA
Columbia, SC
02 April 2021